HEAVILY
INVESTED

DEAN TUTTLE

cabana books

AUSTRALIA

This is a work of fiction.

Names, characters, businesses, places, events and incidents are either the products of the author's imagination or used in a fictitious context. Any resemblance to actual persons, living or dead is purely coincidental.

Cover design:
David Prendergast

Book design:
Cabana Books Australia

To pinchab2 my number 1 fan

ACKNOWLEDGMENTS

Nothing gets created without positive supporters – they are gold.

My love and thanks to you all

To Tomochan, my spark of light, thanks for being there for the ups and downs and the crazy adventures and always believing.
To my mum, Daphne, for giving me the writing bug and so much more.
To my father Alan and brother Sean, thanks for the humour and for maintaining high expectations of me!
To my first draft readers Bryan and Tania, I probably wouldn't have kept going without you!
To my editor, Kate O'Donnell, for lifting my game in the bestest, most collaborative way!
To friends and family, Andrew, Neil, Antony, Carolyn and many more who nudged me along… thanks for your encouragement and I hope you enjoy the final product.

PROLOGUE
Hate Mail

To: cliff.young

Re: investment opportunity

You dirty, lying, stealing, dog...

Cliff flung his iPhone to the ground. It bounced on its corner, went through a hooped wire fence edging the garden-bed and landed in a pile of mulch. He left it there.

Even with a new email account, he couldn't escape his accusers.

He snatched the orange whipper snipper from a pile of gardening implements and wrenched at the starter cord. The motor kicked over a couple of pathetic turns but didn't start.

"Fuck."

He ripped at it again but still it didn't start.

"Fuck! Fuck!"

It was going to be one of those days. As he prepared to yank even harder, he noticed the main switch.

"Argh, dickhead," he twisted the lever from 'Off' to 'Start'.

He shut his eyes, taking a deep breath. A smile formed at the edges of his mouth. How dumb had he just been? Anyone watching would have pissed themselves laughing.

This time he took hold of the starter cord and slowly but firmly dragged it out. The motor coughed into life and the cutting cable whirred.

With his free hand, he lifted the front of his floppy hat to cool his already sweating head. He took his sunglasses from his shirt pocket and put them on. Then he turned to face the long, winding garden path. The grass around it was lush with thick, spreading tufts and tall seed heads, already hiding much of the concrete stepping-stones.

"Alright people, party's over, here I come…"

ONE

January 07

"So, what do you reckon, Jan? Do you like the place?" The real estate agent had a boyish smile.

Jan's face lit up. However, before she could reply, Cliff jumped in.

"Might just have another look at the back. If you can give us a few minutes?"

It was hardly a question and Cliff didn't wait for an answer. He took Jan's elbow, ushering her towards the kitchen and out into the backyard. They crossed the unpainted concrete patio where a faded set of canvas chairs surrounded an equally weather-beaten white plastic table. A bright yellow toy train engine, the type a kid could sit on and ride around using their feet to propel themselves, sat under the table. It looked like a tropical fish hiding under a coral umbrella, the way it sat up at an angle, due to one of its back wheels being missing.

Cliff opened the side door to the garage, its paint flaking off, a jagged hole in the bottom panel where someone had once used too much foot power to open it. The smell of cigarettes and something that could only be described as wet dog blankets hit his nostrils. The same smell had greeted them in each of the bedrooms in the main house.

"You know what that smell is?" he smiled at Jan.

"No?"

"It's the smell of profits."

"Really? Do you think so? How exciting!" Jan clasped her hands together, her sunny face even more radiant than normal.

"Now, have a look here," he took a folded sheet of paper from his pocket.

"I reckon we got a great chance to pick this one up for a really decent price. I mean, it's got solid bones, nothing wrong with it. But that smell puts other buyers off, right? And the garden's another story..."

"I know, it's a jungle at the front."

"Uh-huh," Cliff grinned.

"Who knows what's living in there," she shuddered.

"Yep, that's exactly what everyone else will think. But we both know it will only take a day with a few good mates and a chain saw, right?"

Jan smiled, "If it wasn't for you, Cliffie, there's no way Ken and I would be doing this. But in our eyes, you're a genius. We'd follow you anywhere."

"Don't know about a genius," Cliff chuckled, "Just learned a lot."

He unfolded the page, revealing a printed list of houses. Jan would have seen him show this kind of list at his investor club meetings. The left-hand column had addresses and basic descriptions. The right-hand column showed the sale price and date.

"Now, why this place is so good, is because it's basically the same as all these others nearby. It's just got a few cosmetic challenges, right?" Cliff gave her a wink.

"Mm-hmm," Jan nodded, her eyes fixed on the list.

"For example, number 38, just a few doors down, sold in November for 255."

"Wow."

"Or this one on Acacia Street, that's two blocks away, right? It sold for 259. So, we've got plenty here."

"Great!"

"There's the one we drove by this morning, sold for over 270, just last month."

"Yes, the one with the lovely pool and all the statues around it?"

"Yep, that one, but pools don't add anything out here. They're a hassle for tenants to keep clean so most buyers don't want them. I bought one with a pool and we filled it up and turned it into a cactus garden. Looked sensational. Totally low maintenance!"

Cliff folded the paper away. "So, do you want to go for it?"

Jan gulped. She looked around at the exposed timber framework of the garage, out through the cracked window to the trees and fence beyond. Then her smile returned.

"Well, Kenny, you said it was my call," she took a sealed envelope from her bag and kissed it, "Here's to us my love."

She handed the envelope to Cliff, "Let's do it!"

They crossed the sun burnt clumps of grass and dusty patches of brown dirt that made up the back lawn.

"What a contrast to the front of the house," Jan wrinkled her brows, "Jungle at the front, desert at the back…"

They could hear the agent speaking on his mobile.

"Ok, no problem, I should be back there in about twenty. I'm just showing 32 Brighton to two buyers…"

He smiled at Cliff and Jan as they entered the living room.

"Yes, I know, it's a great one isn't it. Really? Two others? Well it won't last long. Not at this price. Hey, I better go, I'll see you shortly mate."

Jan's hand squeezed Cliff's arm. He knew she was alarmed at the sound of competition for the house, but he'd seen and heard it all many, many times before. As he always told his trainee investors, the only thing that mattered was 'the numbers'. Never let anything else influence the price you pay, especially not anything the selling agent has to say.

"How'd you go?" the agent asked.

"Yeah, certainly a lot of issues…" Cliff whistled.

"Sure, but that's why the price is so good."

"Well, I don't know about that."

"Oh really? What do you think it's worth?"

That was the invitation Cliff wanted. His hand reached to a pocket in the leg of his pants. He pulled out a folded piece of paper with a very similar-looking list to the one he'd shown Jan in the garage. Except that the houses on this list had all sold at substantially lower prices.

"For me the only way to judge a place's value is with the facts..."

"Absolutely."

"And if I compare this place to what else has sold around here recently, same sort of houses, they've sold a lot lower."

"Oh really?"

"Yeah, for example the one across the road, on the corner, it went for only 198."

"Sure, but its fibro and was in a pretty bad state..."

"Bigger land size. Otherwise basically the same house. Three-bedder with a garage. Lots of people like the old clad houses now too, they paint them up nice and cute."

"Fair enough."

"And then there's the brown and white place a few doors up, same side. Went for 195 and its four bedrooms."

"Isn't that the battle-axe block?"

"Yep, but four-bedder. Don't forget, interest rates are making things a lot tougher now."

"Very true. Well, do you want to make an offer?"

"Sure, but it's going to be lower than the seller might expect..."

"That's fine, mate, all offers considered."

"Really?"

"Absolutely. Vendor is in a tight spot and keen to offload."

"There you go." Those were just the kind of words Cliff wanted to hear. He took his time before continuing.

"Well, if you really asked me, I would say this place is worth somewhere around 190... in this market..."

"You're kidding!"

"Nope. What do you reckon the vendor will take?"

"Definitely won't go under 200."

Cliff noticed Jan's eyes widen. It was a pretty huge drop in price he'd just achieved. The property was on the market for 249K.

"Ok," Cliff continued, "what if I meet you halfway at 195?"

Before the agent could reply, Cliff held out the sealed envelope Jan had given him earlier.

"To sweeten the deal, mate, and to show we're committed to a quick sale, we're willing to put our money where our mouth is. It's a cheque for the deposit. Please tell the owner we know it's a low offer, but it's a fair one, and we're serious. They'll get their cash nice and quick, you know, no hassles, no last-minute dicking around."

TWO

Less than an hour later, Cliff turned into McDonalds at Gladesville. He spotted Raj's glossy red GTI, sitting low on its spoked alloys, right in front of the restaurant, in full view of the main window. He accelerated hard. The V8 roared and gravel sprayed as he swung his trusty ute in next to the little, sporty hatch, close enough to freak poor Raj out. Laughing, he leapt out, looking forward to the big bloke going off at him.

As he stepped into the air-conditioned coolness of Maccas, he was disappointed to see Raj and MJ sitting together, both with their backs to the window. Raj would have missed his carpark skills. He dropped into a chair facing them across the varnished table.

"Look at you two sitting together like you're on a date."

"Fuck you. We can both watch the menu from here," Raj dismissed him with a flick of his hand.

"Why, is the menu doing something? Are they showing movies on it, or what?"

"You're an idiot," MJ rolled her eyes, "Why don't you get a coffee. We don't have much time."

"Sure," Cliff jumped up, hitting his knee on a metal cross-bar under the table, "Ouch! Fuck!"

"Ha, ha," Raj's face lit up, "There's another reason it's better on this side."

Cliff hobbled over to the counter. A few moments later he was back with a coffee and an over-sized choc-chip cookie.

"Guess what? Free bikkie."

"What?" Raj threw his hands up.

"She saw me hit my knee and felt sorry for me. I'm telling ya, I have good luck wherever I go."

"You're such a scammer," MJ smiled.

"Ok, down to business, right?" Cliff slapped the table, "Got something to write on?"

MJ pushed her notepad across to him.

"So, latest news," Cliff smirked, "I got Bill to agree to 750 each. For four of his best. Phase One."

"Wow," Raj's eyes widened.

"Nice one," MJ nodded.

"But he was pushing for us to act quick. We got to make a decision now."

"Uh-huh."

"It's a no-brainer, right? Anything like them in the area, even stuff that's nowhere near as good, has sold for 900 or more. We done our homework, we know this shit, yeah?"

"Yep," MJ watched as Cliff scribbled the numbers.

"So, our four, brand new, waterfront units will be worth at least a million each. That's four mill. Probably more, but we'll just say four, you know, to be safe."

"Sure."

"That's like a million bucks gain from day one. And he reckons they'll be finished in less than six months."

"Right…"

"That's like we get one whole unit for free."

"Insane."

"Just like this cookie," Cliff took a bite and grinned.

"But think about this," Raj took the pen from Cliff, his brow furrowed, "We borrow three million to buy them. Three million at 8 percent means two-hundred-and-forty thousand interest per year. Just interest. Plus, there's all the running costs. They'll be high, this is luxury property."

"Sure…"

"Our rent won't come close to covering it. We'll be short at least one hundred thousand a year. Just to hold onto them. I don't have that kind of spare change."

"Yeah but come on. You know the deal. It's exactly the same as our classics. Every time they go up, we go to the bank and revalue them. Don't we?"

"Sure."

"And we make heaps more than the shortfall in rent, right?"

"I know."

"Same as these! If they go up by ten percent in a year, that's four hundred thousand dollars. If it's a bad year and they only go up five percent, that's still two hundred thousand. We're still winning."

"And if it all goes to pot, interest rates keep going up or whatever," MJ mumbled thoughtfully, her chin on her hand, "We flog off one and use the million bucks to pay the interest on the others. That would keep us going for years."

"Exactly Ems!" Cliff bumped fists with her.

"Ok, well here's the only thing," MJ sat back and folded her arms, "Do you think we can borrow three mill? Like, if they're not even fully built yet?"

"Great question Emily-Jane," Cliff did his best impression of a dodgy salesman, "I'm so glad you asked."

"Here we go," Raj shook his head.

"No, no, no, it's simple. Equity, baby."

"Ok, but…"

"Yeah, yeah, I know what you're going to say. But let me finish."

"Righto, go for it."

"I've got forty properties waiting to be revalued. I reckon I'll get two million out of that. I think you guys can handle half a million each, right?"

"Yeah, I can do that," MJ nodded, "I thought you were going to want a million each."

"I know. But I know what you guys can afford."

"Yep, I can do 500K," Raj shrugged.

MJ held up a hand, "But…"

"What?"

"Here's my big question for you, old son. Why are you changing the plan? Why are you, like, going against your own advice?"

"What do you mean?"

"Well, for the last ten years you've invested in little old cheapos in the western suburbs. Piss easy. You've always said 'Stick to the plan. Keep it simple.'"

"I know…"

"And you've made a fortune."

"It's true," chimed in Raj, "Every week you say the same thing to the Club. You love our little classics because they're so simple and safe. You know them backwards. You're an expert. But this is unknown territory. You've always dissed off-the-plan deals. Now you want to do one. For three mill?"

"Why not put our funds into more classics?" MJ shrugged, "Stay focused on what we know so well? Keep our equity for a rainy day."

"Because it's getting harder and harder to do it," Cliff couldn't believe they were still hesitant.

"There's so many investors out there these days, pushing prices up, it takes ages to find a good deal. I just found one for a Club member and it took six weeks. I wish I could have gone for it myself."

"Yeah, you're not wrong," MJ sat back.

"But the main thing, guys," Cliff's eyes were alive, "This is Sydney Harbour waterfront. It doesn't get better than this, anywhere in the world. They're not making any more of it and half the world wants to live there. I've always said the classics were a step, right? Towards something bigger and better. This is the dream coming true."

"Sure," Raj caught MJ's eye and smiled.

"I really want it to be with you guys. So, you know what? Even though I'm putting in two mill and you're each only 500K, you're going to have your own units. I'll have two and you each get one. It's my gift to you guys. I mean it, ok?"

"Woah, take it easy," Raj held up his hands.

"Yeah that's crazy mate, you don't have to do that," MJ shook her head.

"I know, but I want to. I've been planning this for a long time. You guys have been with me the whole ride. From the start. The good times and the shit. I couldn't have done it without you. So, this is my thanks. No more ifs and buts. Right?"

MJ and Raj looked at each other and turned to Cliff in protest.

"I said no more discussion. Shut up and accept."

"Ok," MJ held out her hand, "You're on. Let's make a go of it."

They shook hands, determination on their faces.

"Very generous of you, mate," Raj took Cliff's hand.

MJ slapped Raj on the shoulder, "One small problem... um... very small," she winked at Cliff, "I don't know that we can let you park that little drug-dealer's car on our new water-front property, sorry Rajie."

She raised her little finger causing Cliff to crack up.

"Well if you don't want a lift," Raj got up, "You can take the bus there."

"Ferry, dudes," Cliff gave them a gleeful smile, "Ferry."

"Grab one of these," Bill held out a hard hat.

"Why? You worried it's going to fall down?"

"Ha bloody ha. It's a legal requirement, bud. Anyone enters this site has to wear one."

"Fair enough," Cliff plonked it on his head.

"Come on in," Bill pushed open a tall, wire gate, a heavy chain swinging loose and clinking against the metal frame.

Bill was a solid barrel of a man, with battered boots, black 'stubbies' shorts and a khaki shirt that hung loose except where it moulded around his ample belly. His bearded face was topped by a bright yellow hard hat, completing a picture that a casting studio would have been proud to submit for the role of 'Builder'.

In front of them was a small hill spattered with scrubby weeds and grass. They followed a well-worn path to the top of it. From here the view was stunning.

Bill put his hands on his hips. The hill sloped down to a large, square hole, the size of a building and impressively deep. It was bordered by a fluro-orange safety fence. Beyond that was a half-finished building, all grey cement and exposed steel girders. The stunning bit was the blue water of Sydney harbour, glittering in the sunshine and lapping almost at the base of the building.

Cliff whistled.

"Nice," Raj nodded slowly.

"Yep, those are your units," Bill enjoyed the impact, then shifted his attention to the large hole, "Down here is Phase 2."

"Why have you gone so deep," MJ looked at the mine-like hole, "How many storeys is it going to be?"

"Only three. The excavation is for the underground parking, to service both buildings."

"Gotcha."

"And isn't there going to be a third phase?" asked Cliff.

"Yeah, we've got an option on the site on the left," Bill indicated an aging, harbour-front bungalow, overgrown with trees.

"Really, they'll let you knock it down?"

"Connections, bud," Bill winked.

He headed down the hill towards the building site, gesturing with a sweeping arm, "That'll be your driveway."

"This whole area," he spread his arms, "will be landscaped. Beautiful, lush, park feel."

It was hard to imagine now, but Cliff knew what was possible with good landscaping. It was an exciting point in the project, with construction well under way, but much of the rest of the site a blank canvas. In fact, it probably looked at its worst now, with the earthworks, vehicle tracks everywhere, and the stark, grey concrete of Phase 1. The magic would come with all the 'fine arts' of rendering, painting, tiling, paving and planting. He'd seen the plans and was confident Bill and his team could pull it off. He had a great track record, having built several luxurious unit blocks in the inner suburbs, although this was his first waterfront location.

"I'll take you inside so you can see exactly where the project is at," Bill led them towards an opening under the scaffolding of Phase 1.

Cliff stepped through, expecting a dark and musty interior. He was pleasantly surprised. The far end was completely open, sunshine and blue harbour blazing through in all their glory.

"Wow, that's impressive."

"Yep," Bill was pleased, "It'll be floor to ceiling glass. You're in the lobby. Out front will be a stunning promenade area, to the left opens to the lagoon and on the right, the gym and lap pool. Lift at the back. No walking for these tenants. But I'm afraid we will have to," Bill pointed out the empty lift shaft.

"Geez, couldn't you have put in a trampoline, or something, for us," Cliff smiled.

"Well, we had one, buddy, but I broke it," Bill slapped his tummy.

They chuckled as Bill led them up the stairwell, the limey smell of concrete in their nostrils. On level 1 they stepped through the empty doorway of the first unit. The view had become even better, if that was possible. Again, it looked like the harbour-facing wall would be floor to ceiling glass.

"I want to move in now," Raj spread his arms.

"Bit uncomfortable sleeping on the concrete, bud," Bill responded, "At least wait until we've put the floors down. All Tassie hardwoods, by the way. Plantation stuff, so it'll keep the greenies happy too. Still the best timber in the world if you ask me. Just beautiful."

Bill led them through the floorplan. It had two bedrooms with a large, open plan kitchen and living area that enjoyed the magnificent views.

"This is unit 1 and next door is 2," Bill nodded to his right, "Identical units. Mirror image layout."

"Cool," Cliff caught MJ's eye and she nodded back, clearly impressed.

Up on the next level it was still an open shell. Bill breathed a little heavily.

"These will be 3 and 4. Same as the level below, we're not as far advanced with the internal structure, though."

"Yep, can see that," Cliff smiled.

"So these are our 4 units, are they?" MJ asked.

"Yep, these are your units. If you still want them of course."

"And how many on the next floor?" Raj cocked his head.

"Two more, units 5 and 6."

"Are they better than these?" Raj had the expression of a little boy, faced with a difficult choice at the cake shop.

"Same. Slightly bigger balconies, that's all. But they're not for sale, sorry."

"Chef always keeps back the best," Cliff put his arm around Raj's shoulders, "You know how it is mate."

He tipped the back of Raj's hard hat causing it to fall forward over his eyes.

"Oi!" Raj swung the hat at Cliff, who's laughter went up a notch as he beat a hasty retreat.

"Not necessarily the best," Bill cut in, "Plenty of people don't like living on higher floors. Even with a lift. They've all got different advantages and disadvantages. Main thing is the view and they've all got it. It doesn't get better than this."

"Totes," MJ agreed.

The top floor was girders and unfinished walls. The sun warm on their backs, they savoured the 360-degree panorama.

"Well, these views might be the best," Raj sighed, "But at least our units have a roof over them."

"Exactly buddy," Bill chuckled, "This open-air stuff is over-rated."

They began making their way back down the stairs.

"So you reckon they're five months away, Bill?" MJ asked over her shoulder.

"Well that depends on my Phase 1 buyers. Hopefully that's you guys. As soon as we have the funds, it's full steam ahead. We get all our teams back on board, get back on track, and it's a five-month timetable until you put tenants in. No worries at all."

Back on the ground floor, they paused for a last look through the open lobby to the water.

"Yeah 'cause that's mission critical for us, right?" Cliff fixed an eye on Bill. "We're borrowing to raise the funds so we'll be paying interest on our loans, with no income from rent to cover it. Not until they're completed."

"Yep, I know mate," Bill squinted, a hand shading his eyes, "I understand your position better than anybody. Basically, you're being our banker. Because the real banks won't talk to us anymore. That's why you're getting the bloody amazing discount we're giving you. We're not a charity. We're paying you to get us out of a hole."

"Literally, when it comes to Phase 2," MJ grinned.

They all knew the situation and there was no need to go over it. Bill had hit a bunch of delays. Wealthy neighbours had kicked up a fuss until the council imposed last minute changes to his plans. This caused a row with the earth moving contractor that ended up at tribunal. His other suppliers wanted more money too. After six months of hold ups and cost blow outs, Bill was out of funds and they all began pulling their teams and equipment off the site.

He'd gone to his bank, begging for an additional loan. But they sniffed trouble and refused to advance another dollar. Bill, however, was convinced they wanted to send him bankrupt so they could steal the project for themselves. Neither he nor Cliff trusted banks further than you could throw them. In better times they'd laughed plenty over the crazy stories they'd heard of dodgy tactics, even outright corruption.

"So, if you guys want in," Bill continued, "Time is of the essence. We need the funds right away."

"Oh, we're in alright," Cliff assured him, "I've got a batch of houses up for refinance, should be done in a week or so. These guys are both ready to go with their funds."

"Great. Well, let's go and talk business somewhere more

comfortable," Bill gestured towards the exit.

They sat around a long, white-clothed table looking out at the shimmering water of Rozelle Bay and contemplating the straight-line geometry of the Anzac Bridge, slicing its way through the middle of their view, pulsating with endless, streaming traffic. The table was covered with the remains of a seafood feast. Broken crab shells in baskets, their pink and white legs strewn about, empty oysters stacked three layers high, piles of prawn shells, spilling off plates and floating in finger bowls, lobster heads, legs and antennae staring blankly from platters, pieces of lemon, salad leaves, chips and onion rings scattered across the white cloth.

"That was awesome," Cliff leaned back in his chair, stretching his arms in the air.

"Yeah, bloody great feast," MJ patted her stomach.

"And amazing location," Raj finished off the round of appreciation.

"Glad you guys enjoyed it," Bill wiped some sauce from the corner of his mouth with his napkin. "You know the same architect who designed this place has done Blue, don't you?"

"No, you're kidding?" Cliff was wide-eyed.

"Yep, Charles Shepparton."

"Wow, really?" MJ and Raj echoed.

"Charlie built the Horizon Tower at Bondi. He did some amazing work for the restaurant quarter at the new casino, then Mirvac commissioned him to create this. His best yet, I reckon."

"Very cool," Raj nodded.

"We wanted a real name. You know, for the prestige it brings to the project, but also someone who could do something with the amazing view. And I reckon he's nailed it."

"You're not wrong," Cliff looked over the restaurant with new appreciation for the soaring, brushed metal beams that outlined the curves of its ceiling. The design was truly impressive, curve rising above curve, to culminate in the magnificent frame that opened to the harbour. Three stories of glass ensured the panorama had maximum impact.

The table Bill had booked sat squarely in the middle of the frame. Tall glass panels had been rolled away, opening to the glittering harbour, a gentle wafting breeze and the occasional squawking cockatoo.

"Ok. So guys," Bill leaned in, "We need to get down to brass tacks. You've seen the project. You had a good look over what we're doing. You've seen the quality. I think it's obvious it's top drawer?"

"Of course, mate," Cliff nodded.

"You've seen our other projects, right? You know we'll put in quality finishes. Only high-class stuff. I mean, Charlie will kick our arses if we don't."

"Totally! No worries there, mate. These two have seen your warehouse conversion and loved it, right guys?"

"Yeah, awesome," MJ sat back nodding.

"Cheers," Bill smiled, "Well, I know I'm talking to the best when it comes to doing your research and understanding the market. Which reminds me..."

Bill reached down for his leather briefcase and pulled out a print-out of a Real Estate dot com listing.

"Just got word from the agent this place sold for 990."

"Wow, is that right?" Cliff took the ad from him.

It was a two-bedroom unit in the eighties era, blue-grey block behind Bill's site. It claimed 'stunning views' but, in truth, they were in between buildings and nothing like the uninterrupted, panoramas of Blue's Phase 1.

"So I don't think you should have any concerns about the value of your investment," Bill cocked his head, "Just think what they'll be worth in five months' time, completed."

"I think we're convinced mate," MJ chuckled.

"Fantastic. So here's the thing. If you want in, we've got to be quick. My partners are seeing the same thing we are, and they're already questioning the price. Not to mention, if we don't restart ASAP, we risk losing the whole project to the bank."

Bill turned to Cliff, "So I'm afraid 'In a couple of weeks' just isn't going to cut it. How quickly can you really move?"

Cliff swallowed, "Well, ah... I don't know for sure, mate. I mean I could go see ABC tomorrow. Push hard."

"Yep?"

"They don't seem to take very long. You know, they do online valuations these days. Pretty quick."

"Yeah, mine did it the same day," Raj nodded, "I was pretty impressed."

"I mean, how soon do you need the cash Bill? What's your actual timeline?"

"Today would be great..." Bill smiled, "But, really, it's got to be this week or not at all."

"Ok, no worries. We'll get onto it then."

"Fantastic. Last thing, then, I've got some paperwork for you."

He plonked three stapled documents on the table, "These are the contracts."

As Bill fished a pen from his briefcase, Cliff seized the initiative, "Thanks mate. We'll take them with us, have a look over and get straight back to you."

"Beautiful," Bill dropped the pen back in his case.

"Well, it's all happening," MJ stretched.

"Sure is," Cliff got up, "I'm very, very excited. Thanks for the great feed, mate."

Bill rose too and held out a hand, "No worries, buddy. Glad you enjoyed it."

THREE

On the radio Foo Fighters rasped out 'Best of You' as Cliff headed for home. It had been a fantastic day. The opportunity in front of him was amazing, the returns incredible. Most exciting of all, he'd begun building a portfolio of premium, waterfront properties. Awesome properties. It was a dream coming true.

Yet... He turned the volume down to focus his mind. What was really going on with Bill?

He'd never seen the big fella acting desperate. A risk? An opportunity? No, no, he was a mate.

He flicked his indicator on, swinging into the right lane to head for the office.

Maybe he could make it happen today. Could he push the bank hard enough? Get them to revalue his properties this afternoon and - at the very least - make the funds available tomorrow? Just how much clout did he have? It was certainly worth finding out.

Scrolling his contacts, he quickly found the number for his Office Manager, Lara, and hit 'call'.

She answered with a loud, "Achtung! Klivvies Klimbers Klup!" Then giggled in her normal voice.

Cliff cracked up. He often tried to take the piss out of her Scottish accent. Always failed. Only yesterday he'd had another go, teasing her about the way she said 'phone'.

'Ken yar storp shootin on yer fooorrn please!"

Lara had only rolled her eyes and told him he sounded German.

"You know what," Cliff retorted at his mobile, "You're actually easier to understand in German."

"Ja, wirklich, ist das so?"

"What?!"

"Ha, ha."

"You're so funny."

"Danke. Anythink to plees…"

"How do you say 'smartarse dipshit' in German?"

"Um, let me see… Klivvie Y-"

"Actually, forget it. I really need your help with something urgent. I'm on my way in."

"Oh no, we'll have to pack in the party."

"Yep, put the booze back in the fridge," Cliff chuckled, "Although, if you have a couple lines of speed racked up that might actually help."

"Ooh!"

"Seriously, though, I need you to grab all the files on the properties we picked for refinance last week."

"Ok…"

"There should be about forty."

"Yeah, sure, I know the ones."

"Make sure all the paperwork's there. Especially rock-solid evidence of higher sales. Work your magic. Make sure they can't argue with it."

"Okie dokie. How soon do you need it done?"

"I'm calling ABC now, see if we can go in this arvo."

"Woah, no mucking around. Alright! I'm onto it!"

"You're awesome, thanks. See you soon."

Cliff cruised through the traffic at a good speed. He scanned ahead and behind for any sign of police, before skipping back through his contacts for Dermott, his bank manager's number.

"ABC Bank, Professional Property Loans, Tracy speaking."

It was Dermott's assistant.

"Hey Tracy, its Cliff Young."

"Oh, hi Cliff, how are you going?"

"Fantastic thanks, Trace. Is the big boss there?"

"No, I'm sorry he's stepped out for some lunch. Can I get him to call you when he gets back in?"

"Well, actually, it's kinda urgent. I need to set up a meeting for this afternoon. I know it's crazy, I'm really sorry, but I've got to jump on something today. Do you reckon I could come straight in?"

"Oh right, well, let me put you through to his mobile. You're probably best talking to him directly, save wasting any time, and he can let you know what he can manage today. Alright love?"

"That's great, thank you."

Cliff sat on a comfy leather chair in front of Dermott's expansive desk, which occupied the entire back corner of the Professional Property Loans office. This was an area of the bank only seen by customers with large loan portfolios. It was headed up by Dermott who managed half a dozen lending specialists in addition to his trusty assistant, Tracy. To Cliff they all looked super hard-working, perhaps even a tad sleep-deprived, with multiple computer screens and large stacks of forms piled on their desks.

Dermott was a tall, lanky man with the exaggerated movements of a comedian. He smiled easily and had a real sense of fun, almost goofiness. He was, however, a lot sharper than his outward manner suggested, and always dressed immaculately in a dark suit.

Cliff, mobile phone to his ear, was finishing a conversation, as Dermott looked on bemused.

"That's fantastic, see you soon," Cliff hung up and smiled at Dermott.

"Lara's ten minutes away. She's got everything ready to go."

"Terrific! You've got a good one there. Where can I get such a well organized assistant?"

With a guffaw, he directed this last bit towards Tracy who was placing a bundle of manila folders on his desk.

"Mine just drops all the work on my desk for me to do myself!"

"Well, you see Cliff probably pays his assistant more than dog biscuits," Tracy winked at Cliff.

"Hey, it's awesome of you guys to see me at short notice like this, so I reckon you are both terrific," Cliff beamed.

"Well, now you know how special you are," Tracy charmed back. "Still, I reckon a bottle of Grange won't go astray after this, don't you think Dermott?"

"Absolutely," Dermott's face crinkled into a smile.

With a cackle and a slap of Cliff's shoulder, Tracy made her way back to her desk.

"So, tell me a little more about this venture. You're building waterfront units now?"

"Yeah, it's the completion stage of an absolutely prime development, mate. Three mill gets us well over four mill worth of units. Hard to say no to."

"Sure."

"Best thing is they're designed by Charles Shepparton. Totally stunning," Cliff took one of Bill's glossy brochures from his briefcase and handed it to Dermott. "He did the Horizon Tower at Bondi and a bunch of award-winning projects. A big name architect."

"Yes, I've come across him. Very nice. How come you're getting such a good price? If you don't mind my asking?"

"The developer needs quick funds. They overspent their budget. But they're so close to being finished, it's a no-brainer for them. Sell some units cheaply, get the project finished and make a killing on the rest. A classic win-win."

"And you're the man with the cash to do it. Nice position."

What intrigued Cliff about Dermott was that he'd never done any property investing of his own. Yet he clearly loved it. It was as if it was good enough for him to live out the adventure through his clients. Perhaps, that way, he could have his cake and eat it too. He could experience the thrill of investing, knowing that his own finances were comfortably safe.

"So, here's the thing," Cliff sat forward, "As I mentioned on the phone, I need to get two million to the developer. Ideally today, or tomorrow at the latest. I know it's a big ask. But we've discussed the refinances before and I know you're happy with them. I mean there's a ton of equity there. We've done this heaps of times before and we've got all the paperwork ready to go. So I thought if anyone could work some magic on it, it would be you guys."

As if on cue, Lara entered, smiling cheerfully at Tracy, "Afternoon!"

"They're just over there, plotting away…"

Dermott jumped up and arranged a second chair for Lara.

"Good timing, welcome," he leaned in and gave her a kiss on the cheek.

"Thanks! How are you, Dermott?"

Lara unburdened herself of two very fat laptop bags, thumping two piles of documents on the desk, "It's all here, forty houses."

"Fantastic," Dermott took the top folder, "Let's have a look."

A large, sunny photo of the house filled the cover, its address in bold above. Below, a quick, defining sentence, '3-bedroom family home on large corner block'.

Dermott flicked to the second page, a detailed list of all its features.

"You guys," he beamed, "You've got everything in exactly the right order for our valuation software."

"We try," Lara smiled.

The following pages were where she had just been putting all her effort, before printing and racing over to Dermott's office. They contained examples of similar properties, nearby the target property, their selling prices in bold. She and Cliff watched as Dermott scanned through.

The sale prices were consistently above 275 thousand, some even above 300 thousand. Yep, they can't argue with that. Surely. Cliff shot Lara a smile.

The final page was titled, 'For consideration by our banks.'

He saw Dermott's eyes flicker over it and noticed him shift in his seat. It was working. They'd used the plural 'banks' deliberately. It was a subtle reminder that, despite the amicable relations, Dermott was in competition for Cliff's business.

Below the title was a single, bold phrase:

'REVALUATION TARGET: $275,000 - $300,000'

"Yep, looks great," Dermott smiled at Lara, "Everything we need."

He turned to Cliff, patting the nearest stack of folders, "This makes our job really easy. They're all basically the same aren't they?"

"Exactly the same," Cliff grinned, "We like to keep it simple."

"I'll get Jordan onto them right away," Dermott picked up the first pile.

Before he could walk off, Cliff lowered his voice, "You know we'd like to push for one hundred percent on those, yeah?"

Dermott smiled, "Shouldn't be a problem. Give me a sec."

With a wink he headed over to Jordan's desk at the far end of the office.

"Jordan, old son, your expertise is needed."

"Oh, yeah?"

Dermott sat down, his head disappearing behind the grey, carpeted partitions that surrounded Jordan's desk, their conversation becoming low and indistinct.

Soon, however, Dermott strode back, "Those should be fine."

He ferried the second pile over to Jordan, returning this time via Tracy's workstation.

"Trace, sweetheart, would you mind grabbing us forty loan apps," a sigh betrayed just how much work was going to be involved.

Lara jumped in, "Actually, I have those all filled out already, Dermott."

She reached into one of the laptop bags and pulled out a wad of bank forms.

"And don't worry," she brandished the top form, "We used the new template."

"Well, holy dooly, you guys are amazing!"

Dermott looked like a school kid who'd just been let out early for the holidays.

"That's sensational. I'd forgotten I gave you those. Have you done them all?"

"Yep. It was the least we could do, since we're asking you to do them in one day!"

Cliff and Lara stepped out of the lift on the ground floor. They dared not make eye contact as they crossed the lobby. As soon as they reached the street, they hi-fived.

"Woohoo!" Lara whooped.

"Yeah!!!" Cliff embraced her, lifting her off her feet and spinning her around in a full circle.

His bank account had just gone up by two million dollars. Not bad for a few hour's work. The funds were in the form of a 'line of credit', a loan against the extra equity in his forty houses.

Jordan – or more accurately Jordan's computer - had accepted that each of the properties were now worth 275 thousand. That was roughly fifty thousand dollars increase per house.

FOUR

A text message beeped from his pocket as Cliff hurried along the riverside walkway. He carried an esky in one hand, a picnic basket in the other and a backpack on his shoulder. He put the basket down so he could grab his mobile.

Good, Mandy was still ten minutes away. That would give him just enough time to load up the water taxi, then go back and meet her at the ferry.

He and Mandy had been together for nearly ten years. From day one she'd been completely disparaging of marriage, so it had taken Cliff until just recently to summon the courage to propose to her. To his great surprise, she'd burst into tears, blubbering that she had thought he was never going to ask her. So now they were happily engaged.

Mandy worked as a Producer for a large music promoter in the city. It was one of those cool jobs that made great conversation at parties. A lot more so than property investing, Cliff often grumbled. He'd watched her work her way up from 'shit-kicker' roles, putting up with appalling treatment, long hours and low pay, until finally she had been recognised and given more responsibility. Cliff was proud of her and enjoyed hearing her inside stories, especially the 'dirt' on celebrities she worked with.

Today, like most days, she was taking public transport to and from work. She liked to make the extra effort to take a Rivercat ferry, instead of the train, which meant she had to get a bus for the remainder of the journey from the wharf to home. Cliff knew this final bus leg could be a pain, almost always late, jam packed and very slow. So, whenever possible, he made the detour to pick her up and drive them both home.

However, today, he had something different up his sleeve. The idea had hit him while celebrating the refinances with Lara. She'd loved it and offered to help.

First up, Lara had directed Cliff to an upmarket deli in the eastern suburbs. Here, Cliff nodded while the French owner filled his basket with a dizzy range of 'organic', 'artisan' and absolutely 'gastronomique' treats.

"Ah, of course, peat-smoked salmon. From Stony Bay. Tassie. You must have it."

"Sure…"

"Sounds amazing," Lara re-assured him.

"Tastes better," the proprietor winked at her.

"Oh my god, this one," he handed her a truffle-infused goats cheese from New Zealand's South Island.

There were gooseberries organically grown in the Blue Mountains by a bloke called 'Pierre'. Fair Trade chocolate from a community co-op in New Guinea. Hand-ground, organic rye crisp-breads from Anton's bakery in South Australia (or was that Pierre?)

The list had gone on. Until that afternoon, Cliff hadn't known it was possible to spend over five hundred dollars on a picnic for two.

Next stop, the famous Doyle's kiosk at the fish markets. Here they bought a dozen wild oysters.

"I'm disappointed," Cliff shrugged, "They didn't give us the full story on how their mate, Rob, is the only guy on the planet to know about a secret cave, just off the coast of Cronulla, where the world's purest oysters grow…"

Then they headed across the Anzac Bridge to find a bottle shop. If the food shopping had been eye-opening for Cliff, then this would be the day's most 'sobering' experience.

"Haven't you ever wanted to walk into a bottle shop and say, 'What's your most expensive bottle?' And then buy it?!"

"Never greatly thought about it, but yeah it sounds like fun."

"I reckon I want to do it just once - and today is the day. Scary thing is, I've got no idea how high it could go."

"Well, maybe we shouldn't have picked a bottle shop in Balmain then."

"You reckon? Like, what do you reckon? Over five hundred?"

"Let's find out. I'll stand by to call an ambulance..."

"I've heard of a bottle of Grange going for over five hundred. I wonder if they'll have any of that..."

Inside the timber-paneled shop, a rotund assistant greeted them, his eyes smiling from behind thick glasses, "Hi. How you going?"

"Hi," Cliff grinned back. He turned to Lara, speaking under his breath, "I don't know how to ask this without sounding like a wanker."

"Well then, just be a wanker for a day and enjoy it."

"You're right," he turned back to the shop assistant, with a little swagger.

"Mate, just out of interest, what's your most expensive bottle of wine?"

"What type of wine were you after?"

Cliff was taken off guard. He'd just wanted a price. He knew nothing about types of wine.

"Um, maybe sparkling?" he looked to Lara for support.

Lara, however, was grinning vacantly, "Sure..."

"Don't you think bubbles would be good?"

"Yes, absolutely. Does Mandy like sparkling?"

"Yeah, definitely."

"Ok great then."

Cliff returned to the shop assistant, "Why don't you take us through your top sparkling wines. Starting with the most expensive."

Then Cliff realised why Lara had been lost for words. The shop assistant turned to the darkly polished display-cabinet behind him. Locked with heavy iron bars, it could have been a set piece from a historical, convict movie.

He made no move to open it, simply pointing through the bars to a bottle on the top shelf. Gun-metal foil wrapped its near-black glass. A simple, grey label was printed with white text. The overall effect was of polished titanium.

Below it was a printed tag: 'Krug Clos d'Ambonnay (1995) $4,999.'

"We have this bottle of Krug for five grand. How's that sound?" he smiled.

"Geez that's incredible. A fair bit more than I had in mind, I must admit," Cliff's throat was dry, "What makes a bottle of wine that expensive?"

"It's the only one in Australia. You won't find it anywhere else. There's not many in the world, in fact. The 1995's become legendary. We just happen to have a few rather wealthy wine lovers in the area so we stock some rare and collectables."

"Wow, how could you drink it though?"

"Well, most don't. They invest. The value goes up all the time, because they aren't making any more and, of course, they do eventually get drunk, so there's less and less of them."

"Classic investment," Cliff chuckled.

"This one, though," the assistant tapped the display-cabined, "Is perfect to be drunk right now. It probably won't get any better."

"So that's like the most perfect champagne in the world right now?"

"Yep, pretty much."

"Is the price negotiable?"

"Nope."

The sales assistant laughed whole-heartedly. Then it dawned on him that he just might have a serious buyer.

"Like I say, it's an investment, the price is actually set by the world wine exchange. It's a one-off, like a rose diamond, you know? But I could throw in these crystal-cut glasses if you really wanted to take it. They're worth a couple of hundred."

"Ok, done."

A burst of high-pitched laughter came from Lara.

"It's an investment, a one-off, like a rose diamond," Cliff smiled at her.

"Yeah, but you're going to drink it tonight."

Cliff spotted Mandy stepping down the gang plank and onto the jetty. Perfect timing. He waved and she smiled back, both her hands full with work bags. As soon as she was through the ticket turnstile, he stepped up to her, gave her a smiling kiss on the lips and took one of her bags.

"How's your day?"

Mandy snuggled into him, "Good, now that I'm with you."

She kissed him again, lingeringly this time.

Cliff lost himself, momentarily, in her smile, her deep brown eyes sparkling up at him, her button nose and baby-sized mouth, her perfectly white teeth, all wrapped in the softest, silky brown hair.

He grinned, "Are you up for a surprise? Today's pick up is a bit different."

"Uh, oh, what have you done?"

"It's a surprise. You just have to do what you're told, ok?"

"Not what's-its pizza place again?"

"Hey, come on, it wasn't that bad."

He put an arm around her, but Mandy leaned back on her heals.

"Yeah, but, but, but... they weren't exactly 'Sydney's best pizzas' were they? Probably not even southwest Parramatta's best pizza..."

She laughed at Cliff's indignant look.

"No, it's not Wicksie's pizza, ok? It's almost as good, though."

"What?"

With a cheeky smile, he took her hand, "So come on and stop complaining. You have to be open to the flow, you know... Let the Universe surprise you..."

"The Universe yes. You, I'm not so sure..."

Hand in hand they set off in the direction of the water taxi jetty. Despite her protests, Cliff knew she was excited. She loved surprises.

"Here we are," he nodded towards the fast-looking black and

yellow pod bouncing at the end of the jetty.

The driver waved, "Welcome!"

"We're taking a water taxi?" Mandy was openly excited now, "Where are we going?"

"Jump in and make yourself comfortable. All will be revealed."

The driver took her hand to help her on board. Cliff followed, giving him a pat on the shoulder, "Thanks for waiting mate."

"No worries mate. So, we just set a course for Birchgrove?"

"Yep, perfect."

Cliff joined Mandy, looking over the side at the lapping water of the Parramatta River, soft and blue in the late afternoon sun.

"I thought it was a great night for a picnic on the harbour. What you reckon?"

"This is heaps of fun, yeah! What's at Birchgrove?"

Before he could answer, they were thrown backward, grabbing at the handrail as the boat roared off.

"Bit more grunt than the ferry, hey!" Cliff laughed.

They scrambled into seats at the back of the boat. The bubble-like interior was deceptively large, capable of carrying about twenty passengers, Cliff reckoned. It meant there was plenty of room for them to get cosy down the back and enjoy having it all to themselves. Exactly as Cliff had hoped.

"I just achieved one of my dreams," he beamed, "And I wanted to celebrate it with you."

"Really?"

"You know I've been talking about doing a water front development for ages? Well, I just added two units to the portfolio."

"Wow, really?"

"Yeah. But you have to see these to believe them. They're pretty insane. Not finished building yet, but the location."

"Sounds amazing."

"So I thought this was the best way to show you."

"Thanks sweetheart," Mandy kissed him, "That's so nice."

The water taxi bounced along, the sun setting behind them. At last the river opened up and became Sydney Harbour. On all sides, the shore was lined with the gleaming white walls, expansive glass windows, balconies, manicured lawns, jetties and quaint boathouses of the fortunate few.

They swung towards Birchgrove and Cliff spotted the cleared land and concrete structure of Blue's Phase 1, rising above the low-set, historical house on its right. He lifted the picnic basket and esky onto the seat between them.

"I know you and all your celeb pals, love your organic, greenie shit. So I grabbed something I thought you might get into."

"Wow, this looks great," Mandy picked through the contents, "Yum!"

"Probably a bit more than most celebs could afford, actually," Cliff chuckled lifting the Krug champagne from the esky.

He carefully unwrapped the bottle and slowly, gingerly, began to ease the cork out, "Now, it's time for a very special toast, my beautiful fiancée. To achieving our dreams…"

With a pop, the cork flew out, hitting the canopy of the water taxi, bouncing down and smacking Cliff on the bridge of the nose. He flinched, the bottle slipping from his hand.

"No!"

Before it hit the deck, Mandy grabbed it between feet and hands.

"Save!"

"Oh my god, you have no idea how important that save was!"

Cliff hugged her, then covered her face with kisses.

Mandy laughed, "You're such a romantic, aren't you?"

She took his hands, "Now we can still make that toast to our dreams."

"Not really romantic…" Cliff took in several deep breaths, "I'll tell you how much that champers cost later."

He filled their glasses.

"You see that block going up over there?"

"Uh-ha."

"We own a couple of those units."

"Those ones right there? Oh my god, you've really gone to the next level."

"Yep."

"Congratulations, sweetie."

They sipped champagne and dug into the basket of gourmet goodies. The world around them softened and deepened in the colours of a perfect evening.

Cliff hugged Mandy tight, "This investment is going to change everything."

FIVE

1996

Life had not always been French champagne and oysters for Cliff.

He'd grown up in the rough and tumble of outer Western Sydney, his mum and dad unemployed, their house originally part of a work injury compensation package given to Cliff's grandfather.

'Pops' and 'gran' had lived with them until, not long after Cliff started high school, pops passed away and gran eventually moved into a nursing home. The house had passed to his dad, Tommy, and his mum, Nancy. Cliff's memories were of loud TV and even louder, alcohol-fueled arguments.

Tommy and his mates got up to various 'projects' to make extra cash. Trucks pulled up late at night, boxes unloaded into the garage, as stealthily as a bunch of half-drunk blokes could manage. Such deliveries were followed by more late-night visits from strangers, muttered deals brokered over stubbies in the backyard.

Most of all, however, his dad and his rambunctious band of mates were committed to making their fortunes at the local TAB betting shop. This habit, more than anything else, lit the fuse of his mum's wrath.

Tommy would get back, later in the evening, stumble into the bedroom, shut the door and switch on the TV. Cliff could smell the alcohol a room away. Moments later, he'd hear his mum's footsteps, marching down the hall. With a loud yank, she'd rip the bedroom door open. Cliff would brace himself.

"How much did you lose?"

Silence.

"I said how much did you lose this time?"

It always amazed Cliff that, although his mum knew exactly what the answer was and knew exactly how pushing Tommy at this point was going to end, she kept at him. She must have been so angry that all she cared about was telling him.

Cliff couldn't remember his dad ever hitting his mum. But Tommy did hit walls, punch in doors and smash household objects. Once he even kicked the television so hard it hit the wall and shattered. It only made him angrier.

Nancy, for her part, gave as good as she got. She stood her ground, yelling at him, driving home just how much of a foolish, child of a man she thought he was.

She, too, was capable of turning any handy object into a projectile. In her rage she'd hurled plates of food, beer bottles and even small appliances at him. In happier times, Tommy would proudly show off his 'war wounds'. They included a scar above his right eye and a bump on the back of his head where the hair no longer grew, leaving a small, perfectly square, bald spot in his otherwise bushy head.

Cliff could remember being scared by their fights as a youngster. However, over time, they became a familiar routine. Since no-one was ever killed, he eventually became immune. Truth to tell, teenage Cliff was more embarrassed by what the neighbours must have been thinking than concerned for his own safety. Sometimes he'd yell at his parents to shut up. Most of the time, he slammed his door, turned up his music and tried to ignore it.

"I know where you can get your hands on a Rexie for nothing," MJ told Raj with a gleam in her eyes.

It made sense to Cliff that he would find school friends with a different outlook to his mum and dad. With footy team mates, Raj and MJ, he shared not only a love of the game, but a driving ambition to go far in life. The three day-dreamed of making piles of money, having successful careers, maybe even going into business together.

So, when MJ swaggered over, grinning like the proverbial satisfied cat, and announced their first golden opportunity, it was like fate had opened its door.

"Where?" Raj raised an eyebrow.

"Shel's mum's kicking her boyfriend out. He's had a '78 on bricks in her backyard for two years. He done fuck all with it. Now she's making him get everything out and he doesn't know what to do with the fucking thing."

The three laughed at the ex-boyfriend's predicament. They sat in their usual break-time spot, beneath a cluster of tall gums that grew just within the tall, barbed-wire perimeter fence of the school.

Cliff turned to Raj, "There you go, mate. You've been telling us for ages how you can make a swifty out of fixing up cars. This is perfect."

"Well I don't know what the condition's like. If it's been there for two years, it's probably rusted as shit."

"Ah bullshit! You told us you could fix up anything," MJ kicked at Raj's school bag, "Now's your chance."

"How much does he want for it?"

"I told you he has to get rid of it. He's got nowhere to put it."

"Serious dudes," Cliff held up his hands, "This could be our first break. Can we come check it out, Ems?"

"Yeah sure. Come over this arvo."

"So, here's the plan. If Raj says it's ok, we offer this guy a hundred bucks for it, right? If he cracks the shits, we just tell him to forget it and deal with it himself. He'll have no choice."

They chuckled.

Cliff turned to MJ, "Once we got it, do you think her mum will let us leave it there?"

"I don't know man," MJ stretched, "I reckon she wants to do some big clean up or something."

"Ok, well if she won't I'll have a talk to my dad. If we cut him in maybe he'll let us work on it in the garage. How much do you reckon we can make Rajie?"

"I don't know I have to see it first. But you can sell those things for over three grand."

"Serious?"

"Yeah that's without rego but it's got to be running good."

"Sick!" Cliff tossed a dry twig at the fence. "Kelvin's dad's got a towie. So we can get it over to my place if we have to."

"Ok just one thing," Raj frowned, "Where do we get a hundred bucks from?"

"That's only like thirty bucks each," Cliff was astounded at Raj's lack of imagination, "You telling me you can't get thirty bucks off your mum and dad when you tell them how much we're gonna make?"

Raj shrugged.

"Your old man's always looking for a way to make extra dosh. Tell him he's investing in his son's first business!"

"Well, we will see."

Cliff's dad, Tommy, was sunk deep into the sofa, watching The Simpsons. Cliff had heard him laughing from out on the street and was glad he was in a good mood.

"Hey dad, I need thirty bucks so I can make us a shitload."

"What?"

"I need thirty bucks, like now, and I'll make us a grand."

"What? Come on buddy, I'm watching Simpsons. Can you ask me later?"

"No, no, no, I need it now. I'm serious. I can make us a thousand."

Tommy sat up, pressing mute on the TV remote, "What are you talking about, matey? I'm not giving you thirty bucks for some dodgy scam. Thirty bucks is a lot of money. So stop mucking around, alright?"

"No, no, it's legit. Raj, MJ and me are starting our business. First project's fixing up a rexie. Pick it up for a hundred bucks, sell it for three grand. I'm serious. But it has to be today. Oh, and I might need to store it here. In the garage."

"Huh? Listen, buddy, no-one buys anything for a hundred bucks and sells it for three grand unless it's crooked. So steer clear."

"No this is ok. Raj knows how to fix them and he knows how much they sell for. You know he's the shit when it comes to cars. He'll sus it out."

"I don't care if he's Michael Schumacher, if it sounds too good to be true, then it is. Anyway, even if I wanted to, I don't have thirty bucks to give you, sorry."

He un-muted the TV and slumped back into the sofa. The sound of Bart and Lisa arguing with their parents filled the living room.

"Come on dad, please, it's fucking perfect. I promise-"

His dad held up his hand, "Watch your mouth, buddy. I'm the only one who swears in my house, ok?"

"We wanna start our business. I told you already. I'm gonna make us shitloads of dosh. I'm not gonna sit around on my arse and wait..."

Cliff's voice trailed off. He knew he'd said the wrong thing.

His dad stood up and glared at him, "Like what? Like me?"

Nancy came through the back door, pushing the fly screen open with a full washing basket, "What's going on?"

"Nothing," Cliff turned and headed for his room, "I just wanted thirty bucks so I could do something useful with my life."

"What do you want to do?"

"Fix up a car. A rexie. Make some money to start our business."

Tommy had been holding himself back but now he exploded, "He's not getting any money for any bullshit scam. I've already said it. End of story! Ok?"

His mum put the washing basket down on the kitchen table and came back into the living room, "Well, hang on, if there's something he wants to do, and if it's useful and legit, then, you know, let's talk about it."

She picked up his dad's wallet from the sideboard.

"Hang on!" Tommy was outraged.

"Its legit mum," Cliff sensed the chance.

"Put that down!"

"Hang on, Tommy," Nancy held up her hand, "You're only going to blow it off down the TAB. Let Cliffie have a go. Fair's fair."

She pulled three ten-dollar bills from his wallet and handed them to Cliff. Tommy lunged for them, but Nancy was too quick.

"Leave him alone. He deserves to have a go and he deserves our support."

"Fucking hell," Tommy threw his arms up in resignation, turned away in disgust and slumped back into the sofa. He angrily stabbed at the TV remote until the volume was ear-splittingly loud.

Cliff took the opportunity to slip out the front door.

An angry dog slammed against the inside of the fence, growling, claws screeching on metal, as the three mates approached. It was enough to make them think twice about going in. The racket, however, soon brought Shelley out of the house.

"Scud! Shut up! Come here! Come here, I said. Stupid mutt."

They heard her wrestling the dog, then eventually bolting a backyard gate. After a moment, her head appeared through the front gate.

"Hey."

She led them into the house without a word. In the living room Cliff became aware of a frosty atmosphere. Shel's mum was sitting on the sofa, her bare feet pulled up underneath her, a cigarette in her left hand, reading a Homes and Gardens magazine. Two cats curled into the cushions around her. The carpet was covered with cardboard boxes, some bursting at the seams, others only part filled.

Her boyfriend was in the kitchen, leaning against the sink, an angry look on his face. All the cupboard doors were open, the kitchen tops and most of the floor covered with glassware, crockery, appliances and boxes of food. Lined up on the counter top, next to the sink, was a row of empty 'tallies' - 700ml bottles – of VB.

"Well what the fuck's this? Play group?" he laughed with a smoker's cackle.

They all avoided eye contact with him.

"Don't mind me kids," he continued, "I won't bite. Come on in, make yourselves at home. Join the party. Do you and your mates want a beer MJ?"

"No thanks mate," MJ cleared her throat.

"C'mon I thought you liked being one of the boys? All work and no play makes Johnny a boring footy player. Or Janie, I should say."

He held a bottle out to MJ.

"Leave her alone she doesn't want one," Shelley frowned.

"Ok, no worries. You run along now and play together. But Shel darling - we've told you - no orgies until you're 18, ok?"

Again that hoarse cough-laugh.

"Shut your dirty fucking mouth," Shel's mum threatened from the sofa, fixing her ex with a deadly stare.

"Ok, ok woman. I'm just trying to have a little fun here. Trying to lighten things up a bit. Jesus Christ it needs it."

"Well go have your fun elsewhere and don't talk about my daughter ever again. Ok?"

"Ok darling. I'll shut up. Just 'cause she brings half the footy team home doesn't mean she's going to be like her mum…"

A glass shattered with a loud crash against a kitchen cupboard door. Shelley's mum was on her feet now, cats scattered to the nearest exits.

"What did you say? What did you say? You piece of shit. Pack your boxes and get the fuck out of here. And don't say another thing. Dad's gonna be here soon and he'll kick your arse if he finds you."

"Your dad? I'm so scared…"

"He's more of a man than you are. He'll break you in pieces."

The boyfriend squared up, grabbing an empty tallie and advancing into the living room.

"You shut up, you stupid slut! Sit down and shut the fuck up. Before I do something I shouldn't in front of these nice children."

Raj whispered to MJ and Cliff, "Let's go."

"No, no, please," the boyfriend was all fake smile, "Don't let our little carry-on worry you. We're just mucking around, right? You guys stay and do whatever you want. Go have some fun now, ok?"

Cliff felt Raj tug at his shoulder, but he couldn't walk away. Not from opportunity. A chance to start their business. He had to give it a go.

"Actually, we came over to see you mate," Cliff tried to sound as relaxed as he could.

"Me?"

"Yeah, we heard you had an old RX7 you didn't want anymore. We thought, maybe, we could take it off your hands."

"Is that right?"

"Yeah, only if you don't want it, you know."

"Well, fuck me. You wanna do me a favour, hey? I wonder who put you up to this?"

The boyfriend scanned the room. Silence.

He seemed to chill a little, becoming thoughtful, "That thing's worth a grand you know."

"Bullshit it is," scoffed Shel's mum.

"What would you know, you dumb bitch? If you weren't so stupid, I could have sold it and given you half."

"I told you already, you get it out of here today or it's going to scrap."

"Fuck me," he turned back into the kitchen, kicking the base of a cupboard, "You know I have nowhere to put it right now. What do you want me to do?"

"I don't care. You just get rid of it today."

"Maybe we can have a quick look?" Cliff suggested.

Raj stared at him wide-eyed. MJ looked at the floor. The boyfriend, to Cliff's great surprise, nodded and led them out the back.

An hour later they'd gone all over the wrecked sports car. The mood had relaxed. The boyfriend enjoyed getting under the hood, even crawling beneath the car, opening panels, unbolting and testing parts, debating everything that needed doing to the car. There was a lot. He laughed his rasping cough-laugh every time they found a new problem. Most of all, he laughed when Raj talked about how he could fix each one.

"I've had her for two years, mate, I can tell you it's not that simple."

So, at the end of the inspection, Cliff was more than a little surprised when Raj stood up and announced, "Yep, I think it's doable."

"Ok cool," Cliff turned to the boyfriend, "We'd like to give it a go mate. But it's up to you. Whether you're cool with giving it to us or not?"

The boyfriend looked pained. Cliff could see his inner turmoil, fidgeting with a socket spanner as he spoke, "It's worth a grand you know."

Raj shook his head, "There's way too much to do."

"Yeah mate," Cliff sucked air through his teeth, "It's just a school project."

The boyfriend, head down in thought, walked around to the front of the car. He folded his arms, then tapped the spanner on his chin, looking fondly at the grease-blackened engine.

"This is the model they all want. Five speed, rotary, all original, you know?"

"If it was driving, mate, but you said it yourself, it's a massive job. Who knows if it can even be fixed," Cliff put on his most worried face.

"Hmm."

The more torn the boyfriend looked, the more Cliff found himself enjoying the game. It came naturally to him. Now it was time to play his trump card.

He took out the fat bundle of notes and coins wrapped in a cloth bag, the hundred dollars they'd each contributed to. It clinked appealingly.

"Look, the best I can do is a hundred bucks, mate."

The boyfriend looked up, surprised.

"It's my dad's money so I'll get my arse kicked. But, hey, that's cool. If you want to take it, that's the best I can do."

It was as if Cliff had whacked him with a magic wand. The boyfriend's face lit up and he tugged on his straggly goatie.

"Alright, no worries, if you want to pay a hundred for it, we can do that. No worries."

He held out a hand to Cliff.

That was all it took. Cliff insisted on getting the original paperwork and a handwritten receipt to formalize the sale. That was when he finally learned the boyfriend's name. Trent. Then it was done, his first business deal closed successfully.

As the three mates walked away from the house and the sound of Shelley's dog savaging the fence, MJ held out her hand for a high five.

"Yeah!" Cliff smashed it.

Raj followed, slapping MJ's hand with his right and Cliff's with his left. They formed a huddle, arms around each other's shoulders, bouncing up and down in a circle, chanting, just like they did after scoring a try at footy. It was the start of their first business venture, their first chance to make some real money.

Beneath the joyful celebrations, however, Cliff felt a nag of guilt. They'd taken advantage of Trent.

"We're gonna spray it Ferrari red, ok, and put decals down the sides," MJ slapped Raj on the back, hard enough to wind him, then gripped Cliff around the neck with a muscled arm, "It'll put another fucking grand on the price!"

"Too bloody right," Cliff laughed as he ducked out of the choke, his spirits rising again, Trent quickly forgotten, "Let's make this thing sick."

It took a year. They worked afternoons after school and weekends when they didn't have homework, family stuff or football. They begged and borrowed tools from friends and family. They worked their shadiest connections to get free parts. When they couldn't, they squeezed parents and siblings for loans. Worst case, they found odd jobs, part time, and used their own precious savings. Then they'd haggle with the wreckers, as best they could, for cheap second-hand parts.

At last came the day when the motor purred and the gearbox shifted without a clunk. Then they set about the body work, replacing rust-gutted panels, hammering others straight, bog-filling smaller dents and sanding it all back smoothly. It was a long and frustrating battle just to get its famous pop-up headlights working, but they did it. Finally, with spray gear borrowed from one of MJ's cousins, they transformed the speedy curves to a bright, glossy red.

Six weeks after completing their HSC exams and officially leaving school, the three friends proudly submitted their ad and accompanying photos to the Trading Post. Five days later it sold for an unbelievable $5000. The best possible celebration of the start of their new lives.

SIX
1997

It certainly seemed that way to Cliff as he and Raj set his new lawn mower down with a grunt on the footpath in front of his house.

"Awesome mate, thanks," Cliff stepped back from the mower to admire it, "Might not look like that much, but this baby is the start. The beginning of a million-dollar fuckin' empire."

He turned to smile at Raj, but his mate had already gone back into the van.

"Come on man, I've got to get this back to my dad."

Cliff hurried over so Raj could hand him his whipper snipper. Raj hopped out and swung the battered left door closed, wobbling it into place. Next he carefully aligned the right door before ramming it home with the full force of his shoulder. It was a procedure Cliff knew well, but it still made him smile. The van had been the centre-piece of Raj's family, and the butt of many jokes from his friends, for as long as Cliff had known him. Today, however, he could only be grateful for it.

"Thanks mate, you're a legend. And so is your dad's van."

Raj held up a finger as he got into the cab. The van started with a rattle and then a high-pitched whine. A cloud of black smoke blew out the back as Raj put it into gear and drove off.

Cliff lay the whipper snipper down and scuttled up the driveway into the garage. He grabbed the battered, metal jerry can his neighbour over the back fence, Jerzy, an elderly, red-faced Polish man, had given him as a gift of encouragement when Cliff had mentioned starting his own mowing business.

"I'ff got a new one now, bright, shiny one," the old man had winked as he handed it over the fence to Cliff, his hand shaking a little with age.

As he skipped for the door, Cliff snatched his old Magpies cap from where it hung on a rusty nail in the wall and a set of yellow ear muffs he'd once 'borrowed' from woodwork class.

His mum and dad's house had no lawn whatsoever, being concrete pavers at the front and a dust bowl at the back. So, Cliff picked up the whipper snipper and headed across the road to an open parkland that formed the corridor for the main electricity lines servicing this part of Sydney. About a dozen high voltage lines looped from tower to tower. At the base of each tower the grass grew long and lush.

He donned his sunnies and ear muffs and slung the whipper snipper over his shoulder. This would be great practice. He began at the base of the first tower, loving how the grass melted away with each pass.

He'd almost finished the last side of the tower when he heard a voice behind him. He could only just hear it over the whirr of the whipper snipper and through the dull cushioning of his ear muffs, but it was a familiar voice. Then an unmistakable laugh followed by phlegmy coughing.

He turned around, removing his ear muffs, to find Trent standing only inches behind him, so close he could smell the alcohol on his breath. Behind Trent stood another bloke with a shaven head and a tallie of VB in his hand. Trent pushed Cliff so he stumbled and dropped the whipper snipper.

"Don't you say g'day to old mates?" he squinted.

"I didn't hear you blokes," Cliff tried to buy some time. Despite Trent's words he knew this wasn't going to be an exchange of pleasantries between old 'mates'.

"So, I heard you sold the Rexie."

"Yeah thanks mate we did. It took us a long time, you know."

"I heard you made five grand out of it."

"Yeah but, you know, it cost us more than that. In parts and getting it sprayed, you know."

"Fuck off. Don't feed me shit mate. You gave me a hundred bucks for it. That's bullshit."

"Yep that's bullshit right there," his skinhead mate echoed.

"So, I reckon you owe me some money," Trent squared up.

Cliff edged backwards but found himself up against the steel base of the electricity tower.

"You sold it fair and square mate. You didn't have to sell it. No-one made you," he tried to level.

With the speed of a striking snake, Trent seized Cliff around the neck, forcing him against the tower, "I didn't sell it. I was forced to. That's not a sale. That's bullshit."

"Hey mate, take it easy, ok."

Cliff felt any chance of avoiding violence slipping away fast. Especially with the skinhead's voice chiming in from the background, "Fuckin smash 'im, Trennie."

They grappled, Trent getting an arm around Cliff's neck. His breath, hot against the side of Cliff's face, was an over-powering mix of alcohol and stale cigarettes.

"I only want half the cash, ok matey? But you're gonna give it to me, ok? Half the cash."

"I gave my share to my dad, I don't have any money, alright?"

In rage, Trent threw a series of punches which Cliff tried his best to twist and duck out of.

"You - fucking - get - me - my - money!"

Finally, Cliff broke free, pushed Trent away and began to run. He didn't count on the skinhead, though.

For a drunk it was an extremely sharp throw, the VB bottle thudding into the back of Cliff's head before shattering on the ground. The shocking flash of pain overwhelmed Cliff, he was conscious of falling and then nothing more.

He opened his eyes to find his mum looking down at him, panic on her face.

"Oh my god, are you alright?"

"Yeah, yeah," he reassured her. And himself.

He was on the grass next to the tower and his head hurt. He sat up, a little dizzy and slowly got to his feet. He looked around for Trent and his skinhead mate but they were nowhere to be seen. Then he noticed his whipper snipper was gone.

"Yeah sweetie, they took it," Nancy gave him a pitying look, "They took your mower from the front as well. Before we realised it, they were gone. Pricks. Did you know them?"

When the cops tracked Trent down, he denied any knowledge of the stolen mower and whipper snipper and there was nothing more they could, or would, do.

"Told you, buddy," his dad had been unimpressed, "They'd have gone to Cash Converters the same day. There's only one way to deal with a little piece of shit like that. Between me and the boys, his face and a piece of gal pipe."

The cops, however, weren't divulging any details of where Trent was staying and it was proving hard to get anything from the neighbourhood network. MJ wasn't hanging out with Shel anymore, so she and her mum had no interest in helping either.

After a while Cliff got tired of talking about it. He obviously wasn't meant to have a business. And he hated the gleam of satisfaction he could see in his dad's eyes.

Life hadn't progressed so well for his mates either. MJ's natural sporting flair had always been legendary. So much so, the school had let her play in the boy's footie team, where she'd ended up top scorer in her first season. Unfortunately, her dreams of Olympic glory at Sydney 2000 in her favourite sport, Taekwondo, had begun to fade after failing to win a crucial tournament. Since then, the coach seemed to write her off. In frustration, MJ went to work in her uncle's landscaping business and spent most of her free time at the pub.

Raj, who had studied endless hours, for years and years, in the hope of going to university and having a career in Finance, had narrowly missed the required score. Instead, he'd enrolled at TAFE to do a mechanical trade. He continued to work for his dad, to pay his way, up at 5am every day to battle the traffic across Western Sydney in search of bargain supplies.

Cliff managed to get some shifts at his local Starbucks, serving customers and cleaning up in the kitchen. But they came randomly, at short notice, when a regular staff member couldn't make it. The rest of the time he bummed around, hanging out with MJ and other former school mates, drinking a lot, going to parties and getting stoned.

Eventually the day came when he was woken by a loud knock. Before he could shake off his hazy, alcohol-heavy sleep, his dad swung the door open.

"Time you did something useful, mate. If you're going to stay here, you need to contribute. You're an adult."

"Huh? Do you mind letting me wake up first?"

Tommy tossed the Centrelink forms on the bed, "Fill those in."

Cliff showered and dressed slowly, his head still hurting, then sat down at the dining table, right hand wrapped around a large mug of instant coffee, his left flipping through the forms.

"No, no, no," he shook his head, the questions seemed endless.

He shuffled into the living room and found the cordless phone lying on the sofa. He picked it up and dialed MJ.

"Hey, I'm sick of this shit Ems. We're wasting time. We're meant to be fucking getting our business going. Instead we just get pissed all the time."

"I know, it's bullshit, hey?" MJ chuckled.

"Seriously doofus. You know your uncle said I could work for him if I wanted? I'm in. Let's make some cash and have another go at a fucking car or something."

"Yeah?"

It occurred to Cliff that the best revenge on Trent, his skinhead mate and everyone else who wanted to pull him down, would be to make lots of money, build a kick-arse business and leave them behind.

He decided the lawn mower incident was a good lesson learnt, a funny story to tell one day when he was successful. He'd just be more careful to keep his wins to himself in the future.

The idea grew stronger, becoming a driving force, as he worked hard and sweated in the hot midday sun, or stretched the aches out of his back and rubbed his blue knuckles against the cold of an early, rainy morning. MJ's uncle, Arthur, could only give him a few shifts, again to fill in for full timers when needed, but he made the most of them, watching the experienced guys closely and learning. Together with the work at Starbucks, he was able to put a decent wad of cash in his dad's hand every fortnight and stride off with his head held high.

Then one Saturday morning everything changed.

He was up early for one of Arthur's gigs.

"The client wants a big clean up, paving and the works," Arthur's deep voice rumbled down the line, "But the dickhead wants to work with us, to try and keep his costs down."

"Oh yeah?" Cliff smiled at the idea.

"It's fucking annoying, mate, believe me, he'll be looking over your shoulders the whole time."

"Ah, yeah," Cliff could imagine it now. It would make things tense.

"On top of that he won't have any idea what he's doing. So he's just gonna slow us down and the whole job's gonna end up taking longer and costing more. Fuckwit."

"Shit."

"Do your best mate. Don't give him any reasons to ask for a discount, ok? He's gonna pay for every fucking hour we're there."

From the moment he arrived on site, however, Cliff was pleasantly surprised.

Not by the look of the place. It was a typical home for the area, a small, run-down, single-story house on a large block. The yards at front and back were a shambles of overgrown trees, weeds the size of bushes and hip-high grass. Out-of-control vines buried the garage and garden shed. Somewhere inside the jungle, a fence separated the house from its neighbours at the back and down either side.

The first surprise was pulled up to the front kerb. A bright new, fawn-coloured Pajero 4WD shimmered in the sunshine. Not the wheels you'd expect to belong to a tight-arsed local.

"G'day mate, come on in!"

A voice called out as Cliff was inspecting the car. He looked up to see a man in a white cap, big smile and equally broad paunch, stride down the front path and hold out his hand.

"Welcome. I'm Allen."

A similar aged, but glowingly fit-looking woman emerged from the house, carrying half a dozen take-away coffees in a cardboard holder.

"Hi, I'm Wendy, Allen's wife."

Wendy was darkly tanned and when she smiled her teeth were a brilliant white in the sunshine. She wore a tight-fitting outfit that looked more like she was going to the gym than working on house renovations, except for a leather tool belt slung around her hips. She reminded Cliff of a presenter off a TV renovation show and he tried not to smile at the thought.

Wendy placed the tray down on an old rusty garden table, the grass around it growing so high it poked up through the umbrella hole.

"Sorry it's just Maccas coffee. But we need something to get us going on a Saturday morning, hey!"

She handed Cliff a cup, which he gladly accepted. Then she jogged over to the Pajero, grabbed a fat Macdonald's bag from the front seat and jogged back. She emptied its contents onto the table, a pile of paper-wrapped egg and bacon Macmuffins.

"I bet no-one's had time for brekkie, so please dig in."

Allen grabbed one, unwrapped it with relish and took a bite.

"Cheers," he mumbled happily through a full mouth. Cliff felt a rush of hunger and followed Allen's lead.

"Mmm, awesome, thanks," he got out between chews, nodding and smiling with Allen and instantly feeling at home with this strange couple.

"Nice day for working outside," Allen said when they had eventually finished eating.

"Yeah, great day for it," Cliff agreed.

The place was only a suburb away from his own home, so Cliff had walked there, arriving a little early.

"Looks like we've got plenty to do over here…"

"Oh yeah, we've got our work cut out," Allen laughed, "But once we get going it should move pretty quickly. Just doing the basics, you know. We're not making the Hanging Gardens of Babylon."

Cliff laughed. Although he didn't actually know the reference, he got the general idea. He'd noticed the 'Sold' sign on the front fence.

"You just bought the place, did you?"

"Yeah that's right. I know it looks like a bit of a shocker, but we could see the potential. You know, it won't take too much to make it look pretty darn good."

"For sure," Cliff was not so sure.

"Wendy and her dad are looking after the inside. They're great when it comes to painting and all that. So, it's us on the outside. I got the skip delivered yesterday. We'll get all the clearing done this morning, I reckon, then get onto prepping for the paving. Tomorrow we lay it all and done!"

"Sounds like a plan," Cliff nodded. He was intrigued, "So are you guys moving in?"

"No, no, no," Allen shook his head, "It's an investment."

He caught Wendy's eye and the two of them seemed amused at the idea of moving into the house.

"This is our business," Wendy saw the question-mark on Cliff's face, "We like to fix places up and sell them. We're flippers!"

"Yeah, right."

"We live in the city. In Potts Point. We both have jobs and we do this part time. It's our retirement plan," she laughed.

"Right. But why would you come out here and do it? Like, I mean, if you don't mind my asking, I would have thought you'd be better off investing in Potts Point?"

"Well, you would have thought so, wouldn't you," Allen had a smile in his voice, "The interesting thing is, prices in inner Sydney are not going up these days. But out here they're selling like hot cakes."

"Is that right?"

"Yup, you must have seen the convoys of cars driving around every Saturday? They're going to open houses and auctions."

"Yeah, now that you mention it, I've seen them. Never really thought about it before."

"Well of course you wouldn't if you weren't looking to buy a house. But let me tell you, you are living amongst a gold rush right now."

Cliff was fascinated. He sensed that Fortune had given him a rare opportunity to discover something important. A door had just opened halfway and he wanted to go inside. Trouble was, just at that moment, the company ute pulled up, MJ in the passenger seat with Manu, one of the senior guys, at the wheel. Both were pumping fists and singing along to Black Hole Sun turned up loud.

"Hmm," Cliff thought to himself as he strolled over to help his mates unload, "I bet this 'gold rush' is great for people from Potts Point, who already have lots of money and can cash in out here."

No-one Cliff knew was making any money out of houses in Mount Druitt.

They put in two big, sweaty, scratchy days of clearing and landscaping. By the end of it, the place looked a little 'naked' but remarkably transformed, nonetheless. The house itself appeared so much bigger, more solid, symmetrical and appealing. It had gone from being a dump to something you would want to buy.

Cliff was impressed. He had to admit Allen and Wendy knew what they were doing.

Most of all, though, he was inspired. His two customers had been so cheerfully open and willing to share everything they were doing with him. He now had a plan.

He lingered until his two work mates had driven off, waving, before he turned to Allen and Wendy.

"I just wanted to say thanks to you both, it's been incredible. I've learnt so much. You guys have really opened my eyes."

Wendy laughed with delight and gave him a warm hug.

"That's a pleasure, mate," Allen held out a hand and shook Cliff's happily.

He fished into his pocket, took out his wallet and found a card which he handed to Cliff.

"That's my details, if you ever want to get in touch for more advice."

It was nearly three weeks later when Cliff decided to take Allen up on his offer. In that time, he had spent every free moment investigating properties for sale in the area. He had stood out the front of real estate agencies, looking at the ads in their windows. He had bought the Saturday papers and grabbed the free local newspapers that were lobbed over his mum and dad's fence on Wednesdays. By the end of three weeks he was confused.

"Hello," came Allen's familiar voice.

"Hi Allen, its Cliff here, mate. Do you remember-"

"Cliff! Yeah, of course I do. What's up mate, how can I help you?"

"You gave me your card and, you know, you said I could give you a call about the house flipping..."

"Absolutely, mate."

"It's just that I've been looking at what's for sale out here and I can't make any sense of it. I mean, I just can't seem to find the kind of place you said I should look for."

Allen chuckled, "You've discovered that real estate agents don't always tell the truth, hey? Quick, better put that on the 6 o'clock news!"

"Yeah," Cliff laughed along, "I mean, I realise that, you know, what you're saying about agents and all, but are you saying I am looking in the wrong place? I guess I don't know where else to look…"

"Well, no, you're not necessarily looking in the wrong place. But there's a process you have to go through, to get to the real information. I'm assuming you're talking about price, right?"

"Yeah, there's nothing near 70K for sale. Except a place that's completely burnt out."

Allen erupted in laughter, "Yep I know the one well. You're right to dismiss it, what a nightmare that would be!"

"Yeah, that's what I figured."

"Look, I tell you what. We're heading out your way on the weekend. There's a few bits and pieces to spruce up around the Emerton place for the Open House. But we also want to start looking for our next one. So why don't you come along with us? If you're not working, I mean. It would be really good for you."

"Yeah, sure, that would be fantastic."

"Ok great. Well, give me a call on Friday afternoon and we'll work out the details."

"Awesome, thank you so much."

Saturday was a grey day, rain drizzling steadily. The Pajero pulled up outside a brown, colorbond fence on a deserted suburban street.

Graffiti covered, its metal panels bowed and buckled over at a severe angle. A grey-brown, cement-tiled roof poked above the scrappy tops of bottle brush trees. Allen edged forward until they reached the driveway. The gate had long since fallen off its hinges and lay buried in long grass and weeds. They all leaned forward to view the house.

It was low set, clad in flaking, white-painted timber boards. Two battered sofas adorned a concrete veranda. To the side of the house was a carport, its fibreglass roof sagging. However, there was no room for a car. A landslide of junk cascaded from the back and spilled out at the front. Cliff could make out broken chairs, sheets of cardboard, piles of magazines, old mattresses, guttering, even a cracked porcelain toilet. Caught in the avalanche were several wheelie bins, overflowing with rubbish.

"Now you can see why it went for such a bargain," Wendy announced from the back seat. (They had insisted Cliff sit in the front to get the best view).

"Only 65K," she looked up from a black exercise book that sat open on her lap.

"It's one that got away as far as we're concerned," Allen lamented, "It's really perfect."

"Perfect?" Cliff couldn't help laughing.

"Yeah I know it seems crazy but it's true. It needs a big clean up. That's it. No major damage. It's actually a nice house underneath all that."

"Absolutely," Wendy agreed, "A coat of paint, inside and out, a little 'tlc' in the garden, like a new lawn and a few neat plants and Bob's your uncle."

"And a new fence," Cliff joined in.

"Nope. We'd just rip it out and not have one," Allen shook his head.

"Oh, ok," Cliff was learning more and more.

"Yeah, no point wasting money," Wendy added, "Anyway, if you've done a nice job on the house, why hide it!"

"So how come you guys didn't buy it?"

"Because we can also be fooled by real estate agents," Allen smiled. "Believe it or not, this place was advertised in the local paper for 115K."

"They used a photo of the back of the house. Made it look really neat, you know, hid all the disaster zones. Sly buggers!" Wendy growled with mock outrage.

"So, we figured it would probably find a buyer and we never even looked at it."

"Yeah, right."

"The first we knew was when Gary told us his St Mary's office had sold a place for 65K."

"That's right. Even he was caught out by it, wasn't he?" Wendy snapped her notebook shut.

Allen turned to Cliff, "Gary is our 'guy on the inside'. He's an agent we've known for a long time. We always use him to sell our houses, so he knows he stands to benefit by looking after us. He gives us real information, like what properties are actually selling for, what sellers are really thinking. He even tells us about properties *before* they come onto the market. So, we get the first shot at them."

"Everything he tells us goes in here," Wendy patted the cover of her exercise book. It's the key to our success – knowledge."

"It puts us in a fantastic position when it comes to negotiating a deal," Allen enthused, "That's what I meant by knowing the real values. Not believing what the agents advertise."

"Pretty nifty, you guys," Cliff was impressed.

"We've got one more to show you," Allen shifted the gears into drive and pulled out from the curb, "If you have another ten minutes?"

"Yeah, sure, I'm up for as many as you like!"

They made their way through the winding streets until they came to a bright brick house, neatly fenced with a freshly paved driveway. Its red-tiled roof sported a shiny solar hot water system.

Allen pulled in across the street from it.

"So, here's proof you don't always have to buy a total dog to get the right price. Guess how much this one sold for."

"I don't know. Sounds like it went cheap?"

"70K."

"Really? Wow. How does that happen?"

"Patience. You make lots of offers and you're patient. Every now and then you get one. The buyer was an investor just like us. They would've put in a low offer, backing it up with evidence, just like we do."

"So, you just make offers on everything?"

"No, not everything. That's where Gary comes in. He puts us onto properties that might have a reason to go cheaper. Sometimes they're in a state like that last one and no buyer wants to go near it."

"What about this one?"

"Turns out it was a deceased estate. The kids just wanted to sell it and split the money. They must have got impatient and taken the low offer."

A few minutes later, Cliff waved goodbye to Allen and Wendy at their Emerton house.

"Thanks guys!"

As he walked home, Cliff looked at the world with new eyes. He peered over fences and through gates. He assessed the state of roofs, guttering, paint and cladding.

He smiled to himself, passing a place with three rusting car bodies in the front yard and what looked like a scrap yard out the back.

"Gold mine," he chuckled.

SEVEN

"Hello?" A strong male voice answered.

For a moment, Cliff felt his confidence drain. What was he doing? He wasn't ready to buy a house!

He sucked in a deep breath and re-focused on his plan, "G'day, is that Angelo?"

"Yeah mate, how can I help you?"

"I'm interested in the place you've got for sale in Blackett."

"Which one?"

"The one that says great investment or first home. It's a four bedder."

"Oh yeah, what would you like to know?"

"I'd like to have a look at it. Can you give me the address?"

"Sure. It's 34 Coleman Street. Would you like to arrange an inspection? I've actually got a number of others in the area if you are interested?"

"Yeah, sure that would be good. How is tomorrow?"

"Let me find out and give you a call back. I've got your number on my screen. What was your name again?"

"Cliff."

"Ok, no worries, Cliff mate. I'll call around the owners and see what I can set up. Are we talking morning or afternoon?"

"Either would be fine."

"Ok, give me a few minutes and I'll call you back."

Cliff hung up. It was as simple as that. He was on the road to being a property investor.

He soon found the pattern was the same. Each agent invited him to inspect more houses than just the one he was interested in. So as soon as he had three tours booked in for the next day he stopped.

He sat back on his bed and stretched, enjoying the feeling of power. The agents were really fighting for his business, setting up the inspections, fitting into his schedule and offering to drive him around.

"I mean, I could be a real buyer."

That last thought deflated Cliff. His biggest hurdle was always going to be finance. He needed a bank loan. Which meant he needed a deposit and probably a full-time job. Right now, he had neither.

"Hmm," he contemplated his small, box of a room. This was where people with rich parents had the advantage. He sucked his pen, making some slurping, clicking sounds with his tongue. Then he flicked the pen across the room, swung his legs off the bed and picked up his phone. He found MJ's uncle's number and hit dial.

"G'day Cliffie mate, what's up?"

"G'day Arthur. How you going?"

"Good matey, what's up?"

"Just wondering if I can get some more shifts, mate? I need to make more money."

"Don't we all brother. I'm giving you everything I've got, matey. I mean everything that you are suitable for, you know? We're just bloody quiet right now mate."

"Yeah, right. I mean I'm up for doing other stuff you know, I'm happy to learn whatever."

"Sure matey. Trouble is I've got the blokes who can do the skilled work already, you know? I can't justify paying someone to teach you, you know what I mean?"

"Yeah I understand mate. Please just keep me in mind if anything comes up."

"Of course I will, buddy. But you know what I reckon. If you want better work you should go get yourself a trade, you know? Go join Raj at TAFE. You'll set yourself up for life. You got plenty of time matey. I've been trying to tell MJ the same."

"Thanks. I'm sure you are probably right. I'm just trying to set myself up in another way. That's all."

"Well don't do anything stupid either. You've got all the time in the world. Just take it easy, work your way up. It's the best way in the end, mate, I can tell you."

"Thanks Arthur, I appreciate it."

Cliff was frustrated. He scrolled through his mobile contacts and found Raj.

"Hey Cliffie."

"Mate, where have you been? You never call me no more. You gone on tour in the van? Hit the road to Queensland or something?"

"Just busy with TAFE mate."

"Well I've got a plan for us, Rajie. You won't have to bother about TAFE again. We're gonna be rich bro!"

"Uh-oh, another one of your plans. I don't wanna get my head kicked in ok."

"Get over it, you idiot. They kicked my head in not yours. This is safe as houses mate. Literally."

"What is it?"

"I met this dude. Lives in bloody Double Bay, somewhere around there. Rich-as, right? You know what he does to make his money?"

"What? We're not dealing drugs ok."

"I told you it's safe. Totally legit. He's a property investor. He buys houses cheap, fixes them up and sells them and makes a fucking fortune. It's called 'flipping'".

"Yeah, I know, I've read about it."

"Well, I've been working with this guy. He's shown me everything he does. Exactly what to do. It's totally sick bro. We can do it. I know we can. Do you know where he buys his houses? Guess."

"I don't know... Near the beach? Bondi area? I've heard, like, around the Olympic site is going off?"

"Out here mate. Mount Druitt."

"Serious?"

"Yeah he reckons it's the best place in Sydney. Says it's a gold mine. He's even told me all the numbers, you know, exactly what he buys for, how much he spends and what he makes. It's crazy. But it's real. I've already checked it out."

"Ok, so how do you buy a house? You need money, right? You need money to make money."

"Yeah but we only need enough for a deposit. Plus a little to fix it up and cover legal costs and stuff. Like maybe twelve grand."

Raj whistled.

"It's not that much between three of us. Four grand each. Maybe not even, if we fix it up cheaper. Do you have dosh saved?"

"Nope. I work for my family. I don't get paid. You know my situation. They support me through TAFE and I work in the shop to pay them back."

"Yeah, ok, I'm the same, anything extra I make pays the bills here. They just don't bother to put me through TAFE or nothing."

"You don't want to go to TAFE."

"Yeah I know. I'm just saying. So, can't you borrow off your old man?"

"Come on man, no way."

"Give him a cut. It's the best investment he will ever make. Tell him. He's a businessman he'll get it."

"He's already putting me through TAFE man. Plus there's my sister. He's saving up for her wedding. He doesn't have any extra to throw around. Even if he did, he's not going to risk it in a scheme we've come up with."

"Ok no worries. You know what, it's still easy. It's two or three car flips for us just like we did with the Rexie."

"That will take us three years, dude!"

"Not if we do them all at the same time. One at each of our places. Get your mates at TAFE to help."

"I dunno, man, no-one's got the time."

"Fuck man, this is like the most awesome opportunity ever. It's like those stories you hear about famous people who make millions. They don't bitch about their time and shit. They just work their butts off and do whatever it takes."

"Yeah, yeah," Raj laughed, "Go back to your TV shows."

"Come on dude, let's do it. When we make our first million you can pay your dad back twenty times over. Fuck, you can buy him ten shops and he can retire. Watch cricket and smoke pot all day."

"It's not pot, dickhead."

Cliff laughed. He could never pass up a chance to wind Raj up. Raj's dad smoked an Indian blend of herbal cigarettes that were totally legal.

"I'd love to do this with you ok," Raj was conciliatory, "But it's a big risk, whatever you say. How much is a house? It's not twelve grand. So, we're going to be in some huge debt. If it goes wrong, for whatever reason, then we are stuck with debt over our heads and that could be for life. It's serious man."

"Nothing can go wrong, Rajie. We buy a house with a loan. We fix it up and sell it for more than we paid. Then we pay off the loan and keep the profit. Where's the risk?"

"Ok, well you show me the numbers sometime. I am interested. I just can't drop TAFE it would be too insulting to my parents. I can't do anything right now. Ok?"

"Ok, no worries, Rajie," Cliff could tell his friend could be pushed no further, "Take it easy mate."

He flicked to MJ's number.

"Hey Cliffie old son."

"What's up groover?"

"Ah, mate, just sitting here watching these dick-wads get beaten again."

"What, are you at the game?"

"Nope, down the Toppie with the gang."

"Geez you should seriously take your bed down there and move in."

MJ laughed, "I reckon I should. I spend enough money here they could at least let me sleep in a corner. Oh yeah, hang on, I already do that sometimes."

Cliff cracked up, "You're a bad, bad girl."

"Hey, I try my best. So, what's up? How you finding it with Arthur?"

"Great. I love it. Just wish he could give me more work. You know, I only get a few shifts here and there."

"Yeah, you're never gonna retire. He farms it out, tries to spread it round. But he's a tight arse. Hang on-"

There was a loud noise from the crowd in the pub, then MJ came back, "Fucking losers, why do I bother? No, look, Artie's alright, you know. If you don't have anything better to do. It's good, honest work."

"Yeah, absolutely. I asked him today for more shifts but he said he had to use the experienced guys first. I mean, fair enough. But if you're talking to him, put in a word for me, yeah?"

"No worries. How come you wanna make more dosh, you got a girl or something?"

"No, don't be stupid, still with Mrs Palmer and her five daughters." MJ laughed.

"Don't worry I'd tell you if the status changed. No, I've got a new plan for us Ems. I've found something that's gonna make us rich as. Serious. But I'll tell you when you're not watching footy. Give me a buzz when you can chat, yeah?"

"Ok mate, sounds bloody interesting. It's not another car job, though, is it? That one almost killed us."

"No doofus, it's not another car. This is fucking serious. Totally safe, totally legit. Call me tomorrow ok?"

"No worries old son, will do."

"Alright. Go the magpies!"

"Bloody dead ducks is what they are. This will be the fourth hiding in a row."

"Hang in there, you never know, miracles can happen."

Cliff hung up. He could tell the chances of MJ coming to the party with half the deposit were slim.

"So, it's down to me," he tapped his phone against his chin, "I've got to do it myself and show them the way."

That night he tossed and turned, his head busy. How was he going to make twelve thousand dollars? Quickly? He went over and over his options, who he could borrow from, what he could sell, where he could get more work, but nothing seemed viable. At least nothing legal. The fact of the matter was, in Cliff's experience of life, the only thing that could make decent money quickly was crime.

By morning he was exhausted and struggled sleepily out of bed. He'd played out so many scenarios in his head. Stealing cars, dealing drugs, burglary...

Maybe his dad was right. Maybe the wealthy classes on the north shore deserved to be robbed. Maybe that was the only way a boy from the western suburbs could even up the score. Knock off a couple of luxury cars, rebirth them quietly in a garage in the back blocks of Mount Druitt... and Bob's your uncle. Twelve grand. More. From then on, do everything legit and who would ever know?

The trouble was, Cliff would know. And his family would know. Which meant they would know they were right all along. He couldn't do it. He had sworn for too long that he was going to do things differently.

He slumped back down on his bed, with a sigh. He might as well cancel the real estate inspections. He'd just have to wait for his chance in the future.

Allen's words came back to him, urging him to act quickly, before the prices went up further. Before everyone else got on the bandwagon and the opportunity was gone. He rolled over to face the wall and closed his eyes. How frustrating it was, to see a pot of gold but not be able to reach it.

When he eventually got up, he headed for the kitchen to make a coffee. He would cancel the estate agents, then maybe go get a Trading Post and start looking for his first, fully legit car reno.

On his way past the living room he noticed the TV was still on and his Dad had fallen asleep on the sofa, the remote fallen to the floor beside him. He walked over and quietly switched the TV off.

His Dad breathed with a gurgle and a rasp, his mouth half open, his long, greying hair matted and his chin spattered with white stubble. Several empty tallies stood on the coffee table and a couple more on the floor.

"Yep," Cliff thought to himself, "It's not so easy, hey."

He walked into his parent's bedroom. His mum lay diagonally across the bed, clasping his Dad's pillow and snoring. Cliff went to the dresser and pulled out a thick, brown, woolen blanket, then headed back to the living room. He quietly unfolded the blanket and spread it over his Dad.

Cliff stood there, looking down at the man who'd brought him up. He felt a resolve strengthen within him. He would find a way. He would be the one to show his family and friends that it could be done.

Back in his room he changed into his neatest jeans and a collared shirt, grabbed the newspaper with the agents' details and an old geography notebook that he'd ripped the used pages out of. He pulled his mobile phone off its charger and slipped everything into a black backpack, picked up his house key and headed out the front door.

By early afternoon Cliff had been taken around by two agents, inspected nine houses in the area and filled three pages of his notebook with their details. A good thing, he thought, because the nine houses were already a blur in his memory.

He'd also managed to milk the agents for information about recent sales, adding every new piece of info to his notes. His confidence was rising, already feeling the power of knowledge, convinced that Allen and Wendy had set him on the right path.

The last agent of the day was the first he'd rung the previous day.

Angelo was a burly, middle-aged bloke with abundant curly, black hair which he habitually matted down with the palm of his hand. His most striking feature was his rich and resonant voice. It filled the space around him when he spoke. And he spoke a lot.

There seemed nothing that Angelo didn't fire up with authority about. But he wasn't overpowering. He just took a joyful interest in all things and loved to share it with anyone who gave him half a chance.

So, at the end of the tour, when Angelo asked him about his finances, Cliff found himself admitting his true position.

"I haven't got any yet," he shrugged.

"Righto, well you know who's the best, don't you?"

"Um, not really…"

"Are you after a no deposit loan?"

"What do you mean?" Cliff was taken aback. Could he mean what it just sounded like?

"Well, you're investing right?"

"Yeah, that's it."

"So, you don't want to be spending any of your own money if you can help it. That's the best way when you're investing. Keep up-front costs to a minimum so you can get onto the next one. Right?"

"Sure."

"Well as I'm sure you already know, all the banks are offering very high LVRs right now, some up to 95%. You know what an LVR is of course?"

"No…"

"Ok. It's a term the banks use. Stands for loan-to-value-ratio. It used to be 80% for residential property. That means you had to put up 20% of the price - or value - of the house as a deposit and then the bank would lend you 80%. Got it?"

"Yeah, ok."

"But these days the banks are falling over themselves to write loans. So, they've increased the LVR they're willing to give you. Which is great news for investors because you don't have to put up as much money for a deposit."

"Sounds good."

"Like I said, up until recently the best was 95%. But now one of the banks is, quite incredibly, lending 100%. Imagine that! Shows you how good they think the market is, right?"

"Yeah, sure, that's awesome."

Angelo pulled a fat card holder from his inside jacket pocket. He flipped through until he found what he was looking for.

"You want to grab your notebook and write this down," he advised Cliff.

"Speak to Tom Bresciano at True Blue, St Mary's."

He read out the contact details for Cliff to note down. "He's a mate of mine and I can vouch for him. He's the best around. He really knows his stuff and he will give you good advice. And quite frankly, Cliff, there is no better deal than his 100% loan."

Cliff did not need convincing. It would completely solve his problem. His throat was tight as he asked, "What do you need to qualify, do you know if there is anything special?"

"Nope. The usual stuff. Employment history. A good credit record, I guess. But you know, even that isn't so important these days."

"Ok cool."

"I mean you just have to think like a bank for a minute. All they care about is that you can pay it back, right? So, do you have a full-time job?"

"Yeah." For the first time Cliff lied. The opportunity seemed so priceless, he couldn't jeopardise it now. Besides, he had a plan for the problem of a full-time job.

"Tick," Angelo continued, "Do you have an employer who will give you a good reference?"

"Sure."

"Tick. Do you have any bad debts that you haven't paid?"

"No."

"Tick. There you have it. That's all they care about."

"Right. Awesome. Thanks for the tip."

"No worries at all mate. That's what I'm here for. To help customers. Not just with finding the right property but with the whole process. Make it easy for them. You know, it's a win-win situation. If I can help you get the loan you need, then you can buy a property from me. Right?"

"Yeah, definitely mate. Can I ask you one more thing then?"

"Fire away. Anything I can help you with is a pleasure, buddy."

"Do you have a property sales report for the area?"

"I do indeed. Hold on a moment and I'll get Robyn to make a copy."

Angelo popped out to the reception area. Cliff could hear him give instructions to his receptionist. A moment later he returned, brandishing three photocopied pages.

"Here's all the sales in the area for the last three months. It's for agents use, so it's the best, most up-to-date information you can get."

"Wow, fantastic. Thanks!"

"No worries at all," Angelo smiled, pleased that, once again, he could be a font of wisdom.

'True Blue Residential Home Loan Offer' was printed in bold across the front page of the thick wad that sat on Cliff's lap. He read it over and over again as the train clicked and clacked and swayed side to side on its way from St Mary's back to Mt Druitt.

His Monday morning had been busy. At 9am he'd called and set up a meeting with Tom Bresciano at True Blue Home Loans. Then he'd jumped on a bus and a train to meet him at his St Mary's branch.

Angelo had been right about the 100% loan. It was the only one of its kind, Tom had proudly told him.

In fact, he had insisted Cliff apply for an $80,000 loan even though Cliff was adamant he was not going to pay more than $70,000 for any house.

"No, no, this way we can loan you your buying costs too," Tom had smiled cheerfully, "You know, taxes, legal costs and all."

"Really?"

"Absolutely, mate. Anyway, you just might find a place you really want that's over your budget. You never know, prices are going up all the time round here."

Cliff couldn't believe it. It was as if the more he asked for, the happier the bank was to loan it to him. If he really could get this loan, he would need no money of his own to buy his first property. He could get started right away. The reason he still had a big 'if' in his mind, was because he had lied to Tom Bresciano about one important detail - having a full-time job.

He rang MJ.

A sleepy voice answered.

"Hey Cliffie, it's kind of early. I was going to call you later."

"Early? What the fuck? Come on, I need a favour."

"Ok, ok, what's up?"

"I need you to have a chat to Arthur for me."

"Yeah, you already asked me, you dick."

Cliff hunched into the side of the train to keep the other passengers from overhearing, "No, I need him to give me a reference for a bank loan."

"A loan?"

"Yeah, I'm taking out a mortgage."

"What?"

"I'll explain the whole thing later, ok? Please just help me out here. I need Arthur to tell them I'm full-time. Do you reckon you can ask him that?"

"Yeah I suppose. Probably."

"Thanks Ems. Can you do it now? Please?"

"Sure old son. Leave it with me and I'll talk to him."

"You're a legend."

The train pulled into Mt Druitt and Cliff got off. He sauntered to the end of the platform, jogged across the tracks and leapt a low wire fence onto the street. Then he set off on the long walk through the back streets of Mt Druitt to Arthur's place.

A gravel driveway led into the main yard of the landscaping business. It was a wide area with piles of materials like pavers, rocks and various grades of sand. At the back of the site was the warehouse which housed tools, more expensive materials and the offices.

The roller door was up and Cliff stepped inside. He looked over towards the large internal window of Arthur's office. Just as he did so, Arthur looked up from his desk. His stern eyes met Cliff's.

"Cliff! Come in here a sec."

Cliff hastened across the warehouse and into the office. Arthur gestured to close the door behind him.

"Hi Arthur, how's it going?"

"Mate, I just spoke to MJ and she asked me to lie on your behalf. I don't like being put in this kind of position. What's going on?"

"Oh, sorry. I didn't mean, you know… I didn't want to ask you to do anything you didn't want to do. It's just that I'm applying for a home loan and, you know, like, I'm supposed to have a full-time job to get it. Since I've been working here pretty regularly, I was hoping you would, maybe, just tell them it's full-time. You know?"

"Oh yeah?"

"But, I mean, if you don't want to, that's no dramas."

"So, this is why you were asking me for more shifts?"

"Yeah that's right. I wanted to save up a deposit quicker. But now it's ok because I've found a bank that will loan me the full amount."

"Jesus. They make life easy for your generation. So why are you buying a house at your age?"

"I'm going to renovate it and sell it for a profit. I've been learning all about it and I've worked it out."

"You're a go-ahead young bloke, I've got to give you that. But do you really know what you're doing, matey? Do you know how much interest you will have to pay? If you don't earn enough to pay the interest, you'll lose the whole thing and I can't guarantee you regular work, I've already told you that. Do you understand the risk? If you can't meet your repayments the bank will take the house off you and they'll still come after you for the rest of the debt, for the rest of your life, until you pay it off."

"I know, I understand how it works. I've crunched the numbers and I know I can make it work. I know how much I have to buy the house for, I know how much I can spend fixing it up and I know what I can sell it for. So, you know, it's just maths."

Cliff was surprised at his own level of confidence.

"You don't want to be too cocky, bud. People a lot older and wiser than you have lost everything they owned thinking they knew all there was to know about the property market. The world is full of sharks, matey. If something sounds too good to be true, then you can bet your bottom dollar it is."

"Sure. I'm not jumping in blindly, Arthur. I've checked it out. I'm determined to prove it can be done."

"So, what kind of house, whereabouts? Around here?"

"Yeah around here. This area is perfect for flipping. There are cheap places that are solid, you know, structurally, but look like a dog's breakfast. You know the ones, where there's an old bloke who's lost his marbles or a cat lady who's trashed the place…"

"Yep, I've seen a few, you're not wrong," Arthur chuckled.

"If you pick the right one, you can clean it up and make it look great. Then you sell it for what the good ones sell for. If you done it right, there's enough margin to make a win. At the moment the market is hot."

"Bloody right. I've seen it. Just haven't known how to get into it myself. So, I'm gonna watch what you do, old son, and if you don't lose your shirt I might be right behind you."

Cliff smiled with relief at the sudden change of tone.

Arthur leaned back in his chair, his face creasing into a smile, "Good on you, matey, always glad to see someone having a go. Just let me know what you want me to write and I'll give you that letter for the bank."

"That's awesome, thanks so much Arthur!"

"No worries. Just take it easy, ok buddy?"

"Sure, I'm keeping my eyes open."

"If you need any gear for the reno just ask me."

"Wow, thanks very much."

"Oh, and I'll give you a good price on materials too," Arthur winked at him. He stood up and held out his hand.

"Good luck."

Cliff could have leapt in the air and shouted for joy as he made his way out of the yard and back down the gravel driveway to the main road. All his ducks were in a row. With a bounce in his step, he hastened towards Mt Druitt shopping centre and Angelo's real estate office. He had decided to give Angelo a go at being his 'preferred' agent, just like Allen and Wendy had theirs.

It took a week for True Blue to approve his 80K loan. Bingo.

Now all he needed was some dough for the renovations. How cheap could he do it? Allen and Wendy spent about five grand on theirs. Cliff reckoned he could do better. He had lots of mates… Still he would need some budget.

He called his old manager at Starbucks. It turned out she'd moved to open a new branch at Penrith Plaza and promised to give him shifts whenever she had a gap to fill. Arthur began using him more often too. Cliff was on a roll.

His days and nights filled up, the money started flowing in and for the first time in his life he began to save.

Then Angelo rang.

"Dharruk said 'yes'".

"No way."

"Yep," even Angelo's voice had a high note of disbelief.

Of the many houses they'd inspected, Cliff felt like two had 'spoken to him'. Angelo had advised him to put offers in straight away, even before his loan had been formally approved. Since Cliff's offers were low, Angelo reckoned it would be a while before he got a taker.

Both sellers had tried to negotiate a higher price, of course. However, Cliff, figuring that he wasn't ready anyway, had stuck to his 70K offers. After that there had been no word.

So Angelo's news came as a real surprise.

"He's tired of waiting for a better price and needs the money."

"Ok..." Cliff thought about the implications. "We said it was subject to a builder's inspection, didn't we?"

"Absolutely right, buddy."

"Alright, well let's organise that. If it fails the inspection we can pull out, right?"

"Of course. You haven't signed anything, it's only an offer."

"Ok cool. Can I call you back once I've organised someone?"

"Of course."

"It's a pretty good price, right?"

"It's a bloody good price!"

EIGHT

"D'you want one of my muffins?"

She was a petite girl with nice curves. From the front her green Starbucks apron covered her mini skirt, making it look like she could have nothing else on except her black tights. The cuteness was completed by sparkling green eyes beneath a dark brown fringe and a cheeky smile.

"I burnt the tops," she gave Cliff a pained look, "So we can't sell them."

Then her eyes lit up again, "But they're still yummy!"

Cliff was endeared the moment he'd looked up.

"Sure, thanks, I'll give one a go."

With a giggle, she crossed the floor to where Cliff was sitting at the staff table, took a moment to choose the right muffin from her baking tray and put it down in front of him.

"That one's not too badly charred."

"Great, thanks. Char-grilled, hey?"

"I know. I think David's pissed off with me. But I was dealing with customers, no-one else was at the front."

"He'll get over it. We chuck out heaps at the end of the day anyway."

"Yeah, right. I feel better now, thanks!"

Cliff pulled the burnt top off the muffin and took a bite of the base,

"Mmm, tastes great."

She laughed, "Hey, I can't stay. But I'm Mandy."

She held out a hand.

"Great to meet you. I'm Cliff."

"You're new, aren't you?"

"Yeah I've been at Mount Druitt store. I wanted more shifts so they started me here about a week ago. I've seen you around just not had a chance to say hello."

"Yeah, I know, always busy, busy."

"We should catch up when you're on a break or something."

"Yeah, cool. Actually," she lowered her voice, "We're having a party at my new house. Do you want to come?"

Mandy fished a small square of paper from her apron pocket and handed it to Cliff. It was a photocopy, the edges a little skew where it had been cut out by hand. The heading yelled in bold, punk font:

'Hot, Hot, Hot, House Warming Party!'

Below was a cartoon of a three-piece girl rock band. The one in the centre, kicking a keyboard out of her way, hands stretched high in the air, brown hair flying, was clearly Mandy.

On a cold Saturday morning they gathered, their breath forming puffs of vapour as they stood, hands in pockets, in the front yard. There was Cliff, Arthur, MJ and Angelo in a circle, while Arthur's mate, Dez, crawled under the house with a torch, tapping and knocking and occasionally cursing. He'd agreed to do the inspection for two cases of Crownies.

"Can we have a look around while Dez does his thing?" Arthur asked Angelo.

"Of course, mate, feel free."

First impressions of the house, looking in from the street, were not so bad. In fact, it didn't appear to match Cliff's target of a 'dog's breakfast' at all. The roof was bright red tiles, the brick walls looked clean and un-cracked, and a neat hoop fence ran along the top of a low brick wall at the front. A freshly paved path ran from the front gate to the porch.

Angelo led the way up the steps to the front door. As he opened it and Cliff, Arthur and MJ stepped inside, it became clear why the house had struggled to find a buyer. MJ whistled and Arthur cackled with laughter.

It looked like a war zone. The grey carpet of the living room was filthy and worn threadbare, pock marked with holes and cigarette burns. A pile of rubble, shattered tiles, broken sheets of plasterboard, dirty carpet pieces and other rubbish formed a mountain in one corner. A light bulb hung by its cord through the middle of a gaping hole in the ceiling. There were cracks and holes in all the walls, one of them bigger than two people, its jagged edges revealing the timber bracing of the wall structure behind, rusty nails sticking out like claws. Paint peeled and hung in long strips from ceiling and walls. The smell of generations of cigarettes thick in the air.

Beyond the living room was the kitchen. Or at least what used to be a kitchen. Everything had been ripped out, leaving only dirty, exposed fibre cement wall linings, with pipes twisting across them. More pipes poked through holes in the floor where they had been cut off. The floor was covered with faded yellow lino tiles, many of them buckled and ripped and some completely missing, exposing squares of dirty, glue-covered floor base.

MJ squatted down and examined a piece of exposed floor, "That's asbestos I reckon."

Arthur came over and dug at it with the toe of his boot.

"Yep that's asbestos mate."

"I reckon these walls are all asbestos, Cliffie mate," MJ looked closely into a crack in the wall where, by the outline of dirty silicon and a pair of pipes snapped off at the wall, it was obvious the kitchen sink had once been.

"How can you tell?" Cliff frowned.

"It always is in these old places," Arthur gave him a look of sympathy.

"If you look closely, you can see there's a black fleck through it. That's the asbestos fibres," MJ had broken a small piece off and crumbled it between finger and thumb.

"I thought you weren't supposed to touch it, you idiot."

"I'm not breathing it in, I'm just showing you a little piece, old son."

"Yeah, be careful love, better leave it alone," Arthur nodded.

MJ dropped it in a corner.

They left the kitchen and headed into the main hallway. The feel changed completely. The carpets had all been removed, leaving a solid-looking timber floor.

"Timber's in good nick," Arthur nodded.

"Yeah and someone's done some work already," MJ pointed out the walls.

There were large patches of smoothly sanded plaster where previously there must have been holes, probably just like the ones in the living room.

The bedrooms were the same. Walls and ceilings were professionally patched. Exposed floorboards were, by and large, in good shape. There was only one spot in a corner where you could see the old boards had been cut and fresh timber boards put in to fill the hole.

"Someone's already done half your work, mate," Arthur smiled at Cliff. "These floors are Cypress Pine. Very nice. They'll come up beautifully when you polish them."

"Hey, sweet," MJ called out from the bathroom.

They headed across to join her. The bathroom had been fully renovated. White tiles shone and chrome fixtures sparkled. Everything looked good quality. The walls above the tiles and the ceiling were yet to be painted but they had been plastered and sanded back ready to go.

"Fantastic," Arthur was genuinely impressed. "So they got halfway and didn't want to keep going, hey."

"Yep," Cliff nodded, "They ran out of money and had a fight over it. Now they just want to get rid of it."

"Which is your win, matey" Arthur winked at him. He lowered his voice to a confidential whisper. "How much did you say you're paying for it?"

"70."

"Geez that's good," Arthur shook his head. He patted Cliff on the shoulder and led the way out the bathroom and through the laundry door to the backyard.

Here they could see what had become of the old kitchen. It was piled up against the back wall in a heap of broken cupboards, shattered tiles and twisted copper piping with the old sink sitting on top like a boat riding on a storm swell of rubble.

The rest of the backyard was in fine shape. What looked like a brand new timber fence separated the house from its neighbours and a shiny aluminium shed stood against it. A brick paved path led to a brand new rotary clothes-line in the centre of the lawn.

"Wow, you're getting a lot," MJ looked around, "Even this is new," she walked over and pointed at the hot water tank that sat on a slab against the back corner of the house. It was clean and all its labels still fresh.

"Yeah I know," Cliff enthused, "Inside, all I really have to do is deal with the kitchen and living room. Then paint throughout and polish up the floors."

"Too right," Arthur agreed.

"Then outside, I'm thinking all it needs is a good clean up. Lawn and garden beds, you know, put in some natives, keep it simple, give it a good mow, and done!"

"I think you're right, mate. When you think about it, it's almost done for ya. Let's see what Dez says first though."

As Dez walked over to them, brushing his clothes down, Cliff thought he noticed a brief, silent communication between him and Arthur. A little smirk on Arthur's face, a raised eyebrow from his mate. But before Cliff could think any more of it, Dez put a hand on his shoulder, brows furrowed.

"She's alright, mate. Good structurally, piers are fine, no sign of termites. Roofs good too. You've seen the kitchen and main room inside, right, but it's all superficial stuff. Some signs of damp under the kitchen floor but nothing major to worry about, it's all dry now."

"Great. Whew!"

"There's just one issue you'll need to get your head around," Dez knitted his brows even deeper.

"Oh yeah?"

"Come and have a look at this."

He led them around the far side of the house to a trapdoor in the bottom of the wall.

"This is the easiest way to get in," Dez opened the trapdoor and, torch in hand, squeezed through under the house.

"Come on in and have a look."

Cliff knelt and crawled in through the trapdoor. It was semi dark, with shafts of light coming in through air vents and various gaps where structures like the steps and porch met the walls. It felt dusty and Cliff could feel cobwebs sticking to the back of his head and ears as he crawled deeper inside. Dez shone his torch onto an object ahead of them. It was somewhere approximately beneath the first bedroom, Cliff guessed. The clearance under the house decreased in that direction and the object was jammed in, filling the gap between floor and ground.

"Someone's stuffed a mattress down here," Dez turned his head towards Cliff. "A long time ago I'd say."

"Right," Cliff was not yet sure what the issue was.

"Trouble is it's gone rotten and..." The expression on Dez's face showed he must have got too close to it in his earlier inspection, "There's rats living in it."

"Yeah, right." Cliff suddenly felt vulnerable. He scanned all around, peering into the grey, dusty, light for any signs of movement.

"Someone's gonna have to get that out and it ain't gonna be a fun job," Dez smiled at Cliff, his face close enough for Cliff to feel his warm breath.

"I wonder how they got it in here."

"I'd say there was once more of a gap where the garden beds are now at the front. See that's all backfilled along there," Dez ran his torch along the front side of the house, revealing a wall of dusty rubble filling the gap between floor and ground.

"Either that, or it fell through the hole they made in the bedroom floor," Dez chuckled at his own leap of imagination as he shone his torch up at the floorboards under the second bedroom. This was the freshly patched section Cliff had seen earlier from above.

"Great!" Cliff smiled at Dez.

"Only thing you can do is get someone to fumigate and kill the rats. Then you'll have to get in there, cut it up and drag it all out in pieces. Loads of fun."

Dez gestured to the trapdoor and they both backed out. They were greeted by concerned looks from Arthur and MJ.

Cliff shrugged, "A bit of fun to look forward to guys."

He was a little shaken but recovered as he brushed the cobwebs off in the light of day. Arthur slapped him on the back and MJ ruffled his hair with a cackle, "You'll be right old son."

Arthur looked him squarely in the eyes, "You've got a good project here, matey. You can make a winner out of this, don't worry."

Next came the paperwork, more than Cliff had ever wanted to see in his entire life. Contracts, loans, tax and stamp duties, insurances, bank accounts, agent agreements, solicitor agreements... an endless stream of documents to be read over until his head hurt. Cliff quickly became deeply grateful, and in truth utterly dependent upon, Garth his solicitor. He was another contact provided by Angelo.

"The best bloody lawyer this side of Blacktown. You won't go wrong mate."

Whether or not this was true Cliff would never know. In fact, his first impulse had been to run a mile when, in their initial meeting, Garth had outlined his fees. Cliff's landscaping work earned him a hundred dollars a day. His Starbucks job paid fourteen an hour. So, when Garth looked him in the eye and explained that his conveyancing work would cost $150 *per hour*, Cliff had gone cold.

With a lump in his throat and a quavering voice he'd asked, "So, um, how many hours is it going to take, all up, to get it done?"

"Ah, it's hard to say. Depends mate, on what's involved, what we turn up, or what the other side throws at us. You know, if we find issues when we do the title search, or if there's terms the seller's not going to agree with. All these things are unpredictable until we start."

"Right."

Cliff imagined days turning into weeks, every hour adding another $150 to the meter. He had always feared he would hit a stumbling block. Things had been going too well. He might have bought the property for a good price but now he was going to end up in a lifetime of debt to his lawyer.

Garth saw the expression on his face and laughed, "Look, don't worry, I'm sure it will be fine. Most jobs are straightforward. If it's a simple, standard exchange, we come in at about $1500. That's for everything including your searches."

"Oh, ok, whew!"

"No stress, alright? We do this all the time. If there's any issues, we'll discuss it with you first. Otherwise relax and leave it to us."

That wasn't easy for Cliff to do, though. When the contracts were ready, Garth called him in for their next meeting. The lawyer smiled at him from behind a pile of papers.

"Are you happy to sign it?"

"Yeah. I mean, I think so. It's a standard thing, right?"

"Well, yes, but you need to check that you are happy with the terms."

"Right. Well are there any I should worry about? I mean I haven't done one of these before."

"I know, I know. That's why I'm here to help you. Let me go through it with you."

"Ah, no, that's alright," Cliff held up his hands in panic and began putting the contract back into his bag. "I'll be fine to look over it myself."

Garth shook his head and smiled warmly, "It's included in the fifteen hundred, ok?"

"Oh really?"

"Yep. I'll let you know if it's ever likely to go over. In the meantime, let me help you, alright?"

"You sure?"

"That's what we're here for."

Garth took him step by step through the contract, explaining the key points and anything that Cliff might want to think about or negotiate on. He did the same with the mortgage documents, the bank loan conditions and a bunch of government forms. Eventually, Garth's fee started to feel cheaper and cheaper. Perhaps Angelo had been right about him, he really did seem like the best.

NINE

"Fucking first one, mate," MJ smiled through a mouthful of chicken burger.

Silverchair blasted Freak from a chunky yellow boombox just inside the laundry door, its power cable stretched to the limit.

"How's it feel?" Raj nodded to the music.

Cliff scanned his new backyard and sighed. He'd come straight from a shift, still wearing his Starbucks shirt. MJ pointed at it.

"You won't need that much longer, hey?"

"Don't get too far ahead Ems. So far all I've done is get myself into hock. And it's getting bigger every day."

"Time to renovate. Then flip it," Raj flicked a chip high in the air.

"Yeah mate, let's get it done," MJ sat up.

"Who's in?"

"Fucking everybody, old son," MJ shrugged like it was obvious, "Half our class has got trades now. If they don't then someone in their family does. Words out, local boy's having a go."

"Yep," Raj stretched, "They all want to put in."

"Awesome. Big weekend then!"

"No, no, no," MJ held up her hands, "This is a big project dude. You got to plan."

"Yeah, yeah, we can make a list or whatever. But if everyone knows what they're doing..."

Raj chuckled. MJ held out a fist to him, "Told you."

"What?" Cliff hated being laughed at.

"This is you all over, man. 'Let's have a barbie and knock it over in a day'. You got to be professional now."

"Ok, ok, like what?"

"You remember Skids? From footy?"

Cliff nodded.

"We ran into him at Westfield. His big bro has a building company. He said he'd come over give you some advice. Maybe draw up a schedule and everything for you."

"I can't afford to, Ems, I'm losing money every day it sits there now. I need to fix it and sell it and pay this loan out."

"Dude..."

"Just say yes," Raj slapped him on the shoulder.

In the end, Cliff was awe-struck.

"No, no, no! That's dumb shit. You gotta be smart. Time is money, right? You know what I'm saying? I've seen too many dickheads, mate. You start fucking around putting in the kitchen then you realise you don't have any electrics. You got to pull it all out again. Duh! Motherfucker!"

Reggie, Skids' older brother, was a giant of a man, his muscles rippling out of the tiny singlet and shorts he happily wore in winter.

"Dumb, mate, dumb. Get all your fixes done first, yeah?" he squinted hard at Cliff.

"Yep, right," Cliff had to nod.

"Give them time to dry. Plan, you know mate? Plan. I've been doing this for years. Then I see some idiot 'giving it a go'. You know what I mean? Fuck."

Reggie turned abruptly and walked into the kitchen, the floor creaking under him.

"Fuck me. This is a twenty-grand job. Easy."

"Really," Cliff's heart sank.

"I'll do it for you don't worry," he put a baseball-mitt of a hand on

Cliff's shoulder. "Don't worry mate. I'll take care of it. But it's twenty easy. It's a fucking mess."

Cliff cleared his throat, "I can't afford that. No way. That's why I'm going to, you know, do it myself."

Reggie threw his hands up, "Fuck!"

"I know mate. But I've got no choice."

"Mate, you can't afford to fuck it up. That's what you can't afford."

The big man stomped down the hallway to the bathroom.

"Jesus," he shook his head as he knocked on the white tiles. They sparkled in the flouro lighting, a highlight of the almost completed bathroom.

Then, before Cliff could stop him, Reggie pulled a screwdriver from his belt, poked it into the grout above the top row, drove it down and levered.

"No!" Cliff yelled.

A large patch of tiles creaked and buckled away from the wall.

"See! See, mate? It's shit. You can't sell this place like this. It's total shit."

"Woah," Raj was wide eyed.

Reggie put a heavy arm around Cliff and gave him a sympathetic smile, "Mate, I'll take care of all this, don't worry. We'll get it done properly."

"Well, just hang on, though…"

"Don't stress, it's got to come off anyway."

He led Cliff into the first bedroom, sighed, and made his way to the third, the others following closely behind.

"Oh my God, what the fuck?" Reggie stared at the patched floorboards, where the previous owner had filled a hole.

He began stomping them. Cliff braced for the cracking.

It was MJ who took her life into her hands, shoulder charged Reggie out of the way and stood with her arms spread in protection of the offending piece of floor.

"Mate, please," she yelled at Reggie, "We just wanted your advice. We didn't want you to come and take the place apart."

The big builder's back heaved with several breaths, his body seeming to expand a little more each time. Muscles taught, he turned and stared at MJ. Then with a growl, he thrust a finger in her face.

MJ gulped but did not back away. No-one dared move or speak. At last Reggie's mouth twisted into a smile and he began to laugh.

"Ok. Ok. Settle down love. I was just showing youse. You know? It's easy for me to spot it. The rubbish. I was just showing youse."

"Yeah," Skids moved next to his brother, "Don't worry Ems. Reg knows what he's doing. He's the best around. This shit's got to be fixed anyway. He'll do an awesome job here Cliffie, mate. Don't worry."

"Well…"

"I don't want you to make mistakes. You know, put up with rubbish. I want you to have the best, Cliff old son," Reggie crossed over to Cliff and ruffled his hair.

"I tell you what," MJ jumped in, "Before we decide whether or not we can afford anything let's get the full picture. I mean we've got a pro here. Let's make the most of it. Right Cliffie?"

"Um," Cliff's eyes narrowed.

"Too right," Skids nodded.

"Let's all go outside and talk it through. Come on. I mean you need to check out the outside too, right Reg?"

"Of course, love."

"You haven't checked out the street view yet. That's important, right? First impressions."

"Uh-huh," Reggie was nodding.

"Then… maybe you can talk us through everything you'd do. Tell us exactly what and how much. What do you reckon, should we all go outside and check it out?"

As she turned, MJ gave Cliff a sly wink and led the way to the front door.

The fall-out from 'Cyclone Reggie', was a pretty decent renovation plan. Cliff couldn't say it had been worth it, but he had to admit there were plenty of things he wouldn't have thought of. Not if MJ hadn't milked the big fellow for as much inside knowledge as she could get, before thanking him profusely and promising to get back to him 'asap'.

Next day, Cliff and Raj set out in the van. First stop was a massive auction house for kitchens a few suburbs south of Mount Druitt. They picked up great looking cupboards and appliances at a fraction of their retail price.

They scored second-hand pavers, bricks and tiles from a demolition site, free to anyone who wanted them. They bought returned paint from Bunnings at half the price of new paint. Maybe it was a tint or two wrong for the original buyer, but Cliff didn't care. He wasn't exactly a decorator, but he knew most people liked their walls a shade of white.

While Cliff and Raj went shopping, MJ and two old school mates took to the walls in the living room, knocking out broken plasterboard sheets. When Cliff got back, MJ called him over to the kitchen with a chuckle.

"Have a look at this, old son."

Cliff was surprised to find they had already removed all the floor covering.

"You know how we said it was asbestos?"

"Yeah, I know," Cliff couldn't believe they'd gone ahead and worked on it. Although he wasn't looking forward to it, he'd always planned to tackle the job himself. He'd already bought full-body plastic cover-alls and a respirator.

MJ led Cliff to the backyard where the old sheets of floor covering were stacked against the fence. She pointed to a stencil that could be seen broken up across most pieces and clearly legible on a few.

"Have a read."

"'Hardy's Floor and Wall. Contains No Asbestos.' Ah, wow. Thank god!"

"Yeah, we lifted a couple of lino tiles to check it out and saw this."

"So, ah, what happened to that black fibre being, like, absolutely, one hundred percent, fucking definitely asbestos?"

Cliff picked up a small piece and threw it at MJ, "You doofus!"

After two days, following Cyclone Reggie's advice, they had prepped all the walls and floors in the living room and kitchen, patching and sealing gaps as they went. Cliff was chuffed with how neatly they managed it.

Also thanks to Reggie, Cliff got an electrician to install power points in the kitchen and rewire a new ceiling light and fan in the living room. He had to admit he probably would have left all these to last, after re-sheeting the walls, plastering, painting and tiling which would have been a small disaster.

There was one last thing. Cliff knew he had to deal with the mattress under the house. He'd been putting it off. But he didn't like the idea of an army of rats under his feet and he worried they might pop out when everyone came over for the big reno weekend.

"Hey Rajie!" Cliff called from the back door.

Raj's head poked out of the garage.

"Yeah?"

"Can you get your cousin to come out and do that spraying tomorrow?"

"Hey?"

"You know, the rats under the house."

'Oh yeah, sure," Raj smiled broadly. He took out his mobile, held it up, and disappeared back into the garage.

Friday morning, Sunni the pest controller turned up early, good as his word. He set rat baits under the house and told Cliff they would most likely eat them and then tunnel deeply into the mattress 'nest' to die.

Sunni's disposition matched his name and with a beaming smile he told Cliff he would have to get mattress and dead rats out within twenty-four hours or else the house would stink like a mortuary.

TEN

Cliffs knees bounced up and down as he sat in the carriage. He was on his way to meet MJ and Raj at the Top Pub in Penrith. They planned to have a quick drink before heading to Mandy's party. Cliff was thinking about her sparkling, cheeky eyes. Her gentle face and those soft lips. Her taught little bod made his throat dry up. Would she still be interested? Had she been keen at all, or was she just flirty? He took a deep breath and stretched. He would find out soon enough.

Stepping into the buzz of the Toppie, however, he saw his plans were threatened. MJ sat amongst a group of locals, decked out in black and white caps, scarves and shirts, watching the Western Sydney Magpies kick off on the big screen. The table was filling fast with empty beer glasses as they cheered at the sight of their star halfback limbering up.

"Maggies! Here we go, here we go, here we go!"

Next moment they were hurling abuse at a close-up of an Eastern Suburbs player.

"Hey, we're not watching the game all night, we're going to the party, right?"

"Yeah matey, after the game," MJ poured Cliff a beer from a jug.

"That'll be too late, I'm not missing the party."

"Me neither," Raj grinned, "Uni chicks!"

"You know what's going to happen anyway," Cliff nodded towards the screen.

"Yeah, yeah, I know. Ok, listen, if they are down by three tries or more at half time we go."

In the end, it took only twenty minutes before MJ threw her hands up in disgust. Easts players slammed chests and hugged as MJ kicked her stool away and headed to the back bar.

Here the barman, a stocky Chinese guy, winked at her and gestured to two cartons of Crown lager sitting on the counter-top.

"Thanks T-bone!"

The barman gave a thumbs up. MJ picked up one carton and nodded at Cliff to take the other.

"Two? How pissed are we getting?" Raj was wide-eyed.

"One for the party and one for on the way," MJ chuckled, "It's a long walk."

"What's with that guy's name? T-bone?" Cliff nodded back towards the bar.

"Yeah, I know, funny hey. He's gay, right. Story is one day a customer called him a 'Chinese faggot' and he picked up the guy's steak and slammed it in his face. When the guy got up swinging, T-bone took him down with some serious kung-fu."

"Awesome."

The house was concealed by a tall hedge, but loud music and voices gave the party away. They went in the open gate and up the front path lined by rows of tea-light candles flickering in jars.

"Who are you?" a tall guy with a long pony-tail sussed them from the veranda.

"Who are you?" MJ called back.

"No, love," pony-tail squared up, "I don't recognize you, so who are you?"

"We're the fucking drug squad," MJ made a gun with her hands, "Get on the ground!"

Raj pulled her back, "Shut up, idiot."

"Sorry," Cliff stepped up onto the veranda, "She's just mucking around. We're friends of Mandy."

"Oh cool. I'm Grant."

Cliff shook hands. "I'm Cliff, this is Raj and the weirdo is MJ."

A girl in gothic make-up, a tight-fitting leather bodysuit and glossy black hair appeared at the front door.

"Oh my god, Cliff! I didn't think you would come," she took her wig off.

"Mandy!" Cliff laughed, "Wow I didn't recognize you."

"We're being rock stars. Come on in. The bands gonna do a song."

They followed Mandy in. Grant and his circle of friends came in too. In the living room the sofa and chairs had been turned to face the far wall, where the band was set up in front of a window. On the left a tall, red-head in a black tutu and fishnets held an electric guitar. On the right a petite girl with spiky, blonde hair stood behind a pile of what looked like broken appliances and industrial junk. She held one microphone and handed a second to Mandy who took her position behind a keyboard.

Mandy threw some switches on the keyboard and then all three girls took out their mobile phones, pressed some buttons and held the phones to their mics. After a moment, a distorted feedback began to build up. As the screeching and hissing got louder, the girls managed to conjure an oscillating rhythm from it and their audience cheered and punched the air in time. The short, blonde girl picked up a metal bar and began hitting a steel bin, thumping out a metallic beat. Mandy gave a long, low "Aaahh" into her microphone as the red-head strummed guitar. The wall of sound was intense.

Cliff felt an elbow in his side.

"What the fuck?" MJ shouted in his ear. Cliff laughed.

The spiky blonde had picked up a second metal bar and was now playing on an old TV as well as the steel bin, belting out a lively rhythm. She was clearly talented. Mandy threw a switch on her keyboard and started playing. Despite the layers of white noise and industrial thumping, the tune was familiar. As soon as she started singing, Cliff recognized a distorted version of the Violent Femmes' Blister in the

Sun. The room, as one, heaved into dancing and singing along.

Cliff jumped up and down with them. He turned to face MJ and Raj, "Yeah!"

MJ rolled her eyes.

But Cliff kept at it until she started bouncing up and down too, beer held high. The room became a mosh pit, limbs flying, hair everywhere, people laughing hysterically and screaming along to the lyrics. As the song reached a climax, the three girls took up metal bars and began smashing the pile of appliances. The audience joined in kicking TVs over and stomping on broken bits of furniture, framed paintings and plastic boxes.

The pile was quickly flattened, bits and pieces scattered across the floor, as the song finished with a few final screeches of feedback.

"Thank you!" Mandy yelled into her microphone.

Her eyes met Cliff's as he laughed at the chaos. She smiled back.

The small crowd clapped as Mandy hugged her friends in turn. When she got to Cliff she whispered, "I'm having a drink! Come join us."

She grabbed a bottle of wine from the kitchen and led the way into the backyard, a small group following her. It was dark out the back, except for a warm glow from a clump of tea lights on a table in the middle of the lawn. Mandy handed Cliff a glass and filled it. Then one for herself.

"Thanks for coming," she giggled.

Cliff loved how she could be so cutely shy after giving such an epic performance.

"That was intense, man. I've never seen anything like it."

"That's our assessment."

"What do you mean?"

"We're all doing music. That's our final piece for the year."

"Wow. How do they assess that?"

"Long story. It's about deconstruction mostly."

"Fuck, I got no idea."

"Don't worry. It's bullshit really. Kind of a lark we get to do it, but."

"Yeah, it is pretty funny."

"So, are you studying or anything? Or just working at Starbucks?"

"Yeah," Cliff hesitated, "I'm also landscaping. I'm getting into flipping houses."

"Whoa! What?"

"Yeah, I've just started. Just got my first one and about to renovate it."

"That's mad. That's like so different to uni."

"Yeah, I know. I feel like I'm from another planet. I wouldn't have a clue what you guys are doing or even what to ask you about it."

"Here," she chuckled as she re-filled his glass, "I'm glad you came. Cheers."

They clinked glasses.

"Sorry we're so weird, but. You must be wondering what you got yourself into."

"No, no. It's fun."

"Well I think it's cool to meet different people. It's much more interesting."

They were on their second bottle when an uproar of excited voices came from inside.

"What the hell's going on in there?" Mandy looked up.

Cliff thought he could hear MJ's voice at the centre of it.

"I'll check it out," he offered, concealing his panic.

As he entered the back door, his worst fears were realised. MJ and Grant were locked in a fight in the middle of the living room, with a crowd of revelers cheering them on.

"MJ!" Cliff rushed to grab her, but Raj quickly stepped forward.

"It's ok! They're playing drinking games. It's a wrestling challenge."

Mandy came up beside Cliff and took his arm with both hands, snuggling just a little into him. Cliff savoured her warmth. MJ made a lightning quick move, twisting Grant, grabbing his leg, flipping him on his back and pinning him. She jumped up punching the air.

"You drink! You drink!"

As the crowd applauded, she reached down and helped Grant up, patting him on the back and making sure he was ok. Arms around each other, they turned to the kitchen where someone handed Grant a bottle of VB.

"Scull, scull, scull!" MJ led the chant until Grant had emptied the bottle. The room cheered his effort.

Cliff felt Mandy tug on his arm, pulling him into the middle of the living room.

"Ok, this is for the uni students," Mandy announced, "I'm gonna get one back!"

"No, no, no," Cliff held up his hands.

"It's ok," she whispered, "I fight with my brothers all the time, I'm tough."

"Where's Grant?" she looked around the room, "You were so bloody weak, now it's down to me to save our reputation!"

Her friends clapped, "Let's go Mandy!"

MJ cackled, "Come on Cliff, don't get your arse whipped old son."

Mandy took up a wrestling stance.

Cliff knew there was no way out now. Might as well have fun. He slapped his thighs and chest in a dodgy haka. It got him a laugh from the crowd.

Next thing Mandy grabbed his arms and swung him around. She was a lot stronger than he'd expected. She put in a trip and he almost went over, clinging onto her shoulder to stay upright. The room went wild. He saw the smile on her face and knew she was loving it.

"Ok," he gave her a little nod and set his stance.

"Oh yeah?"

She pulled hard, spinning him off balance. But this time Cliff used all his strength, dragging her in towards him, turning her around and wrapping her up in his arms. Then he sat backwards, taking her down with him.

In an instant she twisted around and was on top of him.

"Ha ha!" she grit her teeth, straining to force his arms to the ground.

Cliff feared his manhood was under threat. He gripped her wrists and rolled her over. Their faces ended up so close he could feel her breath as she struggled against him. Her eyes glinted with excitement. He thought about kissing her, it would be perfect. Instead he summoned his strength, pushed her arms to the floor and took the victory.

"Two nil, two nil," MJ ran around the living room, two fingers in the air. Raj smiled and shook his head.

MJ called out from the kitchen, "Your skull Mandy!"

Just then there was a terrible coughing and retching. They all turned to see Grant, bent over the back of the sofa, throwing up.

"Oh fuck," Mandy ran to the kitchen.

A group of friends hurried to assist her, while others helped Grant out onto the front veranda. With that, the party died.

The lights came on, the music went down and most of the dazed revelers slowly but surely called out their goodbyes and weaved their way down the front path. Mandy and a small group of her most committed friends, sleeves rolled up, mopped and scrubbed at Grant's spew.

"Let me help you," Cliff ripped a handful of paper towel from a quickly shrinking roll.

"No, no," Mandy panicked, "I don't want you doing it!"

"It's ok, many hands make it quicker," Cliff smiled, scooping at a pool of vomit on the seat of the sofa, "Anyway, it's my mate who made him drink so much."

The spew had gone everywhere, down the back of the sofa, between the cushions and all over the carpet.

"Don't be silly. Grant is just piss weak."

Her friends chuckled. It was Mandy's two band mates plus a tall girl with pigtails. A fourth girl looked like she might be Indian, quite beautiful in a body-hugging red dress.

As Cliff chucked his paper towel in the kitchen bin, Mandy whispered in his ear, "You can stay over if you want."

"Great, thanks," Cliff smiled, feeling his breath tighten.

Once the cleanup was done, the tall girl in pigtails announced, "Right, its tea time."

"That sounds great," Mandy blew out an exhausted sigh.

"You sit down, I'll help her," the Indian girl bounced into the kitchen.

"I'll just see what the guys are up to," Cliff told Mandy.

He found MJ and Raj in a circle of party-goers on the front lawn.

"I'm gonna stay," he put a hand on MJ's shoulder.

"Nice one," she winked at him, "Don't worry about us old son, we'll be fine. I'll have one last beer and we'll take off."

As Cliff turned, MJ slapped him on the backside, "Smooth operator, ah-ha!"

Raj giggled.

Back inside Cliff found Mandy and her two band members sitting amongst a pile of cushions on the floor. Mandy patted a cushion next to her and smiled.

He sat down and she touched his hand, "These are my two partners in crime. Angie," she gestured to the tall red head in a tutu.

Cliff reached out a hand, "Nice to meet you."

"And Tess."

Cliff shook hands with the spiky blonde, "Hey. Loved your drumming."

Then he felt foolish, "Not sure if that's what you call it, though?"

"Yeah, drumming, percussion, you know, rhythm. Whatever," she smiled, the light catching star-shaped studs in her lower teeth.

"This is Cliff," Mandy put her arm around his shoulder, "We work together at Starbucks, hey."

"We know," Angie smiled at Cliff, "She hasn't stopped talking about you all week."

"Rubbish!" Mandy frowned.

Angie and Tess were distracted by something behind Cliff and Mandy. He could see they were struggling to hold back smiles. A muffled grunt came from behind him. He and Mandy turned around simultaneously.

The tall pig-tailed girl was up on the kitchen counter, her legs apart, hands on her breasts, exaggerated look of ecstasy on her face, while the Indian girl held a banana at her crotch and theatrically mimed 'shagging' her. As their eyes met Cliff's they froze like rabbits caught in the headlights.

Awkward silence. Finally, the Indian girl erupted in laughter. It caused everyone else to lose it as well. The girls in the kitchen buckled over, in uncontrollable fits. Cliff laughed along too. Finally, as the laughter settled down, the Indian girl held up her banana.

"Sorry."

Then she and pigtails burst out hysterically again.

Mandy stood up.

"And these two are my house mates, Nicki and Romina. All class."

Tess rolled a joint and the girls sat around talking, long into the early hours. At last, when Cliff thought it was never going to happen, Angie and Tess got up, hugged everyone and headed home. Not long after that Nicki and Romina yawned goodnight and went to their rooms, leaving Cliff and Mandy alone in the living room.

Mandy gave him her pained smile, "You survived!"

He grinned back. Then his look changed to one of adoration. He leaned in and they kissed. They slid down amongst the cushions on the living room floor. Cliff felt like the wrestling had given him an idea of what Mandy liked and he pinned her arms down hard as he kissed her.

"Mmm," she responded, grabbing onto his arms and kissing him back. Cliff reached for the front zip of her leather top but she pushed him off and sat up. Then she smiled mischievously and slowly pulled the zip down herself. Her beautifully round breasts tumbled out, held only by a lacy, black bra.

"Wow," Cliff leaned in to kiss them. Mandy put a finger to his lips and stood up. She took Cliff's hand and led him, kissing as they went, into her room and shut the door as quietly as she could.

ELEVEN

Cliff's head hurt despite the Panadols. They'd been stretched out on Mandy's sofa, her head in his lap, a warm mug of instant coffee in his hand, when he'd remembered the day's big mission.

"Ah, shit, I have to go. You're not going to believe what I've got to do, so I probably shouldn't even tell you. But believe me, I'd rather stay here with you."

He kissed her long and slow before setting off down the empty street. Every few steps he turned and waved until he took a corner and she went out of sight.

Now he approached his new house with great apprehension, carrying one of Arthur's chainsaws over his shoulder. It was the method everyone had agreed would be best.

He placed four torches in strategic positions under the house to light the area around the mattress as he crawled his way towards it. Once he was in position, he donned a set of safety glasses and strapped on a dust mask. Then he fired up the chainsaw.

It bit into the mattress and instantly covered him in a cloud of dust and pieces of foam. He had never been totally convinced about this approach and now he coughed and spat dirt despite the mask.

"Fuck this thing!"

The guys at work had been so convincing and Cliff couldn't think of a better option right now. His head was pounding and he just wanted to get it over with. So, he pulled the trigger and cut in deeper. He squinted, keeping his mouth firmly shut as the storm of dust and foam covered him.

Eventually he reduced the mattress to bite size pieces, scattered everywhere under the house. All the while he'd been bracing himself for dead rats. He grimaced at the thought and his stomach turned as he imagined pieces of rat flying all over him. However, it never happened and he completed the job without seeing a sign of them. This both relieved and worried him. What had happened to them? Were they hidden somewhere else? Had the poisoning not worked?

Slowly, he gathered all the pieces of mattress and dragged them over to the trapdoor, throwing them into a pile outside. Finally, the under house was clear. He took the brightest of his four torches and examined every corner but could not see any sign of rats. Eventually he called it quits and backed painfully out the trapdoor. As he stood up to dust himself off, he realised he was being watched.

MJ, Raj, Arthur and two of the guys from landscaping, Chris and Manu, beamed back at him.

"There he is! The Texas chainsaw mattress killer," Arthur laughed.

Everyone cracked up.

"What the fuck are you all doing here?"

"We couldn't miss this one mate," Chris slapped him on the shoulder.

"Hold up the chainsaw Cliffie," MJ aimed an instant camera.

"So you can laugh at me?"

"Come on old son, perfect start to the reno series."

Cliff shook his head but held the chainsaw up on his hip Rambo-style. MJ snapped the shot.

"Brilliant matey," Arthur grinned at him, "We never thought you'd do it."

"What do you mean?"

"When MJ told us you were going ahead," Manu chuckled, "We couldn't miss it mate."

"What? So, you were bullshitting me?"

"Of course, mate."

"Who the fuck takes a chainsaw under the house?" MJ laughed.

"I can't believe you guys. I can't believe you would tell me to do it. I am fucking covered in shit, look at me."

They shook with laughter.

"What about the rats? Did you make that up too?"

"Did you find any?"

"Well, a hard-earned thirst needs a big cold beer mate," Arthur nodded at Chris, who had an esky at his feet.

"Bloody hell," Cliff took the VB tallie.

Then came the first big weekend. Saturday kicked off with a surprise text from Angelo.

'On me way. Not missing out on the fun.'

Now, he shuffled through the open front door puffing under the weight of his shiny, chrome, Italian coffee machine.

"Where do you want it, mate?"

Cliff jogged over and helped him carry it out the back door. He'd made a table using an old door and milk-crates and already laid out drinks and biscuits. Angelo snorted as he pushed aside Cliff's instant coffee to make way for a jumbo bag of coffee beans.

"I'm telling you mate, the single most important thing to keep the troops happy."

Cliff ran off in search of an extension cable.

Mandy had insisted she wanted to be involved, so when she arrived, Cliff teamed her up with Raj's sister, Yasmine, to be his first painting team. He wanted to get started early so they'd get two coats in before the end of the day. Two old mates from school, Dan and Wes, tackled a second room. Cliff figured he could help with painting when he wasn't managing some other part of the operation.

Arthur's brother, Ronnie, took control of the kitchen. He was an experienced carpenter and brought his bed saw and trestles with him. Raj and Deep, his mate from TAFE, joined Ronnie. All three loved their power tools and in no time the auction kitchen was cut to size and fitted in place. Cliff was blown away. By afternoon they were connecting plumbing to the new sink.

Outdoors progress was just as good. Arthur, MJ, Chris and Manu ripped through the overgrown bushes, cleared the lanes down either side and mowed the lawns in record time. They were not short of gear, since Arthur had thrown open his shop. Naturally, they'd picked the biggest ride-on mower in the stable.

Angelo joined them when he was not at the coffee machine or on the phone. Although, when he did, he spent most of the time talking to Arthur while the other three did the work.

After the clearing was done, they got into repairing the cracked concrete patios, front and back, leaving them to dry for painting the next day. Then they were ready to start re-building garden beds around the front of the house.

This is where Arthur and Angelo really came through for Cliff. Between them they'd seen hundreds of properties prepared for sale.

They kept things simple, wide beds with native shrubs from Arthur's collection of salvaged plants. They picked ones with bright yellow, pink and red leaf tips, making for an eye-catching display. Keeping them below a metre in height helped make the house look larger in contrast.

Finally, they topped the beds with a crushed white gravel, setting off the dull red brick work of the house and providing a neat frame to the overall picture.

Cliff smiled as he watched them put the finishing touches to the first pair of beds.

"Amazing work guys. I'm gonna fire up the barbie."

The seller had left a big old fridge in the garage which Cliff had crammed with meat and beers. A sweaty Angelo looked only too happy to down tools and stroll over to help him. By the time things were smoking, the others had gathered. Beers were cracked, make-shift chairs found, and celebrations began.

They'd barely settled in when voices called out from the front. Cliff looked up to see two heads poking around the side of the house.

A tall bloke, sunnies on his head, esky in one hand, waved, "How you going? We're from next door."

"Awesome," Cliff stood up.

"Thought we'd say g'day."

"Yeah, come and join us."

"Looks like a great party!" A round-faced woman grinned over the opposite side fence, then laughed in a high pitch.

Behind her stood a leather-tanned bloke, beaming through gappy teeth and two teenage boys, caps reversed, shirtless and 'don't give a shit' looks on their faces.

"Well come on over," Cliff called back.

"I've been baking puddings. I'll bring them over. Shouldn't kill anybody!" Another burst of shrill laughter.

Hands shaken, beers shared, jokes cracked, chops charred, puddings devoured… and the revels went on into the night.

Next day the weather had turned cold with a light drizzle in the air. It must have rained in the early hours because the roads and yards were soaked. Cliff felt slow and full of aches as he made his way up the front path to the door of his house. Inside was gloomy so he flicked on the light switch. Nothing.

"Damn."

It had been working perfectly since Cliff had it installed. Hopefully it was just the globe.

His phone beeped. "Sorry mate me backs stuffed. You'll have to do without me today." It was Angelo.

Cliff chuckled. He wasn't surprised. The usually enthusiastic agent had looked exhausted by the end of the day and had insisted on taking his coffee machine home with him when he left. Despite his assurances he'd be back in the morning, Cliff had quietly bet he wouldn't see him.

Cliff looked around the near-finished kitchen and stretched. There were empty beer stubbies all over the new cupboards. He started gathering them into a cardboard box. Something felt wrong. Probably just his hangover combined with the grey day.

He had a thought and tried the kitchen light. Also nothing.

"Ah, no, no…"

That was all he needed. No power would seriously stuff renovation day two. He had to get everything finished today. Cliff put the box down and hastened outside to the fuse panel.

"Yep," the mains had tripped. He flipped it back on. Hopefully just a one-off. Then he noticed the garage door.

"Oh shit." The roller was half-way up. Had they left it that way all night? Crap! He rushed over. All Ronnie's power tools… Arthur's mower. He couldn't afford to replace those.

Once inside he sighed with relief. The mower was there and the bed saw and tool boxes sat where they had been the night before.

"Thank fuck."

His phone beeped again. "OMG who sat on my head all night. Be there soon haha."

"No worries slack arse," Cliff typed back to MJ, "Just had a heart attack but all good."

The rain had started to pound on the garage roof, so Cliff pulled down the roller door. He flicked on the light and grabbed the tins of paint they'd need for the second coats. He was bracing himself to duck out the side door and run through the rain to the main house when the light went out.

"Nooo!"

He ran across the lawn, paints in hand, into the house. His phone was ringing.

"Hey, yeah?"

"Hey buddy, it's Arthur. No point coming today matey."

"Ah, yeah, I guess so."

"Don't worry we'll polish it off next weekend. Shit happens."

"Yep. No worries. Thanks for yesterday."

"Too easy bud."

Arthur hung up. It was true they couldn't do anything outside. Cliff wasn't too worried, it was just finishing off patios, garden beds and re-paving the front path. He could handle it himself if he had to.

"What the hell is that?"

Cliff could hear a drumming coming from the direction of the bedrooms. But then a loud hoot from the front took his attention. The van bounced up the driveway. MJ jumped out the passenger side, coffees in hand and ran for the cover of the front porch, Raj following behind.

"Here ya go, old son," MJ held out a polystyrene cup.

"Cheers."

"Shit day, hey man. Bugger," Raj's brows furrowed.

"Yeah it sucks. We can't do anything outside. But hopefully we can finish off inside."

"If anyone shows up…" MJ chuckled as she headed off down the hallway, "I reckon Dan and Wes were pretty smashed last night."

"So, what's the plan?" Raj wandered into the kitchen. "Let's get some music happening, it's such a depressing day."

He clicked the boom box on.

"Oh yeah," Cliff remembered, "We've got no power."

"What?"

"Yeah it keeps tripping."

"Hey, shit, check at this!" MJ called out.

"What's up?"

"Fuck."

"What?"

"Oh my fucking god."

"What is it?" Cliff jogged down the hall.

MJ was looking up at the ceiling of bedroom three. A dark patch had formed and long drips of water were peeling off and falling.

"Oh shit. There's a fucking leak."

Raj's head poked through the doorway, "Oh no. No way."

"Fuck!"

They watched as the dark patch expanded.

Cliff carefully straightened himself up into the roof cavity. He twisted to his left and shone Raj's torch over the beams above bedroom three.

"Can you see it?" MJ's voice rang out from below.

"Yep."

Water was not just dripping, it was trickling and streaming down at several points along the main rafter where the roof made an L-shape to create bedroom three. Cliff turned to his right, scanning the torch along the furthest beams.

"Oh, fucking hell."

"What?"

"It's doing the same thing on the other side, above the living room."

"Ah shit dude."

"Yep, it's running down like a fucking river."

"Ah no way, that's fucked," MJ laughed in a high pitch. "I'm sorry, I know it's not funny. But shit…"

"No, it's not."

"I know, I know. Sorry. So have a look down between the ceiling joists…"

Cliff stepped off the ladder and onto the nearest beam so he could get a better angle.

"Can you see what I'm talking about?" MJ continued.

"Yeah. Holy shit."

"See there's wires everywhere? Lying in pools of water now?"

"Uh-huh."

"That's why the power's shorting. I wouldn't touch a fucking thing, man."

"Yep" Cliff's teeth were clenched. This had to be a nightmare. It couldn't be happening. He stepped back down the ladder and headed into the living room, unable to look at either MJ or Raj.

"Well I don't know what to do," Cliff's voice shook, "This has just trashed all our plastering and painting. No-one's turned up. And we've got no fucking power anyway."

There was no way he could afford all this. The repairs. How much would they cost? And above all, the lost time. He was out of money. He had to get the house onto the market.

MJ put an arm around him and pulled him into a hug.

"Come on man. We'll fix it up."

"Yeah bro," Raj patted his shoulder, "This is a really shit situation but we'll get through it."

Cliff felt a drop of water splatter on the back of his head. He looked up.

"Aargh! Fucking hell!"

Sure enough a dark patch had formed on the living room ceiling now too and drops of water were beginning to fall. The plasterboard was visibly bulging downwards.

Cliff spun about the living room. In an angry flash he thought about kicking all the plaster walls in and tearing the place apart. Instead he stomped out the front door, slamming it behind him.

Out on the street, already drenched, he caught the eye of his neighbour. It was the leathery bloke from the night before. Still shirtless, he lounged in an old deck chair on his front veranda. He gave Cliff a tired wave and his signature gappy smile. Cliff held up a hand.

"Hey mate," he mumbled as he wandered off down the street.

How could he have been caught out like this? What an arsehole the seller was.

"No, actually…"

He took his phone out, found Arthur's recent call and hit dial.

"Cliffie?"

"Hey Arthur. Quick question."

"Sure buddy?"

"Your mate who did the building inspection… what was his name?"

"Dez?"

"Yeah, Dez. Shouldn't he have checked out the roof?"

"Well, I think he did. Didn't he?"

"I dunno. But it's leaking like a sieve."

"Oh jeez mate, really?"

"Yeah, it's trashed everything."

"Ah matey, that's no good."

"Yeah... yeah it's pretty bad."

"Sorry to hear buddy. I'm surprised Dezzie didn't pick it up for ya."

"Well maybe he shouldn't have been fucking around making up shit about rats in mattresses... you know?"

"Ok, matey, I know you're upset, but you got to remember he did it for a case of beer. Right?"

"Yeah, right, I guess..."

"You know what I'm saying?"

"Yeah. Shit. Sorry to bother you Arthur. I'm just pretty devastated, you know?"

"Sure matey. Well, hang in there. You'll be right."

An hour later Cliff sat in the park across from his parent's house. He was soaked to the core and shivered. But all he could think about was what he'd gotten himself into and how to get out of it. They'd all been right, everyone who'd told him he was an idiot. He was well and truly in over his head now.

His phone rang. It was MJ.

"Yeah?"

"Hey, Cliffie where are you?"

"Why?"

"Well, we could use another pair of hands, you know? We're up on your roof with a bunch of tarps. Be good to get it done before it pours again."

"Oh really?"

"Yeah. Arthur's here too."

"So I got a thousand," Raj tossed a Metrobank card on the table.

"Nice one," Mandy clapped, "Plus MJ's and your two new ones Cliffie, that's $3500. How we doing?"

"I've got to make the first interest payment this week," Cliff wrote numbers on an empty burger wrapper.

"Roof repairs are three and a half alone. Those guys are chasing me every fucking day."

"Better fix them up dude I reckon they're fucking Angels."

"Yeah I know, Ems. I'm waiting for them to show up with bats."

"Holy shit," Raj shook his head.

"Then there's re-plastering. We can do that ourselves, right?"

"Sure, but we don't have Ronnie."

"I know so I need to pay a tiler. Also, got to fix up fucking Cyclone Reggie's work in the bathroom."

"God yeah," MJ rocked back in her chair and laughed.

"Plus electrician. That's not cheap."

"Yep."

"And the floors. That's a big one to come," Raj leaned in to read Cliff's scribbles.

"I'm gonna have to do it myself I reckon. I don't want to, everyone tells me it sucks."

"Well you'll have to hire the gear anyway. That's a cost."

"Yeah I know. And it'll take more time, which I can't afford. There's going to be at least one more interest payment before I can off load it. Maybe two."

"So where are you at?" Mandy grabbed the burger wrapper from Cliff, "Show me your accounts."

They all laughed.

"I don't know how the fuck you've managed to get four credit cards approved dude," MJ picked up her own wrapper, "Here's my financial position Mr Bank!"

"Well I won't get any more. And I'm still about two and a half down. I've tried every bank, building society, every fucking shonk agency in the western suburbs."

"Yeah well I struggled to get mine, old son, and I know I'll never get another."

"Here you go," Mandy pulled an envelope from her bag, "Surprise."

"What you get?" Cliff frowned.

"I tried for a few myself," Mandy smiled, "And I just got one off

Indi. Only $500 cash advance, sorry, but it's the best I could do."

"No, no, no. That's cool," Cliff held up a hand, "I couldn't take it off you."

"Yes, you can! I want to help."

"No serious."

"Yes serious." Mandy pushed the envelope at him.

"Really?"

"Just take it. And make sure you give it back to me when you sell."

"Of course I will. Thanks," Cliff kissed her.

It felt wrong, but he needed all the help he could get. It would be fine once he could sell and get all this off his back.

"Well now I'm only two grand down."

"Yay," Mandy stretched.

"Well, to be honest, I'm still stuffed. Keep trying please guys. Not you, though," he hugged Mandy into him.

Cliff had a new worry. His mum never called him to come home 'urgently'. She sounded frightened. And clearly wanted him there while his dad was out. What was happening?

He jogged as fast as he could. Finally, into their street, through the gate, up the steps and, out of breath, knocked on the door.

"Hey," his mum smiled.

"Hi."

"Come in quick."

"What's happening?"

"I've got something for you.".

"What's going on?"

"Here." It was a fat wad of cash.

"Woah…"

"I got it for you sweetie."

"Um, how?"

"Never mind," she gave him a wink.

"No. What have you done?"

"It's ok."

"Mum?!"

"I hocked my ring."

"What?"

"It's ok. You'll give it back, right?"

"Yeah... but..."

"It's fine."

"No. No way. You can't do that mum."

"I can," she smiled, a little painfully, "He'll never even notice."

"No," Cliff held up his hands, "No mum. That's crazy. I would never want you to do that."

"I know. But I wanted to do it. Ok?"

"No, let's go get it back. Come on mum."

"Cliffie, I want to do this for you. I love how you are trying to do something for yourself. This is the only thing I've got to give you. Take it, ok?"

"Mum..."

"Before he gets back. Quick."

"I'll make sure I pay you straight back."

"I know." She put her arms around his neck, "I know you will. That's why I'm happy to do it."

The chunky wad, still in her hand, felt like it was burning through Cliff's skin.

Three Sundays later it was all done. As the sun's rays got longer, Cliff, Raj, MJ, Mandy, Arthur and Shaun, the last remaining school mate, swept up, wiped down and began to pack away their tools. Cliff fetched two cartons of beer from the van. He stopped in the living room and looked around. The house looked like new. It was amazing.

"I wish I had more than beers to thank you all," he felt tears welling, "This place is unbelievable."

"Beers are fine by me," Shaun smiled.

Raj put his hand on Cliff's shoulder, "It is really amazing. Remember how it looked a few weeks ago."

"I know, I can't believe it."

Cliff ripped open a carton and started handing out stubbies.

"Cheers guys. I mean, I don't think I deserve it. I'm definitely very, very lucky to have you all as mates."

Bottles clinked.

Arthur held his up, "Matey, it's good to see a young local having a go. Good luck to you buddy."

"Thanks Arthur. For everything."

"Oh, and when you make your first million don't forget us, alright?"

TWELVE

When Cliff first signed the contract to buy the house, Raj had given him, as a celebration gift, a magazine called 'Professional Property Investor'. Cliff had been so busy with the purchasing process and then organizing the renovations, that he hadn't even opened it.

Now, as he lay in bed on Monday morning, his eye fell on the magazine. It sat buried under a stack of folders and loose papers on his shelves. He smiled, stretching his arms high above his head.

"Yep, that's me, professional property investor."

He pulled the magazine out from under the stack of paperwork and dropped back into bed. As he flipped through the pages, however, his enthusiasm waned. The stories were about large, ultra-modern unit developments, canal estates and harbor-front mansions. Their selling prices were all in the millions. It seemed a very long way from where he was, renovating a cheap little house in outer Mount Druitt.

He was about to slap the magazine shut and toss it back on the shelf, when he noticed a story that looked different to all the others.

'Billie-The-Battler: From Zero to A Million Dollars in Three Years.'

The main photo showed a young Asian guy, smiling broadly, dressed in T-shirt and trackies, standing in front of a simple, fibro house that could easily have been in Mount Druitt.

"Oh yeah," Cliff was focused again.

Billie was born to Chinese immigrant parents who lived in the outer suburbs of Melbourne. He'd struggled to find work when he left school, become disillusioned and started hanging out with the wrong crowd. However, he hadn't missed the booming property prices all around him. He'd been amazed at how much money some people must have been making while everyone else struggled to pay their rent. He wanted a piece of the action. He did the maths and realized there was no job he could get that would pay him enough to keep pace with the rising price of houses. So, it just made sense to do whatever was necessary to buy one. The problem was he had no money, no respectable job and his parents scraped by on a pension.

In the end, he came up with a crazy idea. He approached sellers and told them he would pay ten thousand dollars more than the best offer they had. There was only one small catch: they would have to loan him ten thousand dollars to use as a deposit.

Of course, he was dismissed as a scam artist each time he called or knocked on a door. But he didn't give up, he knew he only needed one and he was convinced he was offering a good deal. It would make both parties winners. So, he pounded the pavement, knocked on doors, dropped notes in letterboxes and argued with agents. Eventually he found a seller willing to accept the logic and go for it. This gave Billie the deposit he needed. Then, with a family friend agreeing to stretch the truth and say Billie worked full-time in his restaurant, he was able to secure his first bank loan.

Cliff chuckled. It sounded just like his own story. Billie's first house was incredibly similar to his. Just like Cliff, Billie did a low cost clean up and renovation to transform the house and make it look a lot more valuable.

To Cliffs surprise, however, Billie did not sell the house. Instead, he said, he was inspired by the legendary American real estate guru, Ray Kirshwood, who's slogan was 'never sell!' So he rented it out.

Billie's plan was to hold onto the property because he reckoned its value would go up so much it would outdo any other way of getting rich.

The other thing Cliff found amazing was that as soon as it was fixed up and rented out, Billie went to a new bank and asked them to value the house. He couldn't believe his luck when the new bank told him it was worth much more than he'd paid for it and, if he wanted, he could borrow most of the increased value.

It meant he instantly had a deposit to buy another one. This time he didn't need to make any bonus ten-thousand-dollar offer, he just bought the best property he could find at the lowest price he could get. Then he fixed it up and rented it out. He did this several times in the space of the first year. Each time he found a new bank to value the property higher, giving him access to more funds to buy yet another house.

In the space of three years, Billie bought fourteen properties. Collectively, because their prices had continued to rise, he had over a million dollars of value, over and above his loans. In other words, if he sold them all today, he would end up a millionaire!

Cliff's mind raced. Was he making a mistake by selling his house? Was there a better way of doing this? Until now he hadn't any clear plan for getting seriously rich. Allen and Wendy's idea was great and had made them money. But it felt more like a job. A fun job for sure. But it didn't offer a step by step way to make a million – ridiculously quickly. Before he closed the magazine, he fumbled around for a pen under the table next to his bed and circled the name 'Ray Kirshwood'.

Next day, when Angelo rang to discuss putting the house on the market, Cliff surprised him.

"Mate, just out of interest, how much could you rent it for?"

"Oh, you're thinking of keeping it?"

"Maybe. Just want to know the numbers for now."

"Well, I'd say we could get $200 a week no dramas."

"Really, that's pretty good."

It was enough to service his mortgage. First box ticked.

"Right now, you'd have no trouble getting a tenant either. There's lots of people looking and the place looks fantastic. A lot better than the average rentie out here."

"Ok cool. And you reckon I could sell it for 120, right?"

"Yeah, that's the ballpark, mate."

"Hmm, I wonder if the banks will agree."

"Only one way to find out!"

"That's what I reckon Angelo. Let me check it out and I'll tell you if we're selling or renting, ok?"

Cliff put his mobile back in his jacket pocket as he made his way inside the glass doors of Westfield Mount Druitt. Lots of banks had branches here and he had no idea which to choose. So, he just picked the first one. ABC Bank.

"Morning," the assistant looked at him warily. Cliff had got used to it, he knew he didn't look like a great candidate.

"Can I speak to someone about a loan, please?"

"I'm sorry all our loan managers are busy at the moment, would you like to make an appointment for another time?"

"I'm happy to wait since I've come all the way. I'm just looking for the right bank to refinance my property with."

Cliff had picked up the term 'refinance' from the article about Billie. He used it like bait on a hook.

"Oh, I see," her eyebrows lifted, "Let me just check and see if anyone can fit you in." She headed through a door behind her. A moment later she reappeared, followed by a tall guy in a neat suit.

"This is our loans manager, Saleh Ibrahim, he is happy to see you now, in between appointments." She smiled with a little too much effort.

Saleh stuck out a long arm, "Come on through."

He seemed to understand what Cliff was doing without needing to go into the details. He ordered an immediate revaluation and, as an unexpected bonus, offered to give Cliff the bank's 'professional' loan package with a discounted interest rate, if the refinance worked out ok.

Later that afternoon, Saleh's valuer nodded politely as Cliff walked him around his freshly renovated house. He made sure to point out all the improvements they'd made to the original.

Inspired by Allen and Wendy, Cliff had memorized the details of a few nearby properties that had recently sold for a high price. He was surprised by how much interest the valuer showed and ended up writing the addresses down for him.

"If we'd done this yesterday, it wouldn't have been so bloody hot. I told you," Cliff's dad, Tommy, wiped the sweat from his forehead.

Cliff was sweating too as he lifted another concrete flagstone and stood it on its end, exposing an ant colony in the dry soil beneath.

"I know but I had to go to the bank yesterday. It was important."

Tommy grunted unimpressed. The two of them lifted the flagstone and carried it across to a pile that was growing against the side fence. So far, they had cleared about half the old, crumbling back patio, an area that had become a useless no-mans-land for the storage of junk. It was a family joke the number of times his mum had complained about it and Tommy, sneaking off to do something else, had promised to fix it up 'one day'.

So, when Cliff was picking up a free pile of bricks from a demolition site for his investment house, his eyes had fallen on a stack of cream-coloured clay pavers, in excellent condition. He knew they'd be perfect for his mum and dad's place and asked if he could take them too.

Tommy had never liked Cliff's property investing venture. Even as Cliff overcame each hurdle and the renovations got underway, he'd refused to take an interest or even talk about it.

When pushed, he'd snapped, "I'm not helping my own son dig his way into a pile of debt and ruin his life. You do what you like but leave me out of it. Ok?"

It seemed to have pushed them even further apart. So Cliff was stoked to be doing the paving together. Despite the grumbling, he could tell his dad was enjoying himself. And for his part he was keen to show off his new knowledge and skills.

"We can use these to make a driveway," Tommy eyed the pile of battered, concrete flagstones.

"It'd be better to pour a slab," Cliff squinted, "Lay some decent pavers on top. Honestly, these are a bit shit."

"They'd be better than nothing."

"Nah, I'd use the good ones as steppers from the laundry to the washing line. The rest we should chuck."

Cliff's mobile rang in his pocket.

"Hello, Cliff Young."

"Hi Cliff, its Saleh Ibrahim from ABC Bank, Mount Druitt. How are you?"

"Hi Saleh, good thanks mate."

"I've got the valuation back, Cliff. It's come in at 130."

"130 thousand?"

"Yes, that's right."

"Wow." Cliff's heart beat faster. He'd spent nearly 90 thousand buying and fixing the place up, including the roof disaster. So, according to Saleh Ibrahim, he'd just made a profit of 40 grand.

"So that's definite then?"

"Yep. We can't quite match your current lender's 100% loan, I'm afraid. But we can go to 97%. That's 126,100 dollars we can loan you. Let me know if you want to go ahead?"

Cliff didn't have to think long. He'd already decided, if the revaluation came back anywhere above 120, he would give Billie the Battler's system a go. This was a solid green light. He could pay off all his debts, get his mum's ring back and still have a deposit to buy another one and start building his portfolio. Maybe he could get to fourteen houses in three years too!

"Would love to Saleh."

"Great, Cliff, well you can come in whenever you're ready and we can finalise."

"Awesome, I'll see you this afternoon!"

"Look forward to seeing you Cliff. I hope we can start a long and happy relationship with you and help you to prosper."

Cliff hung up. "Wow."

Then he saw his dad's eyes. Tommy dropped his shovel, turned and walked inside.

"Hey, dad, what's wrong?"

"I thought we were doing the paving today."

Cliff hurried after him. His mum looked up, alarmed, from behind the kitchen bench. Tommy slammed the bathroom door behind him.

"We are dad. I'm sorry. That call was really good news. I just got excited, you know? I wanted to seal the deal straight away. But I can leave it to tomorrow. That's fine."

His dad opened the door.

"That's alright, matey, you've got more important things you want to do."

"No, no, I promise you I'd rather do the paving with you. I can go into the bank tomorrow. No worries at all."

"You sure?"

"Yeah, let's do it, I'm keen to see it done."

Tommy fished his work shirt out of the washing basket and pulled it back on. With a slap of Cliff's shoulder, he headed back outside. Cliff winked at his mum, her mouth still open.

As they set to work on the next flagstone, Cliff had an extra bounce in his step.

"My plan seems to be working, dad. The renovations have paid off pretty nicely. If it keeps going this way, I might just make some serious money. If I do, I'd love you to get involved. Maybe you can do a house too."

Tommy chuckled as he kicked at his shovel, "That ain't never going to happen."

Cliff quickly became a legend amongst a growing circle of people who knew what he was up to. He had sworn to keep his money-making ventures secret following the RX7 disaster, but there was no way he could contain things with all the renovation helpers, neighbours, friends and work connections and their extended circles of friends and family. By the time Cliff had renovated his second house and put a happy tenant in it, it was obvious he was doing something big. Barely six months later he re-valued both properties, got even more equity from the bank and bought two more houses. Another six months later he did it again.

Billie's strategy was working better than Cliff could have hoped. It was insane. In eighteen months he had gone from unemployed, his lawn mowing business stolen before he could even get started, to owning a portfolio of six houses worth nearly a million dollars.

"And you still don't have a fucking car," Raj frowned as he climbed into the passenger seat of the van.

"It's all tied up in the houses, man. Every dollar I make goes into buying more of them."

They were off house hunting. This time, however, it was for Raj. Now that his scheme was proving such a winner, Cliff badly wanted his mates to follow him and reap the same rewards.

Arthur, as good as his word, had been the first. Then, amazingly, MJ had snuck up on all of them, talking two workmates into buying an investment house as a joint venture. Now it was Raj's turn.

Cliff opened his battered notebook and turned to a new page headed 'Rajie'.

"Let's go shopping!" He slapped the outside of his door.

With a squelch of tires, Raj accelerated towards North St Mary's and his financial future.

Cliff wished he could get everyone who'd helped and supported him onto the bandwagon: the landscaping crew, his boss at Starbucks, his old school mates and footy mates, at least the good ones who'd stuck around. Even all his new neighbours – and there were lots of them! Most of all, he wanted his dad to do it. That would be amazing. All his life Tommy had tried dodgy ways to get ahead. Now Cliff had come up with a 'scam' that was actually working and making him rich. He would love to see his dad enjoying it too.

"The trouble is you can talk to people as much as you like. But they don't get it. Or they don't trust it, you know? It's only the ones who've actually been involved and seen what we do. Those people start to believe it and take action. Like you!"

He punched Raj in the shoulder.

"Hey man, I'm fucking driving."

"I'm fucking driving, I'm fucking driving," Cliff leaned across and messed his hair with both hands.

Raj swerved wildly into the oncoming lane, "Stop it, you idiot!"

Cliff could see there were no other cars coming so he kept it up until Raj hit the brakes, throwing them both forward.

Raj started slapping him, "You dumb fuck, what are you doing, I could crash!"

Cliff was laughing so hard he could barely hold up his arms to defend himself. Eventually Raj let up. They sat for a moment, breathing heavily and staring out the windscreen.

A loud hoot came from behind.

"Come on, man. You're stopped in the middle of the road."

Raj pushed the hand shift into gear, "You're a fucking idiot, man, I don't know why anyone would trust you with anything. I mean, what the fuck am I doing?"

Cliff chuckled, "Because you know I'm right. You hate to admit it, but you know I'm right."

"You're a risk taker."

"Someone has to do it. Then you all follow. If I didn't do it, you'd be working at your dad's two-dollar shop for the rest of your life."

"Bullshit."

"It's true."

"You're so up yourself."

"Come on man, think about it. I wanna get everyone we know involved. All the good people. I've worked this shit out. Maybe I got lucky, whatever, but I've found it. I want everyone to get on it. Everyone out here, you know, it could change their lives."

"Maybe you should take people house hunting with you. Show them exactly what you do from the start. Like those guys did for you."

"Allen and Wendy? Yeah. Good idea."

"Why don't you start a club or something?"

"A club?"

"Yeah, like you have people join up and they come along checking out houses and you show them all the ins and outs, just like those guys showed you. That's how you got started."

"Yeah, true."

"It could be like those motoring clubs, you know, where everyone goes for a Sunday drive. Except you end up driving around Mt Druitt," Raj laughed.

"That's hilarious," Cliff cracked up, "But it's an awesome idea. Let's do it."

Over a barrel of hot chicken wings and several beers, Cliff, Raj and MJ cemented the idea. They called the club 'Cliffies Climbers'. Anyone interested in 'climbing' with them could come along on a Saturday morning tour. They'd show them exactly what kind of property to look for and all the steps in the process. At the end of the tour, they'd head over to whichever house was currently under renovations for a BBQ.

Cliff loved the idea of doing for others exactly what Allen and Wendy had done for him. Since taking the plunge and buying his first investment house, everything had gone according to plan. Better than planned. Prices kept going up. The bank kept revaluing his portfolio higher. At first it seemed crazy, but Cliff had got used to it by now. He wanted others to share in the craziness. He could see how his home patch, this rough old town of Mount Druitt and its locals, could change their lives and create a better future for the whole place. They were his people and he was on a mission.

He even thought of approaching Centrelink and offering to take unemployed people along. He was convinced it was the best way out of poverty. Maybe, if the club was successful, they could do projects for charities. One out of every ten houses could be a charity house where all the profits went to support a local cause.

Raj and MJ were fired up too and the word spread quickly. The first Saturday morning there were twenty-four people waiting for them in the shopping centre carpark.

"This is mad," MJ laughed, "Where'd you all come from?"

They signed everyone up and took their ten-dollar membership fee with a "Welcome to Cliffies Climbers!"

They hadn't thought much about the logistics of a large group. The best they could do was swap mobile numbers in case someone got lost. Pulling out of the carpark, Cliff, Raj and MJ looked back and laughed as a mini traffic jam formed behind them with seven cars trying to stay on their tail.

The day was a resounding success. They visited four houses for sale, meeting Angelo at each one. Then they drove past some of Cliff's completed renovations, including his very first house. It was hilarious to watch neighbours come out and scratch their heads as eight cars pulled up and a small crowd gathered outside. If any neighbours showed an interest, they invited them to join the club. Then the convoy headed to MJ's renovation for the first Cliffies Climbers BBQ.

When the next weekend came around there were more than forty people and the one after that a crowd of over fifty waited in the car park. At this point they decided to break the day up into shifts with Cliff, MJ and Raj each leading a different group and poor Angelo having to show each house three times.

The weekend after that, membership topped one hundred, a huge crowd waiting in the car park for the first shift. The guys knew the plan would have to change. So, when one of the new members said she worked at the nearby golf club where there was a function room that was hardly used, they jumped at the idea. Cliffies Climbers started meeting on a Wednesday night at the golf club. Members could sign up for the Saturday morning tours which were limited to a group of twenty. This seemed fair and everyone agreed to the new plan.

Cliff, totally unexpectedly, found himself presenting from stage with a microphone to the ever-growing crowd. It was a role he'd never imagined for himself but one he came to enjoy. He kept things simple and just talked through his crazy journey so far. It seemed like the members never tired of hearing it over and over. However, he also began to get others to give presentations. It started with Angelo and then his solicitor Garth. He made MJ and Raj do a spot each. He got audience members to come up and share their goals and dreams.

Later on, they invited industry experts to teach the audience about their specialist fields. They never had trouble finding business-people to come and speak to a room full of highly motivated, budding property investors. Bill was one of these experts and ended up joining the club and giving regular presentations on property development. It was a great chance to showcase his own latest developments, of course, but he also made sure to give good insights and advice to the members.

Despite the large numbers, the club became a tight knit group of people who were committed to supporting each other in turning their financial lives around. Everyone had something amazing or touching to share. For Cliff, the best part was watching members take the leap and buy a house, renovate and discover to their joy how much money they had made when they refinanced. He and his team were there for them when they stumbled. So were the other more experienced club members, everyone helping each other to climb up the ladder. Whether it was choosing properties, making offers, finding cheap supplies or advice on loans or legal issues. When new members shared their success stories, how they had made fifty, sixty or even seventy thousand dollars profit with their first property, the excitement in the room was palpable.

The club grew in other ways too. They opened an office in Mount Druitt on a busy strip near the old station. It became a hub for all of Cliffs property buying and renovating, as well as the administration of Cliffies Climbers.

Shortly after setting up the office he took the advice of supportive members and advertised for an office manager. He picked Lara for her enthusiasm and cocky confidence. Also, as he admitted to MJ, "'Cause I love that accent and, I mean, she's hot. Right?"

Eventually the night came when Cliff announced he had acquired his 50th property. To loud whoops and cheers he proudly told his audience that the bank had valued him at a net worth of over $4 million. Not bad for a young bloke only a few years out of Mt Druitt

High who had never held a proper job.

As two hundred people rose to their feet to applaud, Cliff found he was genuinely choked with emotion. Tears welling in his eyes, he had to take a break before returning to the stage.

THIRTEEN

January 07

The morning after Cliff's night out on the harbour with Mandy, Lara sat in front of his desk, a silky green, floral dress not quite covering her golden tanned knees.

"I can't believe you almost dropped it," her eyes wide with imagining the moment, "That would've been hilarious!"

"For you maybe."

"So... did it taste like five thousand dollars?"

"You know what, it could have been a twenty-buck bottle. I would have no idea."

"Oh my god!"

"But..."

"But what?"

"In that moment, out on the harbour, with the sun setting and celebrating the achievement of my dream. That made it worthwhile. Yeah... One hundred percent."

"Hmm. That's really awesome," Lara's eyes glistened and she looked away.

Before they could say any more, MJ burst through the door, carrying two cartons of soft drinks.

"Morning!" she held the door open with her back, "Softies were on special, so I stocked up on ten cartons for the club."

"Nice work," Cliff grabbed them.

"Shit news, hey," MJ called from the stairwell as she headed down to get the next load.

"What?"

"Interest rates."

Cliff had forgotten to check and now his heart beat a little faster.

MJ reappeared with two more cartons and a copy of the morning's paper on top. From several paces away Cliff could read the headline: 'More Pain.'

"Yep they've gone up half a percent. Again." She handed over her load and headed back down for more.

Cliff stacked the cartons in the storeroom and took the paper. The last two days had been so busy followed by such an amazing night with Mandy that interest rates had completely slipped his mind. Today was the first Tuesday of the month, the day any change in rates was announced by the Reserve Bank.

The first increase had come a year earlier when the chief of the Reserve Bank warned that the property market was getting 'over heated'. No-one in Cliffs world had paid much attention and indeed nothing had seemed to change. Some club members had debated fixing the interest rate on their loans, but Cliffs approach to investment, waiting for values to go up and then refinancing and using the additional funds to buy more properties, meant that his loans had to be flexible. He'd told them fixing wasn't for him.

Six months later, rates had gone up again. Then a further half a percent last month. That brought an outcry in the news about hurting battlers in Australia's mortgage belts, especially Western Sydney. So everyone reckoned the Reserve Bank wouldn't dare do it again.

"They can't keep pushing them up, it's bullshit," Cliff tossed the paper onto a shelf.

"Why would they want to hurt the economy like this?" Lara frowned.

"Exactly. But most of all why would they want to hurt the voters they need so badly? Especially out here, right? They're going to cop a flogging for this."

"It's so cruel," Lara's rolled 'r' punched the word out with extra, angry oomph, "You encourage people to buy houses. Make it the 'Great Aussie Dream'. Then you start making repayments harder and harder. Eventually people aren't going to be able to keep up and they'll lose their homes. What's the point of that?"

"You know what it's going to do, right? It just means people like us will be able to snap up properties even cheaper. And make even more out of them."

"You're nice. Taking advantage of other people's misfortune."

"No, no, hang on. I'm realistic. I don't like it. I'm not saying it's good. I'm just saying that's what will happen."

"One more!" MJ thrust two cartons through the door and ran back down the stairs.

Cliff took the boxes to the storeroom, "I was speaking to Bill about the nineteen eighties. That's when people ended up making the most money."

"Oh, so you mean 'greed is good'?!"

"No, you know interest rates went up to nearly twenty percent?"

"What?"

"Yeah. Imagine that. But you know what he said? Investors were ok because rents went up just as much. But owners suffered. People couldn't pay their mortgages and the banks took their houses. They ended up selling them off cheap at auction. That's when the smart investors bought them up, held onto them and eventually rates came back down and they were sitting pretty."

"Wow, so you're happy rates are going up? I learn a lot sitting in this office."

"No, don't get me wrong. I don't want rates to go up. I just borrowed two million bucks yesterday. Think about the interest on that. All I'm saying is it doesn't have to be the end of the world. If you're smart there's always an upside."

MJ carried the last two cartons into the storeroom.

"Did you read it?"

"I read the headline."

Lara cut in, "But he was just explaining how their pain is our gain."

"Fuck you," Cliff pulled a face at her.

Lara gave him two fingers.

MJ remained serious, "The worry is if prices start coming down. Then we're stuffed."

"You're such a drama queen. You're freaking out because we paid down on Blue yesterday."

"I'm not freaking out. I'm just saying."

"Prices aren't coming down. Supply and demand remember. There's millions of people wanting to buy houses and no-one's making any more land. Just because interest rates go up half a percent isn't going to stop people needing a home."

"Sure. I just reckon we might need a plan."

"Da da! That's where I come in," Lara pulled the latest Australian Property Investor magazine from her bag and waved it. "This is what I wanted to tell you about, Cliff."

"Hang on, since when did you start reading about property investing? I thought you just liked to watch."

"I like to stay informed, ok?"

"Nice," MJ nodded.

"So what's happening? There's a really, really big real estate racket going doon in Edinburgh?" Cliff rolled all his r's with glee.

"Ye can take my shit hoose, but ye'll never take my freedom!" MJ pumped her fists.

"Ha dee bloody ha, that's all you lot know about Scotland, isn't it? Shut up and have a look."

She flipped through the pages, "Guess who's having a seminar for the first time in five years?"

"A seminar?"

"Guess! If there was one seminar in the whole world you would want to go to, who's would that be?"

FOURTEEN

Cliff, MJ, Raj and Lara sprung from the cab, opening and slamming the doors in time as if choreographed by a movie director. Their spirits were high despite a long flight. They had, of course, played up all the way, annoying every passenger within four rows. They'd made captain's announcements into their handsets, fought over card games and re-enacted safety demos. When Cliff pulled the life vest out from under Raj's seat, put it on and cried out that he was drowning, an annoyed flight attendant had threatened to report them on landing.

The free alcohol didn't help things either and soon enough the giggles started up again. By the time they reached San Francisco they were the adult equivalent of exhausted kids at the end of a cake and cordial-fueled birthday party.

But stepping out of the airport, into the chilly autumn air and taking in the new sights, sounds and smells quickly reinvigorated them. They called out thanks to the taxi driver and headed into their hotel, an ornately renovated building dating back to the Gold Rush days.

The first night was spent exploring the city and dining out in the heart of the Italian district on what they all agreed was the best pizza they had ever eaten.

Flushed with red wine, glorious pizza and new discoveries, they gave each other a group hug in the lift. MJ and Raj got out first, singing good night as they made their way to their rooms. Cliff and Lara got out on the next floor. Feeling a little tipsy Cliff opened his arms for a final hug. Lara embraced him warmly. Then she kissed him full on the lips. With a broad smile, she wished him good night and sauntered off to her room.

Cliff stood transfixed, admiring her long, perfectly sculptured legs and well-toned behind. He could still taste her mouth. He savoured the fleeting touch of warm breath and taught body. Then he turned and weaved his way down the corridor to his room.

It had been Mandy's idea for him to take Lara along. Unfortunately, the seminar clashed with the tour of a band she was managing, and despite Cliff's best efforts to persuade her, she had insisted her team needed her in Sydney. The band was a big name and would require all her talents and experience. She told Cliff it would be a nice reward for the hard work Lara had put in over the years.

Cliff was super impressed by Mandy's selflessness. But he also felt a little hurt, even jealous, that she didn't seem to care enough about this significant milestone for him. Now, however, he felt a different sensation. The frisson of freedom.

Next day was the seminar, held at the convention centre around the corner from the hotel. They grabbed coffee from a food truck along the way and arrived early. The cavernous, glass-walled foyer was already buzzing.

"Woah," Cliff stopped and took in the scene, "He's like eighty something and he's still a fucking rock star! How good is this."

"Impressive," Lara nodded.

"There goes your chances of having a one-on-one with the big fella," MJ laughed as she slapped Cliffs shoulder.

"Seriously, how good must this guy be? After all this time he still pulls a crowd like this."

Raj put an arm around Cliff from the other side, "We're here buddy. We're actually here."

Cliff hugged his two best mates tight.

"Turn around you big goobers," Lara called from behind them.

She snapped their photo, a thumbs up from Cliff, MJ secretly holding two fingers up behind his head, Raj chuckling and a giant Ray Kirshwood smiling from a banner.

The presentation was an eye-opener for the four Aussies. Beginning with a black out, a wave of excitement rippled through the audience. Then a high energy video pumped across huge screens. Finally, smoke and lasers filled the air as a rich, booming voice acclaimed the return of Ray Kirshwood.

RK himself turned out to be smaller and fatter than Cliff had imagined, but a total dynamo nonetheless. His enthusiasm could have run a small power station and his strong, well-timbred voice filled every corner of the large auditorium. Most unexpected of all, though, was the audience participation. They became one, massive, cheer squad partnering Ray in the overall performance. They answered every rhetorical question, they broke out into spontaneous cheers, drum-roll-like bursts of clapping and foot stamping, even Mexican waves. They held up placards and unfurled banners across entire rows of fans. They knew all his favourite sayings and, when he held the microphone out, they recited them in one voice like the audience at a rock concert filling in the lines of a famous chorus.

Following morning tea break, however, things started to take a different turn. It became clear that RK was not going to stick to his well-known message. He had warned them, during the first session, that his presentation was going to be completely different. In fact, he'd told them he was going to shock them to their very core.

This, in itself, was not exactly unexpected coming from an over-the-top investment spruiker and it was unlikely anyone really did anticipate any major surprises. So, when RK finally came to the point, and told his audience that he was here, for the first time in his life, to advise them NOT to invest in real estate, Cliff along with the rest of the audience waited for the twist, the clever, alternative take that would ultimately lead back to a smart, new way to invest in real estate.

But they were disappointed.

"Do you like bubbles, people? Yeah, they're fun, right? Kids love bubbles, love to chase them. But no-one likes bubbles when they pop. It's messy. Right? Well, unfortunately, I'm here to tell you that we're all inside of a big bubble, people. And it's about to pop."

Ray nodded slowly, "It's about to get real messy. Real, real messy. Do you know what I'm talking about? No, of course you don't. No-one talks about this. No-one wants to hear it. But someone has to say it.

Let me explain. You know I've always taught you there are two kinds of debt, right? There is…"

Ray cocked an ear. The audience responded with, "Good debt!"

He laughed, "That's right 'good debt' and there is…"

"Bad debt!"

"That's it, good debt and bad debt. It's one of my most fundamental teachings, right? Well, now I'm here to tell you that there's also plain 'dumb debt'. Dumb debt that's going to take us all down. Down to hell."

Ray finished with his finger pointing down to an imaginary hell and allowed his words to soak in. Then he continued in a low tone.

"You've all heard of someone, maybe a friend or relative, who's bought a brand-new house lately. Maybe somewhere here in California. The bank's given them one hundred percent of the money, up front. And the builder hasn't even started! Or maybe a couple of lovely pensioners. Should be living quietly in retirement. But, no, they've gone to a real estate seminar. Not one of mine, mind you!"

Ray waved a finger in the air.

"The bank's gone and loaned them all the money they need to buy a brand new, four-bedroom, ritzy ditz house and they're on the pension. They don't get enough weekly to even come close to paying back that loan. So, what happens? The bank loans them even more, so they can use this second loan to pay back the interest on their first loan. Then a third loan to pay back the second. They do it for unemployed people, don't even check their details. Why? Why would normal, decent folks do something so stupid? Why would bankers, who should be smart people, do something so dumb? Because everyone's drunk the Kool Aid, people. Their heads are filled with dreams of riches. Their judgement is clouded by fast talking, snake-oil-selling loan dealers. Everyone thinks house prices are just gonna keep on going up. Right? Right?"

Ray held out his mic to give the audience a chance to answer, but no-one dared.

"Wrong! Eventually prices are gonna stop. Then what's gonna happen? There's a big change coming, people. A reversal of everything we take for granted. A terrible time of suffering for many. And for you and me, investors, a dangerous time indeed. A time when the fat cats become food for the feral dogs."

He hammered out these last words with relish. Then, when he continued, he spoke quietly, with a great sense of compassion.

"I'm here to tell you to build a financial storm shelter people. Take lots of provisions, make things as comfortable for yourself and your loved ones as you can, then go inside, lie low and don't venture out into the coming tornado."

Ray began pacing the front of the stage with purpose.

"If this comes as a surprise to you, you can celebrate in the fact that you are no different to anybody else across this great country of ours."

He held up a finger, "Then you can stop celebrating. You can stop celebrating because now you know something they don't and you can do something different. Ain't that worth the price of a ticket?!"

Ray cocked a wicked smile at his audience. It provoked some laughter, but it was nervous. He became confidential again.

"You know what I've been buying these last five years? Do you know?"

He paused to build suspense.

"Yep, I bet you'd like to know what I've been buying. Well, I'll tell you what I haven't been buying. Real estate."

He let the audience take in the impact of these words.

"That's right, Ray Kirshwood has not been buying real estate. Holy crap, the sky has fallen!"

The audience laughed, but still with uncertainty.

"After lunch, I'll tell you what I have been buying," he winked at the front row. "Then we'll talk about how we're gonna make a fat fucking fortune! How's that? You thought Ray had deserted you? You thought there was no silver lining? Don't be fucking crazy. After lunch we're gonna have some fun ok?!"

At last the audience was relieved of the stress of the previous half an hour and erupted in cheers. Music blasted, Ray waved as he walked off stage and the lights came back up. As everyone filed out to lunch, buzzing with excited chatter, clouds of bubbles drifted down from the ceiling and cloaked them. The irony was lost on no-one.

Lunch was served from a collection of retro New York hot dog carts, parked throughout the foyer. The fillings, though, were anything but traditional.

"Woah, vegetarian tofu-bratwurst? We're seriously in California," Raj scratched his head.

"Well, I don't care who 'Cajun' is, I'm not touching his 'pulled-pork'..." MJ was mid 'wank' gesture when a woman with curly blonde hair stepped up and touched her and Cliff on the shoulders.

"Well, hi! I just had to say hello. I could hear those wonderful Aussie accents. I'm Andi and this is my husband, Paul."

Andi quickly became fascinated by what Cliff and his mates were doing in the Australian property market.

"Holy hell, that's incredible! Did you hear that Paul? They've got their own investor club. That's totally unreal guys. How long have you been doing this for?"

Lifted by her enthusiasm, they boasted about Cliff's achievements, from the size of his property portfolio, to the founding of the club and now their venture into the stunning waterfront development Blue. Pretty soon a small crowd had gathered, smiling and nodding every time Andi exploded with another "Wow!"

A tall, young man in an impeccably fitted dark suit, who had been standing at the back of the throng, pushed his way forward, apologizing as he went. He was followed by an equally immaculate young woman who smiled at everyone they pushed past.

"Please forgive me, I'm very sorry to interrupt," he put a hand on Andi's shoulder and then turned to Cliff.

"That's one hell of a story you have. I believe you should meet RK. Would you like to meet up with him?"

For a moment Cliff didn't quite compute.

"Oh, I'm terribly sorry," the young guy, who looked a bit like an early Pierce Brosnan, offered his business card, "I'm Ronnie Campion, I work for Mr Kirshwood."

Ronnie put his hand on the padded shoulder of his beautiful accomplice, "And this is Catherina. We both work with Mr Kirshwood and we just know he'd love to meet you. If you're willing, that is?"

At last Cliff realized what was on offer.

"Oh, you mean Ray? I mean, Mr Ray… Mr Kirshwood, I mean."

"Yes, absolutely. I know he'd love to meet you and hear all about your amazing success."

Catherina's smile was bright like the sun.

Cliff turned to the others for support.

Raj made a decision, "That would be amazing, we'd love to meet him."

The Australians followed their guides to a door behind the registration tables. Ronnie swiped a card and gestured them in. They found themselves moving along a stark, echoing corridor through the back of house. After many twists and turns they entered a plush area with carpet and timber paneling on the walls. Flat screens showed different views of the stage and auditorium, currently empty. They could hear raised voices and laughter.

Ronnie asked them to wait a moment and disappeared through a door signed 'Green Room 1'.

A few minutes later he reappeared, smiling, "Come on in. Mr Kirshwood is available now."

Inside, people crowded onto a long sofa that ran the full length of one side wall, others leaned next to the door and still more stood in groups in each corner. Everyone was focused on Ray Kirshwood who sat on a tall stool at a round-top table, a glass in one hand, a half-finished bottle of Jack Daniels gripped in the other. Several empty glasses covered the table. Ray was reaching the climax of a story.

"He looked at me and his eyes kinda went big, you know. In fact, he did, you know, like Charlie Chaplin," Ray acted out an exaggerated double-take and rasped with laughter, the cue for the room to crack up in support.

"And he said, he said, 'Hang on. You mean you are Ray Kirshwood? Ray Kirshwood, the Property Guy? The Ray Kirshwood who is famous for saying I'll Never, Ever, Pay More than Half Price for a Property??'"

Ray ran his eyes around his audience, a wicked smile on his face, "And I nodded and said 'You fucking bet your half-priced bottom dollar I am!'"

He threw his head back in a belly laugh and the room erupted.

"Oh my god, excuse my French," Ray took in his new visitors, "You guys must be the Aussies. I'm so sorry I get carried away with my stupid stories. It's these guys fault," he wagged a finger at the people sitting on the long sofa, "They always egg me on, you know."

Cliff, Raj, MJ and Lara smiled, not quite sure what to say.

"Well, come on in!" Ray waved, "Welcome! Or should I say 'Giday mate'?!"

Chuckles rippled through the room.

"Have a drink!" Ray held out the bottle of Jack Daniels.

Before Cliff could decline, MJ gave a high-pitched chortle, "Alright, why not!"

"There must be clean glasses around here somewhere."

Everyone looked around in vain until Ronnie stepped forward and grabbed a handful from Ray's table, "I'll wash some up, Ray."

"Great thinking!"

"Now, which of you folks has bought a hundred properties?"

Raj, MJ and Lara all pointed at Cliff.

"A man after my own heart," Ray held out a hand.

Cliff shook it earnestly, "Well, you've actually been my greatest inspiration and mentor."

"Is that a fact? You mean you guys have even heard of me all the way over there? Or 'down under' there, I should say," he snorted.

"He's read all your books," Lara smiled.

"Well, you know what guys? I mean, I'm really touched, you know. I mean, this doesn't happen every day, right? You know what I'd really like?"

"What?"

"I'd really like you... to join me... on stage for this afternoon's session. What do you say?"

"Woah!" Cliff held up his hands.

"No, seriously, it will be great. These people need to hear from someone other than boring old me anyway, right? Someone, somewhere else in the world, doing good. It will be an inspiration. Absolutely an inspiration. Will you do it?"

"Well, I don't know...".

"Come on, it'll be fun! You're a speaker, right? You've got your own club, your own fans, you'll be great. Have you got a book you want to plug? Here's your best chance!"

"No, really, my club's tiny. It's not like this at all. I'm not a professional presenter or anything."

"Hey, don't worry. We'll make it easy for you. You'll have a blast. Ronnie, can we make this happen?"

"Absolutely, Ray. I'll go tell the AV guys."

The first half of the afternoon session was a blur for Cliff. The great revelation from Ray was precious metal. Gold and silver. He'd been stock piling at very low prices and he urged everyone to get into it now before the big crash comes. While everything else went to shit, he predicted, gold and silver would sky-rocket to unimaginable heights.

Cliff, however, didn't take in much. Ronnie had moved the four mates to front row seats where Cliff could easily get to the stage when Ray introduced him. He sat waiting for his moment, like an executionee at the foot of the guillotine.

When it eventually came, adrenalin kicked in. He bounced up on stage and shook hands with Ray.

"This guy," Ray put an arm around Cliff, breathing heavily with the effort of his performance, "This guy is an Aussie investing legend. He's living proof that what we do here can work anywhere."

Cheers from the audience.

"Tell me, Cliff, how old are you buddy?"

"Ah, twenty-eight, Ray."

"Twenty-eight, huh? Twenty-eight, people!"

More applause.

"And in your long and illustrious career in real estate…" Ray chuckled, "How many properties have you managed to buy using our techniques? Hang on…"

Ray turned to the audience, "I want you people to guess. How many do you think this young man has bought? Not 10. No, not 20. Not even 50… Tell them Cliff".

"One hundred. Well, just over…"

"One hundred!"

The crowd erupted. Cliff felt his heart pounding as they rose to their feet in a standing ovation.

Ray held up his hands to settle them down. It took several goes before he could speak again.

"Wow. Amazing, hey? Tell us a little about how you managed to do this Cliff. Are Mom and Pop rich?"

Cliff smiled and steadied himself with a few deep breaths. He related his story as briefly as he could, making sure to mention the inspiration he got from Ray's books along the way.

"Now I don't mean to put a downer on things, Cliff," Ray became serious, "However, I'm going to say this. I'm going to say this because it's important. And anyway, I know you know I'm right."

"Um, yeah, no worries."

"Australia will not be immune. We've already shown how the same strategies work over there as here. Well, the same dark forces are at work as well. Right? I mean, everything is connected these days, right?"

"Yep, true."

So, I'm going to say this. Be careful. Build your storm shelter. Build other income streams. I know you're doing that, right? You've built a club, right?"

"Yeah, that's right," Cliff nodded, not wanting to contradict Ray by pointing out that his club was not an 'income stream'. Either way, he wasn't fussed. Ray clearly knew very little about the Australian property market.

"You see people. The smart ones are doing it. You wanna follow the smart ones. And they don't come much smarter than this young man here. Please thank our special guest from Down Under!"

Ray shook Cliff's hand elaborately, "Thank you so much, it's been a blast having you Cliff."

As they made their way out of the auditorium, people patted Cliff on the shoulder. Others reached out and shook his hand, congratulating him. Some gave him their business cards. Although, when they asked for his, he had to apologise that he didn't actually have any.

As they reached the street, he heard his name called out excitedly. He turned to see Andi running up pulling Paul along by the arm.

"That was so great, Cliff. Wow! Congratulations!"

"Yeah, thanks Andi."

"Hey, I don't mean to be too forward or anything, but are you guys busy tonight? If not, can we take you out for dinner?"

"Well," Cliff looked at the others who shrugged, "Sure. Thanks."

The night started at a bar in busy Fisherman's Wharf where they drank beer, tried the famous clam chowder and munched on the biggest bowl of French fries the Australians had ever seen. Then they took a cable car to an area called Russian Hill and walked along narrow streets lined with old-world terraced houses, washed in white and soft shades of pink and yellow, punctuated with bright flower-pots.

They found a restaurant that had been converted out of the square, brick box of an old electrical substation. Waiters yelled out greetings over the hubbub as they weaved between tightly packed tables. The friends slurped Mojitos then tucked into plates of spicy food and local wines. By the end of dinner, the volume in the restaurant had become crazy. Cliff could only laugh as he watched MJ trying to make a point over and over with everyone else going "What??"

When Andi suggested they head to a bar in another part of town, they all whooped with excitement.

In a happy haze, Cliff watched as the taxi glided through several underpasses. The streets became wider and the area took on a seedier, more industrial feel with dilapidated houses and unit blocks set amongst old warehouses. Eventually, they pulled up outside a corner bar, music rumbling from within and a scattering of people on the street out front.

Inside was packed with revelers. After buying drinks, they followed Andi and Paul up a steep flight of stairs to a low-lit floor where a jazz band thumped out their rhythms on a small stage. In front of them, couples swung through well practiced steps, individuals gyrated solo and many others stretched back on lounges along the walls or squashed in around tables.

Lara yelled, "Alright! Let's dance!"

She grabbed Cliff's arm and beckoned the others to follow. They ended up in a circle, grooving and jumping about.

Hours later, high and exhausted on dancing not to mention plenty more rounds of beer, wine and cocktails, they headed back down to the street. Andi put the Australians into the first taxi and told the driver to take them back to their hotel.

They weaved through the lobby, MJ singing and drumming on anything she could find.

"Wild Thing!"

The others supported her with air guitars. They piled in the elevator and gave each other a big hug. MJ and Raj got out on their floor, MJ still singing down the corridor and Raj warning against any early wake up calls.

Cliff and Lara got out on their floor. As Lara walked off, Cliff remembered the taste of her kiss.

"Hey Lara. One more good night hug," he held his arms out, "It's been such an amazing experience."

She turned and smiled. Then sauntered, model-like, towards him. She leaned in and kissed him but avoided the embrace.

"Well why don't we have one more drink then?"

Cliff felt a swelling in his groin. "Yeah, sure," he smiled into her bright eyes. "Let's raid my mini bar. I always wanted to serve up cocktails in my hotel suite."

"Sounds good, Mr Bond."

She followed him down the corridor and waited while he found his key. They looked at each other for an uncertain moment until he gestured for her to go in. They giggled. Lara looked around at the suite and plonked herself on a sofa looking out at the glittering city lights.

"Well, this is all very nice. Fitting for a legendary investor from Down Under…"

FIFTEEN
January 08

It was almost a year later and Cliff sat in his usual chair, opposite Dermott at ABC Bank. This time, however, Cliff was slumped forward, his head buried in his hands. He sighed deeply, then looked up at Dermott with one eye through his fingers.

"You *know* what's going on. Interest rates have gone up and everyone's trying to sell. So, prices have been pushed down. Temporarily! It's a cycle. If we try to sell houses now, there won't be any buyers. We'll have to flog them off at rock bottom, ridiculous, prices. I lose and the bank loses. It's dumb!"

"I know mate, but my hands are tied."

"Especially if we sell them all at once. Can you imagine? There's no way you'll get enough to cover the mortgages. Forget me. Leave me out of the picture for a minute, ok? Just think about what's good for the bank. You lose a fortune selling them for less than the mortgages. Then most of the new buyers will probably go to other banks. You lose twice."

"I understand mate..."

"Whereas if you wait just a bit. Until the market recovers – which it will – then you don't lose any money. You keep all your business. You keep a great customer. Someone who has serviced these loans for years without a single issue up until now. Someone capable of growing the portfolio bigger and bigger and taking you guys along with me. You know it makes sense."

"Cliff, like I said mate, the issue is the line of credit. We extended you two million dollars a year ago. That's a lot of money. The bank needs to see you servicing that loan. When you don't, they get very nervous."

"I've told you what's happened. Construction has been delayed. It's killing me too. Bill's had some unforeseen problems. But he's on top of it. You know these units will get built. It's a great project. When they're finished, the rents start coming in. Plus, there's going to be a heap of equity."

"Sure, but that doesn't help us right now, Cliff. Your payments started falling behind six months ago. Any other customer, the bank would have foreclosed long ago. We're trying to work with you. We really are, Cliff. But with the market turning the way it has, the guys in head office are getting jumpy and they're on my back the second they sniff a risk."

"I could always take the whole lot to another bank, Dermott. There's not many investors around with a portfolio like mine."

Cliff was bluffing. He'd already tried to refinance. Together with MJ, Raj and Lara, he had marched into meeting rooms at all the major banks and most of the minors, placing towers of plastic folders on the Lending Manager's desk each time. However, after the initial 'wow', their enthusiasm had waned as the numbers were coldly crunched. Each bank found the portfolio was no longer worth the loans that were written against it. So, in the end, they all politely declined.

Dermott put his hands on his desk, a sympathetic look on his face, "It's up to you Cliff. If you can find another lender, it might buy you a little more time. Trouble is, with prices falling, you don't have any equity left."

Cliff knew he was beaten. His problems had started after returning from San Francisco. Interest rates had gone up again. Then again. The Reserve Bank had decided Australians were borrowing too much, too easily, making the property market way too hot. So, they applied their buckets of cold water.

The effects were dramatic. First thing Cliff noticed was the number of 'For Sale' signs popping up around Western Sydney. It seemed like every street had a couple and each time you went back there were new ones. Next thing was the phone calls. Real estate agents began chasing him over low offers he had once made, sometimes many months before. The vendors who had previously dismissed them were now willing to accept.

For Cliff, though, the first big blow had come when he'd gone in to organize his next batch of refinances with ABC. He'd wanted to take advantage of the 'motivated vendors' who were accepting his low offers. So, it had come as a rude shock, when Jordan, Dermott's appraisal guru, had sat Cliff down, turned his computer screen around and shown Cliff that the bank's valuation of his properties had not increased. In fact, the values had gone down. There was no way they could let him borrow any more.

Dermott leaned forward, holding up Cliff's foreclosure notice. He pointed to the last item in the list of unpaid accounts, "Cliff, can you make this payment? If you do, I'll have another talk to head office. I'll try and get them to look at the bigger picture as far as your history and the size of your portfolio goes. Maybe I can get you a little more holiday on the rest. But only if you make this one."

"Ok mate. Let me see what I can do. Maybe I can juggle some things around."

"Ok, excellent mate. When do you think you'll make the payment?"

"Can you give me to Monday?"

"Of course, mate."

Dermott stood up and held out his hand, "Thanks Cliff, we're here to help, mate."

The truth was Cliff had no idea where he was going to find any more money. He had already maxed out multiple credit cards, taken out personal loans from other banks, and borrowed from friends and connections. With rates now at 8 percent, his outstanding interest on Blue was growing fast. He desperately needed the units finished and earning rent.

As he climbed into his car Cliff was fuming. What the fuck was Bill doing? He felt like he'd been way too accommodating, just rolling along with the builder's excuses, delay after delay. He grabbed his mobile, found Bill's number, hit dial and pressed speaker phone.

"G'day Cliffie."

"How you going, mate?"

"Getting there, buddy. What's up?"

"What exactly is happening with Blue mate? I'm in a really tight spot."

Bill sighed, "I know mate, I'm sorry."

"I can't pay the bank with 'sorry' any more mate."

"Yep, I know, buddy. We're making good progress though, I told you. There's light at the end of the tunnel now."

"When, though? I mean exactly when?"

"Like I said before, Cliff, I can't give you an exact. We've sorted most of the issues now. And there's been a lot of them. I admit I got some things wrong. But we're moving forward now."

"Do you remember how quick I got you that two million?"

"Yeah I do."

"Well, I put my arse on the line for it. Now I'm in deep shit myself. I've had to find six month's interest without any tenants. Do you know how much that is?"

"Yep, I know matey. All I can say is this is the construction industry. There's no absolute guarantees. That's the reality."

"Well maybe you should be covering my interest while we wait, Bill."

"Look Cliff, when all's done maybe I'll do that. But right now, we're not in a position. No-one's made a cent yet. You know that."

"Geez mate you've put me in a hard spot. I'm out of time Bill. I think Blue's stuffed me."

"Hang in there, bud. We're getting close."

"Yeah, well, just, I don't know… update me every day so I know what's going on, ok?"

"Sure buddy. I can do that."

"Ok mate."

Cliff hung up and threw the phone on the passenger seat, "Aaaaargh!!!"

He suddenly noticed the car in front of him had stopped at the lights. He stomped on the brake pedal. The car shuddered and screeched, wheels locking into a skid and the back fishtailing into the oncoming lane. A small truck swerved to avoid him and blasted its horn. He caught a glimpse of the driver's hand in the air, yelling something Cliff could only imagine. He stopped millimetres from the bumper of the car in front.

He took a deep breath and tried to relax.

He couldn't. His mind was racing. He needed to talk and thought about calling Mandy. Instead he chose MJ. She would be sharing his frustrations with Bill. Besides Mandy was at work.

"Hey, Cliffie old son, what's up?"

"Just about took out a Camry and a three-ton truck."

"Good going. Are you alright?"

"Yeah, sort of… Near miss. Not like the bank meeting."

"Oh shit, really?"

"They're foreclosing on me."

"Fucking hell mate."

"Yeah. Fucking Bill, you know he still won't give a deadline. Just says it's getting there. He has no fucking idea what he's doing to us."

"Uh-huh," MJ was clearly holding back her own anger with the situation at Blue.

"You alright Ems? Are you surviving?"

"No. Of course not. I've borrowed 500 grand against a construction site."

'Yeah I know. Bank wants me to pay up by Monday or they pull the pin. Fuckwits."

"Yeah I won't be far behind you. What you going to do?"

"I've got no idea, Ems. I really don't know. Maybe we should sell Blue. As is. Just try and get our money back."

"Mate I'd do it if we could. I'd be happy to get my money back."

"I'm headed to the office now. Want to meet there?"

"Yeah no worries."

Cliff bounded up the concrete steps to their first level office. It wasn't with enthusiasm, though. It was with the blind, grit-your-teeth determination of 'ripping off a Band-Aid.' He had another reason, apart from meeting MJ, to come into the office today. He had to talk to Lara. It was a conversation he had been putting off for a long time.

She looked up from her computer and smiled, "Hey!"

"Hey Lara!"

"How's Derrr-mott?"

Ever since Dermott had mentioned having a Scottish ancestor, Lara had enjoyed giving the r's in his name an extra roll. It always got a laugh from Cliff.

"Yeah he's... whatever."

"Oh?"

"Meeting was a shocker."

"Oh no?"

"Yep. I'm seriously stuffed if I don't get a miracle quickly."

"What happened?"

"They're foreclosing. Taking my whole portfolio."

"Oh my god."

"It's Blue. I can't revalue any houses so I can't pay the interest on it. Simple as that. Bill doesn't know when it's going to be finished and the bank won't wait any longer."

"Wow."

"I'm going to try and sell it. Just try get the money back and pay out the loan."

"Really? Do you think you can?"

"I don't know. Two mill plus interest. That's a big ask right now."

"Wow, after all that. I'm really sorry."

"Yeah, thanks. But listen, the other thing is… This really sucks and I've been trying to avoid it for a long time now," Cliff screwed up his face, "I'm sorry but I can't afford to keep this office going and I can't afford to keep your job anymore."

"Oh… Ok."

"I've left it as long as I could but I've got no choice now. I'm really sorry."

"Hey, don't worry about me. I'll be fine."

"Of course, I worry. You've been the biggest part of this thing. You've done so much for me."

"It's ok."

"I mean, when I get out of this hole, if I can save the situation…" Cliff gave her a coy smile, "If you're still available, I'll make it up to you. I'll pay you twice what I've been paying you just to get you back."

"I'm not bloody going anywhere, alright?"

"I'm sorry…"

"No, no. I'm not abandoning the ship. I don't care about pay for now. When things get tough, the tough get going. Ok? We'll get out of this hole together."

Lara's face softened, "Then, if you like, you can pay me double. Or maybe even triple…"

They laughed. Cliff wanted to sweep Lara up in a hug.

"I don't know if I can let you do that. You can't work for nothing. How are you going to pay your bills and stuff?"

"Well, I guess a bit of what you do has rubbed off on me after all," she smiled, "I've been saving for a deposit. I have a wee bit of money I can live off."

"Really? You're a sly one!"

He wanted to ask how much. He even wondered if it might be enough to be worth borrowing. Enough to help get him through the current crisis? But he held his tongue. Here was Lara offering to work for him for free and all he could think about was borrowing her life savings to save his own arse.

"So, what do we have to do to sell Blue then?" Lara was always one for action.

"Yep, well, MJ is coming over shortly to talk about it. She was pretty keen too."

"Rightio. And Raj?"

"I haven't spoken to him yet. I don't think he's under as much pressure as MJ and I."

"But you don't actually need them involved for you to sell yours, right?"

"No, of course not. It's just good to talk about it with them, have their support, you know…"

"Sure."

"Trouble is I don't know exactly what state it's in. I haven't been down there for a long time. Been so caught up with everything else. It'd be good to see where it's at. You know, how good it's gonna look to buyers."

"Do you want to go down today?"

"Yeah, let's do it. I'll call MJ and tell her to meet us there instead."

"Ok, cool, I'll grab my things."

It was roughly an hour's drive to Blue, depending on traffic. As they hurtled down the M4 motorway, Lara looked up from a long, thoughtful silence.

"It's about more income, isn't it?"

"Yeah. Why?"

"I mean, you've got plenty of properties. Plenty of assets. But you need more income to keep a hold of them while prices aren't going up."

"Yep. Exactly."

"I often think about Ray Kirshwood."

"Yeah, he predicted everything going pear-shaped, didn't he?"

"Yes, but what he said when we were backstage with him. Remember, he said you should use your club to make an income stream. Like he does."

"I know, I've been thinking about that too."

"Yeah? I mean, maybe you don't have time to write a book right now…" she gave Cliff a smile.

"No, not before Monday!"

"But what I was thinking, you give so much to the club. There'd be no harm in using it to make an income. As long as you give them good value in return. Which you would."

"Are you talking about raising the fees? Trouble is, right now, everyone's struggling so I don't think we could."

"No, no. I'm talking about offering something more to those who want to pay for it."

"Right…"

"I mean, now is actually a very good time for people to start investing, if they have the money, isn't it? What with prices going down?"

"Yeah, that's what's so frustrating."

"I know – for you. But if you can't do it yourself, then maybe you can help other people get started. In a totally hands-on way. You give them personal coaching, step by step through finding the right house, getting finance, fixing it up, renting it, you know, the whole journey."

"Yeah…"

"I mean I'd pay for that. Someone like you helping me get my first investment, making sure I get it right. That's worth a lot. It's like a guarantee of success."

"I'm not sure I can guarantee success anymore. I did what you're talking about with my Dad. Encouraged him. He didn't want to do it, but I never let up. I pushed him until he bought one."

"I know…" Lara touched Cliff's leg.

"I helped him. I pushed him along every step of the way. I thought it would give him financial freedom. You know, I had this dream of him making lots of money, being happy… Now he's struggling because he can't get a revaluation and the rent isn't covering his interest. He blames me every time I see him."

"I know, hon, but that wasn't your fault. It's just bad timing, right? Like some of the club members who bought in the last year. It's bad luck. It doesn't change the fact that you bought a hundred. You do know what you're doing. Don't lose confidence."

"Thanks."

"You're a winner."

Cliff chuckled, "Well, I have been thinking about stuff like that. I mean, I've been thinking about every possible way out."

"Yeah, I'm sure you have."

"Trouble is I don't think it's going to make anywhere near enough in the time I need it. You'd have to build up a business like that over time. I'm out of time."

"Hmm."

"Same as getting a job. I even thought about that."

"No!"

"Uh-huh. That's how fucked up it is. But I'd never earn enough."

"No."

"But... I did have another idea," Cliff smiled.

"Oh yeah? I knew the legendary mind would come up with something."

"Well, it's a crazy idea."

"That's what I want to hear!"

"Ok, well, like you said before, this is a great time to buy. I would be buying if I could. I'm getting all these mad low offers from agents now. It's killing me."

"I know."

"And the quickest way for me to make real money, probably the only way I know of, would be to flip houses."

"Oh yeah?"

"You know, buy low, fix up and sell for a profit."

"Yeah, I know what flipping is, thanks very much."

"Ok, ok, I wasn't sure."

"I've been hanging around a few property investors, you know."

"Ok, geez, touchy."

Lara folded her arms, "Just carry on with your story."

"Ok, well... If I flipped a house every month, I could make about

20 to 30K each time. That would pretty much get me by. The way we do things I reckon we could keep the prices low enough we'd be able to sell them. But you know the big problem, right?"

"What?"

"I can't get any fucking finance to buy a house in the first place. So, I can't flip anything."

"Uh-huh."

"But… There is a way I could, maybe…"

"Ok…"

"I once loaned this guy, this investor, some money. This was a few years ago, when I'd just started making some big revaluations. He gave me something like twenty percent interest on it. Some crazy amount like that. I never understood how he could do it. Or why. I was really sus at first."

"Yeah, sure."

"He tried to explain it to me at the time but I never really got it. But now I realise what he was doing. Now that I'm in the situation I reckon he was in."

"Oh, yeah?"

"Yeah. He obviously couldn't get any finance the regular way, for whatever reason. And back then, it would have been a great buyer's market, just like it is now. He was a flipper and he must have been watching incredible opportunities go by, going crazy.

"So, I reckon he figured out that if he gave people a big enough return on their money, like a frikkin' insanely good return, they might take a risk and loan it to him. Then he could start buying. No bank loan needed."

"Wow."

"And because he was good at it, he'd flip it in, like, the space of a month. Pay them back their money and take his profit."

"Right…"

"So, that meant he only had to pay one month of high interest. Genius, yeah?"

"Um, yeah… If you say so," she smiled.

"Ok try this. To keep it simple, he offers me 24% interest. That's pretty enticing so I go for it. Say he borrows 100K off me to buy a house and renovate it. Then he flips it for 120K. After just a month. So he makes a profit of 18K. Right?"

"Eighteen?"

"20K profit less the two percent interest..."

"Two percent... Not twenty-four?"

"Yeah!"

They turned off the main road, onto an overpass with a panoramic view of the harbour. The sparkling water stretched to the east where, in the distance, it met the city skyline. Cliff and Lara's heads, however, turned to the right, where the harbour folded into many small bays and inlets, including the one that Blue was on.

"What the fuck?"

Cliff lifted himself out of his seat to get a better view.

"They haven't done a thing."

"Oh god. Really?"

"Yeah, it looks just like it did last time I saw it. I can't fucking believe it!"

He swung into the right-hand turning lane, stomped on the accelerator and screeched across three lanes of oncoming traffic, barely making it into the side road that led to Blue. Several cars hooted long and hard.

"Fuck off!" Cliff yelled.

A speed hump loomed up unexpectedly. With a loud, bone-jarring thump the car lurched over it, throwing Cliff and Lara forward then back. Cliff instinctively put an arm out across Lara's chest to protect her.

"Sorry. Sorry."

"Jesus, Cliff, don't get us killed!"

He slowed to a crawl, taking several deep breaths.

"I'm sorry. Just stressed."

Lara gripped his arm, "It's ok. Don't let it get to you."

"Yeah I know. I just can't believe it."

"I know, but you're better off dealing with things when you're in one piece. Rather than from a hospital bed."

"I can't believe Bill. He's been lying all along. How the hell are we going to sell the units like this?"

"Maybe they've been working inside."

"Without a roof? I don't think so."

Cliff turned into the narrow street that led to Blue and pulled up alongside the steel fencing that enclosed the building site. He jumped out, looked left and right to make sure the coast was clear and began climbing the fence.

"Take care," Lara frowned.

The fence had narrow rectangular mesh making it hard to get a proper foothold. As an added deterrent, someone had threaded two strands of barbed wire along the top. Cliff had noticed both these things before leaping up but, fueled by his anger, did not care. In fact, he was happy to take a bit of pain.

When he got to the top, however, the sharpness of the barbs sobered him. He took the time to find safe gaps for his hands. He carefully got one leg up and over the fence and pushed his toes into the mesh on the other side. Then, just as he went to swing his second leg, his toehold gave way. His weight fell backwards, and a barb slashed through his jeans and dug into the back of his thigh.

"Ow! Fuck!"

"Careful," Lara urged.

He clung on painfully and slowly swung his second leg over. Then he dropped to the ground his feet making a loud thump on the compacted dirt. Without looking back, he headed up the hill to get a view of the building site.

"Holy shit!"

The top of Phase 1 was still open walls and exposed girders. The hole in the ground that was Phase 2 was still there. The only difference being it was now filled with water. The ground everywhere was still mud. The harbour view was as beautiful as ever but Cliff didn't notice it.

He pulled out his mobile and dialed Bill. It went to voicemail. He realized he'd never heard it before.

"Bill, listen mate, call me. I'm standing here at Blue right now and I can see nothing has been done. What the fuck mate? Call me."

He hung up. Then he had an extra thought and texted "Call me!"

As he made his way back down the hill, he noticed MJ had arrived. She and Lara were leaning against the side of the station wagon, caught up in serious discussion. They looked up when Cliff approached.

Just then Cliff's mobile rang.

"Bill."

"Yeah bud, just got your message."

"Uh-ha. So, mate, what is going on?"

"I don't understand what you mean, 'what's going on'."

"Well I'm here at Blue right now. It looks just the same as it always did. Nothing has been done here."

"Correct. No work has begun yet. We're about to start, though."

"So when you told me you were getting under way six months ago what was that? Then every time I've spoken to you, you've told me you're getting closer and closer to completion. What fucking bullshit is that?"

"Ok, buddy, settle down. I don't have to cop that language."

"I'm fucking angry mate, what do you expect?"

"Well I think you've misunderstood something. So, let's just talk calmly and professionally or not at all, ok?"

Cliff took the phone away from his ear and looked around despairingly, consumed by frustration he vented at the sky, "What the fuck!!!"

When he put the phone back to his ear Bill had hung up.

"You cunt," Cliff breathed through gritted teeth and hit redial.

"Yes."

"Ok mate, we need to sort this out now. Why have you done nothing here, what's going on?"

"We have not restarted construction yet because there has been a lot to sort out. We've had to put everything back in place after the project literally fell apart. It doesn't happen over night. We've done all that now and we are finally ready. Except for one thing."

"What?"

"Finance. Our bank called in their loans. Even after you paid us and we had plenty of funds to finish the project. They tried to take it for themselves. I told you they were pricks. With your funds we could have finished no worries. But by the time we had all the delays, the legal battles, not to mention the issues with partners and suppliers, the money was going fast. The bank knew we were doing it tough. But they knew the project was gold. They knew it was worth much more than the loans. So, they went after us. Just kept demanding payment and threatening us, sucking the funds out of the project."

"Fucking hell, mate. Why did you keep this from me?"

"There was no point panicking you, Cliff. You had enough problems of your own, buddy. Anyway, we were always working on alternative funding. We got a new bank on board two months ago. There's been a lot of back and forth, paperwork and legals to go through. You know the shit. But we're about to get the refinance from them. That's why I told you we're back on track. It's the most important thing of all and we've finally sorted it. This new bank is good. They want to see the project finished. We can kiss the other pirates goodbye. You have no idea how important that is to the project and how hard it has been to make it happen. That's real progress, bud, and that's what I meant when I said we're moving forward. Believe me it is a big deal."

"Ok mate. I understand. I don't think it helps me right now. Or MJ... or Raj. Because we want to sell the things."

"Really? You've got to hang in matey. No, no, no. You won't be able to sell them like this. Not right now. Not without losing money. If you hang in, the project is still going to be a winner. Big time."

"Well, we're going to have to try. We're out of funds. We've got nothing to hold on with. I told you before, my bank is foreclosing on me mate. MJ's in the same boat. I was hoping you could market them for us. Off the plan. You're set up to do it. We just want our money back. That's it."

"Sorry Cliffie, mate. I can tell you now they won't sell. Not even at half your price. Don't you think we've been trying to sell our own stock? The prestige market has slumped right now, buddy, due to all this shit happening in the US. Everyone's panicking and no-one's buying."

Cliff had heard some talk on the radio about problems in the US housing market and it had reminded him of Ray Kirshwood. But from what he could tell it had nothing to do with Australia. The market here was basically good, interest rates had just slowed things down a bit. Temporarily. If anything, high interest rates were a sign of a booming economy. Once they had made enough impact, which it seemed likely they already had, then the Reserve Bank would drop rates back down and the buyers would return, the market would pick up and the great Aussie property party would continue. Either way, he prided himself on ignoring 'media hype'.

"Right. Well I don't know what to do then mate. If you can't help us, we're in deep shit."

"Just tell your bank to hold on bud. It's a good investment. You know it."

"They're not interested. I've tried."

"Tell you what, if you like, I'll talk to our new bank. See if they'll refinance you. I reckon they would. They're really upbeat about the project, mate. Seriously."

"If you could that would be great. It's urgent for us."

"No worries. Leave it with me, I'll see what I can do."

"Ok mate."

Cliff hung up. He looked at MJ. "Hey."

"So, Bill's fucked us?"

"Pretty much. Says he might be able to get us a refinance though. He got one on the whole project. Reckons he should be able to get his new bank to help us."

"What? No interest until the thing's finished? That's the only thing would help us."

"Maybe. Who knows? He says they're very supportive."

"That'd be good."

Cliff could feel the back of his thigh really smarting now and gave it a massage. His hand came back smeared in blood.

"Shit, what have you done?" Lara peered through the fence.

The leg of his jeans was soaked in red-brown blood. They'd been ripped down to the back of his knee.

"You better get that looked at."

"It'll be ok," Cliff took hold of the fence to start climbing.

"Hold on old son," MJ jogged to the boot of her car and came back with a canvas drop-cloth.

"Use this."

She threw it so it landed over the top of the fence. When Cliff reached it, he straightened it out so it covered the barbed wire, then swung his legs over. Once safely on the other side he threw the drop-cloth back down to MJ.

"Thanks, groover," he climbed down.

"Let me see that cut," Lara walked behind him.

Cliff pulled at the torn fabric and flinched, "Ow! Freaking thing really got me. Bad fence!"

He kicked at the fence with his good leg.

"Punch the barbed wire, that's the bit that got you," MJ chuckled.

"You're going to have to get it cleaned up," Lara frowned, "It could go gangrene or anything."

"You just want to get my pants off..." Cliff couldn't stop himself in time. They looked at each other, lost for words.

"There's a medical centre back up on the main road. Let's drop in there," MJ broke the silence.

An hour later they sat at Macdonald's drinking coffee. Cliff's leg was cleaned and bandaged, although the blood stain was still all over his jeans. The nurse had given him a tetanus shot just in case.

After a thoughtful silence, MJ spoke.

"We need a plan for if Bill's refinance doesn't come through. Cause let's face it, nothing else he's promised has happened."

"Uh-ha. Tell me about it," Cliff stared into his mug.

"Can we sell these things ourselves?"

"Maybe. Maybe through the club?"

"That's a big ask when you've told them all along you're against off-the-plan buying."

"Yeah I know. You're right," Cliff leaned back in his chair, "I've been thinking about something else. I was talking to Lara about it earlier. I want to see if we can do the flip thing. Using private loans."

"Oh yeah?"

"Yeah. I reckon some of the club members might be interested. If we make them a sweet enough offer."

"Like what?"

"Well, think about this. I've got agents calling me with sellers willing to take like 200K for their shitbox house. I reckon even less if I pushed them. You know, do the cash on the table thing."

"Yup."

"So, imagine if we bought a classic for 190K all up, spend no more than 5K renovating, but make it really shmick. We know how to do it. Then sell it for 230, even 240, that's a good flip."

Lara smiled.

"I reckon it's still possible. People still need a home. And they still pay for bright, shiny things. Just need the funds to get started, right?"

"Uh-ha," MJ chewed on her thumb nail.

"So, we offer club members 24 percent for private loans. Cut the banks out and give people a chance to get involved."

"Yeah ok, interesting idea. We'd have to keep on doing them, though."

"Exactly. We just keep on making low offers. Create a pipeline. We could even do a couple at the same time."

"Especially if we make it sort of a hands-on thing for club members," Lara knocked on the table, "You know, we get them to actually work on the project, as a learning experience."

"Yes," Cliff gave her a high five.

"How quick do you reckon you can set it up?" MJ frowned. "Meeting is tomorrow. It would be good to present then."

"You reckon you could?"

"Why not? It's gonna be a long night, that's all."

Cliff chuckled. He had missed his cockiness.

SIXTEEN

The PowerPoint slide filled the screen:

'Solving the Cash Flow Drama'

A cartoon showed a tip truck dumping a pile of bank notes on an unsuspecting businessman, his eyes popping and pointy nose poking up for air. Subtitle: 'Make 'mountains' of interest with Cliffies Climbers Short Term Loans!'

Cliff drew a deep breath and nodded at Mandy who sat behind a laptop to the side of the stage. She gave him a thumbs-up with both hands. A moment later the first chords of 'Eye of the Tiger' blasted out over the sound system.

Cliff was more nervous than he could ever remember being. If he got no takers today, he would have no way out of his financial hole. It was make or break. Most nerve-racking of all, though, was that he had agreed to this ridiculous opening performance.

At 4am it had seemed such a hilarious idea. He'd been putting the finishing touches to the presentation with Lara, MJ, Raj and Mandy.

"I can't believe the sun's coming up soon," Lara yawned.

"I can't believe I'm still here doing this," Mandy shook her hands at her computer screen, "Next time I'm putting my fees up."

"What? From zero to ten times zero?" Raj snorted.

Cliff sank his head in his hands, "Man, I'm so tired, it feels like days ago we came up with this idea. I don't know how the fuck I'm going to have any energy to present it."

"Come on, if you stopped whinging we'd be finished," Raj implored the ceiling, "God!"

"You're right," Cliff sucked in a deep breath, slapped his own face a couple of times then got up and bounced on the spot, "Come on!"

Leaning against the kitchen counter, beer in hand, MJ grinned, "That's it. You're in Round 15 mate."

Cliff gave a short burst of air punches.

"Yeah, yeah, let's do it," MJ held her beer high, "You're down, taken some big hits, but you're not out. Now you're coming back! One last round..."

Raj started Eye of the Tiger, "Da... Da-da-da!"

MJ, Lara and Mandy joined in. Cliff couldn't help smiling as he tried a little more shadow boxing.

"Come on, is that the best you can do?" Raj leapt to his feet, gave his body a little shake out and began dancing about the room, ducking, weaving and throwing punches, belting out Eye of the Tiger as he went.

MJ whooped, "Go Rajie!"

"You're actually really good at that, Raj," Lara laughed, "Have you been practicing?"

That week Mandy had been working on a touring show with dancers backing the main artist, which meant she had piles of costumes lying about. MJ found a silver wig with long, sparkling tassels. She snuck up behind Raj and stuck it on his head.

"Woohoo!" Lara almost fell over.

Raj embraced his new character with gusto, swinging the glittering tassels in a halo of sparkles, punching, feinting, shuffling and spinning about the room, still singing.

Cliff caught Mandy's eye and cracked up.

"We've got the CD in there, somewhere," Mandy pointed at the TV cabinet.

"I reckon that's just what we need," MJ gave her a thumbs up.

After a moment of rummaging through shelves and drawers, she pulled out the Rocky CD and held it high.

"Now we're talking!"

As the music pumped, they all joined Raj singing along, dancing and shadow boxing. Finally, as the track finished, they high fived and hugged, before dropping back into their chairs, out of breath.

Lara turned to the others, "I reckon we should do this for the launch. How amazing would that be!"

"It would be hilarious," Mandy laughed.

"It's not a bad idea," MJ had a beer back in her hand and held it high, "Get everyone excited."

"Let's just get Rajie to do his moves," Cliff folded his arms. It had been an awesome re-energiser just then but doing it himself in front of the club was another story.

"What?" Raj went high pitched, "I'm not doing it on my own,".

"No, it should be the whole team," Lara looked about for support.

"Yeah, definitely," Mandy smiled.

"Yep, agreed. The whole team," MJ nodded. "Rajie can be the star, of course," she ruffled his wig, "But imagine if it was all of us, it would blow people away."

Then she giggled, "Let's make Paul and Garth do it too."

"That would be a scream," Lara's hands went to her mouth.

Mandy touched Cliff's knee, "It's a great way to get people excited. In the mood to buy."

"Ok…" Cliff held up his hands, "But it's got to make sense…"

"It's just a laugh," Lara urged.

"I know, but maybe we should be wearing something. Something to make the point. You know, like tee-shirts with Short Term Loans on them, or something, so people get it."

"Ok, ok. If I can get tee-shirts made, will you do it? Come on, please. It will be so amazing," Lara had her hands together, begging.

Cliff couldn't think how Lara would ever be able to make tee-shirts in time. So he nodded, "Sure. If you can make tee-shirts for us, we'll do it."

"Awesome!" Lara leapt to her feet and held out a hand to Cliff, "Done!"

Sure enough, when Cliff arrived at the golf club later in the afternoon, Lara came running over.

"Check it out!"

Her tee-shirt boasted, 'Cliffies Climbers Short Term Loans'. Plus the tip-truck cartoon. Cliff had to admit it looked great.

So here he was, about to run on stage in his tracksuit, to the Rocky theme, in front of a hundred and fifty unsuspecting club members.

"What the hell," he thought to himself, "Let's go out with a bang."

He turned to make sure the others were still with him, then jogged out on stage, pumped his fists in the air and threw himself into shadow boxing.

Cheers and whoops greeted them and some of the audience even started to clap along. Despite a complete lack of choreography. There was Lara leaping in the air. MJ intent and methodical, stepping through serious boxing moves. Funniest of all, though, were Garth and Paul, Cliff's lawyer and accountant, awkwardly jogging on the spot. With every big moment in the song, they mis-timed punching their fists in the air.

As the chorus kicked in, Raj appeared in a stars-and-stripes cheerleader's outfit, his silver wig glittering in the stage lights. This got the biggest cheer of all. Raj was a familiar character to many in the audience but they had never seen this side of him. With his razzle-dazzle footwork, he danced and punched his way around the stage, reaching out to hi-five people in the front row as he shimmied past. Cliff and the rest of the team simply stopped and clapped along to support Raj, his performance so dynamic.

On the final beat of the song they all unzipped their tops (Garth and Paul fumbled to unbutton their suit jackets a few moments later) and revealed their 'Cliffies Climbers Short Term Loans' tee-shirts.

Enthusiastic applause.

They took each other's hands and bowed low. Then all except Cliff waved and jogged off.

"Well, I honestly don't know how they convinced me to do that," Cliff chuckled, "All I can say is, lack of sleep."

Cliff gestured to where the others had left the stage, "Ladies and gentlemen, that was the Cliffies Climbers Short Term Loans team."

More applause.

"Thank you, thank you," he gave them a coy smile, "I think you can tell today's meeting is going to be a little different."

"Cliffies Climbers Got Talent!"

It was Carlo, one of the regulars who had been coming since the car park days and had already bought a couple of investment houses.

He got a burst of laughter. Another voice sang out "Raj for the Finals!"

This triggered even more laughter.

"Not sure I'd call it talent," Cliff smiled, "But thanks Carlo. You're welcome to come down and give it a go anytime."

"No thanks mate. I'll leave it to the experts," Carlo called back.

Eventually the laughter died down and Cliff seized the moment to get on with the real business of the day.

"So today is the launch of something very special and exciting. I think you've probably all figured out what it's called by now," he smiled as he pushed his chest out and pulled the front of his shirt down.

Laughter rumbled around the audience.

"I know a lot of you are already excited about the idea and I know there are lots of questions. That's why the whole team is here, especially Garth and Paul who can give you guys professional advice. Where are you two?"

Cliff spotted his accountant and solicitor standing behind Mandy's table.

"Have you guys recovered from the dancing?"

"No!" Garth answered with mock offence, while Paul held up both hands in a gesture of 'leave me alone'.

"Weren't they both great?" Cliff initiated a round of applause.

"Especially since we gave them about five seconds notice," he chuckled, "No chance to change their minds."

"Exploitation," Garth called back.

More laughter.

"Anyway, these guys might not be the best dancers in the world, but they are amazing when it comes to finances and legal stuff. They're a huge part of my team, I couldn't have done any of what I've achieved without them. So please make the most of them tonight or even make an appointment, yeah?"

Cliff noticed Mandy had been following along with the PowerPoint and had a slide up with the heading:

'Surround Yourself with the Best Advice'

This one had a cartoon showing two convicts sitting in their prison cell. Convict One is holding up his chains, moaning, "My Life Coach told me don't wait for what you want, just take it! Look where that got me."

Cliff caught Mandy's eye and they shared a smile before he turned back to the audience.

"One of the things I always say is you got to find good advice not bad advice, right? And where does most of the bad advice come from?"

A few voices called out "The media!" A few others, "Real estate agents!"

Then one voice murmured, "Your mother in law."

Cliff cracked up along with everyone else.

"Yeah that's it, your mother in law. Don't take investment advice from her."

He shook his head, then waited, smiling, until the audience re-focused.

"Ok, so the really shit advice usually comes from the media, yeah? You don't want to get caught up in all that media hype. Why? Because they're just trying to sell their papers or TV shows, or sign you up for something, yeah? They don't really know what's going on. They're not professionals, they don't have real experience, they've never actually done this, they're just trying to get everyone scared. Fear sells, right?"

"I mean who here is worried about interest rates right now? Put your hand up if you're worried."

About a quarter of the audience hesitantly raised their hands, then a few more until almost half had their hands up.

Cliff shook his head and held his hand high, "Come on be honest. Only about half of you are being honest!"

Now the rest of the audience joined in.

"That's it," he smiled, "Of course we are all worried. You'd be crazy not to be worried right now if you're an investor. Right? But it's made so much worse by all the headlines, yeah? It's so easy to get caught up in the fear and start running with the sheep and forget that you need to do what? Come on..."

No response.

"Get good advice! Right?" He pointed at the PowerPoint.

Pausing for dramatic effect, Cliff took in the relieved smiles and nods. Inwardly he smiled, thinking he might just be channelling a little Ray Kirshwood.

"So, with all the media hype about interest rates going up and up, who thinks it's a bad time to buy an investment property?"

A few hands went up. However, most didn't and in the end even those first few took them back down again, a little awkwardly.

"Excellent! I'm glad to see you've been learning. Of course, it's not a bad time to buy. It's an awesome time to buy. Why?"

"Prices are going down..."

"Yes!" Cliff pumped his fist.

"It's a buyers' market."

"Absolutely."

"There's bargains right now."

"So true."

"Rates will go back down again, eventually."

"Of course, they will. It's a cycle, right?"

They were with him, nodding along.

"All the great investors we've been inspired by, whether it's Ray

Kirshwood or Robert Allen or Rockefeller, whatever, right, they tell us to do the opposite of what the rest of the market is doing. I mean, what do you reckon Warren Buffett does when the stock market crashes? Sell his shares? Of course not, he buys, right?"

"But here's the thing. You've got to do it right. You've got to have a plan. Interest rates really are a problem right now. They suck. If you buy a property now and rent it out, you're going to have this big gap, you know, this big shortfall between what you make in rent and what you've got to pay the bank in interest. So, if you don't have a plan, you'll come unstuck, yeah?"

He noticed Mandy had clicked over to a slide with a photo of a house with a bank foreclosure sign out the front. Great, she was perfectly in sync.

"Which brings me to our new short-term loans."

The slide changed over to 'Closing the Cash Flow Gap'

"We've come up with a solution. Because one thing we don't do here at Cliffies Climbers is sit on our butts and do nothing. We make a plan. Right?"

The slides changed to "Short Term Loans: How They Work"

"So… our new short-term loans. This is the way to deal with the high interest rates and the cash flow dramas they're giving us… and still go out and buy cheap properties. Sounds good?"

"Yeah!" filled the auditorium.

"Awesome! Here's how it works. We're giving you a chance to invest some of your capital – maybe any equity you've got - with us and earn a massive 24 percent interest on it. Sounds crazy?"

"Yep," came a few responses.

Cliff gave them a cocky smile, "Good. Because it should sound crazy. Until you understand it. Which you will by the time I'm finished."

Applause resounded, as Cliff, feeling ten-foot tall, gave a little bow and strode to the side of stage, where his team was all smiles.

MJ held out a hand, "Great work, old son."

Raj, back in his jeans and black polo shirt, patted Cliff on the shoulder.

"Where's your wig, man?" Cliff threw up his hands.

"Never mind the wig, that was excellent dude."

"Thanks mate. But you really were the star of the show." Cliff took a dummy punch at Raj's stomach, "Getting higher… getting stronger!"

A number of club members who'd started to gather nearby clapped. A red-haired woman, sporting angular red glasses, called out, "Best show ever, Raj!"

Before Raj could respond, however, a couple hastily closed in on Cliff, the man taking hold of Cliff's arm. He was in his thirties, of middle-eastern background, neatly dressed in a pink business shirt tucked into beige tailored pants. He gave Raj and the others an apologetic smile, then focused on Cliff with great intensity.

"Hi Cliff, sorry to interrupt, but would we be able to have a chat?" He spoke softly, his wife smiling and nodding.

Now a tall man, in sleeveless North Face anorak, with bushy greying hair, probably in his fifties, called out from the gathering crowd, "Yes, we'd like to have a talk about the new loans, Cliff."

"Yes, us too," came several echoes.

Two more couples came running over from the far side of the audience, racing to get there first. The first couple, who had the edge because they had been sitting several rows closer to the front, ran up behind the middle-eastern couple.

The husband beamed as he spoke, a little out of breath, in an American accent, "Hey yeah Cliff, we're really interested. Can we have a meeting with you?"

The second couple, who were only a few steps behind, were either Chinese or Korean, Cliff was not sure. The wife, dragging her husband by the arm, called out as soon as they were close enough, "Cliff, we were up the back, but we were first to start coming down! We have cash for this deal!"

The power of her voice silenced everyone else.

"Um," Cliff wasn't sure who he should respond to first.

The Asian lady bent over, hands on hips to take some deep breaths after her mad dash across the auditorium. When she straightened up, she took in the startled looks of the others and burst into a hearty laugh. She mopped her brow theatrically and fanned her face with her hand, "Whew!"

The others laughed too, all realising how ridiculously competitive they'd just been.

Cliff gave a high-pitched chuckle, "Great to see everyone so keen."

Now a thin, almost gaunt, young man in a blue flannel shirt pushed in between two couples, his hands on their shoulders forcing his way through.

"Woah," the American guy tried to shrug him off.

Undeterred, the thin bloke called out to Cliff, "So what I want to know, Cliffie, is what have you got to say to the people who've got no money?"

Cliff was stuck for words again.

The thin bloke continued, "You know, the ones who took your advice a year ago, and now the bloody market has gone to shit and we're sitting up the creek. We don't have any money for your nice twenty-four percent interest lurks. You know, we got suckered in nicely and now we're struggling."

"Simon," a female voice pleaded.

Thin bloke whirled around angrily to find the source of the interruption. She was an attractive young woman, in her twenties, with pale skin and long, brown hair, carrying a small baby in a sling over her shoulder so that it lay against her chest.

"Come over here. Hurry up, come on," Simon, the thin young bloke, hissed at her.

Things were awkward again. Cliff looked around the venue to see where the rest of his team was. Lara and Mandy were setting up tables and chairs on the far side of the stage area. Garth and Paul were also there, laptops and folders under their arms.

He caught MJ's eye and she must have read his mind. She quickly stepped across and gave Simon a warm smile, "Listen mate, we'll all get a chance to talk to Cliffie. We're here to help. Yeah?"

He nodded, "Thanks MJ. We're not all winning at the moment, you know, love? That's all, hey? Some of us are doing it tough. We need help, you know, but I don't know how we can do any of this loans stuff, you know?"

He put his arm around his woman, smiled at her and kissed their baby on the head. When he turned back to MJ there were tears welling in his eyes.

Cliff could feel things falling apart. He pointed to where Lara and Mandy were finishing the setup.

"Ok everyone, we will meet with you all, don't worry. I promise. We're going to do it properly and sit down with each of you, one on one. Ok? You've each got your own situation and you each need your own solutions, right? So, let's head over the other side where the girls are setting up for us."

He led the way across the auditorium, the small crowd following.

"Ok, so we'll get you to form a queue, please guys. You know your order, but it doesn't really matter, everyone will get a chance. So just play nicely!" He chuckled, hoping to lighten them up.

The Asian woman beamed back at him, "You should get Raj, you know, to do his kung-fu move. That will make everyone play nice!"

This time even Simon laughed.

Cliff gestured to Garth and Paul to sit either side of him, "Come on, I need my experts for this."

MJ put a hand on the middle-eastern man's shoulder, "So who was first? I reckon it was this gentleman and his wife."

"Yes, I believe it was us," the man smiled, "But, you know, I think you can speak to this couple first."

"Ah, jeez mate, thanks but that's alright, we can wait," Simon held up his hands.

"No, no, no, you have the baby, its better if you don't have to wait around, you know."

"That's so nice of you," Simon's partner smiled with a gentle wonder.

"Ok, excellent," MJ gave two thumbs up, "That's very nice of you mate."

She turned to Simon and his partner, "You guys head over and see Cliff."

Then she ushered the rest of them back to the tiered seats of the auditorium where they could form a 'queue' sitting down.

"Just so everyone who's meeting with the gurus over there can have a little privacy," she smiled.

Cliff felt his stomach knot. If Simon and his partner were stuck with a house that had gone down in value, meaning they had negative equity, and they were struggling to meet the high interest payments, there really wasn't much he could suggest right now. Once he might have considered giving them some money, to help out until things turned around for them. But he was in such a tight spot himself there was no way he could do that now.

He did remember them from a year or so before, although he would not have recalled their names or details. If the club had helped them get a 'no doc' loan, because their income and savings were too low to get a standard loan, then it was probably through ABC Bank. Trouble was, these days Cliff wasn't in a position to ask any favours of ABC. In fact, he was probably the last person the bank would help right now.

He gestured them to take a seat. His biggest worry was that they'd get so upset and create such a big scene that everyone else got freaked out and put off.

Lara came bouncing over with a paper take-away cup in each hand.

"I got you each a nice cup of tea," she proceeded to empty her pockets of sugar sachets, alternative sweeteners, UHT milk containers and wooden stirrers.

"There we go, every option you could need!"

For a moment, everyone around the table was caught, suspended in Lara's charm.

"She really is amazing", Cliff thought, "All this and I'm not even paying her."

He turned to Simon and his partner, "So, let's see what we can do for you guys. No promises, but we'll do our best, ok?"

He gave them his most encouraging smile, but he feared he must look like a fake.

It was Paul's turn to shine. He leaned in, both elbows on the table, "Why don't we start by getting all the details down correctly, then we can talk about what's the best way to go from there. Does that sound alright?"

"Sure," Simon shrugged.

Paul picked up his pen and adjusted the A4 pad in front of him, "Can I start by getting your names down?"

"Yeah, it's Simon and Angela Bartlett."

"And this is Dylan," Angela smiled and stroked her baby on the back. He seemed to be sleeping oblivious.

Cliff called softly, "Hey Dylan, welcome."

Paul wrote as he spoke, "Great thanks. Now I think I heard you say you had bought the one property, is that right?"

"Yeah."

"Great stuff," Paul smiled at Simon, "It's a big thing you know, just taking that first step. So, well done to you both."

"Yeah, thanks mate."

"Is it a club classic?"

The 'club classic' was the name they had given to the standard three-bedroom house, built during the 1960s and 70s, that was found throughout the area. There were only half a dozen basic designs and almost every house in the area was a variation on one of these.

"Yeah it is. Little fibro classic in Lethbridge Park."

"Awesome. And how much did you pay for it?"

"They were asking 250 and we got it for 225. But that was when the market was up, you know, there was buyers everywhere fighting it out. I mean now I don't reckon we'd get our 225 back."

"It's temporary, though, it's a cycle, right?" Cliff held up his hands.

"Yeah, sure, we understand it's a cycle, you know, but I mean we can't afford to pay our loan right now. Cycle or no cycle. It's not what you said a year ago, you never mentioned it back then, you know, we never planned for it. Have a look at this."

Simon pulled a battered plastic folder from his backpack and took from it a writing pad. He flipped the top pages over until he found a sheet filled with handwriting in black, fine-point texta.

Cliff felt ill as he realised it was his own handwriting. Simon tracked through the points with his finger.

"See, like around about now it was supposed to be valued at 275K. Then we were going to refinance, you know, with one of your other banks. And we were going to use that 50K to help us pay the interest on the main loan. Then it was going to go up again the next year to like 305K and we were going to have that extra 30K to help us keep paying, you know? That was your plan."

"Yes, but no-one knows exactly what's going to happen in the future, right? I always say that. This is hypothetical."

Cliff felt like it was incredibly unfair to be blamed for the unpredictability of the economy and things like interest rates.

"That's why I also say we have to plan for contingencies, yeah?"

"Well, I mean, you've changed your tune from last year. Hasn't he?" Simon turned to Angela.

"Look, let's just stick to getting the details down, for now, then we can look what's best to do in this situation. Is that ok guys?" Paul appealed.

"Of course," Cliff sat back.

"Yeah sure," Simon tightened his lips.

"So how much is the loan then Simon?"

"Because you guys helped us out, the bank let us borrow like a hundred percent of everything, you know. No questions asked. So that was…"

Simon paged back in his pad and found a series of numbers written in blue ballpoint, "240K total costs. That's what they approved us. But we didn't borrow it all," he looked at Angela, "We saved up some and your mum gave us five grand, remember?"

"Yeah," Angela pressed a hand on Simon's leg.

"Then we got the first home buyers grant, you know, so the final loan ended up being only like 220K or something. That's it," he pointed at a number on the pad, "That's what the loan was, $219,538."

"Right, you got the first home buyers grant, which reduced the total loan?"

"Yeah, we qualified for that and the free stamp duty and everything…"

"Ok, great. But you are renting the property out, aren't you?"

"Yeah, I mean, you know…"

"Yeah, we know," Paul smiled and Cliff gave a little chuckle.

"So, in theory the bank would still lend you up to 240K on this particular loan. That's good. How have you been going with paying the interest so far, you say you've been struggling a bit?"

"Yeah of course. We've had to use credit cards lately. Like you told us Cliff."

"Woah, really?"

"Yeah, of course, you always tell the story of how you got your first house, using credit cards, right?"

Simon gave a hollow laugh.

"Ok, so back to finalising the details," Paul cut in, "What is the interest you are currently paying?"

"Yeah, sure, it's here," Simon handed him a bank statement from the same plastic folder.

"Ok, about two grand a month," Paul flipped the statement over, "Yep, eight and a half percent. Crazy isn't it?"

"Yeah, too right mate, it wasn't part of the plan."

"Ok and last thing, what is the rent you are getting?"

"$220 a week."

"Ok cool, about $900 a month. Minus agent's fees and a few other costs of course. So, you guys are ending up a thousand a month short."

"Yeah, at least."

"And you say you're using credit cards to cover that?"

"Yeah, have been."

"How much have you racked up?"

"A lot."

"Hmm, ok. What's your income Simon, are you working?"

"No mate. We're both on Centrelink. I can't work because of my back. And Angie's got the bub of course."

"Yep, sure."

"I mean that was one of the things you guys liked last time, yeah? You liked the fact that a couple on Centrelink could invest in a house, using your plans and ideas. You were really chuffed and encouraged us."

Cliff shifted in his seat.

"So that's why, now, we're kinda going 'what's going on?' You know?"

He patted Angela's hand and smiled painfully at her. Then he leaned in close to his baby, "Hey, little fella."

The little boy was becoming restless, so Simon lifted him out of the sling and onto his lap. He bounced him up and down.

"Yeah, my little matey, your mum and dad were going to be the first Centrelink real estate tycoons."

"Alright, look we'll try and be quick because I can see Dylan is getting tired of all the numbers," Paul smiled.

"No, no he's fine," Simon blew a long raspberry on Dylan's tummy, "Aren't you!" Dylan giggled. "See, he's happy as Larry."

Simon bounced him high in the air, "Up we go!"

"Good to see," Paul chuckled, "So guys, what we've got to do is prioritise things. That way we can have a plan and break things down into achievable steps. Ok?"

"Sounds good," Angela nodded.

"Now, remember these are just my suggestions. You have to make up your own minds and be responsible for you own decisions. Is that agreed?"

"Yeah of course, mate," Simon settled Dylan into his lap.

"First up, we should clear those credit cards. If you do nothing else, that's the first thing I would suggest."

"Ok. How?"

"A two-pronged attack. Number one, we take the bank up on the rest of your loan. Might as well borrow at eight and a half percent rather than the twenty-five percent you are paying on the cards."

"Righto, no worries."

"Number two, we need to increase your income. Somehow. I know you've got a problem with your back and I know it's pretty tough to find work right now. But a couple of hundred a week extra is going to make all the difference."

"Yeah mate, don't think I haven't been looking. There's not a lot around here for someone who can't lift or nothing. And don't forget if I do any work and they find out, Centrelink will take me off the pension, yeah?"

"Ok, so there's one other possibility. We get you into the short-term loans scheme."

"Really?" Cliff was taken aback to hear Paul recommending more debt.

"Uh-ha. There's still a few banks out there willing to give higher valuations for this area. Some are still doing 260 even 270K for a classic house."

"Which banks are these? I can't get that for mine!"

"I know, but that's because you've got a hundred. This is one couple with one house. It's not such a scary proposition for the banks so they just might do it. Might. Especially some of the new, alternative lenders."

"Ok, fair enough. He's good!" Cliff pointed at Paul.

"Anyway," Paul smiled, "If we can get that kind of valuation, you've got another 40K you can borrow. We put it into the Club's short-term loan scheme and you get 24% on it. That's 800 bucks a month. Almost covers your shortfall. I reckon it's worth looking into. If you do?"

"Sure, sounds great," Simon nodded. "If you can make us $800 a month, I reckon we can find the rest, hey?"

"Yeah, why not," Angela smiled, "Where there's a will there's a way!"

"Ok cool. I'll see what I can find out for you. The main thing is to save your house. We don't want to lose that."

Cliff leaned back and stretched. It would be a pretty cool story. Great promotion for the short-term loans.

The rest of the meetings were more straightforward. There was Nabil and his wife Sarah, the middle-eastern couple who had kindly let Simon and Angela go first. They had bought two classics a few years earlier and were stretched by the high interest payments. However, they had recently received an inheritance from Nabil's father. Before the downturn they had thought about using it as a deposit for a third investment house.

"But, with such high interest rates we don't feel we can handle a third mortgage right now," Nabil shrugged. "So, we like the idea of making a passive income from our savings, you know, this small inheritance."

"Yes, why not?" Cliff smiled.

"So naturally we are very attracted by the 24% the club is offering. Our main concern, though, is about the security. I mean, no offence, but it's quite different to putting our money in the bank."

"Let me explain the principle," Garth leaned in, "It's quite simple. Really. Since all the money loaned to a particular project is used to purchase and improve a house, there will always be an asset of equal or greater value. The house. Yes?"

"Yes, sure."

"So, Cliffies Climbers simply issues a 'caveat' over that particular house to each lender. In proportion to how much of the budget they've loaned us. Say you loan us 50K and the total funds borrowed for the first project are 200K, then you'll get a caveat over 25% of the house."

"Ok, yes, we've given you 25% of the project budget so you give us 25% of the house as security."

"Yes, exactly. The caveat's in force until the house is flipped – sold - and you receive your money back plus your interest," Garth rested his hands on the table and smiled.

The idea seemed to make sense to everyone they spoke to that afternoon. But in truth, the one thing that mattered to them all was that Cliff was behind it. They trusted him completely. After all, he was the one who had started the club, with a view to helping them succeed. He'd always been there, encouraging them to overcome their fears and get started on their own investment journey.

Above all, he was the one who had successfully built a portfolio of one hundred houses. He'd gone from Mt Druitt dropout to local hero and multi-millionaire in a few short years. He had the golden Midas touch. This was his project, he was hands-on, and they all wanted to be a part of it.

By the end of the afternoon, there was a healthy pile of signed expressions of interest stacked on the floor beside Cliff. He'd kept a rough tally and reckoned the overall amount on offer was around 500K.

"Wow," he smiled to himself.

He knew, though, that there was still some way to go. They'd have to work quickly and persuasively to get these potential lenders contracted and over the line. But it was a great start.

He stood up and stretched. Just then an older couple approached. The woman, dressed in a brown and beige pants suit, smiled and waved.

"Hi Cliffie, how are you?"

It was Jan, the lady Cliff had helped buy a classic at a great price about a year earlier. He'd thought she was incredibly sweet. He remembered the whole thing well because it was the same day he'd committed to the deal on Blue. That day seemed so long ago now, the memory of it like a movie set in a different period in history, back when the sun shone golden and life was exciting and full of opportunity.

"Hi Jan, great to see you! How are you going?"

"Not too bad thanks Cliffie. I don't know if you remember Ken, my husband?"

Ken was a tall, frail-looking man, with a worried face.

"Yes, great to see you again Ken, how are you?"

Ken shook hands with a soft smile. Cliff thought Jan was also looking a bit older and frailer than he last remembered her. Time must have flown.

"How's the property going? That was a while ago now, hey? I still remember, though, such a great buy."

"Yes, well, that's actually why we wanted to have a little chat with you, Cliffie," Jan lowered her voice, "If you have a moment for us?"

"Yeah, no worries," Cliff turned to Lara, MJ and Mandy who were engaged in high spirited banter behind him. "Hey groovers, can you give us some space, we need to have one more meeting."

"Oh, sure, no problem," Lara broke off from the story she was telling, "Let's go sit in the lobby guys."

"Please take a seat," Cliff smiled. Paul and Garth hastened over, pens and paper at the ready.

"Thanks so much, Cliffie," Jan looked serious. "It's silly, I know, because it was such a good purchase. You really did a wonderful job of negotiating for us and we will always be grateful."

"Very happy to have helped."

"Really you did. We could never have done so well. I mean, I am sure we would never have done it at all, without your help," Jan looked to Ken.

"No, absolutely not," Ken shook his head.

"The trouble is," Jan lowered her voice again, "It's become a little difficult for us, just lately. Like you and everyone here has been saying, the interest rates have gone so high and all."

"I know, who could have thought," Cliff gave a pained smile.

"And of course, we haven't had any increase in value."

"Yep," Paul nodded.

"So, there's no equity there for us. You know, like we were all hoping there would be after a year."

"Mmm," Cliff wished he could tell her exactly how much he shared her pain.

"And, of course, it's especially difficult now Ken is retired."

"That's right," Ken pointed a finger at himself, "Poor old Kenny's going to have to go back to work."

"Surely not?" Paul frowned.

"Well at this rate I will," Ken sat back in his chair, "Not that I would likely find a job…"

"Well that's not what we want," Jan patted Ken's knee, "Is it darling?"

She leaned in, "Always so dramatic this one!"

Cliff laughed. "Did you have any thoughts about what you wanted to do then?"

"Well, yes, actually we were wondering about this new short-term loan deal, the one you've been talking about today."

"Yeah, sure, could be perfect for your scenario. Get you through the tough times until the market turns around and you get that equity."

"Yes, but the problem is, being retired, all we have now is Ken's super. What do you think? Do you think it would be safe to use that?"

Cliff glanced at Paul who simply raised an eyebrow.

He turned back to Jan, "How much would you want to invest?"

"We have about three hundred thousand. In total."

"Right."

Cliff felt a stir of excitement. He could do a lot with that right now. He looked around the table. "Well, I guess the first thing to know is if there are any legal issues. Experts?"

"Has your super vested Ken?" Paul asked, "Has it been paid out to you?"

"Yes, that's right, Paul," Ken cleared his throat.

"Well, in that case, it's yours to do with as you like."

Cliff did a quick calculation in his head, "You'd make 72 thousand interest in a year," he smiled, "That's better than spending it on a boat!"

"Well, yes," Jan grinned at Ken, "It would certainly get us out of trouble with the investment house."

"Not wrong," Cliff tapped his pen on the table, "That's what it's designed for."

SEVENTEEN

Next morning Cliff was up early. He sat at the kitchen table, a mug of coffee and a notepad in front of him, listing his requirements for the short-term loans. He wanted Garth to finish the contracts today, so he needed to make sure he had thought of everything. When and how was the interest paid? Under what circumstances could a lender get their money back? What if a project took longer to flip than expected?

He could hear Mandy in the shower. She was also an early riser, having a long journey into the city each morning. He felt an urge to sneak in with her. It had been a while since they'd been naughty. It seemed like the stress of the last six months had also hurt their sex life.

"Wow, when was the last time?" Cliff put his pen down. What had happened to the fun? Every weekend, as far back as he could think now, had been spent dealing with property shit. Yes, they'd occasionally done the deed, on autopilot, before going to sleep late at night. But where was the crazy, the romantic, the silly, muck-around, loving stuff? The wild, passionate stuff?

"Fuck, it's like we're 'married' before we're married."

He clicked his pen in and out. He had to get this done if there was any hope of Garth completing the contract today. Anyway, Mandy would be in a hurry and would probably just get annoyed.

He crossed to where his mobile phone was charging on the floor next to the TV. He'd started switching it off at night to preserve his sanity. The endless calls had become too much. There were more and more people chasing him, happy to text or even call at any time of night. Club members asking for help, real estate agents flogging properties, random investors wanting to cut deals and, of course, all the suppliers and tradies, property managers, not to mention banks and other financial institutions he owed money to.

"Fuuuuck."

It was as if they had a right to throw respect out the window just because he was late with a payment or had stretched a promise. It wasn't going to change anything. He wasn't going to jump out of bed and find some unexpected money for them. If he hadn't paid yet there was obviously a reason. He had a cash flow problem. Surely they could just wait. Surely it wasn't that strange in business.

Three beeps indicated multiple messages. He selected his inbox. Yep, the usual suspects. Then he noticed his dad had called. He looked at the missed call details and saw it had been after midnight. Bloody hell.

He dialled his voicemail, skipping past three aggressive messages from creditors to get to his dad's.

"Cliffie, give us a call," his dad's voice slurred, "I need to speak to ya urgently little bud, ok, so give ya dad a call. Don't mind, any time. Ok?"

Cliff felt a hot flash of annoyance. With a steely vengeance, he hit the dial button. It was 605am.

His mum answered and Cliff immediately felt bad. "Sorry mum, dad left me a message last night. Sounded urgent. He said I should call straight back whatever time."

"Yeah but you know he's not up this time of day?"

"Yeah I know, it's just he said – "

"Especially when he's been on the booze, right? Bloody fool's been up to who knows what time last night. The telly was still on this morning."

"Ok no worries well just get him to call me back when he's ready,"

Cliff could picture the scene and didn't want to hear any more. "I suppose there was nothing really urgent, so it doesn't matter."

"No Cliffie, there is a problem here. They're gonna take our house."

"What?"

"Yeah, it's all this stuff been happening with the second house. He hasn't been paying the bank, has he. I told you it was madness to get him involved in it. He's not like you. He's an idiot. He's got no idea when it comes to money."

"So, hang on, what the fuck? Who's taking the house? The bank?"

"Yeah the bank. He hasn't been paying the interest or whatever. You know, with all this stuff where it's gone so high now. He's either been spending it down the TAB with his mates or whatever, or else he's just not been making enough to pay it. Either way, I don't know. But he didn't tell me nothing and now I see this letter from the bank saying we have to move out and hand over."

"What the- !"

"It's our home, Cliffie," his mum's voice cracked.

"Ok, so get him out of bed and put him on the phone Mum. I need to find out what's going on."

"Ok, hold on."

He heard his mum's slippers flap-flap down the hall, then the muffled sound of his dad groaning and protesting. His mum's voice was louder and insistent.

Eventually the receiver clunked a few times and his dad breathed angrily, "What bloody time is this?"

"Sorry dad, you said I had to call you any time. It was urgent."

"Yeah but fucking hell–"

"I know, I've got a big day alright? Anyway, I told mum to leave you alone, until she told me what's going on. Is it true? Are they threatening to take the house?"

"Yeah, fucking bank."

"So, it's a repossession order?"

"You know what they're like. Robin Hood and his band of merry bankers. Bunch of thieves."

"Yeah I know, but we can stop it."

"Couldn't lie straight in bed, you know. More bent than a Mardi Gras parade…" His dad coughed and laughed.

"Ok, do you want to talk seriously about it, or just wait until the sheriffs come?"

"Yeah, ok Cliffie, what do we do? I mean you got us into this thing, let's see if you can get us out, hey?"

"Come on, dad."

"What? That's the truth. You kept fucking nagging me on and on. 'You gotta do it, you gotta do it.' Wouldn't fucking let up. Like I was gonna be a millionaire overnight."

"Ok, whatever. I was trying to help you. If you stuck to the plan you would've been fine. You never told me you were in trouble with it. Now I find out when it's too late."

"I told you we were struggling. I told you many times."

"You said it sucked being a landlord. You were joking and mucking around. I didn't know you weren't paying your mortgage."

"Come on matey, you know what's been going on, you've seen all the signs up around here. You know everyone's doing it tough. Except the banks."

"Yeah I know. Cause I'm doing it bloody tough too right now dad."

"Is that right? You in trouble too? Then we got no hope."

Tommy was silent for a moment then began to chuckle. "Jesus Christ hey, out on the street, pushing a shopping trolley around till we kark it. That's our retirement."

Cliff looked around to punch a wall. He took a deep breath and changed tack.

"Come on, we can take our trolleys down to the drains at Rooty Hill and have a water view. Be nice, you know."

His dad laughed, "Yeah great, we can have the family back together again. You won't have to come far for Christmas."

"But seriously Dad. We can stop this from happening. How much is owing? How long have you missed payments for?"

"Ah, well, ever since Centrelink found out about it and put a stop to my pension. That was back in July. So, I don't know…"

"Shit, how did that happen?"

Tommy chuckled again, "Long story. Let's just say the tenant ended up complaining about me."

"Fuck!" Cliff rasped through clenched teeth, "Dad, why do you do this shit? Why do you make it hard all the time?"

Cliff held the receiver away and took a deep breath, "Ok, never mind, we'll sort it. If it's been since July, then it's probably about ten grand by now."

"Sounds about right."

"We'll find a way. But you got to get serious about it. Ok? Will you take it seriously? For my sake? For mum's sake?"

"Yeah, ok, ok."

"Alright. You have to phone them, ok? You have to phone the bank. Today. Tell them you are going to pay them. Tell them you've had some issues, but now you are going to pay them. Can you do that?"

"Sure."

"Today?"

"Yep, don't worry, I'll do it today."

"Ok, you have to. No matter how long they put you on hold, whatever. Ok? You have to get through and tell them."

"Yeah, I understand, Cliffie. Was going to get onto it today anyway. That's why I rang you."

"Ok good. Well, call them, that's step one. Then we'll work out the next step. But it's going to be fine, ok?"

"Yeah, good on you Cliffie. We'll be right."

"Ok, dad. I'll speak to you later today."

"What's wrong?" Mandy was in the bathroom doorway, a towel wrapped around her.

"Ah, just bloody Dad."

"What's he done? Why did he call so early?"

"I called him. He left me a message at half past midnight last night. He's gone and stuffed up his investment house. Idiot."

"Oh god."

"He's not been paying the bloody mortgage. Now the bank wants to foreclose on him."

"Shit."

"Yeah, and don't forget, he used their home as security. So they want to take that too."

"Oh wow, that's terrible," Mandy crossed over to Cliff and ran a hand through his hair. "Can you sort it out?"

"Yeah of course," he smiled weakly, "I'll sort it out in the end. But, fuck, you know, it's hard right now. I've got to get these contracts done today. Everyone's waiting on me. You know?"

"I know. Sometimes I think you push yourself too hard, baby. Why don't you leave the contracts for today?"

"I can't fucking leave them," Cliff exploded.

It was the mountain of pressure, frustration and stress, bursting at the seams. He hadn't told Mandy how badly things were going. She knew the market had turned and he was having to find new ways of making money, but she didn't know how severe the situation was with Blue, or how the bank was on the verge of foreclosing on everything. Cliff didn't want her to panic. He didn't want her to think he was failing. That he didn't have things under control. Now that he had the short-term loans plan, he was convinced he could get himself out of trouble. He could tell her afterwards. She'd be proud of him.

"Woah, ok, I'm just trying to help." Mandy stomped to the bedroom and slammed the door.

"Sorry babe," Cliff buried his head in his hands.

By the afternoon, Cliff had finalised the details of the short-term loan contract with Garth who promised to have it ready first thing in the morning. He'd also chased up his dad to make sure he kept his promise and called the bank. He had.

Trouble was, the bank had said it was too late. They had already taken legal action. He had left it too long and ignored too many notices. At that point, Tommy had sworn at the bank's customer service and hung up.

"Fuck!" Cliff cursed aloud as he drove home from Garth's office, "Why does he do this now? It's like he knows the worst possible time and throws his shit in. Aargh!"

Up ahead he spotted the familiar pink and white sign of Andy's Restaurant. It had become a famous local landmark, set up in a sandstone, colonial-era house by a former TV chef. Cliff read their number off the sign, repeating it until he could type it into his mobile.

"Fuck it, no-one else gives a shit. Why should I?" He put the phone to his ear and waited to make a booking.

Cliff woke at 530am as had become his routine. This time, however, his head hurt and his mouth was dry. He closed his eyes and remembered what an awesome night it had been. Holy shit they had drunk a lot. He became aware of being naked and gently lifted the sheets. Yep, Mandy was naked too. He lingered for a moment, enjoying the perfect, soft curve of her behind. Hmm. He closed his eyes and smiled, life was not that bad. Then he slipped out of bed and headed to the shower.

"Today is the day... we gonna turn this thing around, oh yeah!" Cliff sung his made-up tune as he swung into a parking space in front of Garth's office. Garth's dark blue WRX was already there. Cliff bound up the short flight of concrete steps and pushed the glass door open.

"Morning!"

"Hi mate," Garth emerged from his inner office.

"Thanks for making the early start mate, appreciate it," Cliff shook hands, "How did you go with it?"

"Yep, all done. It's on your email already."

"Awesome! Thanks so much."

"No worries. Here's the print-out." Garth sat down at a small, wooden table that took up most of the space in the common area of the office. Cliff joined him and gratefully took the bundle of paper. They went through it together, page by page, Cliff pleased with everything. He couldn't think of anything Garth had missed.

"Bloody excellent, thanks mate."

"No dramas. Now it's down to you to sign 'em up."

"Yeah, well if they're all still as keen as they were at the meeting that shouldn't be too hard."

"And it's the bit you're good at."

"Yeah thanks, mate." Cliff locked hands with Garth.

"Hey, just by the way I've got a bit of a drama with my Dad. Can you give me some advice?"

"Sure."

"He's managed to get himself a foreclosure notice."

"Geez, really?"

"Yeah. The bank's saying it's too late to pay now it's gone to legal action."

"Oh rubbish. They just say that to scare people."

"Really?"

"Either that, or they're too lazy to deal with it now it's moved to a different department. Either way, it's no problem."

"Great. Had a feeling you would say that," Cliff chuckled. "Trouble is, it's ABC and I don't have any friends there right now. As you can probably imagine."

"Yeah, right. We just need to fight fire with fire. I'll give you a letter. You got five minutes?"

"Yeah, great man."

Garth went to his office and sat down behind his computer. A few minutes later he hit the print button with a flourish. "There we go!"

Garth led Cliff across to the printer and handed him the letter. "It's us acting on your Dad's behalf. Basically, just advising ABC that payment will be made and they should desist from legal action as it is no longer necessary. If they have any concerns, they should contact us, blah, blah, blah. I'd be surprised if we hear any more from them."

"You're a legend," Cliff slapped Garth on the shoulder. "Thanks so much."

"No worries. Just make sure he pays it now, of course. That letter will give him another chance, but it's no good if he doesn't pay it."

"Sure, of course. Understand mate. Thanks again."

Cliff headed home to email the contract to all his prospective lenders. He had begun to call them 'investors' to convey the idea they were a part of the project. It felt like a nice touch.

MJ and Lara turned up to help. MJ was in charge of finding properties to flip. She had her laptop to search realestate.com. But because she knew the online listings were limited and sometimes old, she'd also brought all the local papers plus the property segments from the two main weekend papers. She sat down to scan through them. Her criteria were tough and battle-proven, only a few properties with real potential for a flip made it into her spreadsheet.

Cliff and Lara split the list of prospective club investors, emailed them a contract and began calling. They decided to impose a minimum investment of fifty thousand. It would mean they didn't have to combine too many people to get a project up and running. It would also weed out the tyre-kickers.

First on Cliff's list was the American couple who had approached him right after the club presentation. Husband, Tom, was delighted to hear from Cliff and clearly still interested even after Cliff explained the 50K minimum.

"That suits us just fine," Tom enthused, "Let's see, that would be twelve hundred dollars a month interest, right?"

"Yep, spot on."

"That would be just about perfect to help us pay the mortgage. We've got an investment place up at Umina."

"That's Central Coast, yeah?"

"Right. It's a good little spot, you know. In many ways, it feels just like your Mount Druitt area. Houses are about the same price. They even look pretty much the same. You've got the train right into the city, takes much the same time to commute. But then, here's the kicker, you've got the beach right there. It's beautiful."

"Yeah right, sounds great."

"It seems people are only now starting to discover it, you know. They're going, 'Hang on, we can be the same distance from Sydney, buy a house for the same price, and we can be by the sea. How good's that!'"

"Sounds really good, Tom, maybe the club should check it out."

"I would say so, Cliff."

"Well, tell you what, why don't we get you to do a presentation some time?"

"Sure."

"Great. Ok, well, now with your investment. Are you guys in? We're starting the first project this week, if you want to be a part of it?"

"Yeah, sure, we're ready to go."

"Alright, excellent. How soon can you deposit it? Can you do it today?"

"Yeah, should be doable."

"Fantastic! That's what we like, quick decisions. You know it's the decisive ones do the best, right?"

"Ha ha, so true, man, so true."

"Well if you can do it today, we can include you in the first project. How does that sound Tom?"

"Yeah great, Cliffie. We've got all the info on your email, I'll drop it in your account today. Now what about the contract?"

"Well, if you've got the time you can come out and sign it today. Otherwise, just sign it and put it in the mail, and I'll sign our end and put it in the mail to you."

"Yep, that sounds fine."

"Great, will you let me know once you've made the deposit?"

"Sure, will do."

Cliff hung up and turned to Lara, "Wow, simple as that."

They got three more sign ups between them. Nabil and his wife Sarah committed to $50K and promised to deposit it before the end of the week. Another couple, Lex and his wife Rosemary, also went in for $50K. The ever-enthusiastic Carlo, an original club member, who had held his properties long enough to see their values go up nicely, committed $100K.

"Wow twenty-four grand of interest per year. This will let me buy another one, Cliffie. Sweet! I mean, now's the time, right?"

"You're not wrong, mate," Cliff was quietly spewing. It reminded him of himself only a few years earlier, when he'd been buying houses in a rising market, watching their values grow and laughing at how easy it was to get rich. Now it felt like a cruel irony that he was providing the means for Carlo to make a fortune, while he himself could do nothing. Oh well…

He saved his most important call for last.

"Hi Jan, it's Cliffie Young," he put a warm smile in his voice, "How are you going?"

"Oh, hi Cliffie! I'm very well thank you. How are you going with all your new, exciting projects?"

"Fantastic, thank you Jan. It's all happening here."

"Oh wonderful. Now that's what you're ringing about isn't it? The short term loan thing, I mean, investment."

"Yes, that's right, Jan. Just following up on our little talk at the club. I know you and Ken were interested in investing your super…"

"Yes, that's right, to help us pay for the investment property."

"Exactly. Now, I had another talk with Garth and the good news is there's nothing stopping you from investing your super with us."

"Ok wonderful, that's all completely alright is it then?"

"Yep, completely."

"Ok good, and Cliff, tell me, as far as security goes, there's no risk is there? Really?"

"No, none whatsoever. It's as safe as houses, as they say," Cliff chuckled. "I mean, put it this way, I can't say there is zero risk, there's always some tiny, fraction of risk, right? I can't guarantee we won't have, you know, a terrorist attack or a nuclear meltdown or something crazy. But, really, you have the guarantee of a house. Houses don't go anywhere. They're rock solid. Even safer than having it in a bank, right?"

"Yes, of course, I understand. I know I'm being silly, it's just, you know, it's all we've got and we won't ever be able to get it back if we lost it."

"I understand one hundred percent, Jan. You should be careful. At the same time, you can't do nothing. That's an even bigger risk, right? If you do nothing, you lose your investment house. Maybe more. That's a risk you don't want to take, yeah?"

"Yes, you're right, Cliffie. Of course."

"Alright. Well it's up to you. We've got enough funds now for our first project. But we will want to start the second project pretty soon and that will be your chance. So have a think about it. You've got our email with the contract, haven't you?"

"Yes, yes, we got that thanks Cliff."

"Ok, well, have a look at it and have a think about it. Give me a call if you have any questions at all, anything, alright?"

"Yes, thanks Cliffie, we will do that. And don't worry, Cliffie, I am sure we will go ahead with it."

"Ok, great Jan. Grab opportunity when it's there. You know? That's what all the successful people do. You've already taken some big steps. So just keep going, ok?"

"Thanks Cliff. You're such a great support."

"That's what I'm here for. We'll get there together," Cliff chuckled. "You take care now and I'll speak to you soon."

He hung up and turned to find Lara beaming at him.

"You're so smooth."

"Smooth? It's true, everything I said to her I meant one hundred percent. It's their best way out of the hole. What other way can they get out?"

"I know. That's what makes you smooth. You're genuine."

"I mean some people just need encouragement, right? A little push to get over their fears so they can reap the rewards. I can see what she can't see."

"No, it's good. I'm not having a go," Lara laughed, "You're so serious."

Cliff smiled. "Ok, ok. You know the cool thing?"

"What?"

"We've got enough for our first two projects. If she comes on board with 300 grand it covers the next house. If all goes well, we just keep rolling the funds from one project to the next. We do two houses a month, just what we need."

"Brilliant."

"Our investors get their nice, fat interest every month, and we just keep flipping. Win-win. Right?"

"You're the king of win-win. Look at you. So smug!" She flicked her pen at him.

"Oi! I'm not smug."

"Yes you are. Smug as a bug."

"Ha," Cliff folded his arms.

"Aw, come on, come here."

Cliff cocked his head at her, "What?"

"A hug. For the smug bug…"

"First you attack me, then you offer me a hug?"

"Oh come on, you've done a great job."

Cliff sauntered over and embraced her. As he melted into her body, her smell reminded him of the night in San Francisco. He savoured it.

She stiffened and pushed him away. MJ came back in and sat down at her computer, eyebrows raised.

"Lunch time?" Lara enthused.

The next three days were a blur of house inspections, meetings with would-be investors, calls from agents, offers to owners, amendments with Garth, updates from Paul, inspections with tradies… fuelled by an equal blur of early morning egg and bacon rolls, drive-through chicken burgers and late-night kebabs.

At last Cliff got the call he was waiting for. While they were inspecting a weather-worn, fibro house in Shalvey, an agent rang about a low offer he'd made on a house one suburb away.

"Vendor is keen as mustard. But he's hoping you can compromise a little? You're way below what he paid just a year and a half ago."

"It's a buyer's market," Cliff hit back, "You know the deal. There's loads of places just like it. I mean, no offence mate, but it's true, right?"

"Sure, but even in this market-"

"You know how many times a day my mobile goes off with someone trying to sell me a house? It's ridiculous. So, I'm sorry, I can't go any higher. I'll just go elsewhere."

"Alright, understood."

With investor's money now in the bank, Cliff felt cocky. "I can bring a cash deposit over today if he wants to sign the contract?"

"That's alright Cliff, mate, he's given me instructions to accept your offer, even if you won't compromise. So, the place is yours."

"Fantastic."

Late in the afternoon he got a second acceptance.

"Wow this is too easy," he kicked back in his chair, feet on his desk, feeling his old self returning.

Now he needed more funds. He rang Jan.

"Jan, how are you, it's Cliffie."

"Oh, good thanks Cliffie. How are you love?"

"Very good. How's Ken?"

"Oh, he's grumpy. He's got the flu."

"Oh geez, that's no good. Poor bloke. I hope he's in bed keeping warm."

"Well, you know what? I think it's really just an excuse to have me waiting on him all day. It's 'I need a drink' or 'I need my book' or 'I need my glasses.' I'm run off my feet."

Cliff laughed, "He knows how to make the most of the situation, hey?"

"Tell you what, he just needs a crown on his head, one of them ermine robes around his shoulders and a sceptre in his right hand."

"Well I hope His Lordship gets better soon. It sounds like he's being well looked after."

"You should see the look I'm getting from him right now. His Lordship is not amused."

"I can imagine," Cliff chuckled.

"Anyway, sorry Cliffie, you didn't ring to listen to our silly business. You're a busy man. You want to know about the investment of course?"

"That's right Jan. You know I mentioned we were about to start the second project? Well it's happened quicker than I expected. We're ready to start now. So, if you want in, we'll need your funds right away."

"Oh, gee, ok. Well, let's see, we were going to take the contract to the lawyer next week. Our neighbours recommended us to their lawyer and he seems very good. He's having a look at it for us no charge which is very nice of him. But that's on Wednesday, I think. Yes, Wednesday."

"Sure," Cliff could tell they were not going to move fast. At least not his kind of fast. But he sensed any more pressure would most likely put them off completely.

"Then, you know, if that is all ok, we will probably go ahead with it, Cliffie. But we do want to think about it. I'm sorry to be such a pain, I know Ken is still a little worried about the risks and wants to think it over a little more."

"No dramas."

"Sorry Cliffie. It must be very frustrating for you. We're just two silly oldies worried about our little retirement fund. It must seem so trivial to you."

"No, no, no. Absolutely not. Just take your time. I didn't want you to miss out on the next project that was all. But I'm sure there'll be another one down the track, so don't worry."

"Thank you, Cliffie, you're very understanding."

"Damn!" Cliff thought as he hung up. He dialled Lara.

"Hey darl, I need your help."

"Sure, what's up?"

"Do you have the list of investors handy?"

"Yeah, it's in my bag. Do you need it?"

"Can you call the ones who sounded keen but haven't committed yet. You know, the B list?"

"Yeah sure. What, just see how they're going?"

"No, tell them we're starting project two. I've got another acceptance."

"Wow, that's fast."

"I know. Shows how much of a buyers' market it is. So, we're ready to go. Just need investors. Do your best, put loads of pressure on. Okay? Don't take no for an answer."

"I'll give them the full treatment," Lara put warm honey into her voice, "Ok baby…"

"Yep, that's it, perfect! How could anyone resist you."

The smile still on his face, Cliff dialled Paul. His ever-optimistic accountant was helping some of the potential investors refinance their loans to try and access extra equity.

"Hey mate, how's it all going?"

"No complaints Cliffie. Yourself?"

"Yeah, great mate. We've got the funds committed for the first house flip and now I've got another offer accepted. How you going with the refinances? Anyone looking like having useful equity?"

"Yeah, actually there's a couple. We've found some of the new lenders are still open to higher valuations. There's, um, True Blue and also GoForIt Home Loans, they're really aggressive for new business despite the downturn."

"Yeah, great."

"Funny enough, though, the best valuations are coming out of one of the oldest building societies, New England Permanent. Seems like they haven't updated their software or something. We got 280k for the Moran's place at Dharruk and looks like we might get the same for Simon and Angela."

"Wow, really? That would be excellent for them." Simon's attack on Cliff at the last club meeting still stung. So it was not only great news for Simon and Angela, but also for Cliff's guilty conscience.

"Yes, they should have about 40K to invest. If you still wanted to take theirs?"

"Yeah, great. Well, it's the best thing for them. Perfect win-win situation. When will you know?"

"Today, hopefully, but Monday at the latest I'd say."

"Awesome."

EIGHTEEN

Things were moving fast. They had to. Cliff knew ABC Bank was in the process of foreclosing on him. He'd failed to make the payment he had promised Dermott and had ignored his calls ever since. He didn't know how long it would be, but he knew their legal action was coming.

So, he'd put special conditions on his offers. Since he was paying cash, he wanted a short settlement period. He also wanted immediate access to start renovations as soon as the contracts were signed. This, he hoped, would let him have the houses back on the market within a month. Both sellers so far had agreed to his terms.

Driving into Parramatta to pick Mandy up from the ferry his mobile rang. He glanced down and saw it was Bill. His stomach turned with trepidation. For the last year Bill's calls had brought nothing but bad news and worse surprises. He thought about letting it go to voice mail.

What was the point? He'd rather deal with any new disaster now. How much worse could it get anyway?

"Hey Bill."

"Hey mate, how are you? Are you sitting down?"

"Well I'm driving. That's sitting down. What is it?"

"We're building!"

"Yeah? What do you mean?"

"I mean we have started again. Cranes are moving, concrete's being poured. We've got our money!"

"Holy shit! No kidding?"

"Yep the new bank's come through mate. They've financed the completion as per plans."

"That's bloody great news!"

"Too right it is mate. They love it. They can see the value in it. And they're happy to put their money where their mouth is."

"Well done Bill. I just hope it's not too late for me mate."

"I spoke to them about you too, like I said I would. They'll sort you out too don't worry."

"Really?"

"Really. I sang your praises mate, told them you're the best bloody investor they'd find. Told them what you've achieved, you know, a hundred properties in a few years, the club, all that. You're a professional. They can see that, mate, and they're only too happy to take your business off the hands of ABC Bank."

"Wow. That would be amazing. I'd like to get onto it Bill. Can you put me in touch?"

"Of course, mate. When do you want to meet them?"

"Um, how about tomorrow?"

"Alright, let me give them a call and I'll get right back to you."

"Great thanks."

Cliff woke early. He felt alive and fresh like he'd slept for the first time in years. Mandy lay asleep beside him, so he took care not to move the bed as he got up. After a quick shower, he headed into the living room, his towel wrapped around him.

He opened the curtains and was met by a spectacular golden glow where the sun was about to pop up over the horizon. It bathed the world around in warm hues of yellow and deeper oranges, reflecting off windows and shimmering on roof tops. The sky was a steely blue metallic, while streaks of cloud were painted in a spectrum from yellow to red to pink and purple.

"Wow, that's amazing."

Surely it was a sign. Things were turning around and coming good again. He inhaled deeply and let it out slowly, a breath that contained months and months of pent up emotions. Eyes closed, he let in feelings he'd been holding at bay for so long. His face twisted and tears rolled down his cheeks.

"Oh god, I've been storing this up."

He heard the bed creak and quickly wiped his eyes. He still felt like their relationship depended on him being strong and upbeat. He'd never shared the true depths of his emotions with Mandy, even through these incredibly stressful times. He relaxed when he heard her go straight into the bathroom.

Cliff took the house phone off its cradle on the kitchen wall and dialled his mum.

"Hi Cliffie. You've become a real early bird haven't you."

"Yeah, sorry, it's just I've got so much to do, this is the only time I get."

"That's alright darling, what's up?"

"Just want to know how you guys are going... and if Dad's made that payment on the loan?"

"He hasn't Cliffie. He disappeared on Wednesday, came back near midnight, drunk as a skunk."

"Ah, shit! Are you serious?"

"Yes, I'm sorry hun. We haven't been speaking much lately."

"Well you've got to. You can't let this slide or you really will lose the house. This is really, truly, the last chance. Seriously mum."

"I know. I think he was hoping you'd take care of it and when he heard you were struggling too... Well I think he just hit the deck you know, it floored him and he hasn't got up."

"Right. Is he there now?"

"I'm not waking him up, Cliffie."

"Come on, mum, just put him on. You don't have to say nothing, I'll speak to him. Someone needs to put a rocket up him."

"Sorry Cliffie - no. You don't have to be here, I do. I'm the one has to put up with him for the rest of the day. I'll tell him you called.

He can call you back later on. I'll make sure he does, ok? Ok, sweetie?" Her voice tightened on the last words.

"Ok, ok. But tell me, do you have anything at all? Can he even make any kind of repayment?

"No. Not until Wednesday fortnight."

"Fuuuck!"

"And that's if he doesn't spend it again before I can get there."

"Jesus. What's he thinking?"

"He's not. It's got to a point where he doesn't care anymore. And for me, I can't keep fighting, you know Cliffie. I'm sorry. Why do I have to be the one who keeps on battling away when no-one else gives a shit. If we end up in a trailer park then we end up in a fucking trailer park."

"Ok, don't stress mum. Take it easy. Leave it with me. Ok?"

"Sure. Whatever you want to do is fine with me. Just don't keep pushing because I can't do anything about him. I'm sorry." She finished in a despairing wail.

Cliff was back in fight mode. He ruffled through the piles of paper on the breakfast table until he found the folder for his dad's investment property. He pulled out a copy of a loan statement and checked it had all the details he needed. Next, he dialled into ABC phone banking and selected Cliffies Climbers short term loans account.

The balance was there, two hundred thousand had come in already. Fifty from Tom and Anna, fifty from Nabil and Sarah and one hundred from Carlo. Cliff took a deep breath and pressed "2" to make a payment. He entered the details for his mum and dad's loan and paid the full eleven thousand. He hung up, knowing he had crossed a line.

"Fuck it. Time to fight dirty."

Anyway, he was confident no-one would ever know. He could cut the renovation budget a little on the first property, flip it and everything would be back on track. Eleven grand could be made up.

Mid-morning Cliff turned into the cavernous underground car park of the new Westfield Bondi Junction shopping centre.

"Woah, serious," he whistled at the impressive scale of the complex, its imposing cliff-like walls of rugged, sandstone left exposed where it had recently been carved out of the earth.

At the lift lobby he checked he had three hours of free parking. Cool. His destination was, in fact, several blocks away from the shopping centre but the street parking was eight bucks an hour. Total daylight robbery. He smiled as he stepped through the glass doors onto the street. These days he was happy for any small win.

As he headed down the street towards the offices of Western Progressive Bank, he looked up at the new tower developments on all sides. It was a very different world to the laid-back, sprawling suburban houses of Mount Druitt. Here hundreds of shiny new apartments stacked up on top of each other into the sky. Their gleaming glass balconies looked out to the ocean beyond, as their glass walls mirrored the sun-soaked world around them. The only detraction from their perfectly shiny facades was the large number of 'for lease' signs. These were not lost on Cliff. It was like every second balcony sported one. Maybe the wealthy suburbs had their own problems?

Western Progressive's lobby was a light-filled glass atrium with an ornate steel sculpture suspended from the centre of the roof like a giant, industrial, orchid. Cliff approached a wide reception desk, adorned with vases of real tropical flowers. A concierge wearing a three-piece suit looked up.

"I'm here to see Seb Konig in corporate lending," Cliff read the details from a text message Bill had sent.

"Do you have an appointment sir?"

"Yes, eleven o'clock."

"No problem, sir, you can head up to level nineteen. I'll let him know you are on your way."

"Thanks mate." Cliff followed the concierge's directions through an automatic security gate and into the lift lobby.

He stepped out on level nineteen and was stopped in his tracks by a vast panorama of the harbour city that stretched a hundred and eighty degrees, so vivid in the colours of water, glass, steel and sky that it did not, at first, seem real.   A young, immaculately groomed, woman smiled as he approached the reception desk.

"Good morning sir."

"Wow, what an amazing view," Cliff could not contain himself. "You have a pretty incredible workplace."

"Yes, it's beautiful isn't it," she smiled again.

He wondered if she ever thought it ironic that she worked with her back to it.

"I'm here to see Seb Konig please."

"Yes, sure. Mr Young is it?"

"Yes, Cliff Young."

"No problem Mr Young. Please take a seat and Seb will be with you shortly."

Cliff sat down on a white leather sofa. In front of him a glass coffee table offered a selection of investment-related newspapers and magazines. His eye caught the headline of the Financial Review.

"US Housing Crisis Spreads"

He picked it up but before he could read the article, the door to his left opened. An unusually tall and lanky man in a sharp, black suit stepped out. He had an air of action and efficiency and instantly reached out a long arm to Cliff.

"Cliff! Welcome mate."

Cliff stood up and shook hands. "Thanks. Seb is it?"

"Yes, come on through mate," Seb led the way across the lobby to a glass panelled meeting room. Inside he sat down at the glass-topped boardroom table and gestured Cliff to do likewise.

"Great to meet you Cliff," he smiled, "Thanks for coming in."

"No worries."

"So you want to refinance your portfolio?"

"Yeah, that's right."

"Ok, good stuff. Now I like to cut to the chase. No offence, it's just how I am."

"Sure," Cliff smiled.

"We want your business. And we'll do whatever we have to, to get it."

"Great!" Cliff could not conceal his pleasure.

"We just need to make sure it's legit. You know?"

"Sure. No problem."

"About a hundred houses, yeah?"

"That's right, a hundred exactly."

"Nice. What finance are you looking for?"

"Um, the current bank has them valued, mostly, around 275K. We believe a lot of them are worth more than that. They've all been renovated, you know, fixed up better than the average place out there."

"Free-standing houses?"

"Yep."

"In Sydney? Of course they're worth more than that. Median price is north of half a mill. What LVR?"

"A hundred percent if possible. We're looking to draw out the equity and, you know, maybe buy some more. While the market has slowed down it's a good time to acquire more assets and get ready for things to start going up again, you know, over the next couple of years."

"Abso-fucking-lutely!" Seb punched the air, then leaned forward apologetically, "Sorry mate, excuse me, I'm forever filling up the swear jar."

"No worries," Cliff laughed.

"I do a little investing too," Seb explained, "And finally we have a buyer's market right?"

"Yeah too right."

"Ok," Seb was business-like again, "I can't see any issues Cliff. We'll need to get your financials, make sure everything is kosher, the loans are all up to date, etcetera. Are you aware of any issues at all?"

Cliff gulped. He had been waiting for it to unravel. However, he needed this too badly.

"No, all good," he smiled weakly.

"I'll get Matik, my auditor, to get in touch with your accountant and go through everything anyway. That way, you don't have to muck around with paperwork."

"Great." So as soon as they see the overdue balances, game over, Cliff mulled.

"We'll just need your accountant's details."

"Sure," Cliff hesitated. He needed to speak to Paul before these guys did. "Can I email them to you?"

"Perfect mate."

"Ok cool."

"We'll get all the property details off your accountant as well. Run a valuation on them and let you know," Seb smiled.

"Alright, sounds good." It didn't really. Cliff felt like he had been down this road many times before. The sales guys were enthusiastic, but the valuers would be pessimistic. Once they put his Mount Druitt addresses into their system, they would see the latest sales prices and get warnings about the high number of foreclosures in the area.

Seb must have seen the doubt on Cliff's face.

"Don't worry, mate, we're different to the other banks. You're dealing with people who know how this all works. We're 'big picture' people."

He held out his hand. Cliff shook it warmly, "Thanks Seb, I appreciate it mate."

Cliff had mixed feelings as he sat in the window of MacDonald's, Bondi. Across the road was the beach, the ocean cool in hues of green to turquoise to a deep, royal blue. The breeze had come up and was flicking up white caps out to the horizon. Seagulls hung suspended in the air, occasionally swooping to the white sand below, their 'prey' most likely a half-finished pie or bag of chips.

Cliff hardly tasted his own chips and burger as he chewed slowly, lost in thought. His coffee sat untouched. He knew he was at a turning point. This was surely the last chance he was ever going to get to save his portfolio.

His spirits were lifted by Seb's enthusiasm to win his business. Seb's utter confidence that his bank would find Cliff more equity had set his heart racing with hope. In fact, talking to Seb had felt like talking to a kindred spirit, someone who thought in the same way Cliff did. In Seb's own words, focused on the big picture. So refreshing to hear a banker talk of the current slowdown as an exciting opportunity, rather than a reason to clamp down with excessive caution.

On the other hand, there was the problem of his overdue interest payments. They would surely be a stumbling block. Should he have played hard ball? Told Seb exactly how much he was behind in payments and made that the price Western Progressive would have to pay to secure his business. He doubted it. Not even Seb's double-barrelled optimism would hold up against half a million bucks of unpaid interest.

In that case, the only option was to pay the interest and get his accounts at ABC Bank up to date. He knew exactly where he could get the money. But he didn't like to think about it. Paying out his Dad's overdue interest with Club members' money was one thing. It was such a small amount he could make sure it was never missed. But this...

He swung around to get a pen and paper napkin from the counter to do his calculations. As he did, he met the narrowed, hostile eyes of a tall, wiry, young man. Under a backwards-turned cap, he had a large, pointy nose, his jaw set aggressively. The overall impression was of an angry rat, Cliff thought. The man stepped uncomfortably close, his chest pushing into Cliff's face, providing him a close-up of a female cartoon character on his tee-shirt. She wore a broad smile and nothing else, while brandishing an over-sized pair of scissors in one hand, and a USA flag in the other. The slogan read, 'No More Bush!'

"Sorry mate," Cliff tried stepping around. Instead, the young man grabbed Cliff by the shoulders, leaning close into his face.

"Can you help us out with a fiver, mate?" His strong cockney accent was just like a character on The Bill. Cliff smelled marijuana. "I need to get into the city urgent like."

The Englishman had two mates watching from the doorway, grins on their faces.

"No, sorry mate," Cliff was defensive. He tried to lighten the situation, offering his un-touched cup. "You can have a coffee."

"No, but I'll have a chip," the young man leaned across and grabbed Cliff's half-full bag of fries. He giggled in a high pitch as he returned to his smiling mates, brandishing his prize. The three turned and sauntered across the road to the beach, holding up traffic as they cheerfully dug into the chips.

"Fuckwit," Cliff vented as he looked around the shop for support. All heads went down, customers and staff alike.

He sat back down on his stool, feeling more than a little humiliated. Eventually his thoughts returned to his latest financial challenge. How to pay his outstanding interest.

Across the road, a group of tanned, toned and well-oiled volleyball players leaped and rolled across the sand, tapping, kicking and slamming the ball with boundless energy. Beyond them the sand shimmered with couples nestled on their towels and groups listening to music, eating, drinking and soaking up the sunshine.

"Why am I doing this again?" Cliff thought to himself. "Why didn't I just go on the fucking dole and hang out on the beach all day?"

Then he spotted the Englishman and his two mates near the water's edge. They had three girls with them, dancing in a loose circle, in what looked like a mixture of African tribal ritual and nightclub dance floor.

"Yep. Sometimes you just got to take what you want."

NINETEEN

The flip house pumped with the sounds of 'Relax' by Frankie Goes to Hollywood. The Club working bee was in full swing, the renovation a lot more ambitious than normal. This due, squarely, to the talents and enthusiasm of new club members and best mates, Dougie, the brickie, and Mossie, the chippie.

It was their radio that blared out, tuned to eighties classic hits on Gold FM and it was the thuds of their sledgehammers that pounded along in time. Their mission was to demolish an internal wall between the kitchen and living room. It was an ugly brick wall with a seventies-style circular opening in it. Quite apart from giving the house the feel of a moth-balled Brady Bunch set, it was dirty, tired and pock-marked with chips and missing bricks and two large cracks ran through it diagonally from floor to ceiling. Someone had once attempted to fill them with red-coloured putty, but instead of hiding the cracks, this had only created a large, jagged X as the main feature of the living room.

"Relax, uh-huh!" Mossie sang out, his sledgehammer poised.

"When you wanna come," Dougie crooned in high falsetto and - crunch - their hammers took out another patch of bricks.

"You guys are going great guns," MJ called out as she came through the back fly-screen door, letting it slap shut behind her. She'd set up a 'site office' in the garage from where she was managing the renovations.

"Mate, we'll have this down in a few more minutes," Mossie enthused. Crunch, they struck again.

"Keep this up and we'll let you have your way with the back wall too," MJ nodded, impressed.

"That would be awesome," Cliff was hopeful.

In addition to the internal change, Dougie and Mossie had also tried to convince Cliff, MJ and the rest of the team to let them remove half the back wall of the house, where there was currently only a small, battered aluminium window, its twisted, venetian blind cutting across at a sharp angle. Their plan was to put in glass doors and build a deck, thus creating a magnificent open-plan living area that flowed out to the back yard.

MJ, however, had told them they could start with the internal wall and see how they went. After the meeting she'd quietly explained to Cliff she doubted their enthusiasm would last the distance. It would be much better if they ran out of steam halfway through the internal wall than the external one.

For Cliff, of course, the bigger and better the renovation, the higher his flip price would be and the greater his profit. So, watching the two mates quickly reduce the brick wall to a pile of rubble, which two other willing club members hastened to shovel up and barrow to the skip on the front driveway, filled him with great hope.

"Piece of piss," Mossie smiled and winked at Cliff. Crunch!

Pleased, Cliff headed back down the hallway to where he was working with four of his new investors. Tom and his wife (the Americans who had committed 50K towards the project) and a new couple, Spencer and Ronnie (who had only that week invested 150K) were busy filling and patching the battered gyprock walls and ceilings and scraping back the flaking paintwork. It was hard work but they were all in high spirits, enthusiastic to be hands-on the renovation they had their savings staked in. They were getting to see the reality of their investment, in action, making money. And they were getting a practical lesson in how to flip from the 'master' himself, Cliff Young.

"Good stuff, guys," Cliff revved them up, "Everyone's going great."

"Yeah, we're getting there," Ronnie wiped her forehead.

"Though, I see Raj has already moved onto the BBQ."

"Well, we all know his priorities," Tom smiled under his dust mask.

"Yep, avoiding real work."

The others chuckled.

MJ poked her head through the doorway.

"Got another crew member for the inside team, Cliffie."

Carlo, the old time club member who had enthusiastically invested in the short term loans scheme, came through the door with a flourish, holding up an orbital sander and saluting.

"Private Carlo reporting for duty sir!"

"Hey Carlo, welcome," Tom stopped working and smiled. The others greeted him cheerfully too.

"Well I have to come, don't I?" Carlo looked serious, "This is my investment, I have to put some work into it."

"You too hey?" Tom chuckled, "That's what we're all doing."

"Yeah, you know I think it's the only bank that takes your money and makes you work for free on top of it," Spencer winked at Cliff and laughed.

Cliff smiled but wasn't laughing on the inside. He was alarmed. MJ had unknowingly created a potential disaster. Between them, the three lots of investors had given Cliff 300K and he'd written them each a caveat over the flip house as security. In other words, 300K worth of caveats. Everyone knew he'd bought the house for 190K and once renovated and flipped would maybe get to 240K. If they started talking and comparing notes, they would quickly work out there was a bit of a hole in their security.

"Ems!"

"Yeah?" MJ's head re-appeared in the doorway.

"I think we might mix things up a bit. We're going sweet here. I reckon take Carlo and show him the paints. After lunch he can take the two from inside clean up and get started on the first bedroom.

Plaster should be dry in there by then."

"No, no, it's alright Cliffie. We're on schedule everywhere. Let's stick to the plan. Get one job done and move onto the next. Alright old son?"

"No, no, there's plenty of us here, more than expected, so let's push ahead. Really." He snuck MJ a wink.

"Oh right, that's nice, so you don't want me here," Carlo put on a sulking face.

"No, no, it's not that we don't want you Carlo," Cliff insisted, "You're a great painter, that's all, mate. I wanna use your skills."

"No worries," MJ was clearly still irritated, but she'd realised Cliff was trying to tell her something. "Come on Carlo, let's get you a paint brush, old mate."

"Fine, fine, I know when I'm not wanted, I can handle rejection," Carlo put on a sad-clown face, mimed wiping tears and slumped off towards the door. It made everyone laugh.

"Love you, Carlo," Cliff called after him.

That had been close. Now he just had to keep them separated for the rest of the weekend.

By the time Cliff lay his head back on his pillow at midnight on Sunday, the end of two intense days of renovation, he was exhausted but deeply content. In a weekend, they had turned a bomb of a house into something fantastic. He was certain they would flip it for a great price.

It was bright with fresh paint inside and out. Front and back yards were neat and ready for turf, paths and driveway to go in. Despite all the teasing, Raj had put in a champion effort with his landscaping team clearing the piles of garbage, debris, broken appliances and car parts in both yards and cutting down the overgrown cotton palms that had obscured the front of the house with thick skirts of dead fronds.

The kitchen had been salvaged, broken cupboards patched and painted, benches re-surfaced and tiles painted to look new. Remarkably, given how brand spanking it looked, the only items purchased were the sink, the cupboard door handles and a set of taps. Likewise, the bathroom had been transformed for a minimal budget. Tiles and bath resurfaced with glossy enamel, toilet polished up and given a new seat, vanity repaired and new chrome taps installed.

Most exciting of all, Dougie and Mossie had come through with their promises. Before lunch on day one they completed their internal wall demolition, cut all the exposed brickwork back and rendered it up perfectly. So, MJ gave them the thumbs up and they attacked the back wall with relish. They even slept over Saturday night, playing security guards, since they'd opened up a dirty great hole in the back of the house and not yet filled it with anything.

Next day they installed a timber bi-folding door where the wall had been. Mossie had salvaged it from a renovation he was working on near Parramatta. He expertly fixed its broken panelling and hinges so that by the time they put it up it looked as good as new. Then they began laying out the timbers for the deck and promised to finish it nights during the week. By now Cliff and MJ had total faith they would.

There was much more to be done, but you could see it was going to be a winner. During the coming week they'd bring in professional floor sanders and MJ was going to pour the concrete driveway with her landscaping mates. Then they'd have a final Club working bee on the weekend, focused on the outdoors. Dougie and Mossie should have finished the deck by then so it would be garden beds, turf and paved pathways to go in as well as all the exterior painting, house trims, garage and fences.

Last thing would be giving it an 'X-factor' – Lara's speciality. She had a knack for combing through online bargains, local garage sales, markets and auctions and finding those special touches that gave the place a personality and made it feel more like a home. Whether it was a name for the house, an eye-catching garden feature, a set of retro light shades, vividly patterned curtains or an amusing doormat, the result was always outstanding and Cliff knew it added much value to the finished place.

"Yep, she had real talent…" his thoughts drifted.

Mandy rolled over and snuggled into Cliff. She kissed him on the cheek.

"You've done a great job, darling, well done."

He smiled without opening his eyes, "Mmm thanks."

"I know you've been really stressed hon'. I know you don't like to talk about it."

"Yeah… just a bit, hey…"

"Well, I just want you to know I think you are amazing. It's incredible how you keep coming up with solutions. Like the new loans… the house flipping."

"Hmm…"

"You're working so hard. It's amazing watching you. I've never seen anyone work so hard. I know you will be successful. That's what I wanted to say. I believe in you. I have no doubt you will succeed."

Cliff squeezed her hand. "Thanks, darl…"

"You're a survivor. A fighter. You're my little fighter." She snuggled up tighter.

Cliff felt her warmth and it made him smile. He even felt a little aroused, although he was so exhausted he couldn't think of following through. Anyway, his mind would not stop racing on, trying to plan the next steps, foresee obstacles and how to get around them. He was in the strangest, dissected state, his loins saying one thing, the rest of his body another and his mind somewhere else again, spinning at great speed.

"Hmm, thanks, never give up, hey…"

He just had to, somehow, last until Blue was complete. Then he'd have options. He'd be able to sell his units and pay out that huge debt. Or, if the numbers stacked up, he could hang onto them, rent them and service the debt. Rental was sure to be solid given how stunning the units were going to be.

He'd hang in until the market turned around, his portfolio went back up in value, and he was back in business.

If only. It all came down to Seb and Western Progressive. It really was his last shot. If they would value his portfolio higher than ABC did, refinance and give him the extra equity, then surely he'd have the funds to get through another few months until Bill finished Blue. Seb had given him hope and Cliff had acted on it.

Since his Bondi meeting, he'd worked hard with Lara, Mandy, Paul and Garth to make his portfolio look as good as possible. He'd been inspired by Seb's comment that, since Sydney's median price was over half a million, any freestanding house in the city had to be worth more than ABC's valuations. He took a punt on Seb not knowing the realities of Mount Druitt and expanded their search area for price-comparisons, to include suburbs a little further away, and significantly better than the ones he held his portfolio properties in. These suburbs, like Plumpton and Oxley Park, even St Clair, fell within the same local council, some even had the same postcodes, but were newer, greener and occupied mostly by home-owners rather than tenants and people on housing-commission. Their recent sale prices, despite the current depressed market, were well above 300K. He hardly dared to hope that, with a combination of Seb's positivity, his desire to win Cliff's business off a rival bank, and his focus on inner city, high end properties, he might just go for it.

Cliff smiled as he remembered the moment Mandy gave the portfolio template a Sydney harbour watermark. It instantly made the Mount Druitt classics look a million dollars. They'd all cracked up. What the hell, he'd told them, they had nothing to lose. Hopefully Western Progressive would love it too.

He'd also gone hard on raising more short-term loan investments, the tally now over 500K and pushing nicely towards his target of 900K. He'd accepted that he was going to have to be a 'little dodgy'. He had no other choice. The first 400K was going to be his budget for flipping houses, two at a time. The remaining 500K would have to go towards paying his outstanding debt at ABC.

It was not the agreed use of the funds, Cliff knew. He didn't like thinking about it, but he had to admit it was probably, in fact, a fairly serious crime. But it would only be for a very short time, to put his ABC account in the black and keep Western Progressive happy. Anyway, he would only do it if Seb agreed to the refinance. Then he'd have new equity and the funds would be covered. All good.

He had no intention of ripping anyone off. On the contrary, he was determined to help them all get rich. The 24% interest more than delivered on that!

"It'll be cool."

He became aware of Mandy's warmth and the closeness of her breath. He rolled over and kissed her. "You're a great support. Thanks."

She looked into his eyes. "I just don't want you to think you have to do this. I know you're doing it for us, for our future. But you have to look after yourself too, you know. You don't have to do it all at once. You don't have to work yourself quite so hard."

"I know," he smiled at her. "But at the moment I do. It's getting there, though. We're starting to win again."

"Good." Mandy kissed him.

"I'm your little fighter."

They giggled. Cliff rolled onto his back, closed his eyes and drifted away, at last, into blissful sleep.

The big yellow and green mixer roared, jerked and puffed black exhaust as it backed up to the start of the new driveway. Cliff looked on, sitting on the front brick veranda of the flip house, as the driver opened the stop valve on a heavy black hose he'd uncoiled from the back of the mixer and MJ and two of her mates began spreading the concrete that gushed from it. The two cheerful young blokes had both worked with MJ at her uncle's landscaping company and had followed her into the Climbers Club. The taller of them, Johnny, had already bought two classic houses.

Cliff's phone rang in his pocket. He recognized Seb's Bondi Junction number and hastily answered as he stepped inside the house.

"Cliff Young."

"G'day Cliff. Seb Konig here mate from Western Progressive. How are you going? Is it an ok time to talk?"

"Yep, all good, mate. Everything's going great."

"Fantastic. Well, listen, I've got good news for you. The valuations are looking fine. We reckon we'll find you at least ten percent more on most of those properties. How does that sound?"

"Wow, that's fantastic!"

"Yeah I told you it wouldn't be a problem mate."

"That's awesome. Wow. Thanks very much Seb I appreciate it a lot."

"Not a problem. So, I trust you would like to shift your loans over then?"

"Absolutely. Just one thing, though, will I be able to borrow the full amount? You know, one hundred percent of the equity?"

"Yep, we're happy to offer you that facility. Mortgage insurance will be required, of course, but you can borrow that too."

"Sure, no worries."

"So, Cliff, we'll need to put the applications in, which we can do on your behalf. Just, as I said last time, we need your account statements, ok? Your bank statements for your current loan portfolio. Then, as long as everything is looking good, we should be ready to rock and roll."

"No worries. I'll get Paul to send those across to you. Should be in the next day or so, if that's alright?"

"Perfect. We'll wait to hear from him then."

"Great. Thanks again Seb."

Cliff's heart was racing. He leaned against the kitchen bench top and took in a deep breath. He couldn't believe it. He'd pulled it off. Once again, he had found a way to survive. In the words of Ray Kirshwood, he had been able to 'manufacture' some more wealth, just when he needed it most. He laughed out loud.

Now he knew what he had to do. He made straight for the door, bounced down the veranda steps and out the front gate, calling as he went, "See ya shortly, groovers!"

MJ and her two mates looked up and waved. Cliff jumped in his car and headed for home.

He logged into internet banking. The Short Term Loans account had 640K in it. Good, more than enough to pay out his 500K of overdue interest at ABC. He smiled, imagining the look on Dermott's face when he found out Cliff had successfully paid his debts and moved his business to another bank. He could never forgive Dermott. After all those years of loyalty, to turn so cold, to deny him any leniency, any special treatment, and cause him so much stress.

TWENTY

He'd opened the Short Term Loans account with a much smaller institution, Standard Building Society, in order to keep it well and truly out of the reach of ABC. He was going to have to arrange a transfer. He grabbed his things and headed back to the car.

Standard Building Society was anything but 'standard'. The branding was fluro green. Everything from signage to wall panels, to table-tops, even the staff uniforms screamed out in loud fluro. But that was just the beginning of their break with tradition. When it came to branch design, they had thrown out the old-school teller counters, creating instead 'customer pods'. These were essentially booths, like in a fast food restaurant, where the tellers sat, kind of awkwardly, 'hosting' their customers.

The funny thing, Cliff thought as he walked in through the automatic glass doors and surveyed the situation, was that when it was busy, customers still had to take a number and stand in line, waiting for the next free 'pod', their faces just as grumpy as at any traditional bank.

"Bugger this."

His eyes fixed on a young, blonde girl standing behind a curved counter off to his left. She sported a fluro green jacket and matching ribbons in her hair. Above her was suspended a large, cylindrical sign with the word "HI!" popping out from it in bubble-shaped font. This too was all fluro green plastic, with bright LED lights and, hanging through the centre, two green speakers pumping surprisingly up-tempo electronic dance music. It was like something between a night club bar and a stage set for a magician show.

With a gleam in his eye, Cliff stepped up to her with an enthusiastic, "Hi!"

"Good morning sir, how can I help you?" she smiled with no irony.

He had an urge to do the 'Hi' once more, even bigger, but figured she'd probably never find it funny.

"I've got a really big bank transfer to make and I need to do it urgently. Is there someone can help me?"

"Sure sir, if you'd like to see one of our tellers, they will be able to help you. Just wait for the next available customer pod."

"Ah, no, this is like half a million dollars we are talking, I think I need to see someone more senior," Cliff winked at her.

"Oh, ok no problem. Normally our tellers would look after you with something like that."

"Sure, but this probably isn't so 'normal'. Is there a manager around? Someone senior who can help me? A Master of Ceremonies, maybe?" Cliff gave her a cheeky smile.

"I'll see if the Assistant Manager is available. If you would like to take a seat over there and wait for a moment, I won't be long." She indicated a row of green topped stools at a glass counter.

"Would you like a juice while you wait?" she held up a glass jug filled with a deep green-coloured liquid and ice.

"No thanks," Cliff smiled back. Wow, it really is a bar.

He sat down to wait. Why on earth had he opened an account with this crowd? He remembered he'd been keen to make sure any new funds he acquired were as far removed from ABC Bank as possible.

Yep, far removed, but this was ridiculous. Then he remembered that Lara had opened the account for him.

"Of course," he smiled as it dawned on him, "This would be her kind of joke."

"Excuse me, sir," a husky voice yanked him back to reality. He looked up to see a short, round woman, with arresting blue eyes and a tall crop of spiky, shock-blonde hair. Thankfully, she wasn't wearing a fluro green jacket.

"I'm Rita, the Assistant Manager here. Sam tells me you wanted to discuss a large withdrawal?"

"Yeah, hi, thanks very much. It's a large bank transfer I need to make. It's urgent so I need to know what's the quickest way?"

"I see. What's large?"

"About half a mill."

"Right. Well, we can give you a bank cheque. But you'll have to apply for it. That takes five days processing."

"You mean applying for it, or the whole processing time until it is cleared by the other bank?"

"No, that's just application time. What the other bank does with it is up to them."

Cliff always found it remarkable how happy banks were to take your money but when, on occasion, you needed it back they treated you like you were thieving from them. What the fuck was the need to apply for a cheque?

Of course, he had to admit, on this occasion, it actually wasn't his money. It was the Club investors' money. The thought rattled him for a moment. A pang of guilt that had been lingering, dull and unacknowledged, for a while now, twisted more tightly into a knot deep in his guts. Rationally he knew the bank had no way of knowing this, the account was in his name only. Yet his imagination spun wildly. What if they were onto him somehow? Rita was just the kind of 'kowtow to nobody' type that fitted his nightmare scenario perfectly. He took a deep breath and steadied himself.

"Yeah, see that's not going to work. I've got a really big business deal hanging in the balance and it depends on me getting those funds transferred urgently. Is there another way, like electronic or something?"

"How urgent is 'urgent'?"

"Well, ideally today, but if that's not possible then just ASAP in the next day or so."

Rita sized Cliff up, taking her time. Eventually she gestured to him, "Come sit down in the Lenders Lounge and we'll talk it through."

She didn't wait for Cliff and headed for the far end of the bank, where the tellers' pods ended and two shoulder-height, fluro green panels screened off an area that at first glance looked like it might be a kids' play area.

When Cliff got there, he realized why. The seating consisted of three green donuts. There were also several beanbags in bright yellows and reds. All were loosely arranged around a glass topped coffee table. Sitting on the table was a fluro green, plush toy of a house with a 'For Sale' sign and Standard Building Society logo.

"Grab a seat," Rita offered as she settled on the edge of her donut. Cliff sat down but instantly slid backwards into the hole of the donut. Legs flailing, he scrambled back out.

Rita burst out in a loud, rasping laugh, "Yeah, they take a bit of getting used to these things!"

"Yeah, you're not wrong," Cliff sat carefully on the edge.

Rita grabbed a laptop that sat next to the plush house and pulled it closer to her. She typed for a moment and then asked Cliff for his ID.

"Great, I've got you here," she looked at the screen. "Which bank do you want to transfer the funds to?"

"ABC."

"Ah-ha. Well you just might be in luck."

"Oh really?"

"Yeah," Rita trailed off as she focused on some details on the screen, her face set and serious. She punched in more entries and read some more.

"Hmm…" she looked concerned. Cliff's heart beat faster. Rita typed more and went silent for what seemed an eternity.

Eventually she nodded, "Yeah, here we are…" She looked up at Cliff, "You're in luck."

"Great. What does that mean?"

"Well," Rita leaned in, "We're not supposed to tell anyone this…"

She looked out through the partitions to the rest of the bank and then back to Cliff. "We're actually owned by ABC Bank."

"Oh really?"

"Yeah, see, no-one knows it right? It's one of those marketing experiments. 'Stealth marketing' or some such. Win over a new, younger generation and knock out all the smaller players in the market at the same time. Whatever."

"Yeah, right. Interesting what they get up to, isn't it?"

"Totally. It's my bag, marketing, I'm studying nights."

"Really? Good on you."

"Yeah thanks. Love it. You know, strategies and campaigns. It's all about online now... and then there's above the line... Anyway, enough about me," she burst into a girly, almost coquettish, giggle, reached out and slapped Cliff on the knee.

Cliff chuckled a little uncomfortably. Then the penny dropped. She was flirting with him. He tried, discretely, to shuffle further away. Trouble was he didn't want to fall back down the donut.

Rita leaned in, "The good news for you is this means we can actually do an internal transaction," she winked at him, "Within the family, if you like."

"Nice."

She sat back and beamed at Cliff, "And I'm able to authorize it."

Cliff pulled up outside the flip house. It was midday Friday and the sun was warm overhead. MJ's 4WD was parked on the new driveway. Nosed in behind her, Cliff recognized Nick the plumber's ute. They had been using Nick for all their renovation and maintenance work for years. He was a tall, easy-going guy with a cheeky smile and a great sense of humour. He was also hard-working and available 24/7 to assist Cliff, MJ and Raj with anything they needed. Cliff had recommended him to the Club members and suspected that, by now, he did no other work than theirs.

Also parked in front of the house was a ute belonging to Dwaine the electrician. Originally recommended by Nick, who'd been mates with him since school days, he was another mainstay they'd been using for years of renovations.

"Wow MJ's ripping into it," Cliff thought out loud, "Good on her."

He was feeling the best he had in over a year. He bounced out of the driver's seat and headed for the open gate down the side of the house. In the backyard, he found MJ and her two landscaping mates cleaning and stacking pavers.

"Hey peeps," Cliff called out. They put down their tools as he came over and shook hands.

"You guys are bloody legendary. Leave something for the volunteers to do tomorrow." Cliff's mood was infectious.

MJ, however, was living out her schedules and work plans and felt the need to point out, "If we don't get this prep done, old mate, they won't have anything to do tomorrow, and you won't have a front path by the end of the weekend."

"I know, I know, just joking groover. You're doing an amazing job. But its lunch time now and we're going out. Ok?"

"Sure boss!" Johnny smiled.

MJ gave Cliff a suspicious smile, "What's going on?"

"Ah, just time we had lunch." As Cliff walked off towards the house he called out over his shoulder, "And a little celebration!"

Inside he heard the sounds of Nick hammering in the bathroom and saw the legs of Dwaine's ladder through the furthest bedroom door. "Time for lunch people. Let's take a break."

"Just finishing this screen off," Nick called out.

Dwaine came down the ladder, "G'day mate. How you going?"

"Awesome! How are you mate?" Cliff strode down the corridor, his shoes echoing on the freshly polished floorboards, and shook hands.

"Just replacing some of these light fittings. Lara's asked me to put in new ones she's found."

"Great. Well you can come back to it later. We're all going to grab lunch for a little celebration, so come along with us."

Cliff didn't wait for Dwaine to reply and headed to the bathroom to fetch Nick.

Fifteen minutes later they were seated around a chunky, timber table at the Stationmaster's Steakhouse an old-world country style restaurant, legendary in the area. Cliff had called Lara and Raj to join them and a moment later the 'awesome twosome' of Dougie the brickie and Mossie the chippie walked in grinning.

"Alright!" Mossie circled the table high-fiving everyone.

"Order whatever you want, alright," Cliff announced once they were all settled, "This is my shout and my thanks to you all."

"Wicked!" Dougie chuckled, rocking back in the tall-backed wooden chair, "Do they serve Grange here?"

Everyone laughed. Cliff held up his hands for silence, "Seriously, guys, I just want to say something. It's been a bloody hard patch for me. Fuck, it's been a bloody hard year. Stressful as. Some of you know more about what I've been through, no-one knows everything. But you've all stood by me. You've helped me in so many ways and I will forever be grateful. I've just turned the corner and things are looking up. Basically, I've secured a really, really important re-finance."

"Wow, it's gone through?" Raj looked delighted.

"Congrats mate, is it definite?" MJ was serious.

"Yep, I settled my overdue interest with ABC Wednesday. Paul sent everything through to Western Progressive straight away and I got a call from Seb this morning saying I've got the green light."

"That's amazing. Well done." MJ raised her beer glass.

Cliff held up a finger, "But wait, there's more. We've also… got a buyer for the first flip house!"

"What?" Dougie sat back.

"Really?" Lara smiled in disbelief.

"Yep. How good's that? We haven't even settled on it yet."

The expression on the faces of Dougie, Mossie and MJ's two landscaping mates made him explain further, "We've been doing all the renovations before we've even had to pay for the house, because I negotiated early access as part of the deal."

"That's ridiculous," Nick was confused but impressed. Dwaine shook his head and whistled.

"Yeah, that's even more ridiculous than you are normally. And you are normally pretty ridiculous," Raj kept a straight face as he held up his beer. The rest of the table broke out in laughter.

"It was actually your idea," Cliff smiled at Lara.

"Really? I don't think I did anything."

"Yeah, well it was your idea originally, but it just happened without us having to do anything. One of the club members wants to buy it."

"Wow! No way?"

"Yeah. One of the volunteers from the weekend loved it so much he wants to buy it. Reckons he would never have the time to do a fix-up himself so it's worth paying a bit more for it. He offered 230 and we agreed on 235."

"Didn't you want 250?" MJ looked concerned.

"I hoped we might get close. But when you think about it, this way we don't have to pay any agent fees, advertising, nothing. That's worth a lot. On top of it we have the sale in the bag before we've even settled. So there's almost no cost of funds and we can move right on and do another one. It's worth it!"

"Absolutely," Lara beamed, "So are you going to try and do more like that?"

"Yeah, why not. Next meeting I'll put the word out to Club members. If they're too busy and want a quick way of getting a property, nicely fixed up and ready to rent, they can buy direct from us. It's win-win!"

"Just the way you like it," Lara smiled.

"That's brilliant," Dougie was shaking his head.

Cliff held up his glass, "So I wanted to share all this with you. We're back on the bus again. Time to have some fun!"

He winked at Lara. Mossie whooped, "Yeah!"

They all reached in and clinked glasses.

Some distance away, behind Cliff and unnoticed by anyone at the table, a flat screen TV in the lobby of the restaurant blinked with a breaking news flash, in bold white text on a red graphics bar, 'Bear Stearns Bankrupt, Market Panics'.

TWENTY-ONE

It was a name that, until this moment, was unknown to all but a handful of Australians who worked in finance. It was certainly unknown to Cliff.

Now, however, it was all over people's TV screens as images of frightened New Yorkers, worried about their jobs, their life savings and their homes, were beamed into living rooms across the globe. Few understood what the fuss was all about. However, the impacts were swift. Stock markets tumbled across the globe as world leaders warned of a financial meltdown. The entire system, they said, was on the brink of collapse.

"They reckon it's the biggest fall since the Great Depression," MJ looked intently at Cliff from behind her laptop.

It was early Saturday morning at the flip house and a group had gathered in the garage to sip coffee and talk about the latest disturbing economic news.

"Well, we should just be glad we're not investing in shares, right?" Cliff tried to lighten the mood.

"You don't think property will go the same way?" It was Tom the American. "I mean in the US the whole property market's gone to pot, right?"

"In fact, it's the property market over there that has been the cause of all of this," Raj added.

"Completely different scenario," Cliff held up his hands. It was annoying how infectious negativity could be. He was convinced the Australian property market was not going to be affected by the hype and panic that had overtaken the financial world. He felt like he had good reason to be confident. He'd been following the blog of one of Australia's most successful property investors, Cam Richie, a guy Cliff had huge respect for. Just this morning Cam had posted about the 'financial crisis' and now Cliff used his arguments.

"The US caused this massive property bubble because their lending standards were basically shit. They don't have the government watching over them and keeping things under control like we do."

"True," Tom nodded.

"You know, our banks can't just loan to anyone. American banks were loaning to people who didn't even have a job or were already deep in debt without a hope of paying it off..."

Cliff hesitated for a moment, aware of the irony. Some might suggest this was exactly what Western Progressive had just done for him.

"That's what they were doing over there," he pushed ahead, "They were just, like, assuming the house prices would keep going up forever and they'd be able to keep on increasing their loans forever. Crazy stuff, you know?"

"Yeah, it's a mess," Tom shook his head.

"Over here," Cliff went on, "The banks have to assess people properly. You have to take out mortgage insurance if your deposit is less than twenty percent, right? You all know that. Banks here have to hold a lot more buffer in savings to balance what they're lending. It's a different story, you know? Much stricter, much safer."

Carlo, leaning against the wall of the garage, raised his coffee mug, "Yep, I listen to you, Cliffie, for all my news. Not the TV or the newspapers, all that bullshit. I mean, you have all the knowledge we need. Real knowledge."

The others chuckled in agreement.

Cliff was encouraged, "Thanks Carlo, old mate," he clinked coffee mugs with him, "I mean, house prices in Australia have gone up for good reason, right? We've got lots of immigration, our population is growing fast. Especially somewhere like Sydney. Everyone wants to be here, right? Plus, everyone's popping out babies…"

"Not wrong," MJ chuckled.

"There's no more land being released. Costs of building keep going up. So, of course the prices are gonna go up. In America, prices were only going up because everyone was betting on them, buying whatever and waiting to make a profit, thinking it's never gonna stop."

"It's like the tulips in Holland," Raj smiled cheekily.

They all looked at him, and almost in one voice went, "What?!"

Just then a truck rumbled into the driveway and hooted. It was the landscaping team arriving with the turf and shrubs for planting.

"Righto," MJ yelled as she sprang into action, opening the roller door. "Let's start unloading!"

The day had begun and Raj's tulips were long forgotten.

The outdoor working bee progressed with plenty of sweat and laughter but also an edge of concern that had not been there the previous weekend. Turf was laid, paths paved and garden beds planted with shrubs and finished with wood chips. Dougie and Mossie put the final touches to their deck with a set of steps and two coats of dark stain. It looked sensational. The painting team completed all the trims on house and garage and gave the front fence a fresh white finish. It was the neat belt and buckle that completed the 'outfit'. The house was all dressed up and looked bright, new and expensive.

Cliff was on the street in front of the house taking photos, when Lara and Raj pulled up in his family's van. They'd been to get drinks and snacks to celebrate the completion of the house.

"Wow, how many beers did you get," Cliff was taken aback, "That you needed the van for it?"

"Ha ha," Lara chuckled, "We got a little surprise for the house."

She pulled open the back doors of the van. Inside was a mini house all folded up.

"A cubby house?"

"Yeah! It was on Gumtree, if you pick it up, you can have it. That's why I had to take Raj!"

"Ok…" Cliff was not sure they needed this. After all, the house was already sold.

"Don't worry," Lara put on a grumpy face, "It didn't cost us anything!"

"Yeah but…"

"And I already checked with Mossie. He's happy to knock it together."

"Alright…"

She put an arm around his neck, "Come on, I was thinking it would be a nice little thing for Alfie. Something from us to make a happy first customer. You know how we always used to put in a little welcome pack for our tenants?"

"Yeah, right. Nice idea," Cliff nodded.

He'd forgotten those enthusiastic days when they enjoyed adding extra touches for the sheer pleasure of putting a smile on someone's face. He'd come a long way since then. Too much to deal with, too much stress.

"Then if he wants, Alfie can paint it himself," Lara pointed to the back of the van, "I found a couple of half-used tins of paint he can have."

"You're amazing, as always," Cliff put his arm around her waist and squeezed her. He felt truly blessed.

He jogged back in the front gate and halfway up the path to the open front door. "MJ! We need some hands unloading!"

Mossie was as good as his word. By the time everyone was gathered on the back deck with a drink in their hand, he'd assembled the cubby house with Dougie's assistance. Lara, Raj and a small group of volunteers had, in the meantime, prepared a rectangular area in the back corner of the yard, levelling it, laying sheets of weed mat and covering with left over wood chips. Cubby house now stood on its wood chip base and looked as cute as a hobbit home.

"Come on, I have to show you something," Lara led Alfie by the hand from the garage where he'd been talking to Cliff and MJ, "You two as well!"

"Ta da!" she gestured as Alfie came out onto the back deck.

Everyone cheered.

"A little gift from us to say congratulations on your first house, Alfie," Lara raised her glass, "Cheers!"

Alfie looked overwhelmed. Cliff patted him on the shoulder and shook his hand. "See you tomorrow for the big day, mate!"

Cliff got up early the next morning. It was settlement day for the flip house. Being in the remarkable position of having renovations completed and a buyer already in place, he'd come up with what he considered a brilliant plan. Late the night before he had discussed and eventually agreed on it with Alfie.

He would get Alfie to buy the house directly off the original seller, instead of buying it himself and then on-selling to Alfie. Alfie could pay the 190K to the original seller and then the additional 45K to Cliff to make up the 235K they had agreed on. What was brilliant about this was that they avoided paying stamp duty twice. It would save thousands. There were plenty of other smaller fees and charges they'd also avoid paying twice. Cliff had suggested to Alfie that they share all these savings 50-50.

"Sounds genius," Alfie had nodded, deep in thought.

So as soon as he'd poured himself a strong cup of coffee, Cliff sent an email to Garth asking him to contact the seller's solicitor and change the name on the contract. He knew it would throw a cat among the pigeons, but it was definitely worth it.

Crucially for Cliff, the new plan solved another tricky problem. Right at that moment he didn't actually have enough money to pay for the house. Since he'd used up most of the club investors' funds to pay off his interest at ABC Bank, and a little more to pay off his dad's debt, he was about 60K short. By getting Alfie to buy it directly, Cliff wouldn't have to find a single dollar. Instead, he'd receive his 45K from Alfie as pure profit. Some real cash in his hands at last.

He'd been hoping, of course, he would get the re-valuations through Western Progressive quickly enough to have all the funds he needed. However, since Wednesday, he had not been able to get hold of Seb. By Friday this had started to worry Cliff. Seb had always answered his calls promptly. He liked to think Seb was just busy, perhaps still processing all the revaluations. However, a little voice in the back of his mind was starting to nag at him.

As soon as it was nine o'clock, Cliff dialed Seb. Voicemail again.

"Hi Seb. Cliff Young. Keen to catch up mate. Give me a call please. It's been a few days now and I haven't heard back from you. Cheers mate."

"I hope he hasn't fucked off on holidays," Cliff thought out loud. He leaned his head back on the sofa, looking out the living room windows, across the front lawn to the streetscape beyond.

"What's that?" Mandy called out as she bustled into the kitchen, dressed smartly for work.

"Oh, just this Seb bloke at Western Progressive. I can't get hold of him and I need to make sure the revaluations have gone through."

"Oh, no, are you worried?"

"Not really. I mean he said they were all good. The ABC account's been paid up to date so there should be no issues there. Just funny he hasn't got back to me. I'm thinking maybe he's gone off on holidays or something without mentioning it. You know, typical bloody banker."

"Yeah, that'd be right," Mandy brightened up. She grabbed some bread from the fridge and put two pieces in the toaster.

Cliff's phone rang.

"That'll be him!" Mandy called out cheerfully.

"Hi, this is Cliff. Who? Oh, Alfie, how you going, old mate?"

"Yeah, not so good Cliffie," Alfie cleared his throat a couple of times.

"What's wrong mate?"

Mandy stopped rummaging in the fridge and looked over, alerted by the change in Cliff's voice.

"I'm really sorry Cliffie, but I'm going to have to pull out of the deal mate."

"What do you mean Alfie?"

"I'm freaking out, I'm sorry, this whole market crash has got to me. I was speaking to my accountant and he said I was mad to do it, in this market."

"Woah, hang on Alfie, don't let them stress you. Just calm down mate."

"No, no, Cliffie, I've decided. I'm sorry. I'm pulling out. I don't want to go through with it."

"Well, we've got a deal Alfie. I mean, we agreed on everything just last night."

"I know, I'm sorry mate. I was already freaking out yesterday, I just didn't know how to tell you."

"Ok, well let's talk about it sensibly, Alfie. You're panicking mate. There's nothing to stress about. You've thought this thing through for a long time. We've sat down, we've done the numbers with you, you know it all works. It's a great investment. Why would you want to listen to other people now? People who don't know how it works?"

"Sorry mate. It's just everyone is saying it. It's on the TV every night. The whole economy's crashing. I don't want to get caught in it. Not with my first one, I'll never get another chance."

"Well, what about me mate?" Cliff was suddenly incensed as he considered the implications of what Alfie was doing to him. If Alfie didn't go ahead with the purchase today, Cliff wouldn't have the necessary funds to settle with, and he might actually lose the house. That would be a disaster after they had put so much money and effort into fixing it up.

"I'm depending on you Alfie. I've set this whole deal up so it works for both of us. Today's settlement day. You can't pull out on settlement day."

"I know, I'm sorry Cliffie."

"Well you can't just be 'sorry'. You're leaving me in the shit. Excuse my French, but that's what you're doing."

"I know I'm stuffing you around mate, I'm sorry. I hope you can understand. This is my first one, I can't take the risk. You've made your millions. You'll get through this crash fine. I mean, you'll make even more millions, like you said. I just want to wait it out a bit, before I jump into the middle of a world economic crash. Please understand mate."

"Don't assume I can afford this, Alfie!"

Cliff took a breath. He knew he couldn't let the outside world know how much trouble he was in. That would scare away other club investors. He had to keep cool. Keep up the appearance that everything was rocking along smoothly.

"Listen, Alfie," he said calmly, "Take a moment and just have a little more of a think about it. No pressure, ok? I'll give you a call in an hour. I'm happy to come over and sit down with you and talk it all out. Ok?"

"I honestly don't need to, Cliffie, I've decided."

"Well, listen, just give yourself this chance to think it through. It's too good an opportunity to miss out on. To be honest, mate, you'll never get another one like it. You're getting the best deal we'll probably ever come up with. I was going to flip it for over 250."

"I know mate. I just -"

"Don't turn your back on it just yet. I'll come over and we'll talk it through ok? I don't want you to miss out just because you've been listening to the wrong people and panicking for the wrong reasons. Ok? Absolutely no pressure. If you still don't want to, that's fine. But don't throw this opportunity away without looking at the facts, properly. Ok?"

"Ok, sure, no worries. I'll talk to you in an hour, Cliffie. Thanks mate."

Cliff hung up. "Fuuuuck!"

He dialed Seb's number. Voicemail. "Fuck! Fuck! Fuck!"

"What's happened?" Mandy's hand was on his shoulder.

"He's fucking pulled out," Cliff thumped the cushions of the sofa.

"He can't. Can he?"

"Well, he can. Since we've never signed anything. Just a gentleman's agreement, you know."

"What a dick."

"Fuck yeah. I'm going to talk him around. He can't do this. Fuckwit!"

"I'm sorry I have to go to work darling," Mandy looked pained.

"I know, I know, it's fine. I'll be alright."

"Ok, well try not to stress too much." She kissed him on the top of his head.

"Thanks sweetheart," Cliff stared out the window.

Mandy picked up her laptop bag and headed for the door. Before going out she turned back, worry in her eyes. "I love you and I know you will be fine."

Cliff looked up and smiled weakly.

She blew him a kiss. "Love you."

Cliff's mind was elsewhere. He needed a plan if Alfie really did pull out. What a fuckwit. After all they'd done to make the house awesome for him. Truth to tell, if settlement fell through, it could be a total cluster fuck. The owner could just keep the house, all nicely renovated. Or put the price up. Fuck! He had to buy it somehow. He had to find the funds. Or another buyer...

There were some other Club members who'd expressed interest. It was a pretty good deal. But today?! It was crazy, no-one would be willing to jump in and buy it today.

Then there were the other potential investors. He and Lara had rung them all again on Thursday and Friday and the story had been the same every time. With the news of a crashing world economy, no-one was willing to take the risk. They all wanted to 'wait and see what happened.'

Settlement on the house would cost him 190K plus about 10K worth of other costs, so 200K total.

Club short term loans to date had totaled 650K. He'd used 500K to pay off his debts at ABC. And, of course, he'd used 10K to pay off his Mom and Dad's debt. That left 140K in the account. Roughly 60K short of what he would need if he couldn't turn Alfie around.

"60K, 60K, 60K… Argh!" he jumped up from the sofa and stomped into the kitchen for another coffee.

He'd run out of credit card options. He'd applied to every bank, building society or credit union he knew of, but not one of them approved a new card. ABC must have put warnings on his credit rating. He'd run out of friends and family too. Mainly because he'd got them all into debt as well, encouraging them to invest in properties.

He needed to know what Garth reckoned would happen if they tried to delay settlement. Determined, he crossed the room to grab his phone from the sofa. Just as he did, it rang. Seb!

"Hey Seb, how are you?"

"Hi Cliff. Sorry I haven't replied for a few days. There's been a lot going on here, as you can probably imagine."

"Yeah, of course mate," Cliff had not really thought about it, but yes, of course, Seb would be in the midst of the turmoil, at least as far as the Australian industry was concerned. It would probably be very hectic right now.

"I need to have a chat to you about recent developments. Can you come in?"

"Yeah, sure," Cliff's heart beat faster, this didn't sound good. "Is everything alright?"

"I can't really talk now. It would be best if we catch up face to face. Can you come in this afternoon by any chance?"

"Sure, any time."

"Say midday? Meet you at Jungle Café on the main street? It's just a block up from the office."

"Yeah, no worries. I'll see you there."

Two hours later Cliff walked up the main street of Bondi Junction. He passed the glass-fronted office tower of Western Progressive and kept going until he saw a timber sign for Jungle Café. It was a terrace house (one of the last few) that had been converted. A stone wall topped with a neat hedge enclosed a small courtyard. Here several people sat at round, metal tables, drinking coffee or eating lunch and chatting. The chairs were brightly painted in red, green and yellow and several African wood carvings poked out from between potted trees. Bob Marley jumped and jived, but not too loudly, over the sound system.

Indoors had a funky, lounge feel. Mismatching sofas and old-style armchairs creating alcoves. A zebra print rug covered the floor and the walls featured sepia photographs of colonial era Africa and a collection of animal horn trophies.

In the furthest corner he saw Seb, reading a newspaper, his legs crossed over as he leaned back in a tall armchair. He was amused to see Seb had a pair of dark glasses on. It was all very cloak and dagger.

Cliff walked up and held out his hand, "Hi mate, how you going?"

Seb put the newspaper down hastily and gestured Cliff to sit down in the armchair opposite. His manner was hushed and urgent and Cliff couldn't help obeying.

"Thanks for coming Cliff," Seb leaned in across the small coffee table that separated them.

"No problem," Cliff spoke quietly, caught up in the air of secrecy.

Seb looked at Cliff through his dark glasses, his face creased in regret, "There's no easy way of telling you this. So, I'll just get straight to the point, Cliff. My bank's gone."

"Hey?"

"Yep. Western Progressive no longer exists."

"Like, what do you mean?"

"You see, we were owned by a large US investment bank. Bear Stearns. You might have heard of it." Seb smiled bitterly.

"Holy shit. Seriously?"

"Oh yes. So, I, my friend, no longer have a job."

"You're kidding?"

"Nope. That's the way it rolls here."

"But, shit, how does a bank disappear overnight?"

"Well, it's not completely disappearing. It's been seized by administrators. All assets frozen. All staff will be stood down. It'll hit the news tomorrow."

"Wow."

"We at the top are under secrecy contracts. We're not allowed to tell anyone what's going on. We're even forbidden to call clients. They seized everyone's phones last week."

"What the..."

"Yep. It's heavy shit. I'm good mates with Freddy in security so he sneaked my sim back to me this morning. I wanted to call my best clients and warn them. I honestly like you a lot mate, and I knew you would be stressing out not knowing what was going on."

"Wow," Cliff shook his head, "Thanks." His stare became fixed, "Fuck."

"I'm sorry it's affected you mate. But I'm sure you'll be alright. You're a seasoned investor. Other banks will love you."

"I'm not so sure about that..."

"Come on, chin up, you'll be fine. You've got a hundred fucking properties!"

"Yeah, well it's more like the bank's got them right now. I mean what happens to the whole refinance thing?"

"It'll just fall through. You'll still be with ABC. Just go and find someone else to refinance you. Other banks will kill for your business. Surely?"

"Not so far, mate. I've tried other banks. You guys were the only ones."

"Oh shit, well, I'm sorry."

"Sure. Well, I'm sorry about your job buddy," Cliff knew Seb would be fine, he'd just move to another bank. He held out his hand and Seb shook it. Then Cliff had a thought.

"What about Bill? What's going to happen to him?"

"I can't talk about other clients, mate. But you should be able to work it out. We're shut down, everything's frozen."

Cliff felt a knife plunge through his heart. He was suddenly light-headed and felt like he couldn't breathe. As he got up, he swayed, grabbing the arm of his chair and falling back into it.

"You alright mate?"

"Yeah, I'm fine." He took a deep breath and lifted himself up again. With a nod to Seb, he made his way out of the café, side-stepping to narrowly avoid a waitress carrying a full tray of drinks.

As he drove back out west, Cliff called Bill. His call cut off as if Bill had hung up on him. He tried again and again but got Bill's voicemail each time.

"No, no, no," panic had begun to seize him. He noticed he was way over the speed limit and backed off the accelerator.

"We can do this. Keep cool. We can fucking deal with this."

He knew he had to catch up with Alfie and he remembered he lived somewhere near Winston Hills, north of Parramatta. He took the Cumberland highway exit and found a clearing on the side of the road to pull into. If he could at least get the sale of the flip house to go through, that would be one thing for today. Then tomorrow he could deal with the fact that he'd just lost his refinance and Bill may well have lost his funds to finish the construction of Blue.

"How you going, Cliffie," Alfie answered wearily.

"Yeah, not having the best day mate."

"Yep I'm sorry, I know I'm part of that."

"Sure, well let's get together and have a chat. We can still have a happy ending to your story, mate. At least I hope so."

There was only silence from Alfie. So, Cliff pressed on, "I'm on my way to you now, mate. I'm on the Cumberland. Can you give me directions?"

"Look, Cliffie, I have been thinking about it, like you asked, and the answer is the same. I'm out. Sorry mate."

"Come on, Alfie, let's just sit down and go over the figures. Remember, the only thing that matters is the numbers. You know that. This house was a great investment last week and it's still a great investment this week. Nothing's changed."

"I don't know how you can say that, mate. The fucking world economy just fell apart. Everything's changed. It's all fucking crashing down. They're saying it's like 1929, maybe even worse. You don't think that's going to affect my investment? Come on mate. Tenants aren't going to be able to rent it, nobody's going to want to buy it. I'll be stuck with it and the bank's going to come after me. I can't afford it. I don't have the buffer like you do. To ride it out or whatever."

"Alfie!" Cliff yelled at him. "Pull yourself together, mate! This isn't 1929. This is 2008. It's different. Don't believe all the bullshit. Fuck!"

"Righto mate, I'm going." Alfie hung up.

"What the fuck!" Cliff threw his phone down on the passenger seat with so much force it bounced back up and hit the windscreen, then the ceiling of the car and would have hit Cliff in the face if he didn't bat it away into the back seat.

He slumped forward, banging his forehead into the steering wheel, the pain only firing his anger. He furiously head butted over and over again, pain surging through his head until he could take no more.

"Aaaaargh!"

He stayed there, slumped over the wheel as his body convulsed in desperate sobs. Then he went limp and rested, losing track of time.

He became aware of a car pulling up next to him. He looked up and saw it was a police highway patrol. The cop behind the wheel and his partner in the passenger seat were staring at him. The partner got out and came over to Cliff, his boots crunching on the loose gravel.

"You alright buddy?"

Cliff wound down his window, "Yeah I'm fine thanks mate."

"What you doing?"

"Just making a call. You know, I pulled over so I could make the call."

"Sure buddy, but you looked like you were having a bit of a nap too. You feeling alright?"

"Yeah, I'm fine. Thanks."

The officer peered in through the back window and cast his eyes over the rest of the car.

"I'm going to give you a breath test. You know how this works?" He took the breathalyzer from his pocket.

"Yeah, sure, no worries."

"Good. I'll get you to blow in here until I say stop."

Satisfied with Cliff's zero reading the cops departed with a final stare. His head hurt and he felt pretty stupid. Most of all, he felt incredibly lonely. Cars rushed past and the great, flat expanse of Western Sydney stretched out to the horizon in every direction. Thousands and thousands of houses and people, not one of them knowing or caring that he was sitting here, in pain.

There was nothing to do but pull himself together and try to fix things. He took a deep breath and leaned back in his seat to ponder what to do next.

Settling the flip house was the immediate priority. If Alfie was no longer a buyer, then he had to find another one, or get his hands on 60K in a hurry. He remembered he'd been going to call Garth to see if he could delay the whole thing.

He reached into the back and found his phone on the floor. It had a crack through the screen where it had hit the windshield.

"Damn," Cliff regretted his earlier loss of control. The phone, however, was still working.

"Hi mate," he was calm now.

"Hi Cliff. I've been trying to call you. I got your email about changing the contract. That's going to be tricky."

"Don't worry about that. It's not happening. I just need to delay the whole thing. Can we? Just a couple of days?"

"Well, the trouble with that is we give the seller the option to pull out. Do you want to take that risk?"

"Not really, but I've got no choice."

"Ok, I'll contact the vendor's side. When can I tell them you'll settle?"

"Can we hold it to, say, Thursday?"

Cliff held a flicker of hope that he might get an investor or maybe even a buyer at the Club meeting on Wednesday night.

"Sure, I'll get onto it now."

"Thanks Garth. Sorry for the headache, mate."

"No problem. Look after yourself ok. Oh, and give Lara a call. I rang her looking for you, so I think she's a little worried."

As Cliff looked up Lara's number, he remembered something she'd said. The day he told her she no longer had a job. It set his mind racing. Would she?

"Hey Cliff, are you ok?"

"Yep, I'm fine. Well, not really. It's been an interesting day. Can I come over and see you? I need to ask you a big favour."

"Sure. Should I be worried?"

Somehow Lara always lifted his spirits. "Maybe," he chuckled, "I'll see you in half an hour."

Cliff pulled into the carpark of Lara's block of units in Penrith. He jumped out and bounded up the familiar concrete staircase. The door was already open, so he knocked on it, a playful rhythm, and stepped inside.

"There you are," she smiled at him from behind the kitchen bench. Sleeves rolled up to the elbows, she was busy chopping vegetables.

"You didn't have to make me dinner!"

She gave him a 'you're so funny' smile. "Actually, I was already making risotto. Why don't you stay and have some?"

"What, you mean you don't have a hot date coming over?"

"Not this time. So, I don't mind settling for you."

"You're so nice."

"Anytime," she smiled at him.

"Actually," he seized the opportunity, still so wired and keen to get on with fixing his crumbling world, "'Settling for me' is kind of what I've come to talk to you about..."

"Oh?" she gave him a puzzled look.

"Yeah, I'm in a shit hole right now."

"Yes, you look a wee bit stressed. What's happened?"

"Alfie's pulled out."

"What?"

"Yep."

"He can't do that, can he? Why?"

"He's scared of this whole financial crisis thing."

"Oh, come on, it's been going for ages now, the sky hasn't fallen in. Not for property investing, right?"

"Exactly. But he's been talking to someone, his accountant or whoever, and they've freaked him out. So, he's not buying it. I've done everything I can and he's refusing."

"The little fucker. He made a deal. Right?"

"Yeah, I know, but nothing was on paper. So, there's nothing I can do about it."

"Wow. Ok, so you need another buyer. Not me sorry!" She laughed but then noticed his face was serious.

"Well, not to buy it. But maybe to help me buy it," Cliff's eyes betrayed some of his desperation.

"Right... How?"

"You said you had saved enough for a deposit. I never, ever wanted to ask you this. But I have absolutely no other choice. Is there any chance you could lend it to me? Just for a couple of days?"

"Wow, you are in serious trouble, aren't you?"

"Yes. I just met up with Seb. Western Progressive has shut down. I've got no refinance."

"What the -?"

"Yep. They were American owned."

"Holy cow! The whole bank has closed down?"

"Yep, it will be announced tomorrow."

"Woah."

"So, anyway, if I don't settle today, I might lose the flip house. I'm short 60 grand. Is there any chance you have enough to loan me?"

Lara looked a little stunned. Cliff tried to reassure her, "I promise it's safe and I'll get it back to you straight away."

"Yes, ok, maybe… But I couldn't get it to you today. It's in an online savings account. I'd have to transfer it out to my main account first."

She looked at her watch, "It's before 4, so if I did it now, I would get it by tomorrow. Would that work?"

"It's better than any other option I've got," Cliff looked like he was about to fall to his knees, he opened his arms, "Thank you. Thank you so much."

Next morning Cliff lay on his sofa, staring at the ceiling. He hadn't slept all night, his mind too busy. Eventually he'd stumbled from bed to the sofa so he wouldn't keep Mandy awake with his restlessness.

By now she had gone to work and he knew it must be pretty late. His head throbbed and his body ached. He closed his eyes, trying to get some rest. But it was no good, he just started thinking about his portfolio again. What was he going to do? He had a hundred properties. He'd borrowed on average 275K against each of them. But none of them would sell in the current market for much more than 225K. If he was lucky. If the bank made him sell them all at once, then they'd go for a lot less. He knew only too well, he'd been going to the foreclosure auctions himself.

The situation was desperate. He had never been without any answers. The shortfall between the rent that his houses earned and the interest he had to pay was about 80K each month. Without a refinance he had no hope of covering it. He'd have to flip two houses a month, making at least 40K profit on each. But now, with the financial market in chaos, speculation of more US and European bank failures on the news every night, prophets of doom forecasting a world-wide depression, that was surely impossible.

Of course, once he could sell – or rent out – his units at Blue, the situation would get better. But what was happening with Blue? He swung his legs off the sofa and stood up painfully. Zombie-like he made his way to where his mobile phone was charging on the kitchen bench. He switched it on and as soon as a network connection was made, it beeped to tell him there were messages.

"Yep, I know," he grumbled. He dialed voicemail.

"Hi Cliffie, it's me, give me a call hon." It was his mum. He waited for the next message.

"Hi Cliff. Dermott here from ABC Bank. Give me a call please, it's urgent. Thanks."

"Fuckwit." Cliff hit delete.

"Hey Cliff, Tom here from the club. I sent you guys an email. I need to get my investment back in a little bit of a hurry, bud. Give me a call please."

"Shit. That's all we need," Cliff was alarmed. He realized he hadn't checked his email since the morning before. He thought about waking his laptop and having a look, but the idea of finding any more problems only made him feel sick.

He looked at the time. It was 9:45. He had more than 2 hours before meeting Lara at the bank. He decided to visit his mum and dad.

"Why don't you call before you come?" His mum seemed flustered.

"It's nice to feel welcome," Cliff teased.

"What are you here for? You know your dad's already gone up the TAB with his mates."

"Really? It's early, even for him."

"Yeah, well he spends most of his life up there now. Ever since all this stuff with the houses. It's beyond me."

"Geez, I thought I'd sorted everything for him."

"Nothing is ever sorted with him. Why don't you come into the kitchen and you can talk to me there. I've got a lot to do this morning," she turned and led the way.

"Okie dokie. What are you doing? A party?"

"Don't be stupid. When do we ever have parties?"

Cliff sat on the edge of the breakfast table and watched his mum as she began to empty the contents of the cupboard beneath the sink. She stacked the bigger items next to the fridge. There was a metal bucket crammed full of gloves and rags and a large carton of cleaning products which must have been a bulk purchase. The smaller bits and pieces she piled on the kitchen bench where Cliff could see she had already been emptying other cupboards of plates, bowls, mugs, cups and a multitude of plastic containers, large and small, their lids piled into a salad bowl.

"Spring cleaning?"

"The place is a disgusting mess. Someone has to clean up. No prizes for guessing who."

"Can I give you a hand?"

"No don't be silly. You don't come over here to do the cleaning. Do you want a cuppa?" She picked up a yellow striped mug from the sea of crockery on the bench.

"Sure, thanks. I got your message. So, I came over instead of calling you back."

His mum filled the kettle and flicked it on. "Next time just let me know. Then I won't be in the middle of cleaning," she smiled at him.

"Yeah, no worries. Life's been a bit stressed lately."

"Oh dear."

"I'm still deep in shit with all the properties. Just seem to get deeper and deeper."

His mum looked at him for a moment, grave concern in her eyes. Cliff could see she wanted to say something. Instead, she smiled, "I'm sure you'll dig yourself out. You're good at that."

"I don't know. Maybe not this time." He felt his throat tighten, "I think I'm fucked this time to be honest."

"Oh, come on, don't be negative. You're different. You've got get up and go. Not like some people," she indicated with her head towards their bedroom.

Cliff understood who she meant. "You know, the dumb thing is I think I just wanted to show him there was another way, you know? Show him it was possible to get out of this shit. I think I just wanted him to be proud of me."

"I'm sure he is, underneath it," his mum smiled weakly, lifting the kettle to pour his tea. As she did so, her shirt sleeve slipped up her arm, revealing dark patches of blue, yellow and grey bruising.

Cliff was shocked, "What have you done to your arm?"

"What?" she hastily put the kettle down and stepped back. Cliff, however, was there in a flash and reached out for her arm.

"Let me see."

"Okay, okay," she pulled her sleeve up, exposing heavy bruises all the way from her elbow to her shoulder.

"I slipped when I was cleaning the bathroom and fell against the door."

"Rubbish, let me see," Cliff was sure he had seen the shape of a hand print in the bruising. "Did he do it to you?"

"No, don't be stupid. Come on, drink your tea," she pulled her sleeve back down, turning away to fetch milk from the fridge.

"Mum?"

She spoke, her voice lowered, as she added milk and sugar to his mug, "Don't worry, alright. I'm big and ugly enough to look after myself. Always have been, always will be." She handed him his tea.

"If he hurts you mum, seriously, I'll rip his head off."

"It's ok, just drop it!" she hissed at him.

Cliff was shaken but he could see she didn't want to talk about it. He sat back down on the breakfast table and took a sip from his mug.

"Fucking hell," he shook his head, "As if I don't have enough to worry about already. Have you noticed any of the news lately? The stuff happening in America? One of the big banks went under? Everyone's panicking? Well, I'm a victim of all that shit happening over there."

"Well, if it isn't the real estate tycoon," his Dad's phlegmy voice rasped from behind him.

Cliff turned to see him standing in the kitchen doorway, dressed in long pyjama bottoms and a white singlet.

"I thought you were out?"

"Well you thought wrong. I've been listening to your wimping and whining all morning. Things not working out, hey?"

"No, they're not," Cliff stared at him. He could smell the alcohol across the room. It must have been a big one last night.

"Well, you're not going to be any use with this then," Cliff's dad waived a piece of paper.

"What is it?"

His dad held out the paper, "Go ahead."

"We weren't going to say anything," his mum glared from the kitchen.

"Well he might as well, he's the one got us into it."

Cliff looked at the paper. It was a letter from ABC Bank. They had lowered the valuation of his dad's investment property and were demanding he decrease his loan by fifty thousand dollars immediately to cover it. This would bring the 'loan-to-value ratio' down into the new, acceptable limit. If he didn't, they would foreclose within one week.

"What the-?" Cliff was furious. "They can't do that!"

"Well they are. None of your smart tricks, not even your fancy lawyers' letters, none of it's going to stop them. They want our house and they're going to take it. It was fine before because Pops paid it all off. We were out of the system. They couldn't touch us."

There was utter disgust on his dad's face, "Then you came along, with your naïve little plans, your dreams of being rich. Signed us up with the banks again. Let them get their meat hooks into us… and here we are. They sucked you in good, didn't they? You wanted so badly to be better than everyone else, didn't you? Show us all how good you are and how fucked we are. Well, my little matey, they chewed you up and now they've spat you out. And thanks for fucking it up for the rest of us too."

Cliff couldn't take another word. He leapt off the table grabbing his dad around the neck, slamming him into the wall behind him. Jaw set, eyes popping, he hissed, "I saw mum's arm."

He pushed his dad away violently, turned and stormed out the front door, down the steps and out the front gate.

Cliff pulled into the parking behind Standard Building Society. He was early for Lara, so he tried Bill again. Still no answer. He shot him a text, "Hey mate, call me ASAP. I spoke to Seb."

"Why can't he just call me and tell me what the fuck's happening?"

Cliff sighed and leaned back in his seat, staring up at the ceiling of the car. Bill had already received his refinance from Western Progressive, so fingers crossed he had taken the funds and was still pushing ahead to completion. Maybe he was just flat out busy. That would be great.

His phone rang. He picked it up and stared at the screen. It was Tom. Eventually he put it back down on the passenger seat and let it continue ringing.

"Sorry Tom, I just can't right now," he closed his eyes and waited for the ringing to stop.

At last Lara turned up.

"How did you go?" he asked hopefully.

"Yep, all good," she smiled at him, "I got a cash cheque for 60 grand. More than I ever carried in my purse before. So, look after it ok!"

She laughed but Cliff could see the concern in her eyes.

"Let's go and see spiky," Cliff nodded in the direction of the bank.

"Oh yes, the manager here? She's hilarious isn't she!"

"Actually, the whole place is fucking weird. I had a feeling it was your little joke."

"Would I do something like that? I thought green was your favourite colour?"

Lara chuckled and headed off at pace, leaving Cliff to catch up with her.

TWENTY-TWO

Cliff was incredibly nervous. He used to look forward to Club meetings more than anything else. Now he felt the desperation of a salesman about to approach his last potential customer, all or nothing.

He nodded to MJ who clicked over to the all-important slide, a large photo of the completed flip house:

'Exclusive Opportunity: All Done!'

"Yes, yes, yes. Good evening everyone," Cliff turned on the charm.

"This is very, very special. A unique opportunity for Club members only."

As he smiled at the many familiar faces in his audience, he was pleased to see there was no sign of Alfie. He really didn't want him here tonight, telling everyone he'd pulled out of the first flip purchase and spreading his fears. He also didn't want him telling people how upset Cliff had been about it. It wasn't a good look.

Tonight, he needed to promote the flip houses and try and get a new buyer as quickly as possible without letting on how urgent it really was for him.

He knew there would be a lot of concern over the state of the economy, after the Bear Stearns collapse and the doomsday forecasts in the media. He had to allay these fears.

"Yep, tonight is all about bringing positive back. Who's sick and tired of all the negativity?"

Some hands went up, tentatively.

"Yeah, come on, who's had enough of the doom and gloom? Market crashes and everything? Who wants to get back on track to positive thinking?"

Cliff raised his own hand, nodding encouragingly. Now more and more hands went up until it looked like everyone had joined in, faces lighting up in smiles.

"That's it," Cliff smiled back at them, "The sky hasn't fallen in. Doesn't it make you mad how the media loves to turn every little problem into a major catastrophe? Well, I'll tell you one thing for sure, every cloud has a silver lining. Every market crash is an investment opportunity. Yeah?"

Heads nodded and a voice called out, "Yep, you're spot on, Cliffie."

"Oh yeah. No-one's denying there are challenges right now. We know that. But you have to keep going. Right? And the best way to keep going is to stay positive. To look for the opportunities. That's why we're pushing ahead with the short term loans. What a great opportunity, yeah? And now… we're launching another opportunity."

Cliff pointed to the screen behind him.

"You've got to be bold. Balls of steel, right?" he chuckled and a ripple of laughter went through the audience.

"When times are tough, you step up. Right now, is when the next generation of successful investors is being born. Our next multi-millionaires are out there, right now, buying properties, planting the seeds of their fortunes. To win, you have to act when everyone else is shitting themselves. You have to go against the herd, right? It might feel scary, but deep down you know it's true."

He'd made this point enough times in the past that now, when it was most relevant, he was sure they would go with him.

"That's exactly what Cliffies Climbers are doing. Pushing ahead, creating opportunities when others are too scared to act. I'm very proud to tell you that we've finished the first flip house. Who's been involved in the renovation weekends? Put up your hands."

A good scattering of hands went up. Cliff gave them a clap and the audience followed with hearty applause.

"I'm going to show you the photos and then we'll talk about how you guys can pick it up, one hundred percent complete, beautifully renovated and ready to go, for an exclusive, Club-only, below-market deal."

MJ clicked over to the next slide, a 'before' shot of the kitchen from the living room, dodgy brick archway and all.

"Here we go," Cliff chuckled, "Great look."

He nodded to MJ who clicked to the 'after', wall removed, sparkling kitchen with section of French doors opening to the new deck.

"How about that?"

More applause. Cliff was encouraged and nodded to MJ. They stepped through before and afters of all the rooms and multiple angles on the exterior, the new deck and the cute backyard. Each transformation greeted with applause.

When MJ eventually returned to the 'Exclusive Opportunity: All Done!' slide, the room hummed with excitement.

Carlo stood up in the front row, pointing to the screen, "Buy it people! Bloody worth it. I know, I painted it myself."

His friends laughed and someone called out, "Great job, Carlo."

"Yep," Cliff nodded, "Good work, Carlo, you're a bloody legend. Everyone who worked on it is. Thank you all. An amazing job."

He waited for the congratulations and merriment to settle before continuing, "Now, like I said, we're giving Club members the first chance to buy it. Why? Because you might be waiting to get into the property market, but you just bloody well don't feel like doing all that work. Right?"

There were several nods of agreement and a man in the back row clapped enthusiastically, a big grin on his face.

"Not only that, but if you want to act very quickly, there is a one-off opportunity to reduce a bunch of buying costs and get it for a very, very good price. Come and see me if you're keen."

The presentation finished with a loop of 'bloopers' from the renovation. Many featuring Dougie and Mossie mucking around with power tools, pulling silly faces and generally being idiots. At the end of the slide show, their circle of friends kicked off a chant:

"Dougie-Mossie, Dougie-Mossie…"

Cliff clapped along and when it finished, he thanked Dougie and Mossie and everyone else for their help on the project, bowed, waved and left the stage.

As he packed up, a familiar voice called out, "Hi there, Cliff."

It was Tom. Cliff felt terrible for ignoring his calls. He tried his best to hide his guilt behind an effusive smile, "Hi Tom, how are you?"

"Pretty good thanks Cliff. Listen, do you have a moment to chat?"

"Yeah, of course mate."

"I've been trying to get a hold of you the last couple days. I guess you've been pretty busy."

"Yeah, I have, sorry mate. I've been a bit hammered actually."

"Sure. Well, look, sorry to add another thing to your list, but I need to get my investment funds back. I know you haven't sold the flip house yet, but just hoping you won't miss a little old fifty grand too much. See, my brother's family, back in California, they've been caught up in all this subprime stuff, you know, real estate's crashed something terrible over there. Anyway, he's got a couple of little kids now and he's going to have to walk away from his house, you know, his family home. I want to help him out, you know. I mean when it comes down to it, family is a lot more important than making a piece of extra dough here, right?"

"Yeah, sure mate. It shouldn't be a problem," Cliff felt a hollow in the pit of his stomach. He knew the investor account was empty, the last remaining funds committed to settling the flip house. He had to find a buyer first or get another investor on board to replace Tom ASAP.

"Might take a couple of days, mate, for us to move funds around, but we'll sort it. Ok?" Cliff smiled, trying his best to look untroubled.

"Great thanks Cliff. If you could try and do it as soon as possible, my brother is in a pretty desperate situation."

"Yeah, I understand," Cliff couldn't look at Tom. An unbearable exhaustion over-riding any empathy he might have felt. He continued to pack up. "Actually, if you could send Lara an email, just with all the details, you know, that would be great. We need to keep a track of things that way."

"I already did. I sent you both an email yesterday. You should have it."

Cliff smiled sheepishly, "Oh ok, no worries, I'll ask her to get onto it. Thanks Tom."

He held out his hand. Tom shook it, then turned and left, a little uncertain.

"Hi Cliff."

It was an enthusiastic voice. Cliff looked up to see a boyish young man, with dark, neatly brushed hair and a broad, white-toothed smile. He wore a neat, dark-blue, collared shirt, sunglasses slung around his neck.

"Robbie Simons, and my brother Des," the young man gestured to another young guy, of similar height and features, just a little skinnier, standing behind him.

Robbie held out his hand confidently and Cliff shook it, "Nice to meet you Robbie."

"Likewise, Cliff, likewise. That's a great talk you give."

"Thanks very much," Cliff smiled.

"Really simple, basic stuff." Robbie made a show of looking around and lowering his voice, "So even someone from Mount Druitt would get it, right?"

He and Des laughed. Cliff didn't.

Robbie realized he may have said the wrong thing and became serious, furrowing his brow, "Do you get many people from Mount Druitt coming along?"

"Well, I'm from Mount Druitt," Cliff smiled.

"Yeah, great."

"And most of the original Club members are from Mount Druitt,"

Cliff began to gather his things.

"That's excellent," Robbie nodded, smiling awkwardly.

He cleared his voice and re-gathered himself.

"I wanted to ask you about the house that's for sale."

"Oh yeah?" Cliff put his bag back down.

"Yeah, we invest in the area and would be interested. It looks good."

"Really? Sure."

"Great. Are you taking offers?"

"Absolutely."

"Fantastic!" Robbie turned to his brother, "Des have you got that report mate?"

Des smiled and pulled a small bundle of paper out of his briefcase, "Yeah mate, all here."

Robbie put it down in front of Cliff. "See here, Cliff, we get this from our agent contacts in the area. It's perfectly up to date. A great snapshot of exactly what's happening in the market. Have a look at these houses. It's everything sold in Lethbridge Park and the three nearest suburbs over the last month."

"Oh yeah? Agent's sales report, hey?"

"Yep, we compile them all into one document, add in extra information we gather ourselves, plus the photos. Makes for a perfect picture."

"Hmm, very good work," Cliff was impressed with their diligence. "Have you been coming to the Club for long?"

"Nope, first night tonight. We figured all this stuff out for ourselves. It's pretty basic."

"Good for you."

"Check this out though, down the bottom. It's the averages. So, here you go, average house in Lethbridge Park is selling for just under 200K. Yours is fibro, not brick, right, so below average. Now, I know you've done a bit of a fix up, but like you said you did it on a minimum budget. So, at best let's say the place is worth 200K. Then, when you consider you won't have to pay any agent's marketing fees if we buy it directly off you, you save almost ten grand there. Let's split the saving and we'll offer you 195K." Robbie beamed.

Cliff was staring at the sales report, unable to look at Robbie. He was aware that a small group had gathered around, looking over the brothers' shoulders, waiting for Cliff's response. Meanwhile, Raj and Lara had stopped what they were doing and come over to investigate.

"We're not looking to sell wholesale, mate. 'Robbie' wasn't it?" Cliff eyeballed him. He hadn't really gone blank on his name, just buying time.

"Yeah, Robbie."

"Right, see Robbie, we're going for a retail sale with this one. It's a different market. Different figures. You're looking for a wholesale purchase. That's sort of what we do."

"A house is a house, though. A sale is a sale, right? I mean everyone's actually in the same market."

"Sure, but your way of pricing is a wholesale way. That's what we do. We're not looking to make a wholesale transaction."

Robbie's searching eyes and bright smile were relentless, like a blinding spotlight on a reluctant actor.

"Anyway," Cliff needed to get out of the light, "I've got to go. Thanks for the offer, but it's not a price we would take. Go out to the auctions, put in the hard yards with the agents and I'm sure you'll get your price. Best of luck with it."

He smiled at Robbie, picked up his things and headed for the exit.

In the carpark, Lara and Raj came running over to him.

"Wow, who was that guy?" Lara's brows knitted, incredulous.

"Fucking idiot."

"What was his story?" Raj looked confused.

"He sits there, through the whole presentation, learns everything we do, then he comes over and fucking tries to do it to us. What a dickhead."

"Wasn't he dissing Mount Druitt as well," Lara asked, a defiant look on her face.

"Yeah. Total dick. Hey, do me a favour. He must have signed up tonight to come in. Cancel his membership."

"Sure."

"Send him an email saying sorry it was only a temporary membership or something. Just for one meeting. But actually, we're full at the moment, not taking any new members. Can you make something like that up?"

"Of course, leave it with me."

"Thanks darl. Sorry I have to go. My head is bursting. I think the stress is getting to me."

"Sure, no worries, take care. Get a good night's sleep."

Raj still looked worried. Before Cliff could drive off, he tapped on his window, getting him to wind it down.

"Do you think that report's right? Do you think the prices have already dropped that much?"

"I don't know, Raj. I can't think about it right now. I'm sure he's full of shit."

"You would know, though, wouldn't you?" Lara was surprised.

"Well, I've been a bit too busy to look, lately. MJ will know, we can check with her. She'll have all the up to date stuff. Now I've got to go, sorry guys. Goodnight."

"Goodnight Cliff," Lara waved.

"See ya mate," Raj's eyes were dark with concern.

The streetlights passing overhead had a dim, orange glow. They gave the deserted streets, not a soul to be seen for block after block, mile after mile, an otherworldly feel. It was not, however, strange to Cliff. It had always been his world.

He turned into Ghostgum Crescent, a gently curving suburban street that led into the heart of Dharruk, an outer-lying suburb of Mount Druitt. He pulled up outside a house with a metal hoop fence on top of a low, brick retaining wall. In daylight you would be able to see the bright red and yellow roses that bloomed along the fence line. At night they were dark grey shadows. The street was quiet and only a few lights were on in the surrounding houses.

Cliff sat for a while, looking out at the house, a deep and hollow grief welling inside him. This was his first investment property. He remembered how his first tenants had asked to plant the roses. He'd been so impressed that he'd come and helped them. Together they had suffered the thorns but enjoyed a lot of laughs as well. Peter and Ruth. Cliff remembered how sad he'd been when Ruth became ill and they had to move to Geelong to be close to their son. He didn't know who his tenants were now. His agent handled everything, and Cliff just signed the paperwork.

Yep, there was the small veranda at the front, he'd painted all the trims himself. The brick-lined garden beds they'd built with their bushy Aussie natives still growing happily. He remembered the joke his mates had played on him, making him cut up the mattress under the house with a chainsaw, in terrible fear of rats. Such good, simple fun. The big weekend, everyone working hard all day and celebrating just as hard at night. What a great job they'd done. What a good time it had been.

Now, it might have been for nothing. He looked at the familiar line of the roof, the eves and gutters he'd also painted himself. This was the one, the foundation of his entire portfolio, the beginning of his incredible journey to owning a hundred houses. Yet if he didn't get out of the very deep hole he was in right now, he would lose every single one of them.

Despite the cheerful response of his audience, the night had shown him one thing clearly. With investors like Tom getting nervous and wanting their money back, and sharks like the two brothers circling, he had zero chance of flipping his way out of debt. So, it all came down to Blue. Bill had to finish it so Cliff could sell his units and pay down the worst of his debts. He had no options left, no crafty way out.

The trouble was, he couldn't get hold of Bill. It was infuriating. He looked at his phone. Midnight. Why not? He dialed Bill's number. It rang several times, then clicked over to his far too familiar voicemail.

"Come on Bill," Cliff let loose, "Answer the fucking phone mate.

Aargh! I just want to know what's going on. That's all. Call me."

He hung up and tossed the phone back on the passenger seat. Then, fired up, he put the car in gear, did a three-point turn and headed for Birchgrove.

When he got to Blue, he was pleased to see that progress had been made. The crane had moved from his Phase 1 block to above Phase 2 which was now two stories high. It looked like Phase 1 might be complete, at least structurally. That would be great.

Cliff drove past the tall wire gates at the entry to the site and a little way up the street, turned around and parked amongst other cars, in a spot where he could see anyone coming or going from the site. He pushed his seat right back and settled in to wait. He didn't know what else to do. Hopefully, come the morning, someone would arrive.

Next thing he knew, he was jolted awake by a loud rumbling and heavy vibration that made the whole car shake. He must have fallen asleep. Now the bright, early morning sun stabbed his eyes. He turned to the side, shielding his eyes and discovered the source of the noise and vibration. A gigantic truck and trailer had come to a stop right next to him, its huge wheel towering as high as the roof of Cliff's car. He couldn't see much else, but he could make out voices shouting above the sound of the engine. Eventually the truck began moving again and slowly it swung into the gates of Blue's building site.

"Fantastic," Cliff thought, "there's some action."

He watched as the truck drove in and disappeared over the rise. Two workers in fluro yellow overalls waived it on from their positions, like sentries, either side of the gates. They didn't shut the gate, however, and after only a minute or so another truck, also with an empty trailer rumbled down the narrow street and swung into the building site. Once it was inside the two guys began closing the gates.

Cliff leapt out of the car and headed in their direction, hoping to catch them before they disappeared into the building site. Just as he did so, a white ute arrived from the opposite direction to the trucks and hooted. The two fluro guys stopped closing the gates, waived to the driver and hastily swung them open again. Cliff's heart raced. He recognized the ute with its enclosed tray and oversized wheels. As he jogged closer, he could read the decal on the driver side door, 'BG Constructions.' BG stood for Bill Goodman.

"Bill!" he yelled out, but the ute drove off, over the rise and disappeared. The two workers looked up but continued to shut the gates.

"Hey, how you going, fellas," Cliff called out as he approached, puffing for breath, "I got to catch up with Bill."

The taller one, closing the gate on the left, stepped in front of Cliff putting a hand on his chest, "Who are you mate?"

"Uh, I'm Cliff. Cliff Young. Bill knows who I am."

"Sure mate. Look, I can't let you in without authority. Just wait here a sec, ok?"

With that he finished closing the gate, leaving Cliff standing outside, and locked the chain. The two workmen strolled off up the hill.

Cliff called after them, "Will you let him know I'm here?"

Without turning around the taller man called back, "Yeah mate."

They disappeared over the rise.

Cliff waited an hour, pacing back and forth. He tried calling Bill every few minutes, getting voicemail each time. He could hear voices from the building site and the sounds of engines starting up and vehicles moving. Not a word, however, from Bill. He decided to climb the gate. Remembering his previous experience, he jogged back to the car for some old towels he kept in the boot. They should provide a little protection from the barbed wire.

Back at the gate he was about to throw the first towel carefully into place, when he heard voices approaching. He stopped and waited. Eventually three hard hats popped up over the rise, followed by three heads and eventually three bodies. One of them was Bill. The other two were the workers who had closed the gate on Cliff.

As Bill approached, he chatted to his two mates, looking everywhere but at Cliff. When they got to the gate they stopped and made no attempt to open it. Finally, Bill looked at Cliff, squinting in the bright morning sun.

"G'day mate," he didn't smile.

"Hi Bill. How's it going?"

"Depends what 'it' is. The price of tomatoes is alright, I've heard." His two mates laughed.

Cliff tried to smile but only looked peeved. "Come on, just tell me what's happening. I've been trying to call you for days."

"You certainly have been," Bill didn't look amused but the other two chortled again.

There was an awkward silence. Eventually Bill spoke.

"Alright, sorry mate. I've had the week from hell, that's all. You're not the only one who's been trying to get me. In fact, you're about number 180 on the list."

"I'm just your biggest customer. And I thought, your mate."

"Forgive me, I didn't mean it that way. I would have called you if I could have. I was going to. Just didn't get there."

"So, what's happened? I met with Seb. He's told me about the bank going under. That's the end of my refinance. What about yours? I was hoping you might have secured your funds."

Bill squinted at Cliff and shook his head slowly, "Nope."

"Fuck. Really?"

"Yep. They froze everything that day. Not a chance for us."

"So, what does that mean? You can't finish?"

"That's why these trucks are here. Everyone's pulling their gear out. It's over. So fucking close."

"You're kidding?"

"Nope. You can see for yourself. Phase 1 is almost done. Phase 2 only has the top floor to go. A few weeks away, mate. A few weeks away."

"Fuck," Cliff looked at Bill, he felt shaky, his last strength dissolving. "Fuck, fuck, fuck," he shouted at the sky, before his voice trailed off and he had to grab hold of the gate for support.

He looked up at Bill, who had a sympathetic face. "You know if you're done, I'm done too right?"

"'Course I know that, mate."

"Shit. So fucking close. There's got to be a way. Won't people finish it on credit? Surely? If you're only weeks away."

"No credit left mate. No-one's giving it now. You've seen the almighty cluster-fuck that's going down in America. Everyone's pooing their pants mate."

"Fuck, man, come on. Have you tried? There's got to be a way. Maybe another bank?"

"Nope. I've tried them all. Banks are all the same mate. They're your friend when everything's good. Soon as there's a sniff of a problem, they're not interested. It's just the way it is, mate, I'm bankrupt. I'm finished here. No point crying over it."

Cliff sighed. So, this was it. He looked at Bill, but he had nothing to say. Cliff felt his dizziness coming on again. He half raised a hand to wave, muttered "Okay", turned and made his way back to his car.

Cliff sat in the driver's seat unable to move. He wanted to cry, he wanted to yell in anguish, but he had no energy for either. He wanted someone to help him, someone to come along and say, 'Hey, I've fixed it, it's all going to be okay.' But there wasn't anyone. It was over and he just wanted to fade away.

He watched, numb, as the first big truck drove out of the building site, carrying a large, yellow bulldozer on its trailer. A little while later, the second truck left, with two scissor lifts sitting on its trailer. Finally, Bill and his workmen left, chaining up the gate behind them. Time passed, but nothing more happened.

Cliff had no idea what he should do, or where he should go. He didn't care. He didn't know what time it was and he couldn't be bothered to look. He could tell that most of the day had gone and the sun was starting to get lower in the west.

Eventually, he was moved by an impulse to have one last look at Blue. The towels were still scrunched in a bundle on his lap, so he took them and made for the gates. He pulled himself up and over, oblivious to the barbs that stuck right through the towels, piercing his hands, arms and legs.

Once inside, slowly, almost deliriously, he made his way up and over the rise and down towards Phase 1.

"It's like I'm drunk," he muttered to himself, aware that he was swaying and stumbling as he went.

The site was quite different now. Where there had once been a grey, concrete shell rising out of a dusty, tire-trammeled patch of dirt, there was now a complete unit block. The driveway was not yet paved, but it curved elegantly beneath an impressive, L-shaped awning, held up by sandstone pillars. Tall, glass doors, set in bronze frames led into the marble-tiled lobby. From the driveway, Cliff could see through them, right across the lobby to the blue water of the harbour beyond.

He was surprised to find one of the glass doors unlocked, so he pushed it open and stepped inside. The lobby was cool, yet bathed in light from the two-story high, glass façade that faced the harbour. Cliff was impressed, it felt like a five-star resort. And it was so agonizingly close to complete. Only minor details remained. The lift doors were taped up and Cliff could see where various fittings, such as lights and switches were missing, their wires poking out of holes in walls and ceiling.

He made his way up the stairs. The first unit was open and he went in. Here he found there was a little more to be done. Empty spaces in the kitchen waited for the oven, cook top and other appliances. A row of ceiling panels was missing and lengths of shiny, alloy air-conditioning ducting lay piled against a wall. In every other respect, it was a magnificent apartment, with incredible views through its glass balcony doors, and kitchen and bedroom windows.

"So close, so fucking close."

The next two floors were in similar condition, except the tiling had not been completed in kitchens and bathrooms and fittings like toilets, basins, shower screens and vanities sat in cardboard boxes on the landing. The balcony of the top floor unit had not been finished, hazard tape running across the glass doors. It was all bare concrete with only a makeshift railing of roughly bolted scaffold bars.

Cliff pulled the tape aside and stepped out.

"Wow."

Elbows on the temporary railing, his chin in his hands, he absorbed the expansive harbour. He noticed a small, black speedboat bouncing across the swells, leaving a long, white wake. It reminded him of the afternoon he'd taken Mandy out on a water taxi to show her Blue and tell her his exciting news.

Despair welled up inside him at the thought. "How can everything turn to shit so fast?"

He realized he hadn't called Mandy since staying out all night. She would be worried. He pulled his phone from his pocket, where he'd ignored it all day. There was a long log of missed calls. Yep, Mandy had rung four times and sent a bunch of text messages. So had many others, including Tom, MJ, Lara, Dermott and several numbers he didn't recognise.

His thumb hovered over Mandy's contact, but he couldn't do it. He couldn't face her. How could he tell her what had happened and how he felt right now? He didn't want sympathy and he didn't want to be cheered up. She had never really understood the scale of what he was trying to do. She certainly never knew the extent of his struggle over the last year or how deep in trouble he was. How could he ever convey the desperation he felt right now?

"I'm done. I'm gone. People only have one shot in life," his face contorted in despair, "I've had mine and I fucked it up. I'll never get another one like this, no way."

Who could understand failure on such a grand scale? He'd always enjoyed impressing Mandy. How could he tell her he'd lost everything and was back to being what he'd always been, just a bloke from Mount Druitt with nothing?

He looked at the ground, three stories below. The front of the block had been terraced in sandstone down to the harbour's edge. He watched the clear waters, lapping against the stones. He felt drawn to them, giving in to a fog, a mix of vertigo, despair and utter exhaustion.

He held the smooth metal of the scaffold rail but it was as if it was dissolving, slipping from his grip. He began to totter forwards, conceding defeat.

Just then his phone rang. It broke him out of his trance. His first impulse, however, was to drop the phone and watch it shatter below, then follow it. But he had a second thought.

"No!"

He pushed himself backwards, landing heavily on his behind on the rough concrete.

"Fuck!"

His head had cleared. Adrenalin pumped through his veins, his heart pounding and his body shivering. He took several deep breaths. His mobile was still in his hand, still ringing. Mandy? That would be meaningful.

It wasn't Mandy, though. It was a number he didn't recognize. Probably someone chasing him for money. He felt a surge of anger. Indignation.

"Why can't they fucking leave me alone?!"

He pressed answer, "Who's this?"

"Oh, I'm so sorry, Cliffie. Sorry to interrupt. It's Jan from the Club. I'm terribly sorry to get you at a bad time, love. It's just that we sent you an email and haven't heard back yet. So I thought I would give you a quick call. But I'm sorry to call when you are busy, I can call back another time."

"Ah, no it's ok, Jan. Can you hold on a minute?"

Cliff took the phone away from his ear, his brain trying to catch up with events. He liked Jan. She was sweet. She was the grandmother he always imagined other people in nice families had. A kindly soul, a little slow but with a heart of gold. His anger had subsided. He couldn't take his current predicament out on her.

"Hi Jan. Sorry about that, I'm just a little caught up at the moment."

"No, no, that's quite alright, Cliffie. I can call back another time. When you are not in the middle of something. It's just Ken and I are ready to make that investment. When you are, of course. But we're quite keen. Ok Cliffie?"

"Ok, great. Thanks Jan, I'll speak to you later."

Cliff hung up. He felt fragile and shuffled up against the wall of the balcony. His hands were still shaking.

"Wow," he breathed, "I almost did it. Fucking hell."

He closed his eyes, leaning his head back against the wall. It all felt surreal. The call from Jan echoed around his head. So weird, the timing. Yet something else, indistinct, nagged him about her call. He didn't have the energy to work it out. Eventually he fell into a deep sleep, the kind of lights-out that nature provides as a safety switch to an overheated brain.

The sun sank in the west, casting a golden light across the harbour and the city. Long shadows stretched across the walls and grounds of Blue as Cliff slowly became aware of the cold, hard concrete he'd fallen asleep on.

He was in a fetal position, his head squashed up against a box of tiles. His neck, shoulder, back and knee hurt. He rolled away from the wall and tiles and painfully got to all fours. His head spun a bit, however the fog seemed to have cleared.

He took in the outline of the balcony and the open glass doors that led into the uncompleted unit. It had not been a dream. He really was on the top balcony of Blue. He really had met with Bill and lost all hope of saving everything he'd worked so hard to build up. He got to his feet and looked over the edge of the balcony, holding firmly to the make-shift rail. He really had come close to falling over the edge. For just a moment, he'd really wanted it.

"Ouch, that would have hurt."

He backed away from the edge. His phone lay on the ground beside the box of tiles. He picked it up and automatically looked for messages. There were more missed calls now. Lara again. Mandy again. There was also the last call taken. Jan.

"Wow, that was the weirdest part," he closed his eyes and shook his head. Why had she called him again?

Cliff was jolted by the memory, like a surge of electricity had gone through his mind.

"Wow, maybe there is a fucking God!"

He texted Bill, "Hey mate, how much would you need to finish it?"

Cliff checked to see if he'd left anything else on the balcony, then stepped inside, closing the glass doors behind him. He hurried for the exit, but before he'd crossed the living room his phone rang. It was Bill.

"What, have you found some money?"

"Maybe. How much would you need?"

"Half a mill. At least."

"How about 300K?"

"Yeah, maybe. Could make it work."

"Seriously? You could finish them?"

"Yep. We could. If we started up immediately, before everything gets pulled and everyone moves on."

"OK, I can get the funds quickly. But I'm going to need something for it. Another unit."

"Bullshit!"

"Yeah, another unit, mate."

"No way, I need to sell those to pay off everything. Why would I do it if I still ended up broke?"

"Not one of your Phase Ones. A Phase Two will do. You can give me your worst Phase Two, but I want another unit for it."

"Come off it, mate, they will still be worth over 500 grand."

"Sure. That's a reasonable pay off for my risk. And don't bullshit, you'll end up fine if you get to sell everything completed. Full retail, yeah? You know it. It's a whole lot better than the bank taking everything and leaving you bankrupt."

"Yep, ok, you're right."

"Great. The other thing is, me, MJ and Raj are going to project manage it with you. We're going to sign a contract that says you can't spend a cent without our approval and we're going to release the cash only as needed. Agreed?"

"Um. Alright, we can talk."

"Awesome. It's for everyone's good. We'll work with you and we'll get out of this hole. Ok mate?"

Bill was still processing.

"I'll speak to you tomorrow to confirm everything. We'll meet onsite and I'll bring Garth to draw up the new contracts."

"Uh-huh."

"And Bill –"

"Yeah mate?"

"We'll do this, mate. I'm a winner, I never, ever give up."

Cliff's mind was racing. He checked the time. After 730pm.

"What the hell."

He found Jan's number and dialed.

"Hi Jan, how are you? It's Cliffie. Sorry to call you back so late."

"Oh, hi Cliff. No problem at all. We were just watching TV. It's the new CSI. Do you watch it at all?"

"No, not much lately. I heard it's good though."

"Oh, it's so good!"

"Well," Cliff smiled, "I'll let you get back to it soon. I just wanted to say sorry I was a bit rude on the phone before."

"Oh, no, that's alright, I'm sorry I got you at a bad time, Cliffie."

"Yeah, a slightly awkward moment," Cliff chuckled, "But sorry I sounded a little abrupt, ok?"

"No worries, really."

"Thanks Jan. Look, the other thing is, I just wanted to sort out the investment. We've got a new opportunity but have to act fast."

"Ok, yes of course. Let me get Ken so he can listen in too."

There was a rustle as she put the phone down. Cliff could hear her hurrying Ken up to turn the TV off and come over.

"Hi Cliffie, Ken is here with me now, so he can help make sure I get everything right."

"Ok great, say hi to Ken from me."

"Cliffie says hi," she raised her voice, "He says hi to you, Cliffie says-"

She returned to Cliff, "Oh god, he's losing his hearing now."

"All good. He'll be right."

"Well, he'd be right if he admitted it, you know. But he won't. He's going to be 21 forever."

Cliff laughed. "Alright, no worries, I won't keep you long Jan, so you can get back to CSI. I just need to confirm you want to go ahead with the 300K we talked about?"

"Yes, yes, that's right. If that's still ok?"

"Yep, of course it is. Now how do you want to transfer the funds? Can you do an electronic transfer?"

"Yes, we've spoken to the bank and they can help us at the branch. We just need your banking details to give them."

"Of course. Those are all in the original email I sent you. Do you still have that?"

"Yes, yes, we do Cliffie."

"Ok great, well can you print that out and take it to the branch?"

"Yes, of course we can, good idea."

"Great. When would you be able to do it? It's just we need to act on this new opportunity fast. This week, to be honest, if you are going to be a part of it."

"Sure, sure. We can do it tomorrow if that works for you."

"Yes great. Perfect."

"Now, Cliffie, there's a few questions we have for you. We've got a little list, actually. Do you have the list, Ken? The list with the questions?"

"Ok, no worries. Fire away."

"Ah, here it is. Ken's got it now. Can I go through them with you?"

"Yes, definitely."

"Ok, thanks Cliffie. Firstly, the contract. How do we get the contract signed before we deposit the money?"

"Sure. That's no problem. I'll scan and email it to you tonight."

"Oh, I see, but that will just have your side signed. What about ours?"

"Well, you can just do the same. Sign it, scan it and email it to me. But honestly, I wouldn't worry about it. I trust you and I can get it from you later," Cliff was always surprised at how caught up in minor details his amateur investors could get.

"It's just that our solicitor said we should get the originals of everything and make sure they are witnessed."

"Right. Well, it's just as good if it is emailed these days. You know, it's normal now."

"Hmm, yes, I see. I suppose it's ok, since it's you, Cliffie," Jan still sounded worried. "Now what about the caveat? You know, our security? We really should have that. It's the next thing highlighted on the list."

"Yes, no worries, I can email that to you too."

"Ok good, thanks Cliffie. I'm sure you understand, don't you? I mean it's a lot of money to us. It's everything we've got. We are nervous and just want to make sure we do everything the way our solicitor advised us."

"Of course, I understand. No worries Jan. Is there anything else on your list?"

"Yes, just a few questions about how it works. You know, what we do to get our money back when we need it and so on?"

"Sure..."

"I'm sure you've told us all these things already and I'm sorry to be a nuisance, Cliffie. You've probably got all the answers in your email, haven't you? We just couldn't find some things and wanted to go over them with you, personally, if that's alright?"

"Of course it is," Cliff wished she would just get to the point when she spoke, "Ask me anything Jan."

As she went through her list, checking with Ken at each step, Cliff paced back and forth across the living room. At one point he found himself staring out the glass balcony doors, waiting for Jan to finish reading her notes. In his frustration, he couldn't help thinking, 'I really should throw myself off this balcony... she's never going to stop.' He smiled at his dark humour.

Eventually, however, Jan did get to the end of her list. "Thank you so much Cliffie. We will wait to receive your email tonight. Or, most likely, first thing in the morning when we get up, since we go to bed after CSI. As soon as we've got it, we'll go into the branch and make the deposit. I'll give you a call to let you know it's all done."

"Fantastic."

"Thanks for putting up with all our questions, you are very kind to us. We've never done anything like this before, and we certainly never would if it wasn't for you, Cliffie. We are very lucky to have found you."

Cliff had a spark of hope again. He selected Mandy's number. Sure, she would be upset, furious most likely, when she found out he was safe. He could handle it now, though. He was back in the fight. He pressed dial and made for the exit, a small bounce in his step.

TWENTY-THREE

"No problem, Jan. Thank you so much. Yes, of course we will. I know Cliffie will treat it like it was his own life savings," Lara smiled, "Yes exactly! I think we would all be better off giving our money to him and letting him work his magic on it. Alright, talk to you soon. Bye now."

"All good?" Cliff was hanging on her words.

"Yep, she got everything, she's happy and they've just transferred the funds. She says the bank is saying two days."

"Well, that's heaps better than Standard Building Society. Whew!"

"What's next captain?"

"Bill. Can you call Garth and tell him the meeting's on. I told Bill we'll see him at 12."

The rest of the day was spent at Blue, inside the small demountable site office. Garth brought copies of the new contract between Cliff and Bill. Reluctantly Bill agreed, holding out for only a few minor changes. He was cornered. Garth made the updates immediately on his laptop and Lara reprinted them. By early afternoon Bill had signed. Cliff wasn't mucking around.

Next up, he, Raj, MJ and Bill went step by step, item by item, through everything that remained to be done. MJ created a spreadsheet as they went. By sunset they had a detailed picture of the project with priorities, timelines and estimated costs against everything.

Cliff leaned back in his chair and blew out a long, deep breath.

"What a day."

No-one said any more. Bill did not seem angry, just shell-shocked. Cliff tried to cheer him.

"We'll do this, mate. We'll turn things around." He held out a hand which Bill shook unenthusiastically.

Then he led his team out of the site office. Dark shadows had engulfed Blue, but on the very top of Phase 1, a last golden ray reflected in a window.

'Yep,' Cliff thought, 'That's for me.'

It was the first relaxed weekend Cliff had enjoyed for as long as he could remember. He told Mandy she could decide what they did. He was all hers. It was the least he could do after disappearing for twenty-four hours. Anyway, there was nothing to be done until Jan and Ken's funds cleared, so he might as well take it easy.

After a blissful sleep in, they hit the Riverstone farmers markets. In the shade of two grand old oak trees, they ate bacon and eggs 'fresh from the farm'. They watched squadrons of small children run back and forth, chasing each other with toy pistols, sticks turned into makeshift rifles and one large, plush bunny. They admired the displays of gourmet olive oils, heirloom tomatoes, hand-made lamb sausages, truffles and a myriad other 'farm to table' products. Then, Cliff's favourite, they hit the dodgem car track.

Cliff went for speed and maximum G-force in the corners. Mandy, on the other hand, enjoyed hiding amongst the crowd of other carts, then slamming into Cliff when he least suspected it. Her driving skills, not to mention sneaky tactics, impressed him a lot.

Sunday was equally relaxed. In the afternoon, they headed into Newtown, a funky, inner-city area of Sydney, to a party thrown by one of Mandy's work mates. It was held in a warehouse apartment with great views of the city skyline, beers and wines flowing abundantly and an animated crowd packing living room and balcony. Indie rock was 'turned up to eleven', while arthouse video clips danced across the exposed, brick walls. Not really Cliff's idea of a fun Sunday afternoon, but he was happy to be doing Mandy's thing.

Finally, they were making their farewells, when a young guy, short, but with boy-band good looks, broke away from an intense conversation, offering his hand to Cliff.

"Hi Cliff, I'm Harrison. I work with Mandy. I've been wanting to say hello. Sorry I didn't catch up with you earlier, now you're leaving."

He gave an apologetic smile. Cliff shook his hand warmly, "No that's cool. Good to meet you."

"Yeah definitely. Dumb of me to leave my move so late. Story of my life!" He slapped himself on the forehead theatrically.

Mandy put an arm around Cliff and smiled at Harrison, "Yep, typical."

Harrison folded his arms and hung his head, "Ah, so harsh, so harsh!"

They laughed. Harrison focused on Cliff, "So Mandy tells me lots of really interesting stuff about you. You're in real estate, right? Like property investing and stuff?"

"Yeah, pretty much."

"Wow, so different to our world," he smiled at Mandy.

"It's pretty impressive, man," he nodded at Cliff, "You're a young dude, you know, and already doing all that shit."

"Thanks mate, I appreciate it. Not sure I'm doing all that good a job at the moment, but getting there," he smiled. "What do you do?"

"I sing," Harrison looked serious for a moment, then he broke into a broad, if somewhat pained, smile, "But what do I do to earn money? I'm a sales exec!"

"Nothing wrong with that."

"Well, really, there's a shitload wrong with it, you know, if your heart is in music," Harrison dropped his sales persona, "If that's all you think about, all you wanna do, day in and day out... But then you've got to turn up for work at nine and give your soul to the company for ten, twelve hours a day. Mandy knows," he smiled gently at her, "We talk about this stuff a lot."

"Yeah mate, it must be hard. The life of an artist. But all the good ones struggle, right? Then, when they finally make it, they look back on the hard times and have something to talk about in their TV interviews, right?"

"Totally," Harrison chuckled, "So, what do you think about today's news by the way?"

"Um, what news?" Cliff didn't want to be dragged into a music industry conversation he knew nothing about.

"What news?" Harrison was incredulous. "Just the entire global economic system collapsing!"

"Oh, what do you mean? Like the stuff going on in the US?"

"Fuck yeah! It's bye, bye baby, fucking all over red rover, when the saints come marching home..."

"Ah, yeah, it's been going on for a while now, though. I don't think it's that big and to be honest I don't think it's going to affect us that much."

"Serious? I mean have you seen what's happened today? The two biggest banks in America just collapsed. Fucking Frankie and Fannie or whatever the fuck. I mean who calls a bank those names anyway?"

He turned to Mandy for a laugh, but she was confused.

"Oh, I don't know then..."

Cliff had no idea what Harrison was talking about. He doubted his accuracy, but nonetheless, he was struck with a nauseating fear.

"Yeah, man, let me show you," Harrison took out his iPhone and began tapping keys to look it up. He zoomed in to show Cliff the headlines.

'Market Devastation as Freddie Mac and Fannie Mae Close Doors.'

Cliff tried to remain upbeat until, eventually, they had said their last goodbyes and departed.

In the car Mandy asked, "Is it really bad news?"

"Well, it's more bad stuff, yeah. I don't know how much it will affect us, like I was saying back there. But the shit thing is it delays any chance of recovery. We need the market to get back on track here but it seems like when that stuff's going on over there, everyone here gets scared."

'Yeah, they're all sheep, hey?"

"The big thing is the banks. It's like they're getting paralysed by it and you don't want the Australian banks to start collapsing. Then we'd be in deep shit. And the trouble is they're all so totally connected nowadays."

"Well, don't you go throwing yourself off a building like they do on Wall Street, ok?" Mandy laughed, "Money isn't worth it."

Cliff was stung. He contemplated silently. He could never tell Mandy how close he'd come the other day at Blue. She needed him to be positive. That's what he would be for her, always.

"Don't worry. I'll always come up with a plan."

TWENTY-FOUR

Cliff was getting ready to go to Standard Building Society. It was Monday morning, he was feeling good, everything seemed to be going according to plan.

Shortly after 9am he had gone online and was delighted to see the money deposited by Jan and Ken had cleared into his account. Now he needed to set up a way of accessing the funds quickly and easily. In fact, he reminded himself, he wanted to get all the investor funds out of Standard and into another bank as soon as possible. He just hadn't had a chance yet.

His mobile rang. It was Dermott.

"Can't he leave me alone? I just need a few more weeks."

He pressed end call, grabbed his things and headed to the car.

He stepped inside Standard Building Society cautiously. He was keen to avoid the flirtations of the spiky blonde-haired manager. There were no other customers and no sign of spiky.

"Excellent," he thought, "So far so good."

He made his way to the first 'customer pod' where a sleepy looking teller was sitting, staring at his computer screen.

"Hi mate," Cliff sat down on the fluro-green, vinyl bench.

"Good morning sir," the young teller tried, unsuccessfully, to stifle a yawn.

"You got the dawn shift, hey?"

"Yeah, sorry, just had a late one last night.".

"No worries. Got to have some fun in life."

"Yeah, thanks," the teller gave a little snort of a laugh and sat upright, shaking himself into readiness.

"I need to access some funds I've got with you. But I don't want it to be a palaver. Just whatever is the easiest way, a bank cheque or something like that?"

"Oh, ok, sure. Do you have your card?"

"Yep, here," Cliff took it from his wallet and pushed it across the table to the teller. "I also want to withdraw a little working cash. What's the most I can withdraw today? Again, without causing any hassles?"

"Oh, it's no hassle. Just need to make sure we have the funds available, that's all."

"Great, thanks."

"Now I've got your account," he read from his screen as he spoke, "But I've got a message coming up, saying funds are temporarily not available. It actually says you need to speak with Corporate Services."

"Really? What's that all about?"

"I'm not actually sure. At this branch, our Assistant Manager can help you with that. Would you like me to see if she is available?"

"Yep, ok," Cliff sighed, resigning himself.

The teller picked up his phone and pressed a number.

"Hi. I've got a customer here with a message on his account from Corporate Services. Seems like they've put some kind of block on it. Can you see him? Ok great thanks."

A moment later Rita, aka spiky, the diminutive Assistant Manager, appeared from an internal door. Cliff braced himself.

"Hi you!" she smiled. "Are you causing trouble again?"

"Yeah," Cliff chuckled, "Seems like I am."

Rita sat next to the teller so she could look at his computer. "What's going on?"

"I'm not sure. See this message here. The account can't be

accessed."

"Hmm. I've not seen that before. We'll have to contact head office." She looked up at Cliff, "Is there any reason you can think why they would lock your account?"

"No," Cliff felt like a kid at the headmaster's office. The less he said the better.

Rita took over the teller's phone, consulted his computer for a number and then dialed.

"Hi I need information on an account that's been locked by Corporate. Yep. Thanks."

She rolled her eyes to indicate to Cliff they were putting her on hold. Eventually she spoke again.

"Yes, that's right. It's in the name of Cliff Young."

She relayed his account details and then waited some more.

"Oh really? Ok, I'll let him know. Right."

Her eyes were wide. She covered the phone's microphone and whispered to Cliff, "It's to do with America."

"What?" Cliff was confused.

"Yep, I see. Ok, no problem, I'll let him know." She put the phone down, took a deep breath and shook her head. "Wow, this is a new one."

"What is it?"

"Ok," Rita put a hand out to calm Cliff, "It's about the big crisis going on in America and the world right now. The bank has immediately reviewed a lot of its lending with customers and has moved to increase security. That's all I'm told. But obviously it would be about your business, maybe in America?" She looked at Cliff expectantly.

"I don't have any business in America!" Cliff was exasperated now.

"Right. Well, whatever. But it must be your loans and the bank might need to adjust your position, something like that. It'll be about improving security. You know, with the crisis-"

"I don't have any loans with you! What's going on?" Cliff was now convinced he was the victim of an error. "This is ridiculous!"

"Look. Don't shout at us. I'm just telling you what I've been told," Rita held up a finger to warn Cliff. "You need to contact our Corporate Services directly yourself. They won't tell me any more. I'll give you the number."

She wrote it out on a post-it note and handed it to Cliff with a patronizing smile.

"Great," Cliff took it with a sigh.

As he got up and left, he noticed the time on a digital display that floated like a hologram against the fluro-green wall on his left. Some kind of clever projection effect onto a Perspex panel. He was running late for the meeting at Blue. He would just have to go without any funds.

When Cliff entered the site office at Blue, he stopped dead in his tracks. Bill, MJ and Raj looked up with grim faces. Seated behind the main desk, in a crisp, dark suit, was Dermott from ABC Bank. He wore his usual goofy smile, except this time there was steel in his eyes, where previously there had always been boyish fun.

"Welcome, Cliff. Finally."

"What are you doing here?"

"You've been a hard man to get hold of. If you'd answered my calls, I could have warned you about what was going on," Dermott shrugged and raised his eyebrows to indicate it was beyond his control.

"What's going on?"

"Take a seat," Dermott gestured to a white, plastic chair with a stack of folders on it, "Just chuck all that crap on the floor."

Cliff removed the folders and spun the chair around to sit in reverse position. However, the shape of its back dug painfully into his inner thighs. He stood up again, turned the chair around to face the front and sat down normally.

"Great," Dermott smiled at his antics. "Long story, short. US Banking system collapsed. World markets crashed. Australian banks have panicked."

Dermott gave Cliff a pained look, "Unfortunately that's been really bad for you. Just terrible, terrible timing."

"Uh-huh. So, what, exactly…"

"Well, what I've been trying to call you about for the last week is the bank ordered a revaluation of all property portfolios it considers 'high risk'. You're very much categorized high risk by ABC Bank, I'm afraid. So, after the proverbial shit hit the fan all over the financial world yesterday, they acted immediately this morning."

He leaned forward, concern on his face, "It's Head Office doing it, you understand, completely out of my hands, I'm sorry."

"So, what have they done?" Cliff was still reeling with confusion. He knew a hammer was falling, he just didn't know what hammer or from where.

"Your portfolio's been valued down. Meaning, you either need to cough up a couple of million cash to reduce your loan, or the bank takes all your properties and fire-sales them. I'm guessing you don't have a couple of mill handy?"

Dermott waited only a moment for an answer before continuing.

"The second thing is, in situations like this, the bank seizes anything of yours it can get its hands on. There's a legal process it has to apply through and so on. But in reality, it grabs whatever it has access to. If you read the fine print in your terms and conditions booklet, you'll see it's allowed to do so. Again, I was trying to call you to warn you about this."

"Sure. Look, I've just been busy Dermott, ok?"

"Of course, you have. Trouble is, you had an account within the banking group, right? With one of the subsidiaries? You'll have found it's been frozen. 'Call Corporate Services to discuss', etcetera?"

"So that's what it is. Fucking hell!" Cliff leaned back and stared at the ceiling. They'd well and truly got him now. He looked at Dermott. The man seemed to be savouring the situation too much. Sure, Cliff had ignored his calls and, yes, he'd become a risky customer not servicing his debt very well. However, Dermott seemed personally involved.

"What are you doing here anyway, Dermott?"

"Ah, yes. I was coming to that." Dermott gathered himself. Bill, MJ and Raj shuffled uneasily.

"I'm not, in fact, representing ABC Bank here. I'm here on behalf of a company called DM Holdings. It's a Hong Kong company."

"It's his company," MJ hissed. "DM. Dermott Masters."

"Yep, ok," Dermott gave MJ an annoyed look, "But for all intents and purposes it is a separate entity that has nothing to do with what I do at ABC Bank."

"Ok... and what are you doing here?" Cliff was frustrated.

"Alright, well, if you will let me finish?"

"Sure," Cliff held up his hands.

"DM Holdings is interested in acquiring the development here at Blue."

"What?" Cliff laughed.

"Yes, we've made an offer, which these three guys have accepted. Now it's just a case of coming to an agreement with you," Dermott leaned back in his chair.

"Woah, hang on. What the fuck? You wanna buy us out?" Cliff turned to MJ and Raj, "And you guys have agreed?"

MJ held up a hand, "No, not without your agreement. Only in principle."

"Yeah," Raj tried to assure Cliff, "We've only had a basic discussion and said we'd consider it if you do."

"Well," Bill chuckled, "I think you two were a bit more strongly in favour than that."

"And what's your story anyway?" Cliff turned on Bill.

"I'm done, mate. I'm finished. I've got no choice, so I've chucked my cards in, mate. But let the man finish," he gestured to Dermott.

"Thanks Bill," Dermott leaned forward on the desk. "Here's the thing Cliff. Tell me if I'm wrong, but from everything I know, you've lost your portfolio. You can't pay down your loans. You can't refinance, not with Western Progressive or anyone else you've tried. And now with the disaster in the US you'll never be able to, no way."

"Seems like it."

"It's true, mate," Bill didn't look up as he spoke. "I'm the same. I'm out of funds and I'll never get any more now."

"So," Dermott continued, "The bank's also grabbed your last stash of cash. They'll force you into bankruptcy now. It's just the way it is. There's nothing you can do about it. Then they'll flog off your share of this project, and the lawyers will take it all. You know how it is. They are the only ones who win at the end of the day."

"He's right, mate," MJ sighed.

"Trouble is, your friends here won't be able to sell their shares either. Not with the cloud of bank repossession hanging over it and lawyers buzzing around like flies on a sheep's bum. Not to mention the mud and dirt piling up as the site slowly falls into disrepair. They'll lose big time."

Raj looked at Cliff. There was genuine fear in his eyes. MJ stared at the ceiling. Cliff looked at Dermott, "So, what are you suggesting?"

"Well, we've offered 300K for each of the Phase One units."

"300K?!"

"Yes, but just consider this. The project is incomplete. Every day it sits unfinished, its condition deteriorates and the job of finishing it gets bigger. There's no buyers for it. Not at this end of the market and definitely not while its unfinished. The only potential buyers are other developers and they're going to want to buy the whole project and they're going to offer even less than me."

"Really?"

"Yes, really."

"How do you know this Dermott? I thought you didn't invest in property."

"Well, I never said I didn't. I just don't like to talk about it, that's all. I do things differently."

"You sure do," Bill shook his head.

"Anyway," Dermott was getting irritated, "My offer helps these guys out. Unfortunately, it doesn't really help you, but your situation is different. You are unavoidably going bankrupt. There's no price I could pay that would help you with that. I'm sorry. It's just the way it is. I think you know that, if you are honest."

"Oh yes, I fucking know that," Cliff felt an unbearable weight of despair descending on him. He thought of the club investors. Poor Jan and Ken. And all the others as well. Even Lara had loaned him money. Everything she had.

"So," Dermott looked sympathetically at Cliff, like a doctor delivering bad news and a tough treatment program for it. "You might as well help your mates. MJ and Raj could clear their debts if I buy the whole bundle. Bill won't, unfortunately."

"Nope," Bill stared at the floor.

"Bill is going bankrupt too. He's too deep, like you are. However, he'll get a job with DM Holdings, to finish the project. So, he'll be alright."

"Great," Cliff looked at Bill, "He's the bloke who didn't finish it in the first place."

Bill was stung, "Hey, come on mate."

Cliff leapt up and headed for the door, "If he had of, we wouldn't be in this fucking mess now!"

Bill got to his feet, his face twisted in anger.

"Wait Cliff," Dermott called after him.

Cliff turned at the door, "So what? You want me to sell you my units for a fucking steal, so you can make a fortune and I get to go bankrupt? Why would I do that for you? What have you ever done for me?"

As he thought about Dermott and ABC Bank, it all seemed so devious and twisted. He stepped back into the room and pointed at Dermott, "In fact, I reckon this is fucking illegal what you're doing!"

"Come on Cliff," Dermott stood up, trying to calm him. "There's nothing illegal about this."

"Really? What would your head office at ABC Bank think about it? You've used your knowledge to come here and try and profit. You've fucked over a good customer and now you're here on the side trying to screw him even more. Fuck you!"

"Ok Cliff," Dermott held up his hands, his voice was sharp, "You walk out that door and it's over for everybody here. I'm not doing any deal unless it's for the whole thing. I've already said that. You can let your ego run wild if you like. I understand you're upset. But you walk away now and you fuck your friends. You condemn them to bankruptcy too." Dermott began gathering his things.

Cliff was frozen. He'd already fucked enough people. He looked at Raj who was miserable. He looked at MJ.

MJ shook her head, "You do what you have to, mate. Don't consider us. Honestly. You've got to make your own call Cliffie."

Raj stared at the floor, "Yep, mate, don't do it for us. We'll be fine." His voice quavered and Cliff felt it like a knife in the guts. What had he done to his friends?

"Ok," Cliff considered the situation, he could tell there would be no negotiating over price or terms with Dermott. He held all the cards. Perhaps he could try for time.

"Give me twenty-four hours to think it over."

Dermott looked incredulous, "Are you kidding? In twenty-four hours, god knows, there'll be sheriffs and lawyers and bank auditors crawling all over the place. Come on Cliff, think about it, it's got to be now or never. The bank's moving fast to lock down your assets. Blue may not be direct collateral against any of your loans, but it will take them about two seconds to find it. Once they do, they'll go all out to stop you selling it – and they've got good lawyers. Lots of them."

Cliff hated being cornered. Having no options, no bargaining chips whatsoever. It all felt so wrong. He looked around the room for some kind of support but there was none. His eyes came to rest on a framed picture of the original architect's vision for Blue. It sat on the floor, squashed against the wall by the legs of a portable white board. There it was, the elegant lines of the buildings, the dramatic wave of the front promenade which had never been completed, and the glorious harbour reflecting on the towering glass façade of Phase One.

He stared at it as he spoke, "So how do we do this then?"

"Well," Dermott smiled, pulling the wad of papers back out of his briefcase, "We start by signing a contract. A little something I prepared earlier."

"How do you pay us?"

"However you like. I suggest cash, though, in your case."

"You can pay in cash today?"

"Yep, it's ready to go," Dermott looked pleased with himself.

"Fuck, you were confident."

Dermott pushed the contract across the desk. He leaned back in his chair, his hands knitted behind his head and sighed.

Without reading it, Cliff flipped the contract to the last page. "Pen," he held out a hand.

Dermott looked at him, like he was studying a fascinating insect. "I remember someone once telling me how he negotiated the lowest prices off sellers in Mount Druitt. He'd find the ones who were desperate, had no other options. Maybe their marriage had broken up, or they got sick or lost their job, or maybe they had just been too stupid and paid too much originally and couldn't afford the repayments now. Whatever."

Cliff realized what Dermott was saying. The back of his neck grew hot with anger.

"They couldn't sell for some reason," Dermott continued, "Usually because the property was in a state. It was a dump or renovations were unfinished and looked terrible. Anyway, he'd offer them quick cash. Dangle it in front of them. They'd go for it no matter how low the price."

There was a flicker of a smile at the corners of Dermott's mouth, "Of course, he was really 'helping' them out," he rocked back in his chair and chuckled at the ceiling, "Just like I'm helping out now."

Cliff glared with murderous rage.

Dermott smiled, "Come on Cliff, don't take me so seriously, I'm joking."

Cliff rose slowly. He turned to MJ and Raj. "Sorry guys. I hope I don't fuck things up for you. Please make whatever deal you can with him. But count me out. You can't expect me to let this guy cut my heart out and make me eat it too."

He tossed the contract back at Dermott and walked out.

Dermott called after him, "I'll pick them up at the auction then Cliff."

TWENTY-FIVE

Dermott's predictions proved correct. Cliff's phone rang multiple times as he drove home. He ignored it but checked his messages once he was home. ABC Bank Corporate Services had left three messages, each increasing in urgency. By the third one they were flat out demanding that he contact them or face immediate legal action against his company and assets. Instead, Cliff dropped his phone on the sofa, walked over to the fridge and took out a beer.

When Mandy got home, he was on his sixth. He lay on the sofa with a game show blaring on the TV.

"Hey, hey!"

"Hey, darling," she smiled at him as she crossed the room and dumped some plastic shopping bags on the kitchen top. "How was your day at Blue?"

"Don't ask that question," he did the game show host's voice, "That is not the right question, I'm afraid. Think carefully before you ask your next one. Do you want to phone a friend?"

"Ok, hon, what's the right question then? How many beers have you had?"

"Nope that's an easy question. Just count the empties!"

"Why can't I ask that question? Did you have a bad day?"

"The worst of my life. No, actually that was last week. The second worst of my life. But I'm not really up for talking about it right now, sweetie, is that ok?"

"Sure. I'm sorry you had a bad day. I got some Thai, do you want some?"

"Yeah, bring it on. Beer and Thai. Perfect!"

After dinner Mandy went to bed early and Cliff stayed on the sofa, channel surfing, trying to block out the thoughts that were racing around and around in his head. How was he going to deal with being bankrupt? How was he going to tell people? How was he going to break it to Mandy? What was he going to say at the Club meeting tomorrow night?

Eventually he fell asleep on the sofa.

An insistent banging slowly brought him back to consciousness some hours later. It was early morning, the fresh light streaming in through the open curtains of the living room. Mandy was already at the door.

"Who is it?" she called out.

"New South Wales Sheriff," came a strong, male voice.

Cliff swung his feet to the ground. His head hurt as he tried to straighten himself up.

"It's early," Mandy complained as she opened the door.

"Yes, apologies," came the assertive voice, "I'm here by order of the Supreme Court of New South Wales."

Cliff was by Mandy's side now and she turned to him, deep concern on her face, "What's going on Cliff?"

"I think I know. Let me talk to him." He put his hand on her shoulder and gently moved her back from the door. She looked horrified.

"How can I help you?" Cliff asked.

"This is 44 Simms Avenue, is that correct?" The Sheriff consulted a clipboard.

"Yes, it is."

"It's the registered address of CY Property Holdings, also Cliffies Climbers Investors Club and Cliffies Climbers Investment Fund. Are you aware of that?"

"Yes."

"Are you Cliff Young?"

"Yes I am."

"Ok good. I've got a notice to deliver to you. I am required to read it to you first." He pulled the letter from the clipboard and proceeded to read it word-for-word to Cliff. It was a notice from the courts, granting the request of ABC Bank and requiring that none of Cliff's companies sell any assets until further notice. The Sheriff then handed the letter to Cliff and got him to sign a receipt for it.

"Thanks very much, that will be all then. Good morning, sir. Good morning, young lady. Sorry to have called so early."

He turned and walked back to his car, a white station wagon that was parked across the street, three doors down. Cliff closed the door and turned to Mandy. She waited, expectant.

"Hm. You know I said I had a bad day? Well it was a really bad day. I've lost everything darl. The lot. Houses, Blue, everything I own, everything I don't own, other people's money not just mine," he leaned back against the door and sighed, "Fuck."

"Oh my god."

"I'm sorry I didn't tell you. I'm so sorry. I just couldn't. I didn't want to worry you. I don't know. I didn't want you to think I was a fuck up. But I am."

"No you're not. Don't be silly. But what's happened? Why so suddenly? How's it all gone so badly, like yesterday?"

"Come and sit down," Cliff touched her on the shoulder and shuffled wearily across to the sofa. He felt dizzy and his body ached. Mandy followed and sat next to him.

"It's been going badly for a long time. I mean, you know some of it. But you don't know half of it. I really, honestly, thought I could turn it around though. It's only yesterday my last chance ran out."

"Yeah, I thought you were on top of it."

"You know all this financial crisis stuff that's been going on?"

"Yeah, of course. You said it wasn't affecting you. Just making other people panicky."

"Exactly, everyone else has panicked. The market has shit itself. Totally, you know, no-one wants to buy anything."

"Like Alfie..."

"Uh-huh. Then every time there's another crash overseas, the banks freak out and tighten the screws on me. ABC's been coming after me, I can't borrow anymore, I can't refinance... So, it's been harder and harder to hold onto the properties. Then, yesterday, they fucked me completely."

"What happened?"

"They reduced the value of every property, basically leaving me millions short. Then demanded the money. Obviously, I don't have it, because I've used it to invest in other properties, Blue and all. So now they've frozen my assets and they're planning to take them and declare me bankrupt. That's what the Sheriff was here for."

"I'm sorry, darling," Mandy reached out and took his hands, "I wish I'd known. I mean I knew you were stressed but I thought you had sorted it out. I can't believe you've been going through all this silently by yourself."

She knelt on the sofa and hugged him. He put his arms around her, hugging her back, his head buried in her chest.

After a while he spoke tentatively, a little muffled, "I'm sorry I didn't tell you more. I've just been caught up in it, you know? I think I've been really scared. Stressed. I don't know, I thought you'd think I was useless."

"What? I mean, I already think you're useless most of the time... Why would I have thought it anymore?"

"Hey?" He looked up.

She laughed, "Just joking. Come on, you know I don't care about the money stuff. I'm a hippy at heart. You know me."

She held his face and smiled at him, "You know what I would have done if you had told me?"

"What?"

"Helped you. That's all I would have wanted to do. Helped you in any way I could." Her expression became determined, "But that doesn't matter, I still can. I'm going to help you from now. We'll deal with this together, ok?"

"Hmm. There's nothing left to help with now, really."

"Of course, there is. I can do more than just PowerPoint, you know. I deal with legal stuff all the time at work. I have to handle the biggest dickheads, the most extreme bullshit imaginable. What do you think, I'm in the music industry!"

Cliff smiled. It was not the reaction he had expected. She looked down at him with bright eyes.

"I'm going to take the day off. I'm going to be with you and help you with whatever. First, though, we're going out. So, get ready."

"Where?" Cliff groaned.

"Wallies! We'll talk through everything there."

She was on a mission. Wallies Waffles was where they'd gone on their first 'date', the morning after Mandy's party. Since then it had become their little secret spot for romantic outings. They hadn't gone for a very long time.

"Now get ready! You're in for some Mandy therapy."

Cliff knew there was no stopping her, so he raised himself painfully to his feet.

"Oh, one more thing," Mandy held her hand out. "Give it to me," she indicated his phone.

He willingly surrendered. She switched it off, walked over to the kitchen counter and put it in her bag.

"We'll start by reducing one big, fat cause of stress. For the rest of the day, you can forget about it."

"Ok," Cliff agreed meekly and headed for the shower.

Alive with delighted shrieks, rowdy laughter and enthusiastic chatter, Wallies was a very good candidate for the happiest place on earth. Happy kids and, in many cases, even happier mums, jammed in around brightly coloured tables, scooping, licking and slurping their way through milkshakes, parfaits, sundaes, ice-cream cones and, of course, plates stacked with golden brown, crispy waffles, dripping in syrup and bathing in cream.

It was certainly the coolest shop on Penrith's main street mall, a seedy shopping strip that had once been the centre-piece of the local Council's vision for an attractive shopping oasis. They'd closed it to cars and redeveloped it as a brick-paved pedestrian mall. Unfortunately, the idea failed so miserably that a few years later it was torn up and re-opened to cars, the pedestrians forced back onto its littered footpaths, the street a 'mall' in name only.

This set Wallies apart, like a bright, alien planet amid the vacant shops and rundown discount stores offering container loads of cheap, plastic goods from China. Cliff and Mandy waited in the doorway amongst an eager crowd of would-be customers. Eventually a waitress in 1950s American diner outfit, complete with pink checked skirt, ruffled apron and matching pink side cap, led them to their table.

"A mini tower of banana berry waffles please and two spoons," Mandy beamed at the waitress.

It was their traditional order. She smiled at Cliff, but his expression was fixed. He was lost somewhere behind his eyes.

"Come on," she reached across the table and took his hands, "Life can't be all bad when you're eating waffles."

Cliff could only manage a weak smile, "I don't know how you can be so light-hearted. I've lost everything. Everything and it's not coming back. That was our future, you know? We would have been able to do anything we wanted."

"I know, sweetie, we have to stay-"

"It's fucked. It's really fucked up. I'm in deep shit, you know? I could end up in jail."

He became aware of the table next door. They'd gone quiet, the little boy and little girl staring at him in awe while their mum's raised eyebrows at each other. Two other, older kids, meanwhile, continued to demolish their ice cream bowls oblivious to it all.

Cliff leaned in and lowered his voice, "It's true. I don't know what the bank's going to do, or any of the others I owe. It could get really nasty."

"Ok," Mandy breathed in deeply, "You're freaking me out now. I need to understand more. I thought you just couldn't pay your loans? So, the bank takes the houses. Finished. Why would you go to jail?"

"I don't know. I'm not saying I will. Just, there's other people going to lose money as well. You know, the club investors and all. It's shit. You know, I've given them contracts and caveats and… They think their money is secure but it's not. It's all been taken by the bank, or gone to Blue, you know, it's all gone."

"You mean you've spent it on what you shouldn't have? You've misled them?" Mandy looked at him sharply. She was not angry but her expression demanded frankness.

Cliff looked about uncomfortably, then leaned in, "Yeah they would be able to say that. Yeah. Breach of contract or something, I guess."

Mandy continued to fix Cliff with her gaze. After a moment she softened and placed a hand on his forearm, "I'm on your side. Ok? But I can't help you if you don't tell me everything."

Cliff looked down and sighed, he hadn't allowed himself to think about these things. He'd always pressed on forward, with the end goal in mind, believing he could get through every challenge. Then, once he was successful, he would be able to look after everyone else. There would be no questions about whether he had done the 'right thing' or not because he'd deliver rich rewards to everyone.

"It's true. I used their money for stuff I wasn't supposed to. I'm probably in deep shit for it. Yeah. But I never misled them. I mean, I never meant to. I don't know. If this whole financial crisis didn't happen, I would have made everyone lots of money. Then they would be happy, right?"

"Of course…"

"They'd be thanking me. Instead of suing me,"

"Well, hon," Mandy looked away, like she was trying to find the right words.

"What?"

"You better get some legal advice. That's the most urgent thing. Let's get Garth and Paul down here now. Yeah?"

"Yep. You're right," Cliff sighed.

TWENTY-SIX

Wednesday night's Club meeting came around quickly. Members streamed into the conference room, filling the neatly curving rows of seats. Cliff wasn't sure if it was just his imagination, given his own situation, but he sensed an air of tension. There seemed to be fewer smiles and less banter than usual.

He wiped the thick glass of the projection room window where his breath had misted it. Garth and Paul had told him to stay away from the meeting. He was best off lying low and saying nothing, especially not to the Club members. There was still a slim chance of negotiating with ABC Bank, perhaps staving off bankruptcy proceedings and avoiding legal investigation, but not if he was also being sued by private investors. He had to co-operate, they'd all insisted. However, he couldn't stay away completely.

He held his breath as Mandy took to the small stage.

"Hi everyone. How are we tonight?"

Cliff was pleased to see smiles amongst the audience, even one or two friendly waves.

Mandy had covered for him before, when he had genuinely been sick. She'd also held the fort when he, Raj, MJ and Lara had gone to San Francisco. So Cliff was hopeful the members would not be alarmed.

"Unfortunately, our Cliffie is stuck at home with a nasty lurgy. Poor thing, he's very sorry he can't be here. So, I'm afraid, you've just got me tonight."

She held her hands up, "I know it's disappointing. But think of it this way. We'll all appreciate Cliff even more when he's back next week!"

Cliff noticed Carlo amongst the crowd turning to his wife and brother-in-law and holding up his hands. His family shrugged, shaking their heads. The audience murmur sounded unhappy.

Mandy pushed ahead with the standard PowerPoint presentation. Everyone seemed to settle down and listen to her. It was a familiar routine. Every week Cliff walked them through the Club's simple, achievable steps to building a property portfolio. The effect was always positive and inspiring. Cliff's personal story formed the backbone of the presentation and his real-life examples illustrated each step. His story was remarkable, but its real power came from how ordinary he was, how much he was just like his audience.

Mandy came to the last slides, the ones that promoted the short-term investment scheme. They had decided to leave the slides in, just in case removing any mention of the scheme looked suspicious.

"Alright, we're pretty much done here so we'll have a nice, early night. I think everyone knows about the short term investment plan so I won't go into it. It's full up right now, anyway. So, if you're interested just stay in touch, I'm sure there will be a new opportunity soon. Thanks everyone."

A hand went up at the back of the audience. It was Tom, the American.

"Mandy," he called out, "I have a question please."

"Sure Tom."

Cliff noticed Garth and Paul get to their feet in the front row. They had good, protective instincts.

"There's a few of us want to get our money out," Tom's voice travelled easily to Cliff in the projection room, "But there seems to be some kind of problem."

"Oh really?"

"Yeah, I've been talking to some of the other investors and we're getting kind of worried."

Carlo raised a hand, "Yep, worried."

Now Jan, looking alarmed, was also saying something to Tom.

"Listen Tom," Mandy held up her hands, "Let's have a chat afterwards, instead of calling out across the room at each other. I'm sure we can sort everything out, ok? Cliff's just been really busy and now he's sick. Unfortunately. I'm sure you understand."

"Yep, ok," Tom sat back down.

"Thanks so much everyone," Mandy smiled, "We will look forward to seeing you next week."

Cliff watched as the audience got to their feet, some stretched and yawned, others turned to the people next to them for a chat. Some new faces approached Mandy and cheerfully thanked her. Slowly but surely the room emptied.

Then, just as it seemed like it was all over, Cliff noticed Tom and Jan talking animatedly. A moment later Carlo and his family joined them. A number of people who were on their way out stopped to listen. Amongst them were Nabil and his wife Sarah, two of Cliff's earliest investors.

Nabil called out to Tom, his voice cutting through the hubbub, "This is ridiculous. We should speak to them now. We need answers now."

With that, the group made their way over to Mandy, who was still caught up in a friendly conversation with two new members. Cliff desperately wanted to protect her. He slapped the wall in frustration.

"Shit. This is bad…"

As the unhappy investors gathered behind Mandy, Cliff carefully slid the projection room window open a crack. Nabil was visibly fired up and took the lead.

"Mandy, these people need answers to their questions."

Mandy turned around in surprise.

"Everyone is really stressed because they are being ignored. They need their money back but they are getting no reply. That makes me and all the others very worried. Come on. We need to see them getting their money out safely or else we are all going to panic."

Nabil noticed the young couple, looking freaked out, "I'm very sorry to interrupt. Please forgive me. This is a very important issue and it can't wait, so please forgive us for being rude."

He turned back to Mandy, "Some of these guys have been asking for their money for weeks now and they get no replies. What's going on? You need to look after them. I don't care how sick Cliff is, you can't stress people out like this!"

Cliff could see Mandy was taken aback. Garth and Paul stepped up to flank her.

"Yeah, come on guys," Cliff breathed, "Earn your fucking dough."

"Ok, ok, Nabil," Mandy tried to take control, "Let's just try to keep calm, there's really no need to get stressed, ok? We'll chat through everything and if I can't help you right now, of course I'll make sure Cliff gets back to you and sorts things out. Ok?"

"That's the problem right there," Tom's strong voice cut in before Nabil could respond, "We're not getting any reply from Cliff. Nothing. You know? A day or two you understand someone's busy. More than a week? That's when you start thinking somethings fishy."

"Exactly," Nabil threw his hands up.

"Especially when you've explained to the guy that things are urgent and he's promised to get onto it right away. Then no replies. Not even a simple text, email or nothing. Then we come here tonight and he's sick. Of course, we're going to be worried."

"I understand," Mandy's voice betrayed her nerves.

"It's ridiculous," Nabil was getting more worked up, "You know what it does? It makes everyone want their money back right now."

A number of angry voices called out in agreement.

Spencer and Ronnie had joined the crowd too. Now Lex and Rosemary, an older couple who'd invested the proceeds of Lex's voluntary redundancy payout, came over. Other Club members, non-investors, looked on.

"Yeah, you're right," Spencer told Nabil, "I'm getting worried now."

"You're not wrong," Lex echoed from behind him.

"Listen guys," Garth weighed in, "Obviously Mandy's not in a position to tell you any more right now. Cliff will have to get back to you when he can."

This was petrol on hot coals.

"What?" Ronnie looked at Spencer.

"Yeah that doesn't sound good," Carlo frowned.

"So, what are you saying?" Tom yelled at Garth, "There *is* something wrong?"

"No, no, no, I'm not saying that."

"What the fuck!" Nabil's eyes were wide.

"Woah, guys," Mandy tried to intervene.

Tom pushed forward, pointing aggressively at Garth, "You need to get Cliff on the phone now! I don't care how. You need to get him and we need to speak to him."

"Yeah, that's it, if you can't give us any answers then we need to speak to Cliff. Fair enough," Carlo's hands were in the air.

"Get him on the bloody phone," Spencer insisted.

"Guys, guys, listen!" Garth yelled back at them, "I did not say there was a problem. I said I don't know anything."

He swatted Tom's pointing finger away, "And get your hand out of my face."

"Hey!" Tom shouted, "Don't you touch me!"

"Ok! Ok!" Mandy's face had gone red, "Oh my god."

She grabbed a chair from behind the operations table and jumped up on it.

"Everyone settle down! We don't know anything. We can't tell you any more, don't you get it?"

"Well you represent the Club. You are part of this whole thing. You should know." Nabil shook his finger at her.

"I can't help you. I'm sorry," Mandy's voice broke, tears running down her face. She was shaking precariously on the chair.

"Come on everyone, let's stop attacking Mandy. She isn't the right person," Jan's voice was strong yet calm. Just for a moment it stopped everyone in their tracks.

Cliff, however, did not hear her. He had seen enough and made his resolve. He pushed through the projection room door and hastened over.

"Ok, ok, I'm here."

"Oh my god!" A woman amongst the crowd of onlookers held a hand to her mouth.

"Cliff!" rang out from several directions.

All eyes were on him.

"So, hang on, you were here all the time?" Tom's surprise was edged with anger.

"Listen everyone, I'll explain everything. I was advised not to talk but I can't stay quiet. I'm going to fill you in on everything."

He looked around at the spectators.

"The only thing is, we have to do it confidentially. Let's ask all those who are not involved to please leave the room. Yeah? Then we'll close the doors and sit down and chat. Is that ok?"

"Alright, sure…" Spencer looked scared.

"Yep, ok, let's clear the room and talk," Tom went into action.

The others joined in and the room was quickly emptied of all non-interested parties. Cliff began arranging chairs in a circle at the front of the room. Spencer, Ronnie, Garth, Paul and Mandy all came over and helped.

"Sorry I was hopeless," Mandy whispered as they put down the last chair.

Cliff squeezed her hand, "Don't be stupid. There was nothing else you could do. Sorry I dropped you in it."

Garth and Paul gathered around Cliff. Garth put a hand on his shoulder, "You don't have to say anything. You probably shouldn't."

"It's ok," Cliff smiled.

Everyone took a seat. Cliff gathered his thoughts for a moment.

"First, everyone, I'm very, very sorry for my behavior. There are reasons, I'll explain, which I am sure you will end up understanding."

"It's alright, Cliffie, we know you've been under pressure mate," Carlo gave him a nod.

"Thanks mate. But I am very sorry. I really am. I only ever wanted to help you people. I never wanted to stress you or cause you any problems. I'm really devastated that I have."

"We know that Cliffie," Jan's voice was warm.

"Yeah but you don't know what I've done yet," Cliff shook his head and chuckled regretfully.

Spencer looked about nervously, catching Nabil's eye. The others waited tensely.

"Not really what I've done. What has been done to me is more like it. This financial crisis has affected a lot of things it shouldn't have. Unfortunately, as you all know, it's played havoc with the property market. Which, as you also know, is just a short term thing. But unfortunately, it's had a big effect on the banks... Especially when it comes to someone like me with a big portfolio of investments."

"So, what's happened?" Tom's voice was thin. He coughed to clear his throat.

"They've run scared. I've been struggling for a year to get any new refinances. One of my last hopes was Western Progressive. It was all looking good. But they were owned by a big American bank, right? Now they've shut down completely. Gone. Just like that. I mean, who would have expected a bank to disappear overnight?"

"That was pretty huge," Spencer nodded.

"It's massive. Nothing like that's ever happened before. So they've panicked. All of them. Which means I've been screwed, right? They've dropped all my valuations, demanded I reduce all my loans, which of course means millions of dollars and I can't do it. Not without refinancing. Which, of course, they won't do."

"That's awful," Jan's brows furrowed.

"Surely they can't do that?" Spencer snorted, "I thought once they had valued your property, and given you a loan against it, then that was the agreement. They can't suddenly change it, can they?"

"Well, yes they can. To people like me. Suddenly I'm in a 'high risk' category. Which is ridiculous, you know, because I have been so successful, I've got a track record of investing success. But they don't care. They panic and change the rules."

"Fuckers," Spencer breathed.

"Yeah, mate. They don't give a rat's about people's lives."

"So, what does this mean for us?" Tom was on the edge of his seat.

"Uh-huh," Nabil agreed.

"Well, this is what I'm sorry about," Cliff looked at them one at a time, his face pained, "The bank has seized all my assets. Everything."

"What do you mean?" Tom was panicky now, "Including our investments?"

"Yep, including your investments. They were linked assets, you know. I didn't know they could take them but they did."

"Holy shit," Spencer sat back in his chair.

"So, they're gone?" Nabil's eyes were wide.

"Yep, they're gone Nabil. I'm sorry."

"You can't fucking do that," Tom got up, "What about our protections? What about the properties and the caveats?"

"Well, the bank's dropped all the valuations. They've just basically taken everything they can get their hands on. I'm sorry mate."

"But there were caveats, weren't there?" Jan's eyes were desperate for some comfort.

"I'm afraid they were all linked assets under my name or one of my company names and the bank has seized them. Every cent, in any account, anywhere they could get hold of."

He wasn't going into the issue of caveats and where the money had actually gone. He couldn't afford to. The main thing was to let them know their money was lost. The details would have to be dealt with later.

"Fucking hell," Nabil got up and walked away. Then he turned back, "This was all in your trust Cliff!"

"I know," Cliff held up his hands, "I know my friends. I know that. I am gutted. I'm truly gutted. I've been doing everything I can since this crisis started. Each time I thought I had found a solution I got smashed by the banks with something else. Like I said, I was advised to remain silent about this. But I wanted to be straight with you and let you know."

"Wow," Tom sat down and hung his head. After a moment, he looked up at Cliff, "You know my brother's going to lose his house. Him and his sweet little kids, they've got nowhere to go."

"I've lost everything too, Tom. I'm sorry mate. But listen –"

"No, no, you listen Cliff," it was Lex. His voice shook as he spoke, "We've all put our life savings into this. We've all trusted you. It's never been a game for any of us. You play around with millions. We all get by on the little we've got. So we risked everything when we loaned it to you. You know why? Because we trusted you. That's why."

He shook his head and looked away. Then he took Rosemary's hand and got up to leave, "Come on darling."

"Wait, please Lex," Cliff got to his feet, "Please wait a moment."

Lex and Rosemary stopped but didn't turn around.

"Listen everyone. Like I said, all our money is gone. I'm not going to lie to you. It's the truth. You know, we all take risks when we invest. We know this. You don't get high returns without higher risks. But this is my promise to you. I'm going to do everything in my power to get your money back. Plus interest. Plus bonus interest. You trusted me before, please trust me again. I am the best chance you've got of getting it back. I made millions before, I can do it again."

"Good on you Cliffie," Carlo shook his head.

"Yes, we need something to go on, Cliffie," Jan was still shell-shocked, "This is really devastating. We need some hope. Poor old Ken, I don't know what he'll do."

Tom put his arm around her shoulders and hugged her.

"Well, yeah, it's true. I am your best hope of getting it back. But, you know, you guys are going to have to help me. You're going to have to give me a chance."

"What kind of chance?" Tom was not in a mood to be

magnanimous.

"Here's our best-case scenario, right," Cliff leaned forward, speaking quietly, "If I can negotiate some kind of deal with the bank… I honestly don't know if I can… But if I could, say, buy some time with them. All we need is a chance for the market to recover, right? We all know it's going to recover. Then if I've still got some of my portfolio, if I can refinance it and get myself out of this hole. Then I can repay you guys, no problem. Right?"

"There's a lot of 'ifs' there," Tom shook his head at the floor.

"I know, I know, but it's still the best chance.".

"Sure."

"But this means you guys have to help me. You've got to be patient. Right? If the bank sees there's a bunch of other investors panicking and chasing the same assets, you know, like suing or something, then there's no way they will make a deal with me. Then we have no chance. Do you understand what I'm getting at?"

"Yep," Tom blew out heavily, "You don't want us to take legal action. You want us to leave you alone, even though you've lost all our money."

"Well, no. I want you to give me a chance to get your money back. Different."

"I'd give you some time," Spencer cut in, "Depends how much. So you can at least try and make a deal with the bank."

"Thanks mate."

"Yep, I'll do that too, Cliffie," Carlo leaned back, his arms folded.

"Wow, you guys are generous," Tom glared at them.

"Not generous, mate," Spencer spoke quietly, "Just doing whatever it takes to get my money back."

"Cliffie," Jan's voice was still shaky, "What's the chance of this working? I've got to tell Ken something. He's not come tonight because he's been quite anxious lately. Ever since he finished up at work, you know, he's been quite down. So, I really don't know what to tell him. I need some hope."

Cliff felt awful. He knew their situation. They were the ones he felt worst about.

He got up and crossed the circle to Jan, holding out his arms, "Come on Jan, come here. I'm really sorry this has happened. I'm so sorry."

Jan got to her feet and accepted Cliff's hug. He could feel her shaking.

"Thank you, Cliffie, I know it must be so hard for you too."

Cliff watched Mandy as she slept, her hair disheveled across her face, her lips puffing in and out with each breath. They'd had a drink to unwind after the meeting. In the end, they'd polished off two bottles of red.

Mandy had, at first, been devastated that she'd failed to contain the meeting, causing Cliff to go against legal advice and tell his investors everything.

"Don't be crazy," Cliff had told her, "No-one could have stopped that mob. They were in a frenzy. Paul and Garth couldn't do anything either. There was only one way, I had to come out. It's better that I did, anyway. I'm glad. They had to find out sometime and I feel better it's done."

Eventually, she'd cheered up, grabbed an armful of biscuits and dips from the kitchen, piled them on the coffee table and cracked open the second red. Later, she had dragged Cliff to bed, pulled his clothes off, giggling in his ear, her hands running over his body. Unfortunately, his mind had been so spinning with events at the Club, the bank, the visit from the sheriff, Bill, Dermott, Blue, Jan and Ken… he had been unable to respond physically.

That embarrassed him now, as he gently stroked the hair away from her eye. He'd let his work, business and, basically, money, get in the way of his love life. He had, for a long time now, allowed it to put his most important relationship at risk. He would change his priorities from today. He was truly lucky to have her. She had every right to leave him after he had kept so much from her and gotten himself into such deep trouble. Instead she had done nothing but care for him and support him.

He wandered into the living room. Mandy had hidden his mobile again. She'd insisted he needed to get away from it, to de-stress. However, he was confident he knew her hiding places.

The shallow wooden fruit bowl sitting on the corner of the kitchen bench top hadn't seen any fruit for a long time. Instead, it had become a depository for their mail. Cliff lifted the bundle of unopened bills, local papers and advertising flyers. Nothing.

"Hmm..."

He walked around the kitchen bench to the laundry. The washing basket sat on top of the machine, half filled with dirty towels and clothes. He rummaged through until he felt something solid.

"Yep!"

He pulled out his phone.

It was only 7am and there were already three missed calls. There was also a new text message. From MJ.

'Hey dude I need to fill ya in gimme a call. When ya had ya beauty sleep zzzz ☺'

Cliff smirked, at least MJ hadn't changed. He wandered over to the sofa, sat down and dialed his voice mail.

"Hi Cliffie, it's Jan here, sorry to call so early. I'm just going a little bit bonkers with worry. We're really desperate and hoping you can do something, you know, to help. Please, whatever you can, love. Give me a call thanks."

Cliff shut his eyes and breathed heavily. Grief knotted inside. His voicemail, however, was demanding a selection. He pressed 'next'.

"Hi Cliff, please call Baz from BK home maintenance urgently. It's about your account, mate. It's more than a hundred days overdue. Thanks."

Cliff hit delete. The third message played. Lara's familiar Scottish accent.

"Hi it's me. Can you give me a call like right away? I heard about last night. What the bloody hell is going on Cliff? Why am I the last to hear about it? I'm really worried so call me."

"Shit!" Cliff hung up.

News travelled fast. Lara was the one he dreaded telling the most. She was a friend, someone he really cared for. She'd done so much for him, been so supportive and worked so hard to help him build his business, the Club and every project he had ever done. She'd even kept on working for him when he couldn't pay her!

Most of all, she was the one he had fun with, laughed and mucked around with, probably the one person in the world he most enjoyed hanging out with. Now he was scared to face her. He'd borrowed her entire savings, an amount she must have worked so hard to build up, and he'd lost it.

His thumb hovered over the dial button but he couldn't press it. How do you tell someone who's trusted you completely, who's put their faith in you one hundred percent, that you've lost everything for them?

He'd have to go see her and explain face to face. Try to reassure her that he'd do everything to get her money back.

He looked in on Mandy. She was still asleep. He took the keys from the kitchen top and quietly made his way out the front door.

"Oh, it's you," Lara peered through the crack of her door, the security latch still on.

"Yeah, sorry it's not Brad Pitt."

She unlatched without smiling.

"Come in."

"Thanks. Here you go," Cliff handed her one of the coffees he was holding, her usual skinny cappuccino.

"Thank you. Now tell me what's happening, Cliff. I'm worried sick. It sounds terrible and I'm fearing the worst."

Cliff had to satisfy his curiosity, "Who've you been talking to between 10pm last night and 7am this morning?"

"What do you mean talking to? You forget I get all your emails. There's heaps of them."

"Oh shit, yeah, right. I haven't looked yet. Who's been emailing?"

"Lots of people. Jan. Nabil. What's his name, the other investor, Spencer? Several others from last night. Some of them supportive. Others really, incredibly angry, like they're going to sue you or send a hitman after you. What have you done? Lost everyone's money?"

"Fuck me," Cliff shook his head, "Yeah, I've lost everyone's money. Including yours. I'm so fucking sorry, Lara. I'm really, really sorry."

"You've lost my money too?"

"Yeah."

"Are you serious Cliff? Really?"

"Yes. I'm sorry."

"Jesus Christ," her face went red, her eyes wild. Shaking, she turned away from Cliff and buried her face in her hands, "Oh my god."

Cliff wanted to go to her but he held back, telling himself he had to let the reality set in first.

He spoke quietly, soothingly, "I'm sorry Lara. I'll explain it all to you. Then I swear I'm going to try and get it back. I'm not going to rest until I've got it back. I can do it."

Lara's breathing calmed a little. She went over to the glass balcony doors and stared out of them, her back to Cliff. Eventually she turned to him. The panic had been replaced with hurt.

"What did you do with it? You promised me you would look after it."

"I know, I know. Listen, I've been smashed by this GFC... and by ABC Bank. Totally smashed. They've done me over. I had no idea they could even do what they've done."

"Uh-huh."

"They seized everything in the Standard Building Society account. Can you believe it? They owned them so they could do it somehow. Honestly, if I'd known..."

"So, hang on. That was the investors' money. Not yours. That was the short term loans account."

"Yeah but basically still in my business name. You know, to them it's kind of the same."

"Ok. But I thought all the investors funds were protected by properties? Separate from any of your stuff."

"Well, yeah, but there was only one property so far, don't forget, and it hasn't even settled."

"What properties were the protections on?"

"Ok, that's a long story, but the bottom line is –"

"No, no. I want to know exactly what you've done. Christ sake, Cliff!"

"Ok, ok, like I said it's a long story. Some of those funds went into servicing other properties."

"Your properties?"

"Yeah, but it was only temporary. I had to keep everything going, you know, I was under so much pressure just trying to keep things going. Hanging in until I could refinance. Until fucking Blue was finished. So I could sell it. I mean Bill really fucked me with that."

"So, the investors have caveats over properties that don't exist? They think they have security. They're still hoping they have part of a property. Maybe they've still got a chance. But, in fact, they've got nothing!"

"I know it sounds fucked up. But that's only now that it's all gone to shit. Right? I was never going to rip anyone off. I was trying to keep everything going so I could help everyone in the end. I was always going to make sure everyone did well."

Lara's eyes were steel, "Have you told them?"

"Well, not about the caveats yet. I have to handle it carefully. I don't want to go to jail, you know," he gave her a weak smile.

"Fuck right off, Cliff. This is bullshit. You know it. It's not what I worked for. I thought we were doing something good. Something to help others. This is rubbish. I worked for nothing because I believed in you."

Cliff crossed the room and took Lara by the shoulders. He tried to look into her eyes but she brushed him away.

"Come on Lara. Please. I fucked up. I already said it. But my intentions were good."

"You know, once when I deposited into the Standard account for you, I thought the numbers were odd. It was like we had a lot more funds coming in than were actually there. But we hadn't even settled on one, single property yet. I thought that was weird. But it never occurred to me that you were a dirty, fucking thief."

"Please, Lara. I have been trying to find my way out of a fucking nightmare for more than a year. I've made mistakes, I know. But it's always been about trying to protect what we've got so I could keep helping people. Do you know how shit I'm feeling right now? I seriously want to kill myself rather than tell people I've lost their money. People who trusted me. I'm fucking devastated. I'm fucking torn apart."

Lara turned back. When she looked at Cliff there was compassion in her eyes.

"Ok. But you have to do one thing for me. You have to be honest now. This is the most important thing. You have to tell these people exactly what's going on. Just like you told me. They deserve it. Ok?"

"Yeah of course."

"No, no, not 'of course'. You have to do this."

"Ok, ok, I promise."

"Jan and Tom have been calling me a lot. Carlo too. They've been freaking out, because you weren't returning their calls. You were ignoring them. It was getting obvious something was wrong but you were leaving them in the dark. It's cruel. You have to tell them the truth. It's the right thing to do. Ok?"

"Sure," Cliff reached out to pull Lara into a hug, but she stepped back.

"No, I'm not ready to hug you, sorry. Do the right thing and maybe we can end up being friends again. Alright?"

Cliff spent the rest of the day avoiding people. Mandy re-took control of his mobile. They got him a prepaid phone from a local service station and she allowed him to give the new number to only three people: herself, Garth and Paul. Then she sent him to Bondi beach with strict instructions to de-stress.

"Paul and Garth know everything that needs to be done. Leave it to them. Ok?"

Cliff wondered how he could ever relax, knowing how many people would be trying to contact him, angry and upset with him, desperately trying to get money out of him. Money he didn't have and quite likely would never have again in his life. He tried not to think about it.

There was, at least, something about being told to relax by someone else. A sense of permission. He changed into his board shorts, squelched across the warm sand and dived into the waves. The cool water instantly woke his senses. He splashed over smaller waves and paddled to catch the bigger, breaking ones. Eventually he got out, wandered up the beach and fell asleep on his towel in the shade of a stone wall.

When he woke up he was hungry. He crossed the beachfront road to a New Zealand ice-cream franchise, where a young girl stacked his cone scoop upon scoop in defiance of gravity. He spent the rest of the afternoon walking along the cliff tops from beach to beach until the sun turned golden, hanging low over the mountains in the west.

"You look five years younger!" Mandy squealed, "See, I told you, you needed some Mandy therapy."

"You're not wrong. I want you as a boss all the time," he held her waist and kissed her slowly.

"Hey, something else to make you feel better," she smiled, "Garth has organized a meeting with ABC. You know, their corporate guys. It's all set up for tomorrow. I'll come with you."

TWENTY-SEVEN

"It's got to be here," Mandy scrutinized a print-out of Garth's email.

"I know. Number 280, right?"

"Yep, but there's no sign, nothing."

They were standing in front of a colonial era building in the heart of Parramatta. It had seen better days, rust stains ran from the gutters, windows were cracked, some boarded, while its heavy, chiseled stonework had turned black from exposure to decades of pollution. Not what you would expect for the corporate offices of one of the country's major banks. Strangest of all, there seemed to be no front entrance. There was a set of solid timber doors, but they were firmly locked, no signage to be seen and certainly no inviting lobby.

"I'm calling Garth," Cliff hit dial on his new phone.

"Hey buddy," Garth replied after only one ring.

"Hey mate, we're here but it doesn't look right. Where exactly are we meeting?"

"Ah, yeah. There's a café down the side."

"Ok, sweet," Cliff knew exactly what he was talking about. He and Mandy had already done a 360 of the building and seen the café.

"Catch you in 5," Garth hung up.

They hastened around the corner. The cafe occupied a long, arched terrace, running along the side of the building, a striped canvas awning butting out over the footpath. Inside they found a quiet sanctuary, no other customers around. They settled at a table up the far end.

A waiter in neat blacks took their coffee order. As he wandered off, Mandy shifted and looked into her bag.

"Lara's calling again."

Cliff sucked on his thumbnail, "Leave it. I want to stay focused on this meeting."

Mandy reached into her bag and pressed cancel.

"I'm a bit nervous, hey? I'll catch up with her after."

Mandy gave his hand a gentle squeeze, "You'll be fine. It'll work out."

Garth and Paul arrived.

"Hey boys," Cliff shook their hands, "Thanks for coming."

Garth put a hand on Cliff's shoulder, "No worries, mate. We'll sort something."

"How did they sound when you spoke to them."

"Good, mate. They get it, you know. We'll be fine."

"Chin up! We're all here for you," Paul smiled.

"You guys are awesome. Let's get you some coffees."

He called the waiter over and took their orders.

Garth leaned in, "It's a funny place isn't it? Not what you'd expect for the bank's most high-powered department. It's like they want to keep hidden."

"Yeah, I know," Cliff nodded, "They definitely don't want random visitors. I mean, where's the entrance?"

"Through here."

"The café?"

"Yep, those doors," Garth indicated a pair of internal glass doors, tinted and bronze-framed. Still no signage.

"Wow, like James Bond," Mandy's eyes sparkled.

As she spoke, the glass doors swung open and an impeccably groomed woman, probably in her mid-forties, stepped into the café, followed by a younger man. Both wore dark, corporate outfits, black folders under their arms. Garth stood up and smiled, a little unsure.

The woman gave him a similarly unsure nod.

"Garth?" she asked.

"Yes!" his smile broadened, "It's us."

The two corporates came over, Garth reaching out to take the woman's hand, "Hi Amelia, great to meet you in person."

"Yes, good to meet you too. This is Mitchell, he works with me."

Mitchell smiled and Garth introduced everybody at the table, initiating a flurry of handshaking, before inviting them to sit down.

"Thanks so much for the opportunity to meet up," Garth kicked things off.

"No problem," Amelia smiled.

"What we're most excited about," Garth embraced Amelia and Mitchell with his most charming smile, "Is that we seem to have found exactly the right people at ABC. Finally!"

A wave of polite laughter went around the table.

"Because, you know, there's two ways this whole thing can go. There's the usual disaster, where borrower defaults, assets are liquidated in fire sale and everybody loses. In this case, let's be honest, ABC would end up a very big loser. You put a hundred properties, all exactly the same profile, on mortgagee auction, in the same area, in an already depressed market and you're going to take a very big haircut."

"Of course," Amelia nodded, her expression controlled.

"But the other way things could go, is we approach the situation in a smarter, more strategic way, understanding what's happening in the market, aiming to have everyone end up a winner. Even if it's over a slightly longer term..."

'Yes, correct," Amelia shifted her folder, "Without wanting to sound our own trumpet, your point about finding the right people is valid. There's a very big difference between retail and what we do in corporate."

She gave Garth a smile, "We do understand how the market works and the nature of the investment cycle."

"Exactly," Garth grinned.

Amelia turned to Cliff, "So you understand, Cliff, we can only work with qualifying customers. Now, of course, if we took each of your properties separately, they would simply be retail investments. But a portfolio of a hundred is rather unique. Quite a different thing, it could be argued."

"Right?"

"So, hypothetically speaking," Amelia continued matter of fact, "If we treated them as one project, we're looking at a development in excess of twenty million. It certainly qualifies in terms of scale. We're stretching definitions a little, but I think it can be done."

Cliff tried to remain poker-faced, "Sounds promising."

"Yes, well it's certainly going to take some thinking outside of the box," she sat back and laughed heartily.

The table burst out in unison with her, releasing the built-up tension.

"What we have in mind, Cliff, is this," she paused for effect.

"Yes..?"

"In addition to your hundred houses, you had some other assets, liquid and otherwise, which the bank has exercised its mandate over…"

"Frozen?"

"Exactly. If you were to be treated as a qualifying developer, with your hundred houses being a qualifying project, you understand?"

"Yes?"

"We have a form of insurance we can access, which, basically, insures us against the market price falling below a given level. It's not cheap, especially in the current financial climate," she gave them a knowing smile.

All heads nodded in agreement.

"But your extra assets could be used to buy this cover. It would be sufficient to give us a comfortable 'basement', as we call it, for a limited period of time."

"I see," Cliff's mouth had gone dry. Was there really one more chance to save his portfolio?

"It's all about time, of course. We all understand we're in a crisis right now. Markets have taken a battering, and it's going to take time for things to recover. But recover they will."

"Absolutely," Cliff beamed, allowing himself to breath for what felt like the first time all meeting.

"We're also well aware that what Garth mentioned earlier is true. The timing would be appalling for us to liquidate in an attempt to recover funds."

"Yep," Garth nodded, "It would cause a local market crash all by itself. You'd have even more investors defaulting and it would just spiral."

"So, if we were indeed able to access basement insurance," Amelia focused on Cliff, "We could begin to sell assets slowly, one at a time, over an extended period. This would give the market time to stabilize, and, if you were lucky, perhaps even recover. Although, there is not much sign of that happening right now," she smiled sympathetically.

"Sure. But at least it gives everyone a chance."

"Exactly."

Cliff's eye was drawn to someone entering from the street, someone familiar. Lara. Their eyes met. She was distressed. She remained near the doorway, waving at Cliff to come to her.

Cliff hesitated. He gave her a little wave and mouthed, "Five minutes."

Lara shook her head furiously. Her gestures were even more urgent. By now the table had noticed. Amelia raised her eyebrows in annoyance.

"Sorry everyone," Cliff apologized, "This is Lara. She's my assistant. Come on over, Lara."

Cliff smiled as casually as he could.

"No, no, Cliff, I need to talk to you privately," Lara stayed where she was.

"Oh, ok, no worries. Just hold on a few minutes then. I'll be out shortly. We're making good progress here."

He gave her a thumbs up.

Lara exploded, "No, Cliff, it can't wait. You need to hear this now!"

There was an uncomfortable pause. Cliff was caught by the ferocity of Lara's outburst. Clearly it was urgent. But he couldn't possibly break up the meeting, at such a critical moment. Amelia was in the middle of offering a solution.

He decided it would look bad to give in.

"Sorry, Lara, I need to finish this meeting. Ok? Then I'll catch up with you. You can join us or you can wait for me outside. Ok?"

"Don't you fucking tell me what's important and what's not!"

Lara stormed over to the table, "If you don't want to hear this privately then I'll play it for you now."

Mandy thumped Cliff in the thigh.

He stood up, "Wait, Lara…"

It was too late. Lara held her phone up for all to hear, "This is from Jan."

Her voicemail announced, "You have one saved message…"

Then Jan's voice, "Hi Lara. It's Jan. I don't know what to do, love," her voice broke off.

They could hear her crying for a moment before she took a deep breath and spoke again.

"Ken's killed himself. Do you understand? Ken's taken his own life… after I told him the news. Why won't anyone call me? I've tried and tried… Well, it's too late now…" Her voice trailed off again and the call ended.

Lara looked at Cliff accusingly. The table had fallen into a stunned silence.

"She's been calling you, emailing you, sending you messages. She called me too and I've been calling you, messaging you. You don't answer anyone. You just avoid them. Now look what you've done."

Lara was shaking, tears running down her cheeks. She wiped them with the back of her hand, sniffing loudly.

Everyone shifted in their chairs, avoiding eye contact. Cliff stood frozen. Mandy, finally, leapt into action. She went to Lara, putting an arm around her.

"This is awful, Lara. Come and I'll talk to you about it. Cliff can join us when the meeting is over."

"No, it's ok," Amelia closed her folder and stood up.

She looked at Cliff, "It sounds like you've got some big issues to deal with. We'll let you sort them out, alright?"

With that she turned and headed for the internal door, Mitchell at her heels.

The café fell silent. Cliff felt like he'd been punched in the guts.

"Poor Jan," was all he could mumble.

Lara stood swaying, the tears silently streaming down her face. Were it not for Mandy's hand on her back, it looked like she would topple over.

Garth put a hand on Cliff's shoulder, "Geez mate, you couldn't have known. You can't be responsible for what other people do, you know?"

Lara looked up sharply, "Yes, you can be held responsible if you promised to speak to someone and you didn't."

"Come on Lara," Cliff's voice cracked.

"No, no, don't look at me with your cow eyes. You've been lying to people, deceiving them. It's time you heard it. It's time someone told you straight."

"I have not been lying to people. Or avoiding them. Not on purpose. I've been trying to control something that's way out of control."

"You're the one out of control. You used other people's money for what you shouldn't have and you lost it. Then you avoid them. You ignore them and avoid them to the point that they panic. They get so desperate like poor old Ken and Jan. Shame on you!"

Mandy was shaking her head. Now she spoke, her voice ice.

"You're being unfair Lara. Cliff never meant anyone any harm and you know it."

"Unfair? Am I seriously the only one here who cares about the truth? About what's right? Someone's killed themselves because of what he's done."

"That's bullshit, Lara!"

Garth held up his hands, "Come on everyone, let's take it easy."

He turned to Lara, "We've just blown the last chance we had. Let's settle things down, ok? This guy's been through enough…"

He put a hand on Cliff's shoulder.

"Don't tell me to settle down, Garth. If you didn't want me crashing your little, secret meeting then maybe you shouldn't have sent it to Cliff's email. Given that I'm the only one who ever fucking reads it," she gave a sarcastic cackle.

"So that's how she got here," Mandy's eyes accused Garth.

Lara turned back to Cliff, "I'm sorry I've blown your chance to save your millions. Maybe you should have called me back. Or Jan. Or Tom. Or any of the other poor, stupid idiots who are not smart enough to be sitting around in cafes, discussing how to play with everyone else's money and make themselves even more millions. Or maybe just lose it in the process. Oh well. Oops."

The accusations were landing on Cliff like uppercuts, he knew the truth in them.

"What do you want me to do?"

"The honorable thing! Talk to people, tell the truth. These people put their trust in you, you owe them some loyalty."

Mandy had had enough.

"Loyalty?!" she flung the word back at Lara.

"Yes. Seems like it means nothing around here."

"Yeah it does! You work for Cliff, you know. You're supposed to be on his side. But instead you come in here and ruin his last chance to save everything. That includes everyone else's investments as well. Where's your loyalty? I thought you were supposed to be his friend?"

"Mandy, do you want to talk about loyalty? Do you seriously want to talk about loyalty?" Lara's eyes were wild.

She glared back and forth between Cliff and Mandy, suspended in rage.

Cliff sensed the imminent explosion. He hurried over to Lara, put his arm around her shoulders and tried to lead her towards the exit.

"Come on Lara, let's you and I go for a chat, ok? Come on…"

Lara flung his arm away from her, pushing him backwards into the table. Cups and saucers clanked loudly. "Don't try to shut me up!"

Then she let loose. A year of pent up humiliation bursting its walls.

"I'll tell you about loyalty, Mandy. I'll tell you about fucking loyalty. Your boyfriend, your fiancé now, right? The guy you've chosen to be loyal to, yeah? The guy you obviously put all your faith in. Despite all the evidence in your face."

"Come on, Lara, you know I'm sorry," Cliff reached out.

Lara slapped his hands away, her voice becoming a hiss, as she turned back on Mandy.

"You call me un-loyal? How about your fiancé fucking his office manager? In San Francisco? Did he tell you about that bit of loyalty? Did he?"

She began to choke up, hands flailing, gripping her sides, "His office manager who kept her mouth shut every day for a year… watching you two live it up… I even worked for nothing to save his arse… What an idiot I was."

Her venom spent, Lara turned and made for the exit, swaying a little as she went.

"Where's my sixty grand Cliff…?"

TWENTY-EIGHT
June 2010

Cliff banged his grass catcher out into the green compost bin. It sat like a fat, plastic frog against the neat, white, lattice fence which enclosed a service area behind his customer's garage.

Sweat beaded on his forehead and he could feel it running down his back. His skin itched from the grass cuttings. He felt a sneeze coming on. Nope, it was one of those tickles in the back of your throat that never quite turn into a sneeze.

"A tease sneeze", he chuckled, picking up his whipper snipper and making his way back down the garden path to where he'd left his gear.

Before he reached the back veranda, he slowed, scanning the mulched garden bed to his left. He caught a glimmer of sunshine reflecting off glass.

"Yep, there you are." It was his iPhone, lying amongst the mulch where he'd tossed it earlier that morning, angry at receiving yet another abusive email.

Two years had passed since that day in the café in Parramatta. Dusting his iPhone off, Cliff's mind turned over what he'd had and what he'd lost. The same loop his thoughts had run through thousands of times.

His relationship with Mandy had never recovered. He hadn't seen her for more than a year now. The world he'd built up had finally and completely collapsed that day.

Raj and MJ had both lost their investments too. Cliff knew they blamed him. Garth and Paul simply moved on. His mum and dad were not welcoming.

The bank had taken their investment property, leaving them fifty grand in debt and threatening their home. His mum got a job at Woolworths in a desperate attempt to make extra money. It complicated their social security, though, so in the end her only option had been to clamp down on his Dad. He was forced to give up his gambling entirely, handing over control of his money to her. He wasn't happy.

There was one thing, however, that Cliff was pleased he'd done.

The morning after Parramatta, Cliff sat on his sofa feeling numb. In fact, the only sensation he had was a dull, physical pain, coming from his bruised right cheek bone. The spot where the coffee cup had hit. The one Mandy had thrown at him.

He rubbed it carefully. His relationship with Mandy was in serious trouble. He'd never seen her that upset. She was usually the stoic one. Not yesterday. He'd seen the humiliation in her face. He was glad the cup had hit him.

He'd made no attempt to deny Lara's accusations. Instead, he'd tried to reassure Mandy that it was a one-off, drunken mistake and that it had meant nothing. Eventually Mandy had come home with him. But, as it turned out, only to gather her work things and leave for her friend Romina's place.

Cliff was alone. He had no idea what to do. It was the strangest sensation. He'd always been so active, so focused on his tasks, the pursuit of his goals. Now it seemed he just had to sit there and let things be done to him.

He didn't know what he should be feeling. Guilt? Yes, he felt plenty of that. Shame? Yes. Fear? A little.

He got up and trundled wearily into the kitchen. He found his favourite Batman mug, piled in three teaspoons of Nescafe, another three of sugar, and flicked the kettle on.

Out of habit, he scanned the kitchen top for his mobile and realized Mandy must still have it in her bag.

"I wonder if she did that on purpose?"

While the kettle boiled, he crossed back to the sofa where he'd been sleeping, rummaged through his pile of clothes and found the new phone. He plugged it in to charge next to the TV.

He poured the coffee, stirring it slowly, the action reminding him of standing in another kitchen with a coffee in his hand. Lara's. She was telling him to do the right thing. Talk to Jan. He'd promised her he would. Then he hadn't. Now Ken was dead, poor old bloke. Jan devastated.

He looked across the living room, out the main window. The sun was bright.

"For everyone else this is a normal day," he breathed out long and slow, "Except for me. And Jan."

She would be feeling far worse than he was. He had mostly lost material things. Yes, probably his fiancée too. But he was young, he still had his whole life. Jan, on the other hand, had lost her life partner, the man she'd been with for decades, the man she had planned to retire with and live out the rest of their lives together. She'd lost all that and would never replace it.

He wondered if she was alone now, like he was.

"Maybe... Nah," he shook his head.

He took his coffee and wandered back into the living room. What was his gut telling him? What was the right thing to do?

"I should call her."

It might just help her. So what if he felt like an idiot? Let her abuse him, if there was a chance it could do her some good.

He went over to his phone.

"Shit."

It was the new one, with only three numbers in it. He didn't have Jan's. Garth had his laptop and MJ had all the Club paperwork.

"Damn."

How could he get her number? Mandy wasn't responding to him. Anyway, she would tell him to leave Jan alone. Whereas now it felt really important.

The only other person was Lara. Her number wasn't in his new phone either, but he remembered it.

"What the hell..."

He started typing.

'Hi its Cliff, do you mind giving me Jan's number?'

He hit send.

A moment later, a beep. Eight digits, nothing else.

"Awesome."

He pressed call.

"Hello," came a shaky voice.

"Hi Jan, it's Cliff Young."

"Oh..."

"Yes, I know I'm the last person you want to hear from right now, Jan, I'm really sorry to call you..."

"Are you?"

"Yes, I'm sorry I didn't call you sooner. I'm sorry I'm calling you now, when it's too late. I heard what happened. I just wanted to say sorry."

"Ok."

"No, really Jan, I know I'm the cause of all this. I'm devastated. I wish I could turn back the clock and do things differently. But I can't. I honestly don't know what to say. Except 'I'm sorry' and I know it does no good."

"Why couldn't you have got back to us? With something? Something. When we were so desperate..."

"I'm sorry."

"Just to know... In our hour of need... so we knew what was going on," Jan took a deep breath. "Anyway, it's done now. Poor Ken went mad with worry."

Her voice wavered as she spoke his name.

"I know. I'm sorry Jan. I was under so much pressure. I was fighting for survival. For myself and everyone else, you know? But I made wrong decisions and I've caused this and I'm truly sorry."

Cliff felt his throat tightening. He moved the phone away from his mouth. He had no right to cry.

"Well, what's happened has happened. You can't blame yourself, Cliffie. You always told us it was our decision. You told us there would be risks."

Jan sounded ready to hang up.

"Yes, but I did the wrong thing, Jan. I did."

"What's done is done, love."

"No, I want you to know the whole truth. I used your money for what I shouldn't have. I was so desperate to save all our investments. I thought I could get myself out of trouble and then look after everyone else and no-one would be the wiser. But I was wrong, I shouldn't have taken your money when I did."

"You mean you took it knowing you were likely to lose it?"

"I took it when I was already in trouble and used it to try to fix my own situation. But, please believe me, the reason I did it was I honestly, truly, believed it was the best way to look after everybody. If I had been able to save my portfolio, and get back on track, then I could have looked after everyone, including you guys. I was even planning to give everyone bonuses, you know, that was my plan."

"I don't know Cliff... It sounds all wrong."

"Yes, it was. That's what I'm saying. I did the wrong thing and I wish I hadn't and I'm really sorry. I didn't have any new flip property. I gave everyone caveats over the same property. Then I tried to use the funds to finish a big development. If I had, it would have solved everything. But it was dishonest. It was a mistake."

"I see..."

"Oh my god. It was basically theft. I realise it now."

"Yes."

"I stole everyone's money, I was that desperate. I was obsessed. I shouldn't have. I shouldn't have taken anyone's..."

"That was everything we had, Cliff."

"I know, Jan. I'm so sorry. I wish I could do things over again. I know it's too late to make anything better for you. I know these probably just seem like empty words… But I just wanted to call you. All I could think of was to be totally honest with you. I thought maybe it could help in some small way."

"I don't know what to think."

"That's all, Jan. I don't want you to forgive me but please believe that my apology is from the bottom of my heart."

"Thank you for being honest, I suppose, Cliff."

"That's all, honestly… I just wanted to say it."

Jan's voice was tired, "Well… I accept your apology, alright Cliff? I don't know about forgiveness, just yet, I don't know if Ken would want me to…"

"Of course."

Jan sighed. When she spoke, there was a little warmth amongst the pain.

"Hmm… No. You know, when I think about it like that, I think he would want me to. He'd say anyone who apologises so whole-heartedly deserves forgiveness. So, there you go…"

She took a shaky breath before continuing, "Ken always was a softy. But I don't know what I'll do without him…"

She broke into sobs.

"I'm sorry…" Cliff whispered.

"Just accept our forgiveness, Cliff, and try to do the right thing. Ok, love?"

TWENTY-NINE
Save or Delete

Cliff wiped his iPhone on his pants and squinted at the screen. He moved into the shade of the veranda so he could read it better. It was 1230. He had to pack up and get to his next job.

Since that call to Jan he'd quietly resolved to get everyone's money back, somehow, some day. But as a bankrupt it was no easy mission. Investing was, of course, out of the question. He was broke and would never get a mortgage. He couldn't officially carry out any form of business. Regular jobs had proven hard to get. So, he'd fallen back on the only other thing he'd known, garden maintenance.

He found that his years as an investor had given him a plenty of confidence with people. There wasn't anyone he was afraid of approaching. He spent twenty-five dollars printing a wad of business cards from a vending machine, dressed as neatly as he could and took the train into the wealthy northern suburbs. He knocked on gates and rang doorbells, giving his card to anyone who looked like they had a lawn or garden, promising the best service and price. Cash only.

Within a week, he had ten bookings and by the middle of the next, twenty. He found a loan shark in St Mary's and borrowed enough to buy a second-hand lawn mower, whipper snipper and hire a ute. Then he got busy. After a month, he paid the loan shark out. From then on, his income was his own, and it grew steadily from week to week.

He was lucky. None of the Club investors ended up suing him. They'd been angry and threatened him. Some with his life.

"So, so weird," he shook his head.

Whether they admitted it or not, they hung onto the hope that Cliff would get back on his feet and somehow make their money back. As crazy as that idea was. He'd done it before, they hadn't. So an unspoken agreement formed. Suing Cliff would deny them all this last hope.

Thinking of his old investors reminded Cliff of the abusive message on his phone. The one that had provoked him to toss it into the garden bed earlier that morning.

He selected his email. There it was, still at the top of his inbox.

'You dirty, lying, stealing dog…'

His thumb went to the delete key, but he hesitated, curiosity getting the better of him. Who would write something like that? He opened it and looked at the sender. Simon Bartlett. A familiar name…

"Oh, yes, that's it. The guy with the kid and the attitude."

He looked at the rest of the message:

'You dirty, lying, stealing, dog you still haven't paid back any of MY MONEY!!!'

But then, surprisingly, it continued in a very different tone:

'Ok had to get that off my chest. Now the business. Your gonna love this shit. Oh yeah! I'm flipping houses. Hahaha!

Yes me! The guy you left broke and up shit creek. The guy who was on the dole with a wife and new born kid and no job. Good for nothing. No hoper. I've flipped 4 houses already!!!

I'm doing it like we always said. Like we talked about at the Club but never got around to. One for charity and one for me.

First one was for the Neighbourhood Centre. Made them 70 g-g-grand!!! They don't know what to do with it hahaha!!!

You won't believe the market right now mate. It's serious changed. It's going up like a rocket. But there's still bargains everywhere you look."

Cliff looked up, tapping the phone on his chin, "So, Sydney's turning around, hey? Of course it fucking is."

He took a long breath and went back to reading.

"Oh, yeah, the banks are bending over backwards now ha-dee-ha!!!

Anyway, I'm ready for my next one and I need someone to work with. Thought you might be alright at it hahaha!!!

If your interested give me a call. I've got fifty grand and a heap of bargains to turn into sweet sweet cash.

Cheers mate

Simon

(and Angela and Dylan)'

Cliff felt his heart rate quicken. It was a sensation he hadn't known for a long time. It stirred long forgotten emotions, good ones, like old friends calling out across a great distance.

He selected Simon's number and tapped dial…

ABOUT THE AUTHOR

This is Dean's first novel. It is the realization of a long-held dream. Before *Heavily Invested*, Dean had written a number of playscripts, including *Dial to the Tone*, which won the audience choice at Belvoir Street Theatre's Open House, and an adaptation of *Hamlet* that was toured by the Queensland Arts Council. He also wrote and produced a short film, *Season of Fear*, and co-wrote the online game, *Alternator*, which won the ABC-Screen Australia Serious Games Award in 2009 and went on to be a Finalist for an Earth Hour Award and a United Nations World Environment Day Award.

cabana books
AUSTRALIA